Select praise for internationally bestselling author Rachel Reid

"Rachel Reid's hockey heroes are sexy, hot, and passionate! I've devoured this entire series and I love the flirting, the exploration and the delicious discovery!"

—#1 *New York Times* bestselling author Lauren Blakely

"It was sweet and hot, and the humor and banter gave it balance. I'm really looking forward to more from Rachel Reid."

—*USA TODAY* on *Game Changer*

"*Game Changer* is a provocative, heartwarming story about love, pure and simple, with no labels, no limits, and no regrets. It's a wonderful debut for Reid that is without a doubt one of my favourite MM novels of the year, and I can't wait to read what she comes up with next."

—*What's Better Than Books*

"*Game Changer* balances the light-hearted and the angsty, and is easy to get lost in as escapist fare. [. . .] If you like something sweet and easy and soft, it's more than passably enchanting, and a very nice way to spend some time."

—*All About Romance*

Also available from Rachel Reid

Time to Shine
The Shots You Take

The Game Changers Series

Game Changer
Heated Rivalry
Tough Guy
Common Goal
Role Model
The Long Game
Unrivaled

GAME CHANGER

RACHEL REID

HARLEQUIN

HARLEQUIN®

Recycling programs for this product may not exist in your area.

ISBN-13: 978-1-335-00408-6

Game Changer

First published in 2018. This edition published in 2026.

For questions and comments about the quality of this book, please contact us at CustomerService@Harlequin.com.

Harlequin Enterprises ULC
22 Adelaide St. West, 41st Floor
Toronto, Ontario M5H 4E3, Canada
www.Harlequin.com

HarperCollins Publishers
Macken House, 39/40 Mayor Street Upper,
Dublin 1, D01 C9W8, Ireland
www.HarperCollins.com

Printed in the United Kingdom

26 27 28 29 CPI 10 9 8 7 6 5 4 3

This book is for everyone who encouraged me to try to publish this story, and especially to Matt, who supports me wholeheartedly in all things. And also to the random Gap model who was my physical reference for Kip.

Dear Reader,

My only hope when *Game Changer* was first published in October 2018 was for at least one person to read my book and love my characters.

It was the very beginning of what would become an amazing adventure. With each book that was published in the Game Changers series, I received more love from readers. When the *Heated Rivalry* television series based on those books debuted in November 2025, my characters received more love than I could have ever thought possible. I am truly, enormously blessed and grateful for that love and for my readers.

I wrote these books as a lifelong hockey fan, and as someone who wants the culture of the sport I love to be better. The series is based on an idea: that the bravery of one person could create a ripple effect that benefits others and eventually leads to real change. Each book focuses on at least one hockey player, and the man who makes him braver. Stoic New York captain Scott Hunter is charmed by cute and clever history student Kip Grady. Weary Toronto defenseman Ryan Price reunites with bold and beautiful musician Fabian Salah. Distinguished New York goaltender Eric Bennett falls for witty young bartender Kyle Swift. Miserable Ottawa forward Troy Barrett learns how to smile with adorable social media manager Harris Drover. And, of course, despite their best efforts, Shane Hollander and Ilya Rozanov couldn't stop themselves from falling in love with each other.

I love each and every one of these characters, and as I write this letter in February 2026, it feels like the whole world loves them too. It's an incredible feeling, and I'm very aware that none of what I'm experiencing now would have happened without the enthusiastic support from the early fans of my books. The success of the Game Changers series was largely driven simply by readers recommending the books to their friends and online followers. It was driven by booksellers and librarians, by reviewers and bloggers, and by BookTokers and Bookstagrammers. I will always remember and appreciate that support.

Thank you for the love, and I hope you enjoy having these beautiful special editions on your shelves.

Love,
Rachel

GAME CHANGER

CHAPTER ONE

Tuesday, January 14, was the day Kip Grady learned that loud blenders and hangovers didn't mix.

He hadn't meant to drink so much last night, but Chuck and Jimmy had been in town and he hadn't seen those guys in months. It wasn't like he'd gotten *wrecked*. He *had* been aware that he needed to be at work at six the next morning, but he'd still managed to drink just enough to make the high-powered blenders his mortal enemy.

But he had a job to do. And that job was to make the best damn smoothie he could for the busy-looking woman waiting at the counter.

"Here you are, ma'am." He tried not to wince as he handed the customer her order. "One Green Warrior smoothie with a wheatgrass shot."

He glanced at the clock. Six-thirty. Jesus Christ.

There was no time to rest his head on the inviting pile of oranges that sat on the counter. The weekday morning rush at Straw+Berry tended to be steady right up until nine. Maria was working with him this morning, and that was cool. They worked well together because, while neither of them was particularly invested in this job, they took it seriously and did everything they were supposed to. Plus, she was funny.

"Which of these damn smoothies cures a hangover?" Kip moaned when the shop was briefly empty.

"Um, none. But allegedly the watermelon one."

"Okay. I'm going to make myself a giant watermelon one with, like, five Advils in it."

"I think you mean five 'wellness boosts.'"

Kip did make himself a giant watermelon smoothie, and he did feel slightly better after drinking it. He took *two* Advil.

"So what were you up to last night, anyway?" Maria asked.

"Oh, just hanging out with some college friends."

"Yeah? Are they cute?"

"Nah. I don't know. Not my type." Chuck was big, burly, and bearded. Jimmy was the complete opposite: short, slim, and looked about seven years younger than he actually was.

"Are they super-successful juice-bar baristas too?"

"*They* got jobs in their field. They're both working in Boston. Business something? Insurance? Finance? I don't know. They wear suits to work."

"You wear an apron. That's pretty great."

"Yeah, I'm super proud."

"And a ball cap with a little strawberry embroidered on it. Come on!"

Kip threw a chunk of frozen pineapple at her.

"Tell you what, Kipper. I'm going to be nice and do all the prep work in the back this morning so you can just rest your pretty head when the rush is over."

"Yeah?"

"Yup!"

"You are the best and I love you," he sighed happily.

"I know. Now look alive! We've got businesswomen coming in and they want liquefied kale!"

It was another hour of steady rush before Kip was finally able to enjoy the quiet that Maria had promised him. She went to the back room to chop fruit and vegetables, and he slumped onto a chair he had dragged behind the counter and pressed his face against the wall. It was a nice, cool wall.

He hadn't even realized he had closed his eyes until he was startled by someone clearing their throat. Not aggressively. Just enough to let him know they were there.

He opened his eyes and stood quickly. "Sorry, sir," he stammered. "What can I—?"

Kip's mouth may have dropped open like a cartoon character's. Possibly his jaw was on the floor, and his tongue may have rolled out of his mouth like a carpet. It just so happened that the *hottest man he had ever seen* was standing in front of him.

"Um, what can I get for you?" Kip managed.

The man was tall, blond, and, well, *ripped*. And Kip *knew* he was ripped because he was wearing a ridiculously tight Under Armour zip-up jacket thing and sweatpants. He must have just finished a run, the way his damp hair clung to his forehead and his skin glistened with sweat.

"Good morning," the sweaty man said cheerfully. "Sorry to wake you."

Kip's cheeks flushed. He dipped his head a bit so the brim of the stupid baseball cap would conceal it. *God, the hottest man in the world is standing in front of me and I am wearing an apron and a strawberry baseball cap.*

"You didn't . . . I wasn't . . ." Kip took a breath. *Pull it together!* "Sorry. Had a bit too much fun last night."

The man raised an eyebrow. "On a Monday night?"

"Yeah, well, you know the life of a smoothie maker . . . Live fast, die young, right?"

The man laughed. Kip nearly fell over.

"So what's good here?" the man asked, squinting at the menu.

"Um, there's one with blueberries and pineapple and kale—but you can't taste the kale, I swear! It's good. I like it."

"That would be the . . . Blue Moon Over Brooklyn?"

"Yeah. All the names here are kinda dumb."

The man pointed a long finger at Kip's name tag. "I like *your* name."

Kip glanced at his own name on the tag, as if he didn't know what it said. Like an idiot.

"It's, like, a nickname," he said, as if the hot guy had asked him for further information. Which he had not. But Kip kept talking because that's what he always did. "I mean, everyone calls me Kip. So it *is* my name. But not, like, my *real* name. It's, um . . . Anyway. You want one of those blueberry smoothies?"

"Sounds good," the man said, politely ignoring how fucking dumb Kip was being.

Kip got to work loading the blender with various frozen fruits and fresh kale. Fortunately it required focus, and then the machine was loud enough that he couldn't talk over it. He glanced over it at the man, who was now standing with his hands on his hips, studying the uninspired photos of fruit that decorated the small space. Kip's eyes didn't know where to land, rapidly jumping from broad shoulders to ridiculously huge arms to a muscled back tapering into a trim waist to an ass that was frankly just—

Kip shook his head and turned off the blender. He fumbled for a plastic cup and filled it with blue smoothie. "Here you are, sir."

The man turned, nodded, and handed Kip a folded, slightly damp twenty-dollar bill from the pocket of his sweatpants. He waved his hand when Kip tried to hand him his change. "Keep it."

"Seriously?" Kip asked, watching him take his first sip. Watching his pink lips fit around the straw.

"Yeah." The man smiled. "We'll call it a finder's fee. This is delicious."

Kip smiled back. "Glad you like it. Have a nice day."

The man toasted him with his smoothie cup. "You too, Kip."

Kip felt a little giddy at the sound of his name coming from this man's mouth. As his dream man exited, another man who was not nearly as attractive walked into the shop.

"Holy shit!" the new customer said, jerking a thumb toward the door. "That was Scott Hunter!"

"Huh?"

The man looked at Kip like he was very dumb. "Scott *Hunter*."

"You mean, like, the hockey player guy?" Kip said.

"What?" came a voice from behind him. Maria stood in the doorway to the back room. "Did I seriously miss Scott Hunter?"

"I don't think . . . Do you really think that was him?" Kip asked.

The customer nodded. "Oh yeah. Definitely. Surprised he shows his face around town, the way he's been stinking up the ice lately."

"He's not doing well?" Kip did have *some* awareness of who Scott Hunter was, of course—everyone did, sports fan or not. He was the star center and team captain of the New York Admirals. Three years ago he had led Team USA to Olympic gold. But Kip mostly knew him for his Hugo Boss ads. He was a big fan of those ads.

Kip liked hockey just fine, but he hadn't been following the NHL too closely. Scott Hunter had always been, to his knowledge, celebrated and beloved in this town. The King of New York, really. But apparently Kip had missed something.

"Yeah, he's been terrible this season," the customer continued. "Hasn't scored a goal since November! Don't know what they're paying him all that money for. They should trade the bum."

"Well . . ." Kip said, not sure how to finish. It was ridiculous, but he felt personally offended by this guy's criticisms, and was compelled to defend Scott Hunter. "Maybe he's just going through some stuff."

The customer snorted. "He can go through it in the summer. We're not gonna make the playoffs this year if he keeps this shit up."

Kip still felt inexplicably angry, but shrugged it off and gave the guy his smoothie so he would leave.

When they were alone again, Maria said, "Was Scott Hunter really in here?"

"I don't know. Maybe. I mean, now that that guy mentioned it, I think it had to be. I was kind of distracted by how hot he was, but, yeah, he definitely looked like Hunter. And, uh, he gave me a huge tip."

"How huge? We have to split it, you know."

"Yeah, yeah, I know. It was like a thirteen-dollar tip!"

"What?"

"Well, if it *was* Hunter, that's probably, like, nothing, right? He probably doesn't care about money at all."

"Must be nice."

"Yeah."

"Soooo," Maria said, leaning over into Kip's personal space, "he was hot?"

"Oh my god." Kip grinned. "He was *volcanic*. He didn't look real."

"What was he wearing?"

"Workout clothes. He'd just been running, I think. Really *tight* workout clothes."

"Oh my god."

"Yup."

"I can't believe I missed it. If he comes back, you have to tell me. Even if I'm in the *bathroom*, just get me!"

"Sure, that won't be weird."

Maria started loading the freshly chopped fruit and vegetables into the fridges. Kip helped. They worked quietly for a few minutes.

"Hey," Kip said, "he said my name."

"Who? Hunter? He actually said the word *Kip*?"

"Yeah," Kip said dreamily.

"God, I'll bet when *he* says it, it doesn't even sound dumb."

Kip threw a strawberry at her.

Kip saw the headline the next morning on the train: *Night of the Hunter!* He leaned forward a little to read the front page of the paper of the passenger sitting opposite him. Apparently Hunter had scored a hat trick last night and got two assists in a 7–1 trouncing of Washington. Kip smiled. He felt oddly proud of him.

Yeah, so nice that millionaire superstar had a good night. Sheesh.

The Admirals were playing in New Jersey tonight, the paper said. As Kip walked the two blocks from the train station to Straw+Berry, he thought about the last time he had been to an Admirals game. Must have been at least eight years ago. No, longer, because he'd never seen Hunter play except on television.

Jesus, am I just going to think about Scott Hunter all the time now?

He yawned as he took his key out and unlocked the door to the shop. He needed to find a job with a later start. Getting up before five to be at work before six was ridiculous. Especially for minimum wage.

The morning went the same as most weekdays: steady rush from about seven until nine, and then a bit of quiet before the customers Maria had dubbed the "yoga moms" started to trickle in.

"Your boyfriend had a good night last night," Maria said as she restocked the orange bowl.

"What the hell are you talking about?"

"Scott Hunter. Scored, like, a million goals or something."

"*Three* goals," Kip corrected her, "and two assists."

"Oh, sorry. Didn't realize you were such a hard-core fan."

"I'm not! I read the paper on the way here. It's, like, big news or whatever."

"Oh my god! You are mad crushing on him right now! You went home last night and Google-image-searched Scott Hunter, didn't you?"

"No!" *Yes.*

"Whatever. You are such a fanboy. So cute."

"I hate you."

"You don't."

Maria stacked oranges and Kip swept the floor behind the counter even though it wasn't that dirty. He just hated standing around doing nothing.

At a little past ten, the door opened and Kip was once again faced with Scott Hunter in sweaty workout clothes.

This time Maria was there to witness it. "Holy shit."

Kip elbowed her as subtly as possible.

"Good morning again, Kip," the man who was definitely Scott Hunter said.

"Good morning, um . . . *Jesus.* You're Scott Hunter, right?"

He looked amused. "I am."

"That is so awesome," Maria breathed.

"It's, um . . ." Kip started, then switched courses. "Great game last night."

"Thanks! Thought I might get another one of those blueberry smoothies. When something goes right in my game, I like to try to repeat what I did that day."

"Right," Kip said. Scott's eyes were blue. They were so blue.

"So . . . another blueberry smoothie, please."

"Right!" Kip broke out of his trance and got to work making the smoothie.

Scott Hunter was, once again, wearing an absurdly tight Under Armour jacket and sweatpants. His hair was damp and mussed, and his skin was slightly flushed from exercise. Kip Grady was, once again, wearing a fucking dumb apron and a ball cap with a goddamn strawberry on it. But at least he wasn't hungover this time.

He handed the star athlete his smoothie and tried not to focus too closely on the way his lips wrapped around the straw. It was difficult because Scott was looking *directly at him* as he took his first sip. His lips curved up a bit when he noticed Kip's staring.

"Thanks again, Kip," he said. "Hopefully I'll see you next game day."

He raised the smoothie cup in a farewell salute, and then he left.

When Kip turned to Maria, her jaw was on the floor.

"'Hopefully I'll see you next game day'?" she said. "Are you *kidding* me?"

"What?"

"He's completely into you, Grady!"

Kip turned as red as the strawberry on his hat. "Oh, come on. That's not what he meant."

"Sure it isn't."

"It isn't! He's just superstitious. He means he hopes it works and he has a great game tonight so he'll be back again next game day! That's it!"

"I know that's what he was saying on the *surface*, idiot, but that's not *all* he was saying."

"He's not even . . . Oh my god. I can't believe I'm talking about this. Scott Hunter is *not* into dudes. And he's *definitely* not into dudes who work at smoothie shops."

"If you say so."

"I'm going to go back there and chop the pineapple," Kip grumbled.

"Better check to make sure we have lots of blueberries stocked," Maria singsonged after him.

Kip stood in the living room of his best friend's Tribeca apartment, admiring the view of the Hudson River. He couldn't even imagine what a place like this would cost.

Living in New York City was *expensive*, but Kip had a super impressive strategy that allowed him to work a minimum-wage job *and* manage to file his student loan payments on time each month: He still lived with his parents.

Yes, he was twenty-five. Yes, he had graduated university when he was twenty-two. But the thing was, history majors weren't exactly being snapped up on the job market.

Kip had dreams. Aspirations. He wanted to work at one of the museums. Maybe move on to work at one in Europe one day. Maybe write a book or two. Maybe host a popular television show where he traveled the world and presented different important historic sites to the home viewers. Maybe consult on historical movies in Hollywood . . .

Or maybe turn fruit and vegetables into drinkable mush for busy people on their way to jobs that were actually important.

The owner of the apartment in which he now stood, Elena, had a real job and a life that seemed very adult compared to Kip's. She was a cybersecurity engineer for Equinox Tech, one of the fastest-growing IT companies in the country. Kip did not know what exactly a cybersecurity engineer was, but it seemed to pay very well and it sounded impressive.

Elena was, hands down, the smartest person Kip knew. Besides being brilliant and funny, she was also stunningly beautiful—an unusual combination of her father's Norwegian height and bone structure, and her mother's Lebanese dark hair and olive skin.

Kip's friendship with her back in high school had helped him realize that he wasn't sexually interested in women. Because if he wasn't interested in *her*, well . . .

Anyway, Elena had probably known he was gay before he did. She knew everything before he did.

"You need a roommate?" Kip asked, turning away from the windows.

"No," she said. "Not ever."

They settled themselves on her couch to eat Szechuan food (Elena *did not* cook). Kip had barely taken a bite before Elena casually said, "So. Who is he?"

Noodles slipped from Kip's chopsticks, sliding back into the box they came from. "What? Who? What do you mean?"

"You've had a dreamy look on your face all night. Who are you thinking about?"

Kip's face flushed. He poked at the noodles with his chopsticks. "No one."

"Christopher." Elena liked to use his real name when he was exhausting her.

"You'll laugh."

"That doesn't sound like me."

Kip smiled at that. "It's just . . . You know Scott Hunter?"

"Do I know Scott Hunter? Not personally, no."

"You've heard of him, though."

"Yes."

"Okay. So he's been coming by the shop."

"The smoothie shop?"

"Yeah. The past couple of days. For luck, he says, because he played so well after he got a smoothie yesterday morning. So he came in today and got another one because they are playing again tonight."

"Okay."

"He's just . . . He's really hot, is all."

Elena's lips twitched a bit, but she didn't laugh. "That's exciting."

"Yeah."

They continued to eat in silence. And Kip, who apparently could *not* be cool about this, lasted all of a minute before he blurted out, "He knows my name."

Elena raised an eyebrow.

"He said, 'Good morning, Kip,' when he came in today." Kip tried, but failed, to keep the dopey grin off his face.

"That must have been a thrill."

"Yeah, and, uh, he said he hopes to see me again. You know, like, if the smoothie works, or whatever."

"The magic hockey smoothie?"

"Stop making fun of me."

"I'm not! And I'll tell you what else: We are watching that hockey game tonight."

Kip was embarrassingly nervous watching the hockey game. Every hit Scott took, Kip flinched. Every shot Scott launched at the net, Kip held his breath. He wanted this game to go well for Hunter, and there was no point in kidding himself about why.

At the end of the first period, the score was tied 1–1. Scott stopped on his way into the dressing room for a quick interview. He pulled his helmet off, and his damp hair stuck out in all directions. Kip's heart fluttered. Scott was drenched in sweat, even more so than when he came into the shop after his runs. Kip could see the glisten of it down Scott's neck, into the red collar of his jersey.

Scott was saying words about strong defense and working as a team. His beautiful mouth hovered above the microphone, his blue eyes looking neither at the camera nor at the man interviewing him. It was like he was barely present at this interview, already wherever he'd rather be at that moment.

"He's definitely attractive," Elena said.

"Yeah . . ." Kip breathed.

The game stayed close for the second period. It wasn't until the third period, when Scott scored two goals and assisted on one more, that the Admirals silenced the fans in the Newark arena. Kip was giddy.

"God, he's incredible. That last goal, he probably shot that puck a hundred miles an hour, but it looked like slow motion."

"He's got talented hands," Elena agreed, with a quirk of her lips.

She picked up her phone and typed something. "Next game is Saturday night at home against Tampa Bay," she said. "Are you working on Saturday?"

Kip groaned. "Fuck! I need to be—I've gotta switch shifts! Who's working Saturday?"

He picked up his own phone and texted Maria. Are you working Saturday?

The response came a minute later. Yes?

KIP:
Can I switch with you?

MARIA:
Why?

KIP:
I'm scheduled for Friday. Let's swap. Please?

MARIA:
Is this about Scott Hunter?!

Kip felt dumb, but he still typed, Maybe.

MARIA:
Jesus, Kip.

KIP:
PLEASE?!

MARIA:
Fine.

There was a pause, and she added, You're working with Jeff.

Ugh. Jeff was the worst. Just really lazy and basically stoned all the time. Kip couldn't even believe he still worked there.

But it would be worth it, because when the game ended, the score was 6–2 for the Admirals. Which meant Scott was going to be coming in on Saturday for sure.

Probably for sure.

Almost certainly for sure.

CHAPTER TWO

Kip may have gotten up extra early on Saturday to put some additional care into his appearance.

There had been nothing he could do about his uniform, but he'd at least made sure his nicest jeans were clean, and he had decided to wear the stylish new sneakers he had bought a couple of weeks ago that he could not afford at *all*, but had not been able to resist.

He'd even bothered to fix his hair up a bit, despite knowing he had to slap his stupid ball cap over it. He flossed. He tucked mints into his pocket to cover up his eventual coffee breath.

He arrived at the shop ten minutes early after a relatively relaxing commute, and was not at all surprised to see that he was the first to arrive. He got to work prepping, taking special care to make sure they had the ingredients for Scott's Blue Moon Over Brooklyn smoothie ready.

Twenty minutes after the shop opened at six, Kip was still alone. Again, not a huge surprise given that it was Jeff who was scheduled to work with him, but it was grating.

At six-thirty the phone rang; Jeff was calling in "sick." Kip couldn't even conjure up the energy to be angry, especially since this might mean being all alone in the shop when Scott . . .

You are way too excited about the possibility of a two-minute interaction with a man who is not at all interested in you, Kip.

Saturdays were always way quieter than weekdays. The morning crawled, with just a trickle of customers to break the monotony. Kip ended up pulling out his phone and, of course, reading old articles about Scott Hunter.

There were a lot of articles. Most of them had the same information: Scott had been born and raised in Rochester, and had always been the best player on any team he played for, right from his adolescent days. The articles often highlighted his generous devotion to charities, especially those that help sick children, and described him as an outstanding role model on and off the ice.

The other thing the articles *always* mentioned was that Scott Hunter was one of New York's most eligible bachelors. He had never been linked to a woman for any significant amount of time (interesting), and he tended to dodge any questions about his private life (more interesting).

Kip was busy saving the photos from Scott's *GQ* article onto his phone when the door opened. He scrambled to shove his phone into his pocket as Scott Hunter entered the shop.

It would be ridiculous to say that Scott's face lit up when he saw Kip, but . . . that *really* was what it looked like.

"Kip!" he said, a delighted smile spreading across his sweat-slicked face. "I was worried you might not be working today."

"You were?" Kip asked, too shocked to say anything more intelligent.

"I just mean . . ." And did Scott Hunter seem *embarrassed*? "I like to keep as many things the same in my routine as possible, and you made the other two smoothies, so . . ."

"Must be something about the way I make 'em," Kip said, bravely attempting a flirtatious smile.

"Must be."

Kip gathered the ingredients and started dropping them into the blender. "I watched the game the other night," he said. "That last goal was really something."

"Thanks." Scott sounded like he truly appreciated it. "I felt good about that one."

He smiled at Kip, whose mouth went dry. He turned on the blender before he could say something stupid like, *What do your abs taste like?*

"All alone today?" Scott asked as Kip handed him his usual.

"Yeah, uh, I was supposed to be working with someone, but he called in sick. I don't think he's actually sick. He's kind of useless." Kip cringed inwardly as he said this. *As if Scott Hunter gives a shit about your coworkers.*

"Sorry to hear it," Scott said. "I've had teammates like that."

Kip laughed, because was Scott Hunter seriously comparing their two lines of work?

"You, uh, you mind if I drink this here?" Scott asked, as if there weren't tables and chairs right next to him. "I just . . . have some emails to read." He pulled his phone out of his pocket and waved it in the air.

"Of course, yeah," Kip said, not able to believe his luck. Scott sat at one of the little bistro tables with his back to the door (and his face to Kip). Kip tried hard not to just stare at him as Scott scrolled through emails on his phone, occasionally sipping from his blue smoothie. He was drinking it very slowly, it seemed.

After fifteen minutes, Kip left his station behind the counter and went to work wiping tables that didn't need to be cleaned at all.

When he was at the table next to Scott's, he took a chance and broke the silence. "You sure this isn't going to mess up your game? Breaking routine like this?"

"What? Oh, no. I don't have to do *everything* the same. I mean, I'm not *that* obsessive."

"Sure," Kip said, with a bit of a smirk.

Scott grinned and even laughed. "I probably do seem weird, don't I? Acting like this smoothie is a magic potion or something."

Kip shrugged. "I've read about athletes. You're all nuts, right? Putting your uniforms on a certain way, not changing your socks, not shaving . . ."

Scott pointed an accusing finger at him. "Hey, only in the playoffs, and that is a time-honored tradition!"

"Totally normal, then."

Kip could not believe what he was about to do, but he had to test the waters. Just a little.

"Not saying I mind it," he said, as casually as he could manage. "You guys always look so rugged by the time you hoist the cup. Like a bunch of hot lumberjacks."

There. So that was out there.

Scott looked at him, and Kip could swear the ghost of a smile passed over his lips.

But then Scott stood abruptly, and the smile was gone. "Well, I should get going."

Kip wanted to *die*. He had just been flirting with Scott fucking *Hunter* and now Scott was going to leave forever because what the *hell*, Grady?

"Thanks again, Kip," Scott said. He was kinder than Kip deserved.

But when he got to the door, Scott stopped and turned. "Would you like to go to the game tonight?"

"What?"

"No one is using my tickets. I could give you two, so you can bring . . . someone . . . if you like."

"Are you serious?"

"Why wouldn't I be?"

Kip gaped at the impossibly gorgeous celebrity filling the doorway of the shop, who was offering him a gift for no reason. "If you're sure, I would love to go!"

"I *am* sure, and I'm happy to hear that. Just give them your name at will call."

"Okay. I'll see you tonight, then," Kip said, *like an idiot.*

Scott just smiled and left.

Kip should not have been at all surprised that Scott Hunter's personal seats were *phenomenal.* Six rows from the ice, on the blue line facing the home bench. Just unreal.

"Shit," Elena said. "I know Equinox has a box here, but these seats are way better."

"I can't believe we're here. I can't believe we're using *Scott Hunter's* tickets!"

"It's a weird date, though. You're here with a woman, and he's at work."

"It's *not* a date."

"I'm sure he gives tickets to every smoothie shop clerk."

Kip had been trying not to think too much about why Scott had given him the tickets. "He's just thanking me because he thinks I'm in some way responsible for his hot streak. Like I said, he's nuts."

"Nuts about *you*, maybe."

"Don't be dumb."

"Kip," she said, placing her beer into her cup holder. "You *do* know what you look like, right?"

"What do you—?"

"You're hot, Grady. Extremely hot."

"I'm . . . okay."

"No, listen to me. You are ridiculously good-looking. Do you think I'm happy that you're gay? I am not."

Kip rolled his eyes. "As if. And besides—" he lowered his voice to a whisper, leaning in "—we don't know that Hunter is . . . on my team."

"Don't we?"

"No! I mean . . . I get hints that maybe . . ."

"Like how we're sitting in his personal seats because he *personally* gave you his *personal* tickets when he visited you at work for the third time this week?"

Kip was blushing now. "He's just superstitious," he mumbled, "that's all."

The players came out on the ice to warm up. Kip watched them all skate around, go down on the ice to stretch, take turns lobbing easy shots at their goalies. He tried, but failed, to not pay too much extra attention to #21, Scott Hunter. The man was doing a deep lunging hamstring stretch that showed how flexible he was. Kip imagined what that position might look like without the heavily padded hockey pants.

His undersexed brain took him on a wonderful journey for a few minutes, and he was so distracted that he almost didn't notice when Hunter skated by the glass in front of them—looking like he'd skated right off a promotional poster in his crisp red, white, and blue uniform—and nodded at him.

No. Not at me. Must be at someone sitting behind me.

Kip turned his head. There was no one sitting behind him yet. No one in front of him either.

Huh.

The warm-up wrapped up, the Zambonis came out to clear the ice, and then the spectacle that was the pre-game show started. The lights went out and videos of the Admirals in action were projected onto the ice while rock music blared. There was dry ice and pyrotechnics, and when the players came storming out, the place hit a fever pitch.

Kip was struck by two things: Scott Hunter was a big star. Like, *really* big. A mammoth superstar athlete and this city *loved* him. It seemed like half the people in the crowd were wearing his jersey. And when Scott's name was announced as the game's starting center, the crowd was deafening. He was not just a guy who liked blueberry smoothies and was nice to the shop clerks who made them. This guy *was* New York.

And Kip was here as *his* guest.

Holy fuck.

The other thing that struck him was that Scott commanded a lot of respect from his teammates. Kip could see the way the younger players would glow when he clapped them on the shoulder and complimented them on a good play. Even the referees seemed to like him, giving him little taps on the elbow after they explained a penalty decision to him.

The game was incredible. Scott was incredible. He not only scored a goal each period and assisted on another one, he also made the crowd roar when he leveled a Tampa winger near center ice with a huge hip check. Kip was the most impressed when Scott broke up a fight before it happened, calming his teammate down with a firm hold on his arm and words that Kip wished he could have heard.

It was undeniably sexy to watch Scott displaying so much skill and authority throughout the game. He was spectacular.

"That was so fucking great!" Kip said, far too loudly, as they made their way to the subway after the game. "I want to go to another one! I want to go to all of them!"

"Well, you'll have to wait, superfan," Elena said. "The Admirals hit the road for the next two weeks."

Kip should not have felt as devastated as he did by that news. Suddenly the idea of working an entire shift without seeing Scott seemed unbearable.

When he was at home in bed that night, he couldn't help but wonder if Scott was at all unhappy about going on the road, away from his safe routine.

He was being stupid. Scott was a professional hockey player who was *not* going to be missing his dumb smoothies while on the road. Kip sighed, and resigned himself to at least two weeks of Scott Hunter–free shifts at work.

CHAPTER THREE

Scott watched the island of Manhattan disappear as the plane pushed through the thick clouds that had covered the city for days.

He felt off, but he didn't know why. It had nothing to do with his game because he was playing better than he had all season. The team was on a winning streak, and they were free of any major injuries. Plus, the team's private plane was taking them to Phoenix, which would give them a nice break from the bitter cold of January in New York.

His agent was happy again, at least. A couple of weeks ago Scott had received a very panicked call from Todd Wheeler, the man who had represented him since his college hockey days.

"We're in real trouble here," Todd had said. "The sponsors don't like what they're seeing from you. Gillette is saying they won't renew next year. Even Under Armour is getting nervous. Fucking *Under Armour*, Scott! We can't lose them!"

If the conversation was supposed to have motivated Scott, it hadn't worked. It wasn't like he hadn't known he was playing terribly, or that he had been happy about it.

"Believe me, Todd," Scott had said. "No one is more disappointed in me than I am."

But yesterday Scott had received a very different phone call.

"Whatever you did to get your game back, keep doing it!" a relieved-sounding Todd had said.

Except Scott couldn't keep doing it. He would be on the road for two weeks, mostly playing teams in the Western Conference. The Admirals had seven games scheduled, ending with one in Toronto, before they flew home. Scott never minded being on the road. He liked his teammates, and he wasn't a nervous flyer like some of them. He also, unlike most of the team, didn't have a wife and kids that he had to leave behind.

But for the first time in his career, Scott felt—absurdly—like he was leaving someone behind.

Scott's seatmate, and one of his alternate captains, Carter Vaughan, was particularly excited about their upcoming stop in Los Angeles. He had been seeing Gloria Grey, a very famous and extremely attractive television actress, for a few months now. "Nothing serious," Carter had insisted the last time Scott asked him about her. "Just two beautiful, chill people enjoying each other's company whenever we're in the same city."

Scott thought it might be more than that, but he didn't say anything. He was the last person who should be nosey about other people's love lives.

Carter had his headphones on already. Since there was nothing to look at outside the window, Scott pulled out his book. It was a dumb spy novel, but it was something to pass the time with.

Scott tried to read, but his mind kept wandering. It kept conjuring the image of a charming smoothie shop clerk with stunning hazel eyes and the cutest smile . . .

He turned his head so Carter wouldn't notice his goofy grin.

He had come to the game last night. Kip. Scott had nodded at him, but Kip hadn't done anything in return. Maybe he hadn't seen. Maybe he'd thought Scott was weird.

Either way, it had made Scott absurdly happy to see him sitting in that arena. Happier still to see that he had brought a *female* friend with him, because Kip had implied that he was attracted to men. At least, Scott was pretty sure that was what had happened. He was hopelessly clueless about flirting.

He frowned. Kip might be bisexual. Maybe that woman he had been with *was* his girlfriend. She had certainly looked pretty enough.

Scott was not bisexual. What the world didn't know was that he wasn't straight either. *He'd* known he was gay for a long time. Since he'd played junior, actually. He'd had a terrible crush on a teammate then, one he'd been sure was unrequited. Even if it hadn't been, he'd known Jacob would never act on it. Would never admit it. Making a move on him would only have gotten Scott a black eye, or worse. It could have cost Scott his career if word had gotten out. Because hockey players weren't gay. No NHL player was *ever* gay.

Scott knew, now that he was older and wiser, that there was no way that was true. But it didn't change the fact that no one in the league had ever been openly gay, or even openly bisexual. NHL players married young, had a bunch of kids, and took the family to the cottage in the summer. NHL players golfed and drank and played poker and ate steak and went to strip clubs and slept with puck bunnies and used homophobic slurs liberally.

So Scott kept his love life to himself. Or lack thereof.

It was hard enough to be discreet when you were just an average anybody. It was infinitely harder when you were a superstar athlete. Scott couldn't go online and hook up with random men; he would always be scared one of them would talk to the press. He felt the same way about sex workers. He avoided gay bars and clubs, not that he would necessarily be into that sort of thing anyway. He was a terrible dancer.

Most of his sexual encounters happened during the summers. He would go away to exotic places where people didn't know a damn thing about hockey. Italy, Spain, Brazil, Greece. Places where he was just one of many young, fit men looking for one thing.

Summer had been a long damn time ago.

What Scott didn't do—what he never, *ever* did—was flirt with shop clerks in Manhattan. Because that would be stupid and careless and not at all worth the risk. He would certainly never give them a hint that he was interested in men. Scott had gotten good at concealing that fact; he'd had years of practice, after all.

But there was something about Kip.

Scott couldn't even name it. Obviously he was good-looking (*he's fucking gorgeous, Scott, come on*), with those dimples and those eyes. At the game last night, Scott had finally gotten a glimpse of Kip when he wasn't wearing a ball cap and apron. He'd like to get a much closer look sometime.

Jesus.

So, yes, he was attractive. Lots of men in New York were attractive. Hell, lots of men on Scott's *team* were attractive. So that wasn't the entire reason why Scott couldn't stop thinking about him.

There was just something about him. Scott wanted to talk to him for hours, and find out everything about him. Show him everything. *Give* him everything.

His reason for returning to the shop on game days wasn't a ruse. He sincerely felt that it was important to stick to routines when his game was going well. He had been playing the worst hockey of his career before he'd walked into that shop and Kip had served him that smoothie, and he'd been on fire ever since.

In more ways than one, if he was being honest.

★ ★ ★

"Hey, stranger."

"Hey, Dad," Kip said as he went to the cupboard to grab the cereal box. It was Kip's day off, which meant a rare morning at home.

"I never asked you how the game was the other night," his dad said.

"It was awesome." Kip grinned to himself as he said it. "Really."

Dad sipped his coffee and looked at Kip from where he sat at the little kitchen table. "It was awfully nice of Scott Hunter to give you those tickets."

"It was."

"I don't think there's a person in Brooklyn your mother hasn't told about that."

"God, it's not a big deal."

"We don't have a lot of excitement in our lives." Dad smiled.

Kip joined his father at the same round table he'd been eating breakfast at his whole life.

He loved his parents. He loved this house, but he also desperately wanted to get out on his own.

"How's Elena?" Dad asked.

"Great. You know, completely impressive in every way."

"No job openings for you at Equinox Tech?"

"What the hell would I do at Equinox? I'm just a history nerd like my old man."

"Well, what about the New York Admirals? Are they hiring?"

"Yeah, team historian."

His dad chuckled and leaned back in his chair. "So this thing with Scott Hunter—"

"There is no *thing* with Scott Hunter."

"All right . . ." his dad said in that singsong tone of *Fine, none of my business.*

"Seriously, he just . . . thinks the dumb smoothies I make are good luck or something. Nothing to do with me."

"Your mother will be very disappointed to hear that."

Kip rolled his eyes, but smiled.

"I think Megan's going to be here for dinner tonight," his father said. "Andrew too."

"Oh. Nice." Megan was Kip's big sister, and Andrew was her boyfriend. The two of them lived together in Williamsburg.

Whenever Megan came home for any occasion, it just reminded Kip that she had to *come home*. She was almost four years older than Kip, but still . . .

"You planning on being here tonight?" his dad asked.

"Sure," Kip said, forcing another smile. "Where else would I be?"

Scott slumped against the wall of the steam room, exhausted and frustrated. They should have won this one.

They had played their backup goalie, a kid from Sweden named Tommy Andersson, and it hadn't gone well. But Andersson wasn't to blame. No one had helped him.

Scott ran his hands over his sweat-slick face and into his damp hair.

Scott hadn't even showed up tonight. It had just been a terrible effort by the whole team, and it should have been an easy win.

Coach Murdock had already made them feel ashamed of themselves. He'd walked into the room, shook his head, and walked out—worse than being screamed at.

No one came into the steam room to bother Scott. They knew better.

He sighed and stood up, tightening his towel around his waist. He needed a shower. And something to drink.

He walked into the lounge area, still wearing his towel, and grabbed a bottle of water from the fridge. He downed it in one go, then turned to see Greg Huff sitting on the counter behind him.

"So that was a shit show," Huff said.

"You're not kidding," Scott said. "I don't even know what to say."

"I mean, I'm not the captain, but maybe like, 'Hey, fuck-heads. Stop playing such shitty hockey.' Or something."

Scott smiled a little. "That was more or less what I was thinking."

"Poor Andersson, man. I feel sorry for that kid."

"Yeah . . ." Scott said, looking in the direction of the dressing room. "How's he doing?"

"Wonderful. How do you *think* he's doing?"

"I'll talk to him. *You're* off the hook. Got our only goal tonight. Nice one too."

Huff gave him a lazy salute. "What I'm good for."

It was true. Greg Huff was one of the best sharpshooters in the game. He had incredible aim, and had been an NHL all-star for eight consecutive seasons because of it.

Scott grabbed a Gatorade from the fridge. Huff put out his hands in a catching position, so Scott threw him one as well.

"I'm going to take a shower," Scott said. "But tell Andersson to stick around, all right?"

"Will do."

If Scott could have a whole team of Greg Huffs, he'd be thrilled. Greg was a real dependable, stand-up guy, and a tremendous team presence on and off the ice. Not the flashiest player, and not the biggest guy by a long shot, but a huge contributor to the team.

Scott went to the showers. A couple of other guys were in there. Most of the team had already showered and were getting ready to go back to the San Jose hotel.

One of the guys in the shower was Frank Zullo. He was the only player on the team Scott just didn't like. He was a great defenseman, no question, big and tough and a brutal fighter when necessary. But he was also a bully, and a bit of a creep, really. There were plenty of guys like Zullo in the NHL.

Scott made the water a little hotter, letting it wash away this terrible game. Tomorrow morning they flew to Chicago. They had a night off, then a game the following afternoon. Then a short night flight to Toronto for a game the next evening, and then home to New York.

He left the showers and went to the lockers. He put on some shorts and a T-shirt and went to find Andersson in the dressing room. The young goalie was packing up his gear, looking miserable.

"Hey," Scott said, sitting on the bench beside Andersson's enormous goalie gear bag, "I'm sorry we didn't help you out there tonight."

Andersson huffed an angry laugh. "I fucked up," he said in his heavily accented English.

"We all did."

"I looked like a fucking idiot out there."

"Murdock made the right call, putting you in," Scott said. "I don't blame you a bit. I blame the rest of us. It's just psychological. Putting the backup goalie in makes us cocky, I guess. Like the coach thinks this game should be a walk, so we all believe it, and then . . ."

"Then I look like a fucking idiot."

Scott tilted his head in acknowledgment. "We're all going to be replaying our mistakes tonight when we're in our beds. No one on this team is proud of themselves tonight. But no one blames you either. I need you to know that."

The young goalie gave him a reluctant smile. "Thanks," he said. He stuffed the last of his gear into his bag and stood. "I'm gonna head to the hotel. Replay some of those mistakes. And then I'm gonna forget all about it and get ready for the next game."

"Good man. You're rooming with Burke, right?" Scott asked, just to make conversation as they walked out of the room.

"Yeah."

"Man, I'm sorry. Good luck."

Tommy laughed. "Yeah, thanks. I pretend I can't understand him when I need him to stop talking."

Scott laughed too. Tommy's English was excellent.

"I'm gonna get my stuff together," Scott said. "I'll see you tomorrow, Tommy."

"Goodnight."

Kip scanned the crowded pub until he spotted Shawn sitting alone at a small table. Shawn grinned across the room at him.

"Hey, man," Shawn said, standing and hugging Kip when he reached the table. "Glad you could make it out."

"Been around straight people too much lately," Kip joked, releasing Shawn and settling into the wooden chair across the table from him. It was the same pub they'd been coming to for years—the Kingfisher. It had the same worn, cozy feel of any decades-old English-style pub, with dark wood and dim lighting and beer signs on the walls. A television at the back of the room showed local sports. At a glance it didn't look like a gay bar at all, or at least not what most straight people probably pictured a gay bar being. But the men sat a little closer, and the bartenders were, in Kip's opinion, a little hotter. He loved this place.

"We got a cute server," Shawn said. "You'll like him."

"Aw, I can't compete with you."

Shawn shook his head and raised his pint glass. "Too clean-cut for me. He's all yours."

Shawn was handsome, all dark skin and soft eyes and a warm

smile. He was also an impeccable dresser, always looking like a J.Crew catalog model.

He and Kip had fooled around a bit in college. Nothing too serious, but they had both been eager to experiment. Shawn had a thing for bad boys, though. Despite his straitlaced appearance, he had always been drawn to men with tattoos and an air of danger about them. Kip was just an eager-to-please nerd who couldn't figure his own life out.

Their server stopped by the table, and Shawn hadn't been kidding. Slim, athletic build and blond hair falling in his face—the guy was exactly Kip's type.

Kip gave him a flirty smile as he ordered because he couldn't help himself. He received one in return, and the man introduced himself as Kyle.

Shawn laughed after Kyle left. "Always so fucking smooth."

"As if," Kip said. "I'm a mess most of the time."

"Nah, you're all charm. That boy is already thinking about telling you when his shift ends."

Kip looked over his shoulder toward the bar where Kyle was waiting, presumably for Kip's beer. "Well . . ."

"But first, we have something to talk about," Shawn said.

"What's that?"

"I've been thinking about when we were out with Jimmy and Chuck last week."

"Oh?" Kip could really use that beer.

"First of all, I feel like we maybe ganged up on you when we were—"

"Asking me what the fuck I was doing with my life?"

"*Encouraging* you to pursue your dreams."

"Right."

Kyle, the wonderful angel, came to the table with Kip's pint of local red ale. As he leaned to place the glass on the table, he took the opportunity to rest a hand on Kip's shoulder. Kip felt the tips of his fingers brush the back of his neck. "Let me know if you need anything else," Kyle said, the double meaning lost on no one.

"Look," Kip said to Shawn, after enjoying a parting smile from Kyle, "I know you guys just—"

"I have a proposition for you," Shawn interrupted.

Kip raised an eyebrow. "Those never ended particularly well before."

"A *business* proposition. And I remember a few of those previous times that weren't bad at all."

Kip smiled into his beer. "Me too."

"I *propose*," Shawn said, "that you apply for a better job."

Kip fought the urge to roll his eyes. "Like where?"

"I have a *friend* . . ."

"A friend, huh?"

"He works at the Museum of the City of New York."

Okay. Kip was listening now.

"He told me that they are just about to post an opening for an assistant educator. You know—someone who helps organize school trips and stuff. Teach the little kiddies all about our great city."

Kip slumped back in his chair. "I'm not qualified for that."

Shawn looked at him pointedly. "Do I need to use my Elena voice?"

"No," Kip grumbled.

"You *will* apply for this job, Kip Grady. And you will dazzle them with your charm, and your love of history, and the fact that you have lived here all your life."

"I won't even get an interview!"

"I'm calling Elena."

"Fine. She won't answer. She hates phone calls."

"Apply for the job, Kip."

Kip sighed. *Why not, right?* "Okay. I'll apply. Thanks for letting me know."

"Don't mention it, asshole. Now—" Shawn leaned back and made a show of looking around the bar "—how about you see if our friend Kyle feels like celebrating your glamorous new career."

This time Kip *did* roll his eyes. "I'm not celebrating shit. And . . ." He stopped himself because he wasn't sure what he wanted to say. *I'm holding out for someone else right now. You probably know him—he's the captain of the New York Admirals. You might remember him from* People *magazine's "50 Most Beautiful People" issue? Yeah, I have a crush on him. He's almost definitely heterosexual. Fingers crossed!*

Instead he just said, "I think I'm gonna head home early tonight. But let's see if we can't find *you* someone."

"It wasn't fucking charging! It was a fucking hit! It's *hockey*, you blind mother—"

"That's enough." Scott grasped Zullo firmly by both arms and hauled him away from the referee.

Zullo turned his head and kept screaming. "What, I can't fucking touch anyone now? This not a contact sport anymore? Open your fucking eyes, you—"

"I'll talk to him. Just go to the box, Zullo."

Zullo shook his head. Carter skated over to help escort him to the penalty box. If Zullo kept the yelling up, he'd end up with a game misconduct.

Scott went back to the referee. "Charging, Hal? Really?"

"You telling me I don't know how to do my job, Hunter? I know what I saw." Hal Coleman—one of Scott's favorite referees—only came up to Scott's chest, but he was tough as nails under his calm demeanor. Smart too.

"Well," Scott said, glancing at the penalty box that was now occupied by a fuming Frank Zullo, "won't hurt him to cool off a bit in there anyway."

"He's a real sweetheart," Hal agreed.

Scott looked across the ice to the Chicago bench. "Is Becker all right?"

"I'm going to go check on him. Seems to still be alive." Hal looked pointedly at Scott. "Tell your boy if I see that shit again he's out of the game."

"Noted."

Hal left to head over to the Chicago bench, and Scott headed to the penalty box.

"Couldn't change his mind," he said. "Just take two to cool off and then we'll finish disappointing the home crowd."

"It wasn't charging. No fucking way that was charging," Zullo spat.

"Except the part where you charged him."

"Jesus fucking Christ, Hunter. You fucking serious? You playing for Chicago now? Becker took a dive!"

Scott was already skating back to the bench. "Take two, Frank," he called over his shoulder.

Carter caught up with him. "How much can I slip Hal to suspend Zullo for a few games?"

"Come on," Scott said dryly, "Zullo is perfectly capable of getting suspended without your help."

"Fucking psychopath," Carter muttered. "We're still doing Chicago Cut after the game, right? I *need* those steaks."

"Yeah, yeah."

Hal blew the whistle for the face-off. Scott went down to the circle in their end of the ice to take it, and threw some encouraging words at their goaltender as he skated by the net.

"Good game, Benny!"

"Don't say a damn word. You jinx me and I'm coming after you."

Scott chuckled. Eric Bennett was as mild-mannered as they come off the ice, but once he was in the crease, he was as fierce a competitor as Scott had ever known.

Scott bent down at the circle and put his stick on the ice. He glanced up to meet the eye of his opponent, a star center for Chicago named Clarke.

"If Zullo tries that shit again," Clarke growled, "I'm sending Harvey after him."

"Man, go ahead. Don't know why you'd do that to Harvey, though." Scott smiled.

"Zullo is a piece of shit."

"Now, now. If you can't say something nice . . ."

As soon as Scott won the face-off, he raced down to the opposing team's zone and took a quick pass back from Carter. He launched the puck at the net and watched it sail over the goalie's shoulder for a shorthanded goal.

It felt so fucking good to have his game back.

CHAPTER FOUR

Kip had more than one job.

As well as working at Straw+Berry, he was on a call list for a company that hired servers for events, like fund-raisers and ceremonies. A friend had gotten him on the list, and Kip had worked a couple dozen events over the past year and a half.

He had received a call to see if he was available to work a fund-raiser for one of the children's hospitals Wednesday night, a black-tie cocktail reception with some speakers at Chelsea Piers.

Kip *was* available, and he *really* needed the money. So on Wednesday, he left Straw+Berry at two o'clock with his backpack containing his wadded-up apron and ball cap, and also his black leather shoes, his black dress pants, and a few basic toiletries so he could freshen up before the high-class event.

He got off the train in Chelsea with a couple of hours to kill. The miserable February weather drove him into the nearest Starbucks, where he took his Americano to a table to sit and think about a certain NHL superstar.

He had been kind of hoping the two-week Scott Hunter drought would be enough to end this ridiculous crush. It was unlikely he would be seeing Scott on a regular basis, or at all, for much longer. One bad home game and it would be over. Or maybe Scott had already found a new good luck charm.

Anyway, the drought hadn't ended the crush.

He had tomorrow off at his other job, but would be working Friday. Hopefully Scott would come by, if only because Kip wanted to thank him for the tickets.

When Kip was *really* bored, like right now at his little table in a Starbucks in Chelsea, he would let himself fantasize a bit about what it would be like to date Scott Hunter. For one thing, just having access to that body . . . What would all those muscles feel like under his hands? What would it be like to have the full weight of Scott covering him, pressing him into a mattress? Or against a wall . . .

He wondered what kissing him would be like. If Scott's full, pink lips were as soft as they looked. He wondered how he tasted. What it would be like to run his tongue over those perfect teeth.

And what would it be like to date someone as famous as Scott? As *rich* as Scott. Kip couldn't imagine what it would feel like to have that much money. Even a fraction of that much money. Hell, at the moment Kip couldn't imagine what it would feel like to be able to afford the Starbucks sandwich he had kind of wanted to order with his coffee.

He let himself daydream about going to the games as Scott's boyfriend. Sitting in his usual seat, bursting with pride when Scott did something amazing. They would celebrate Scott's big win at home that night. Together.

Maybe he would greet Scott at the door when he came back from a long road trip. Scott would be so happy to see him . . .

Kip was getting a little hot and bothered in this very public coffee shop.

He sighed and took a sip of coffee that was far too hot. The pain brought him down to earth. *If you put half as much energy into finding an actual, realistic boyfriend as you do into fantasizing about a superstar millionaire who probably isn't even interested in* men, *let alone* you . . .

Kip hadn't gotten any action in . . . a month? No, two months?

God, almost three months.

It was his own fault, really. He hadn't been going out much. He used to, all the time. He'd never been in a relationship that he would call serious, but he used to love the challenge of picking guys up at bars or gyms or even grocery stores. He was naturally flirtatious, or at least he used to be. Something about being twenty-five, living with his parents, and working at a smoothie shop with nothing promising on the horizon had killed his swagger.

He took another sip of coffee that was *still too hot*—how?

There might be a cute guy working with him tonight. Maybe he could break this dry spell.

Scott tugged at his navy tuxedo jacket and fiddled with his cuff links. He hated these events, but wanted to use his celebrity for good, and children's hospitals were a particular favorite cause of his.

He was scheduled to speak tonight, but he wasn't nervous about that. He never minded public speaking, and this would only be a short speech anyway. What he hated was *this*: Being on display for a room of wealthy, fawning donors. Making small talk with tedious people. Wearing a tuxedo. Being mindful of his every move, his every word.

He was tired. The road trip had been long and they had just gotten back this morning. It would be a challenge to stay in a good mood tonight. But he would. Because that was his job.

There was a loud din in the room of people talking and laughing. It was a sea of dark tuxes and mostly dark gowns. In one corner of the room, a trio played mellow jazz music.

He stared into his pilsner glass of beer and realized he was starving. The only food seemed to be on little trays being carried by servers wearing all black. He inched toward one, hoping to snag a shrimp or something.

The server turned, and Scott was shocked to see that it was: "Kip!"

Kip looked just as surprised. He took a step back, and the tray wobbled dangerously on his arm before he quickly grabbed it with his other hand. "Scott! Uh, I mean . . ."

Scott gathered himself and smiled. "Scott is fine."

"I didn't know you were going to be here."

"That makes two of us."

Kip's eyes were stunning, set against all of the black of his uniform. He was more beautiful than Scott remembered, even.

Scott took a couple of things off Kip's tray, just to make it less awkward. "Do you work a lot of these things?" he asked, trying to keep the conversation normal.

"A few. This one was last-minute."

Scott nodded. He desperately tried to think of something else to ask him. But all he could think about was how soft Kip's hair looked.

"Hey," Kip said, "thanks again for the tickets. That was amazing, being there."

"No problem. I'm glad you had a good time. It was nice seeing you there."

"Oh. You saw me?"

"I nodded at you when I skated by. Kind of subtle, I guess."

"Oh! No, I saw. I just . . . didn't think it was meant for me."

"It was," Scott said, far too earnestly. He took a step back and cleared his throat. "Anyway . . ."

"You're probably busy."

"Right. And you're working, obviously."

"Yeah. So . . ."

"I'll let you get to it."

"All right."

Scott placed a hand on Kip's free arm, needing to make contact somehow. "It was nice seeing you, Kip."

"You . . . Yeah, you too. I guess I'll see you around tonight."

Scott nodded and Kip left to serve canapés. A hand landed on Scott's arm immediately, and he turned to talk to one of the event organizers. He felt a lot lighter than he had before.

Scott spent the rest of the evening chatting with different people, but he kept scanning the room for Kip. Their eyes met a couple of times. The first time, Scott quickly looked away, embarrassed. The second time, though, he let his gaze linger, and he was rewarded with an adorable grin from Kip that caused Scott's stomach to flip.

Oh no, Hunter. You are in trouble.

Once Scott had given his speech and had mingled for another hour, he was desperate to get out of his tux. Out of this room.

Except . . .

He caught Kip as he was loading empty glasses onto a tray.

"You have to stay much later?" Scott asked.

"Another hour, maybe? Cleanup isn't too bad this time."

Scott smiled a little. He couldn't think of anything else to say. He just didn't want to leave.

But he *should* leave. Otherwise he might say something dangerous . . .

Scott was a superstitious man. He believed everything happened for a reason, and it couldn't be a coincidence that Kip was here tonight. Fate had thrown them into the same room together. It was an opportunity. Scott just didn't know what to do with it.

"They never have enough food at these things," he said, as casually as he could manage.

Kip looked up from the table he was clearing. "At least you

got to eat *something*," he said. "I've been carrying around trays of food I can't eat all night. I'm starving."

He kept his eyes on Scott's, waiting. And Scott *knew* this was his moment. Right here.

"There's a place a couple of blocks from here that has great burgers," Scott said, still carefully. Not a direct invitation. Not yet. "It's open late."

"Oh?"

"I was thinking of heading there after . . ."

Kip stood straight up to meet Scott's gaze. "Are you asking me to come get a burger with you?"

Scott was absurdly terrified. But goddamn, he wanted this. "Yes."

Kip grinned, showing his dimples. "All right. I'll meet you as soon as I'm done here. At the front doors?"

"Yeah . . ." It suddenly occurred to Scott that he was wearing a tuxedo, and didn't have a change of clothing on him. "An hour, you think?"

Kip shrugged. "Maybe a little less. Maybe longer if you keep distracting me."

"Okay!" It was all Scott could do to keep from clapping his hands together with glee. They were doing this. They were going to get a burger together. He would fix the tuxedo problem and he would let this thing happen.

He didn't think he could get to his apartment and back here on time. No nearby clothing stores were still open, unless . . .

When Kip saw Scott again, he was standing near the front doors of the complex, wearing a gray hooded sweatshirt that had BROOKLYN written across the front, and a black knit hat that said NYC on it. He had a cheap-looking knapsack slung over his shoulder containing, Kip assumed, most of his tuxedo.

"I, uh, I didn't have a change of clothes with me, so I went to a bodega that sold some touristy stuff," Scott explained.

Dressed like he was, you almost couldn't tell he was Scott Hunter. But Kip knew. And he knew that Scott Hunter had frantically bought souvenir clothing so he could *go on a date with him.*

Maybe. Maybe a date.

Kip smiled. "You look good."

He *did*. A little odd, perhaps, in a hoodie, navy tuxedo pants, and dress shoes, but good. Kip was pretty grubby, in the same jeans he'd worn earlier in the day and a black T-shirt he had been wearing under his uniform tonight.

He zipped up his parka before following Scott out into the cold. It was *very* cold.

"You must be freezing," he said. "You sure you want to walk there?"

"I run hot," Scott said with a grin. "I'll be fine."

They walked together through the quiet streets. Not a lot of people out on this frigid Wednesday night. There were a few flurries in the air, but no wind. Despite his claim of not being cold, Scott had shoved his hands into the pocket of his hoodie.

"How was the road trip?" Kip asked, after spending a solid minute trying to think of something to say.

"Good! Went well. We won five of the seven games, should have won the one in San Jose, but that's a rant you don't want to hear."

"You like the travel?"

"I don't mind it. I like some cities more than others. Some cities like *me* more than others . . ."

"They'd all love you if you played for their team."

"Maybe."

They walked another block in silence. Kip still couldn't believe who he was walking with. *He's just a guy. He's just a really hot, enormous guy who's famous and beloved and . . . cold.*

Scott was definitely huffing a bit as they walked. And his shoulders were hunched.

"You all right?" Kip asked.

"Oh, yeah. Just . . . it *is* pretty cold."

Kip smiled. "Yeah, okay, tough guy." He got brave and nudged Scott a bit with his elbow.

Scott laughed and his breath came out in white clouds.

Kip swallowed. "Is the burger place close?"

"Yeah. It's, um . . . Oh. It's right there." Scott pointed across the street.

"Let's get you inside."

They entered and Scott smiled at Kip as the warm air hit them. Kip could not believe how beautiful he was.

They ordered at the counter (Scott paid) and sat at a table in the corner to wait for their food. The restaurant was quiet.

Kip wished he knew what was going on here. Normally when a guy invited him to get some food, or a drink, there were no doubts about where it might lead.

But this wasn't a regular guy. And it was possible that Scott didn't realize this seemed like a date. Maybe he was just . . . lonely.

How in hell could Scott Hunter be lonely?

"You live in Manhattan?" Scott asked suddenly.

"Nah. Brooklyn. Born and raised."

"Ah. I'm from upstate. Rochester."

Kip smiled a little. "I know."

"Right. I, uh, I guess my life is kind of public knowledge."

"Kind of," Kip said, and, feeling brave, added, "but I'll bet you have *some* secrets."

Scott turned pink. It was cute. He fiddled with the straw in his soda cup until it seemed to inspire his next question. "Have you worked at Straw Plus Berry long?"

"Um, actually," Kip said, feigning offense, "it's pronounced Straw *and* Berry, so . . ."

Scott put up his hands and grinned. "Sorry! Didn't mean to insult you."

"That's okay." Kip sighed dramatically. "I'm sure people get your team name wrong all the time."

Scott shook his head, still smiling. "Do you like it? Working there, I mean?"

Kip actually laughed at that. "It's all right. I mean . . . no. I don't really like it."

"Is there something else you would rather be doing?"

"Of course! I just don't know what that is yet. I mean, I have a history degree."

"No kidding? I never finished college."

Kip gave him a gentle smirk again. "I know."

"Right."

"Did you want to? Finish college, I mean?"

Scott seemed surprised by the question. "I . . . Yes. I did. I wanted to finish. To graduate. My mom . . . She would have liked that. And I enjoyed the classes. I've always liked learning."

"What were you studying?"

"A little bit of everything. I couldn't commit to a major, and I didn't need to. The school didn't care what I took, just as long as I performed on the ice."

Kip felt a little sad for him. "Must be weird," he said. "Everyone's wanted a piece of you since you were a teenager. Probably never felt like your life was your own."

Scott looked stunned.

Kip turned red—he'd crossed a line. "Sorry. Jesus, forget I said that, all right? I don't even know you—"

"No!" Scott said. "That's . . . It did feel like that. I don't want to complain, obviously, but . . . Yeah."

"You're allowed to complain."

Scott smiled at him. "I'm really not. It would get me despised by everyone."

"Well, you can complain to me."

The way Scott looked at him then, Kip would never forget it. If they were alone, and if he were someone else and Scott were someone else, he would have expected Scott to lunge across the table and haul him into a hungry kiss.

Instead, burgers were placed in front of them by a server and the moment was gone.

As they ate, Scott's eyes darted around the small restaurant, and it occurred to Kip that he had never taken his winter hat off.

"Worried you'll get recognized?" Kip asked.

"Not worried. I'm just . . . hoping I won't. Not right now." Scott picked up his burger, then put it down without taking another bite. He fiddled with his straw again.

He finally sighed, and turned his eyes up to meet Kip's. "It's just nice. Doing this."

"Hanging out with someone?"

"With you."

Kip was speechless. And Scott looked absolutely *tortured*. His eyes were pleading with Kip to understand him. To not make him spell it out.

"Oh" is what Kip finally said.

Scott's face relaxed a bit. "Um, I'm not . . . good at this," he said. "It's important to me to keep my private life private, and that's increasingly hard to do. So I don't ever . . ."

"Pick up guys?"

Scott flushed a little. Kip loved it. "Yeah."

Kip could not believe that this thing that he had been trying not to pretend was a date was *actually a date*. It was unreal. But suddenly he didn't want to eat another bite of his stupid burger. He wanted to get Scott Hunter somewhere private and let him slam Kip against a wall.

He decided to be bold.

"Is there somewhere we can go?" he asked in a low voice.

"Yeah," Scott said, his voice huskier than it had been a second ago. His eyes a little darker.

Kip wasn't naive. He knew what this was. Hunter wasn't out, and he had to get his action as discreetly as possible. Nothing serious or long-term; he just needed to get off, and Kip was more than happy to help him with that. He was honored that Scott felt he could trust him to keep a secret, really.

"Let's go," Kip said.

CHAPTER FIVE

They dumped the rest of their dinners into the garbage cans and walked out, saying nothing to each other. Scott pulled his phone out when they were outside, calling some sort of car service.

"Should be here in a minute or two," he said after he hung up.

Kip just nodded, buzzing with anticipation.

The car arrived, a black SUV, and they slid into the leather seats behind the partition. Scott sat straight upright with his hands on his knees, not looking at Kip at all. His fingers flexed and curled restlessly.

Kip placed his hand on one of Scott's thighs, feeling the solid muscle under the smooth fabric of his suit pants. He didn't move his hand, but let it rest there as a reassuring presence.

Scott glanced at Kip's hand, then turned to meet his eyes.

"I can keep a secret," Kip said, almost a whisper because he wasn't sure if the driver could hear them. "And I promise I'll make it good for you."

"I know." Scott placed his own hand over Kip's and tangled their fingers. He pressed his lips together, like he was trying to suppress a smile. Like he was *giddy* about this. About *Kip*.

Fucking incredible.

The car took them to a newer building in the Lower East Side. Kip was surprised. He had expected something . . . Well, he knew it had to be near Straw+Berry, but . . . in a fancier neighborhood, maybe? But, he supposed, every neighborhood in Manhattan was getting fancy these days, and this looked like a brand-new building.

It was also, clearly, a very *expensive* building. The lobby reminded Kip of the room that housed the Egyptian temple at the Met—vast and serene, with marble everywhere. Scott led them to the elevator and typed in a code. When the doors opened, they were right in front of Scott's door; there were no other units on the floor. Scott typed in another code and opened the door. They were met with a floor-to-ceiling view of the lights of Brooklyn across the East River.

"Holy shit," Kip murmured, walking, trancelike, toward the windows.

Scott left the lights of the apartment off. He stood behind Kip and said, "The view was definitely a selling point."

"Geez, yeah."

Scott's hand was on Kip's shoulder. Kip waited a beat, then turned to face him. The lights of the city played against Scott's face in the dark. His brow was furrowed, like he was arguing with himself, but his eyes kept landing on Kip's mouth.

Kip decided to take the plunge.

Grabbing a handful of Scott's hoodie, he pulled him down and pressed their lips together. Scott responded immediately with a hungry groan. He parted his lips, then placed his hands on Kip's face as he pushed his tongue into his mouth, kissing him like a starving man. Like he hadn't been with anyone in ages . . .

Kip kissed back, exploring Scott's mouth. Tasting him for the first time. Kip's head swam. *I can't believe this is happening.*

Scott unzipped Kip's parka and slid it off his arms, letting it fall to the floor. His hands fell to Kip's waist and slipped up under his T-shirt. Kip shivered at the sensation of Scott's large, callused hands brushing over his skin.

They kissed for what felt like forever in the dark apartment, until Kip finally asked, breathlessly, "You got a bedroom?"

"Yeah." Scott laughed when he said it. He sounded nervous, but he gestured for Kip to follow him.

He led him through a doorway that revealed a giant bedroom with an even better view of the Brooklyn Bridge than the living room. There was a California king–size bed against the far wall. Aside from that, the room was sparsely decorated, but masculine and impressive.

Scott kept the lighting dim in the room. He smiled shyly before he pulled the souvenir hoodie off over his head and tossed it onto a chair. The white T-shirt he still wore was stretched tight across his chest.

"Is this . . . okay?" Scott asked. "I'm sorry if I'm . . . I don't do this very often."

"It's *really* fucking okay," Kip said, stepping toward Scott and placing one hand on his ridiculous bicep. "Let me take care of you. You can just be Scott from Rochester tonight, all right?"

Scott looked at him with so much gratitude, it was heartbreaking. Then his gaze went to where Kip's hand was on his arm, and his gratitude quickly turned to something else. Scott kissed him, hard, and lifted Kip's T-shirt. Kip took the hint and stepped back to pull his shirt off. Scott did the same, and *good god . . .*

Kip had seen pictures of Scott. Had even seen some shirtless locker-room interviews. But seeing Scott standing in front of him, a wall of muscle and smooth, pale skin . . .

"Fuck," Kip muttered.

Mesmerized, he watched the rise and fall of Scott's massive chest as he breathed. Then he saw that Scott was staring at Kip's naked chest the same way. As if Kip was even in the same league. Sure, Kip kept in shape. He went to the gym whenever he had time. But Scott was . . .

"You are gorgeous," Scott said.

Scott was impressed, apparently.

Kip grinned and bit his bottom lip as he walked backward toward the bed. Scott returned the grin and followed, stopping at the end of the bed as Kip fell back onto the mattress. Kip propped himself up on his elbows and gazed up at Scott in a manner that he hoped was seductive.

"What do you want to do with me?" Kip drawled.

"I don't know. I've . . . There are a lot of things I've thought about."

Kip's mouth dropped open and his cock got uncomfortably harder in his pants. *Scott has been thinking about this. With* me*!*

He instructed himself to keep his cool. This was a once-in-a-lifetime opportunity and he'd be damned if he was going to fuck it up.

"Pick your favorite," he said. "Or, hell, pick your top ten. I've got plenty of time."

Scott moved quickly, covering Kip's body with his own as he took his mouth again. Kip kissed him back eagerly. He couldn't get enough of Scott's mouth, and he wanted Scott to know how much he wanted this. He wanted him to feel confident to do whatever he'd been fantasizing about.

When Scott placed a firm hand on Kip's crotch, gripping his erection through the denim, Kip groaned into his mouth. He jerked his hips up and pressed into Scott's palm. *Yes. Please. Touch me everywhere.*

Scott broke their kiss and looked down at him with wild eyes.

"Do it," Kip breathed. "Whatever you're thinking. Please."

Kip leaned forward to kiss him again, but Scott was already moving down his body. His big hands quickly unfastened Kip's jeans and hauled them down to his thighs. Kip didn't even have a chance to react before Scott was mouthing him through his underwear.

"God! Fuck!" Kip cried out, partly out of surprise and partly because Scott Hunter's beautiful mouth felt so fucking *good*. He stayed propped on his elbows so he could watch, because *holy shit*.

Perhaps encouraged by Kip's enthusiasm, Scott tugged the waistband of his briefs down, freeing Kip's erection. He lowered his lips to the head, then glanced up at Kip as if he was asking permission. Kip nodded, and murmured, "Yes, please."

When Scott wrapped those plush lips around him, enveloping his cock in delicious wet heat, it was all Kip could do to stop himself from thrusting up into his mouth. The only thing that stopped him was his assumption that Scott *probably* didn't have a whole lot of experience sucking cock. Not that he was *bad* at it. He was just a bit frantic, working his mouth on Kip's cock like they were in an alley instead of Scott's home—like he was worried someone might walk in on them at any moment and stop them.

"Hey," Kip said, a little choked, "it's all right. No need to hurry—you, *fuck*, you might wanna slow down if you want me to last."

The tension seemed to leave Scott's shoulders as he slowed his tongue. He was making gorgeous noises, as if *he* was the one being sucked off instead of the other way around, but he would have to stop soon or Kip would be *done*. The whole scene was too fucking much.

Kip placed a hand on the side of Scott's face, and Scott looked up, lips still stretched wide around him.

"What do you want?" Kip asked.

Scott's mouth slid off Kip's cock with a long, obscene drag of his tongue, and Kip's eyes rolled back. *Jesus*. Scott could say literally anything right now and Kip would be down with it.

"I want you to fuck me," Scott said.

"You do?" Kip was certainly down for whatever, but he'd just sort of assumed that the captain of an NHL team might be kind of . . . toppy.

"Yeah," Scott said with a shy smile. "Is that okay? It's . . . it's what I've been thinking about the most."

Kip made a mental note to stop making assumptions about the preferred sexual positions of giant, muscular star athletes. "Fuck yes, it's definitely okay."

Scott grinned.

"Get those pants off." Kip could not *wait* to see all of Scott.

Scott stood and seemed to take him in. Sprawled out on the bed, pants pulled down to mid-thigh, and erect cock wet with Scott's spit, Kip imagined he was quite the picture.

"You too," Scott said finally, voice strained. "Get your clothes off."

Kip quickly removed his sneakers, pants, underwear, and socks, and lay back on the bed, watching Scott.

Scott turned away from Kip as he bent to rid himself of the last of his clothing, giving Kip a great view of his incredible ass. He watched the muscles ripple as Scott tugged his socks off. His eyes trailed down Scott's solid thighs, pale as the rest of him but covered in dark blond hair. He was so strong, so masculine. He was everything Kip had ever dreamed about, almost too perfect to be real.

When he was completely undressed, Scott turned to face the bed.

"You've gotta be kidding me," Kip breathed.

Scott huffed a laugh, as if he was relieved that Kip liked what he saw. Which was ridiculous.

He stretched himself out on the bed beside Kip and brought their mouths together again. Kip had been expecting more of the same urgency, but the way Scott was kissing him now was so tender, like he was savoring him, and Kip lost himself in it.

"God, your mouth," Scott murmured.

Kip smiled against Scott's lips. "I can do other things with it too."

He needed to taste every inch of Scott. He might not get another chance.

Scott caught Kip's bottom lip between his teeth, then released him and whispered, "Show me."

Kip did not need to be told twice. He rolled Scott onto his back and straddled his massive thighs.

"Fuck, you're enormous," Kip said.

"Well, I'm *very* turned on right now."

Kip laughed. "I meant all of you, but yeah. That thing is impressive too."

He leaned forward and pressed a kiss to Scott's collarbone. Scott gasped and arched up, so Kip let his mouth travel down his body, licking the curves of his muscles on his chest and stomach, and along the line of his absurdly defined obliques. The path led him to Scott's cock, which was swollen and begging for attention. Kip ignored it and moved back up to Scott's mouth.

"Bastard," Scott growled, but he kissed Kip wildly.

As an apology, Kip moved his hips so their cocks slid against each other. Scott moaned his approval. "Christ, yes."

Kip repeated the motion a few more times, then pressed a hand on Scott's chest, and sat up. "Lube?"

"Yeah. Just a sec."

Kip dismounted so Scott could roll and reach into the nightstand drawer. He handed the small bottle to Kip.

"Top shelf," Kip commented, examining the label.

"I like to spend big on important things," Scott said dryly.

Kip reached for Scott's cock, stroking it slowly and getting it slick and shiny. Scott's abdominal muscles flexed as he writhed on the bed while Kip caressed his balls and tugged at them gently. Scott swore quietly and arched his back. Kip smiled.

He stroked two slick fingers over Scott's hole, and the NHL all-star *whimpered*.

"Yes, *fuck* . . . God, it's been too long. Too fucking long . . ."

Kip stroked Scott's cock with one hand as he teased his rim with the other. "No one else," he murmured. "Just you and me in this room. Nothing outside that door. Nothing matters but making each other feel good, all right?"

"Yes." Scott didn't so much say it as exhale it. All of his muscles seemed to loosen a bit. His eyes closed, his beautiful long lashes resting against his cheekbones. "Gonna make you feel so good, Kip. Can't wait until you're inside me."

"Me neither. Gonna fuck you like this, I think. You on your back. I wanna see you. Wanna make you come all over that gorgeous body of yours."

"God, yes." Scott sounded a million miles away.

By the time Kip had worked a third finger into him, Scott was breathing hard and his cock was leaking.

"You're so fucking stunning," Kip told him.

"Then fuck me," Scott growled.

"Condom?"

Scott answered by reaching into the drawer again and tossing a condom at him. Kip rolled it on as fast as fucking possible before lining himself up.

He pushed in slowly, and kept a hand on Scott's cock, gently stroking as he entered him. Scott's face gave no indication of pain. Of course not. He was a tough guy. An athlete. A guy who got stitches on the bench and was back on the ice next shift. He could take it.

Scott bent his knees until they were touching his chest, coaxing Kip to push deeper. Kip grabbed Scott's hips and hauled him closer, then he slid back and thrust in, hard and fast. Scott cried out, but he was smiling. He looked ecstatic.

"Just like that," Scott breathed. "Hard. Please."

He hooked a leg over Kip's shoulder, and raised his hips, urging Kip to take him even deeper.

Kip watched, mesmerized, as Scott stroked his own cock. He was already on the verge of shattering, but when Scott murmured Kip's name, Kip lost all control. His rhythm was completely gone, and he was just fucking Scott as hard and fast as he could as his mind broke apart. It was all just too much.

Suddenly, Scott threw his head back, his chin jutted out and his neck muscles strained. His back arched and he came with a gorgeous shudder that Kip would never forget. He spurted, endless and beautiful, against his own stomach and chest, some even hitting his neck. Kip moaned and swore and came on the next thrust, almost screaming with how good it felt.

When the last waves subsided he collapsed on top of Scott, panting and smiling. After a minute, Scott gently maneuvered him so he could reach his mouth, and kissed him.

"Thank you," Scott murmured happily. "You have no idea . . . Thank you."

"You're thanking *me*?"

"I needed that," Scott said. "It's been a long time."

Kip felt brave. "How long?"

"August."

"Are you—?"

"*Early* August."

Kip wanted to ask how that was possible, but the answer might lead into territory that wouldn't make for great post-sex pillow talk. Scott obviously wasn't comfortable picking up men.

What he *really* wanted to know was: *Why now? Why* me*?*

Instead he said, "I should get cleaned up."

"Bathroom's that way," Scott said, gesturing to a door across the room. "I'll use the one in the hall."

Kip got himself cleaned up and walked out of the (incredible) bathroom. Scott was sitting up, propped against the headboard, with a thin sheet over him.

Kip began collecting his clothes. He wouldn't kid himself about what this was. The sex had been great, but Scott would probably like him to leave now.

"Well," he said, "thanks for that."

"You're leaving?" Scott sounded disappointed.

Kip paused, holding his jeans in one hand, his T-shirt in the other. "Yeah, I mean . . ."

"You don't have to," Scott said. "You can stay. I . . . I'd like you to stay. If you want."

Kip stared, gobsmacked, at the gorgeous, sex-rumpled hockey star who was very shyly inviting him to stay the night. He actually looked nervous, as if he thought Kip might turn him down.

Kip dropped the jeans and shirt on the floor, and returned to the bed, grinning. "Don't gotta twist *my* arm."

He sprawled playfully across the width of the bed with his head on Scott's thigh.

"I want to know about you." Scott smiled down at him and began stroking his hair. "Will you tell me something? I can't think of the right questions to ask."

Kip gazed up into his face. "My real name is Christopher, but almost no one calls me that. I'm twenty-five. I . . . I still live with my parents in Brooklyn because I need to pay off my student debt or get a much better job before I can move out."

"Don't be embarrassed about that. I grew up dirt-poor. You think I don't know how lucky I am?"

"Not lucky," Kip said. "You worked hard for everything you have."

"I had help. I got a scholarship to a boarding school with a great hockey program when I was fourteen. I had a free ride to college. I haven't had to think about money for over ten years. I just wish my mom . . ."

"She, um . . . ?"

"Died. Yeah. When I was fifteen."

"I'm sorry."

"Thank you. She was really amazing. I would've liked to have been able to take care of her the way she deserved. Buy her a nice house. All that."

"Only child, right?"

"Yeah," Scott said. "Yeah, it was just the two of us." He cleared his throat. "Anyway. We should probably talk about happier things."

"Don't have to talk at all, if you don't want," Kip said, reaching up to stroke Scott's face. He felt traces of stubble.

Scott smiled at him. "I should sleep soon. I have an early practice tomorrow. Long one too."

"Mm," Kip said, feeling drowsier by the minute as Scott continued to stroke his hair. "You sure you want me to stay?"

"Definitely." The way Scott said it was so warm. So *affectionate*. Kip's heart fluttered.

Uh-oh.

One night, Grady. Don't go getting stupid. Appreciate what you've been given here.

Kip got under the sheet with Scott. He rested his head on Scott's chest, letting the rise and fall of his breathing lull him to sleep.

CHAPTER SIX

Scott blinked awake at the sound of his alarm. It took him a moment to register the weight on his chest that was making it difficult to reach for the phone.

Kip.

Scott grinned as he turned off the alarm and let the memories of the previous night wash over him. He had *done it*! He had successfully picked up a man here in Manhattan. A man he really *liked*. A man who was now naked and sleeping blissfully in his bed, curled against him.

But Scott had to leave. *Fuck.* The car would be here in, what? Forty minutes?

He sighed, and turned to kiss the top of Kip's head before he slipped out from underneath him. Kip made a small noise of sleepy protest, but immediately settled back into a deep slumber.

Scott took a quick shower, and was in the bedroom, pulling on his T-shirt, when he heard rustling.

"Hey," Kip said groggily. He was propped up on an elbow, his hair was all messed up, and one eye was closed. Adorable.

"Sorry to wake you," Scott said. "I need to go. You can stay if you—"

"Nah, I should go. I, um . . ."

"You're working today?"

"No. If I was working today, I would have been late an hour ago. Just . . . I should go home."

"Right."

"Yeah."

Kip was already out of the bed, scooping up his clothes off the floor. He dressed himself quickly, then went into the bathroom.

Scott exhaled. This was unknown territory for him. Kip was hardly his boyfriend, but he wasn't just a one-night stand that Scott had picked up either. At least, not to Scott.

"I'm working tomorrow," Kip said, when he got out of the bathroom. He seemed as unsure as Scott was. "You play tomorrow night, right?"

"Yeah. And Saturday."

"Well, I guess I'll see you tomorrow morning? Unless you think that magic smoothie isn't working anymore."

Scott grinned. "I think it's still working. I'll see you tomorrow morning, then."

"Okay."

Kip left the bedroom and Scott followed. He watched as Kip retrieved his coat and backpack from the floor, and put on his sneakers.

"So, uh . . . have a good practice," Kip said when he was ready to leave.

"Thanks." Scott frowned. Why was this so awkward?

"Tomorrow morning, then."

"Yes. Tomorrow."

Fuck it.

Scott strode over to Kip and kissed him. He held his face in his hands and tried to *show* him what he was feeling, since he couldn't tell him. Kip seemed to hear him, because he kissed back just as fervently, and it was all Scott could do to keep himself from pressing Kip up against a wall, unfastening his jeans, and . . .

"I'll see ya," Kip said, murmuring the words against Scott's lips. "Tomorrow."

Scott reluctantly let him go. He wanted to walk him to the front door, but there was no need. Kip didn't need the codes to leave the building. Besides, it was better that no one saw them together so early in the morning.

After the door closed, Scott threw himself back against a wall, cursing how fucking hard this was. It wasn't just being gay, or being famous. It was both of those things combined and *knowing* that it wasn't possible to openly be who he was in his line of work.

He used to think this was the price. He had been fortunate in so many ways and this was the trade-off. He could rise from poverty to play in the NHL—play in *New York City*, even—and enjoy this dream life that was so close to perfection.

He just couldn't fall in love. Couldn't share with his teammates the stories of dating and marriage and children. He could try to fill that void with everything that made his life exciting and enviable, but that void always remained. Always gnawing away at him.

His first few seasons in the NHL hadn't been so hard. He'd been a kid, not looking for more than an occasional release anyway. The older guys had had families, sure, but Scott had been hanging out with the other young players. As Scott got older, it had started getting harder. At twenty-eight, he was hardly an old man, but in hockey years he was getting up there. Each season that went by, he found it more of a struggle to conceal who he really was.

He wasn't lonely, exactly. He had his teammates, and they were like family. But sometimes he longed for something in his life that had nothing to do with hockey. Nothing to do with being famous.

But his life belonged to too many people: the NHL, the New York Admirals, his agent, his coaches, his sponsors, the press, and the fans. Maybe it was too much to hope for something that could take him away from all of that.

Or maybe that thing had just walked out of his apartment, after a whispered promise that he'd see him tomorrow.

Kip received a text from Elena while he was on the train back to Brooklyn.

Come to this thing with me or we aren't friends anymore.

She sent a link immediately after. It led to an article describing the upcoming Equinox Foundation Gala for STEM Opportunities for Youth, a high-profile annual fund-raiser that brought together a who's who of New York. It wasn't something he'd ever thought *he'd* be attending. Not if he wasn't serving hors d'oeuvres at it, anyway.

Kip read over the article. The gala was in three weeks.

He texted back. I don't have a tux!

Elena replied quickly and, he imagined, irritably. Rent one.

Would Scott be there? He had to have been invited . . .

Kip grinned. The Equinox Gala! Things were looking up! He was still riding the high of the night he had just spent with Scott Hunter. And the possibility of similar nights in the future seemed to be implied when they'd parted . . .

Don't read too much into it. Don't get your hopes up.

It was early in the year. Maybe this would be a turning point for Kip Grady. A gala invitation. A possible job opportunity. A new . . . friend.

He *really* hoped Scott wanted to see him again. Kip's standards were now set ridiculously high after last night, and it would be really hard to go out and pick up just some guy.

Kip made a plan for himself for the rest of the day that involved going to the gym, working on his résumé, and other responsible things that had nothing to do with daydreaming about Scott Hunter.

Kip was working with Maria when Scott came into the shop the next morning.

He couldn't be completely sure, but he thought he detected a hint of disappointment on Scott's face when he saw that Kip wasn't alone.

"Hello again," Scott said, making an obvious effort to sound casual.

"Hey," Kip said, trying not to show how giddy he felt just seeing Scott again. "Long time no see." *Smooth.*

"Right," Scott said.

For a moment, they both just kind of stared at each other, neither of them speaking. Kip wished he could hop over the counter and wrap himself up in Scott. He wanted to kiss him so badly.

"Well," Scott said. "The usual, I guess."

"You got it," Kip said with a little smirk. Scott's lips twitched up a bit too.

Kip made the smoothie and handed it to Scott. He glanced at Maria, who had just been silently watching them both the whole time. He quickly looked away when he felt himself blushing. When he glanced back at Scott, he was blushing too.

"So . . . game tonight and tomorrow night, huh?" Kip asked as if they hadn't already had this conversation.

"Yeah. Then a day off before a short road trip."

"Day off?"

"Mm-hmm," Scott said as he took a sip of smoothie.

"Big plans for the day off?" Kip was trying to be as subtle as possible, which wasn't very subtle at all.

"I was thinking about staying home. Maybe watching a movie." He sounded casual, but Scott's gaze was threatening to melt Kip on the spot.

"Sounds like a good plan."

"I think so," Scott said. "Anyway, I should get going." He handed Kip the usual twenty-dollar bill, and maybe his touch lingered when his fingers met Kip's palm. "See you later, Kip."

"See you . . ." Kip said, his voice faint.

Scott left quickly.

"Oh. My. *God!*" Maria exclaimed.

"What?"

"*What?* What the *hell*, Grady? Are you guys engaged or *what*?"

"I don't know what you're—"

"You need to tell me what I just witnessed."

"Nothing!" Kip knew his face was giving him away. His cheeks still felt flush and he was biting his lip to keep from grinning.

Fortunately he was saved by a customer walking in. Maria gave him a "this isn't over" look before turning to the young woman who was reading the menu above their heads.

Kip unfolded the bill to put it in the cash register and found a tiny slip of paper tucked inside. It almost fluttered to the floor, but he caught it. When he read it, he had to go to the back room so Maria wouldn't see his expression.

The paper had, in very neat handwriting, Scott Hunter's phone number on it, and the word *Sunday* written underneath.

Holy shit. *Holy shit!*

Kip quickly pulled out his phone and entered the number into his contacts. Then he took a photo of the paper, just in case, before he slipped the number carefully into his wallet.

He'd hoped, but hadn't dared to assume, that Scott would want to see him again. Even if it was only for sex, that would be fine. More than fine.

He allowed himself a minute to do a little "Scott Hunter totally wants me" dance in the privacy of the back room before he floated back out to serve people smoothies.

Sunday seemed to take forever to come. Kip had seen Scott again on Saturday when he'd come into Straw+Berry for his usual game-day smoothie, but the shop had been busy and Scott hadn't lingered.

He had probably wanted to leave before anyone recognized him. The chance was pretty good these days, because the whole city was talking about the triumphant return of Scott Hunter. Kip had watched Scott being interviewed after the game, and he had been asked, point-blank, what he attributed the turnaround in his game to.

He had just smiled shyly. "Guess I just found something that reignited me."

Kip had been giddy ever since.

And now it was finally Sunday and he had no idea what to do. He had Scott's number. He had the vague instruction to call Scott today. But he didn't have a time to make the call.

Or should he text him?

But it was only eleven in the morning. Even a text would seem eager at this hour.

Right?

Kip decided to hit the gym. He'd go to the gym, take a shower, eat something, *then* text Scott.

At just after two in the afternoon, he sat on his bed and stared at his phone, wondering what on earth to write. He was overthinking it. All he needed was to let Scott know that he hadn't lost his number, and he would like to see him.

At a loss for something better, he texted, Hey. It's Kip.

He put his phone down. There. Scott would probably get back to him later. He had Kip's number now.

He has my number now!

Kip was about to get up and put on a movie or something when the phone vibrated.

SCOTT:

Good to hear from you, Kip.

Had Scott been *waiting* to hear from him?

Scott sent another message. Was worried you lost my number.

Kip swore to himself. He should have texted earlier.

He was about to write back when his phone rang. Scott's number.

"Scott?"

"Yeah. Hi."

"Hi."

"Sorry for calling. I'm just really slow at typing."

"S'okay."

"Are you busy, or—"

"No! No, it's fine. I, uh, it's nice to hear your voice." Kip cringed. But he could *hear* Scott's smile over the phone.

"You too, Kip. I've been thinking. A lot. About the other night."

Kip lay back on his bed, grinning. "Yeah?"

"Mm. I was hoping you might want to come over later."

"I could probably make myself available," Kip said playfully.

"We could get some food delivered. Watch a movie. It doesn't just have to be—"

"That sounds perfect. As long as it can also include—"

"Oh, it definitely can."

Kip bit his lip. Scott's voice had dropped a bit and gathered some gravel when he'd said that last thing.

"So what time do you want me?" Kip asked, trying his best to match Scott's tone.

"I'm not doing anything right now."

Shit. "You want me to come over now?"

"If you want."

"I do. I want. I'll see you soon."

Kip almost hung up, but then he thought to ask, "Oh. Should I . . . should I bring an overnight bag?"

Scott was silent a moment, and Kip cursed himself for being presumptuous.

"Yeah. Bring one. Absolutely." Scott hung up.

Kip blew out a breath and smiled stupidly at the ceiling. Then he got to work figuring out the fastest route to Scott's.

CHAPTER SEVEN

Scott couldn't sit still while he waited for Kip.

All morning he had been worried that Kip wasn't going to contact him, either because he didn't want to, or because he had lost the number. It had been ridiculous; Kip had seemed very interested in seeing Scott again, and he also seemed smart enough to enter a number into his phone.

Kip was smart. Smart and gorgeous. And a really good kisser.

Scott paced around the apartment, occasionally doing something unnecessary like rearranging the throw pillows on the sofa or straightening a perfectly straight picture on the wall. He stood at his windows and watched the boats in the East River, and the cars going over the bridges at either end of his panoramic view.

He brushed his teeth (again) and checked his hair.

Scott considered his outfit. He was keeping it casual, obviously—he was relaxing at home, after all. But he was wearing his best jeans, and a pale blue T-shirt that he was pretty sure made his eyes look nice. Unfortunately, he also had a pretty big bruise on his right arm, just above his elbow, a fucking two-handed slash from a Buffalo defenseman's stick.

You look fine. Everything is fine.

He went down to the lobby to meet Kip. He timed it well because Kip arrived less than five minutes after.

"Hey," Kip said, shaking off the cold. His cheeks were pink. He was adorable.

"Hey." Scott grinned at him stupidly. He was rewarded with a smile that showed Kip's dimples.

They went to the elevator and made small talk on the ride up. It was tense in a good way. The promise of what was to come crackled between them.

They stepped into Scott's apartment and Scott took Kip's coat. Kip removed his shoes, dropped his backpack, and wandered into the living room. Scott followed him, admiring the way his long-sleeved T-shirt and dark jeans showcased his long, wiry limbs.

"Another win last night," Kip said. "Congrats."

"Oh, yeah. Thanks."

Scott couldn't stand it anymore. He reached for Kip, who came to him immediately. Scott kissed him and an instant calm settled throughout his body. He had needed this so badly. He had been thinking of almost nothing but Kip's mouth for over two days. It was a miracle that he had played as well as he had in the two games since his and Kip's night together.

"I missed you," Scott said. It slipped out, but he didn't regret it. Especially not when he saw the way Kip smiled.

"Yeah?"

"Mm . . . hard guy to forget." He placed his hands on Kip's hips, and gripped his pelvic bone. He stepped even closer so Kip could feel how much he'd missed him.

"Jesus," Kip breathed.

They kissed and grabbed at each other frantically, until Kip went backward over the arm of the couch, and Scott landed on top of him.

"Sorry," Scott said, laughing. "Are you all right?"

"Completely."

Kip gripped Scott's erection through his jeans, and Scott groaned and pressed against his hand.

"Here," Kip said, "let's . . . You sit, and just let me . . ."

He wriggled out from under Scott, who sat on the couch and watched him slide to the floor between his knees. Kip leaned up and kissed him as he opened Scott's jeans. They kept kissing as Kip pulled Scott's dick out and stroked it with loose, lazy fingers.

Fuck, it felt so good. Just to be with someone like this. To be touched. To be worked up and to be given release. He needed more of this in his life.

Kip spotted the bruise on Scott's arm and brushed his fingers over it. "That must have hurt."

"I've had worse."

"I'll make it better." Kip laid soft, open-mouthed kisses over the purple skin. It was cheesy and dumb and Scott loved it.

Kip continued to apply his "remedy" as his fingers played with the hem of Scott's T-shirt. Scott wanted the shirt *off*.

"I think I have a few more bruises," he rumbled. "If you feel like exploring."

"Hmm . . . I'd better have a look."

God, Kip's voice was so fucking sexy when he was turned on, all cracked and breathy. His arousal seemed to unearth his Brooklyn accent, and for some reason Scott found that absurdly hot.

"Can't see any bruises here," Kip teased, kissing his way down to Scott's stomach. "But just to be safe . . ."

"There might b-be—" Scott sucked in a breath. "Might be some lower-body injuries."

Kip laughed against his skin, which made Scott laugh. He licked over Scott's abs, pressing his hands up the insides of Scott's thighs and gently brushing the backs of his fingers over Scott's balls. Scott shuddered.

"Fuck."

"Been thinking about this," Kip murmured, his mouth hovering over Scott's cock. "Didn't get a chance to last time."

"Please" was all Scott could say.

Kip ran his tongue over the head, and pressed against the sensitive skin just under. Scott gripped the sofa to keep himself from accidentally shoving Kip's head down. He ached with the need for release.

But Kip sucked him slowly, relaxed, like they had all the time in the world. Which, Scott supposed, they did. He watched Kip as much as he could, at times losing focus when he did something that made Scott's eyes roll back.

He was so beautiful. Kip. Scott decided to tell him so.

"You're gorgeous." Scott gazed down at him with what must have been a look of pure adoration. "And you're so fucking good at that. Jesus Christ."

Kip grinned around him and redoubled his efforts. He took Scott in almost completely, wrapping his hand around the base and stroking Scott's balls with his fingertips.

Scott was on fire. He felt like he might die. He couldn't think anymore, and could only speak in obscenities.

"Oh fuck. Oh god. I hope you want to fuck me later. God, I've been thinking about that. It was so good the other night . . . Never had it that good before . . . So many things I wanna do with you . . ."

Kip moaned around his cock, and pressed a hand to his own erection through his jeans.

"I'm gonna take care of that," Scott promised. "Soon as you're done, I'm gonna take your cock however you wanna give it to me—Oh—fuck . . . Okay . . . I'm going to . . ."

That was all the warning he could give Kip. His orgasm hit him so hard and so fast, he thrust up a bit and rode the waves of pleasure that rocked through his body as he emptied himself into Kip's perfect mouth.

When it was over, Kip pulled off and rested his head on Scott's thigh.

"Holy fuck," Scott said. "Come here."

Kip went to him and kissed him, and Scott wrapped his arms around him as Kip straddled his lap.

"What do you want?" Scott panted.

"Doesn't matter. Not gonna take long either way."

Scott opened Kip's jeans and took his cock out. At a loss for anything better, Scott spit in his own hand and wrapped it around Kip, mixing it with the precome that was already leaking from the tip.

Kip swore and thrust into Scott's grip. Scott looked down between them, watching his hand move over Kip's swollen, gorgeous cock.

"I want to see you come. I want you to come all over me. Later maybe you could show me how you like it, I could watch you stroke yourself. Fuck, I'd really like that . . ."

Kip made a sudden sharp cry and gave him exactly what he wanted, coming in long streaks against Scott's abs and chest and down Scott's hand.

When Kip opened his eyes, they were hooded, sex-drunk, and his cheeks were flushed. He was the sexiest thing Scott had ever seen.

"Jesus, no wonder you're the team captain," Kip drawled. "You're a great motivator."

Scott laughed and kissed him. "We should get cleaned up."

"Mm," Kip said, falling back onto the couch.

Scott stood and went to get a wet cloth. The edge had been taken off, but it had only ignited his need for *more.*

He returned to the living room to find Kip still sprawled on his back, jeans open, cock wet and softening against his thigh. He had an arm thrown over his eyes.

More. A lot more.

⋆ ⋆ ⋆

Kip flopped onto his back beside Scott, spent and sweaty and happy. They were stretched somewhat diagonally across Scott's giant bed after their second round. It wasn't even dark out yet.

Scott rolled his head in Kip's direction. "You hungry? I'm starving."

Kip laughed. "Yeah. Definitely. But I could use a shower first."

Scott was on his feet in one quick and very athletic move. He held out a hand for Kip, which Kip took, grinning. Scott kissed him after he hauled him to his feet and led him into the spectacular bathroom.

The en suite bathroom was larger than Kip's bedroom. It was larger than his *parents'* bedroom. It had a giant soaker tub in the middle of the room, and behind that, a stone tile wall that hid a corridor-style shower with open ends. The center of the ceiling of the corridor was a giant, rectangular rain shower with pot lights at either end. The walls were all quiet, gray stone tile. It was sexy as all hell.

Scott turned on the shower with some fancy knobs, and water rained down from the ceiling. He stood under it and pulled Kip against him.

Kip loved the shower almost as much as he loved making out with Scott Hunter in it. The water traced Scott's muscles as it flowed down his ridiculous torso. Kip bent to catch one rivulet in his mouth, as it was about to drip from the crease of Scott's thigh, then followed the reverse of its path with his tongue.

"Kip. God." Scott shuddered above him as Kip licked the grooves of his abs. Scott hauled him up and pushed him back against the wall, kissing him wildly.

It was incredible: They'd been doing nothing but getting each other off all afternoon, but they still couldn't keep their hands off each other.

They did manage to clean themselves eventually, using Scott's excellent-smelling (and no doubt expensive) soap and shampoo. By the time they left the shower, the bathroom was thick with steam and Kip was *starving*.

He threw his jeans and T-shirt back on. Scott, to Kip's delight, wore only a towel around his waist as he ordered food on his phone. It didn't surprise Kip that Scott was very comfortable with his body; he had spent a lot of his life wearing nothing, or next to nothing, in locker rooms full of people.

"There's a place nearby that makes amazing ravioli," Scott said. "Sound good?"

"Perfect."

Scott did eventually put some clothes on, and joined Kip on the couch to wait for the food.

"Hey," Kip said, "are you going to that fancy Equinox Gala?"

Scott looked at him curiously. "Yes, I confirmed I would be there. Why?"

"Oh, just . . . I'm going too."

"Working?"

"No! No, I . . . My friend invited me."

"Oh!" Scott said. Then, "Oh god, I'm sorry, Kip. I shouldn't have assumed—"

"Nah, it's okay. I mean, obviously it's weird for someone like me to be attending a gala like that. As a guest, I mean. But Elena—my friend Elena—she works for Equinox and she wants me to be her date."

"Is she the one you brought to the game?"

"Yeah. She's my best friend. Really amazing person."

Scott nodded.

An awkward silence fell. Kip couldn't be sure what Scott was thinking about, but *he* was sure wishing he could be going as Scott's date. He imagined dancing with him in that fancy ballroom, both dressed to the nines, cameras flashing . . .

The dream faded.

"Anyway," Kip said, "I'll be there."

Scott was frowning and looking away. Kip waited for him to say the words Kip had known were coming, but dreaded hearing. *This has been fun, but I don't want you getting any ideas . . .*

Instead, Scott stood and asked, "Would you like something to drink? A beer or something?"

"Sure," Kip said, surprised but trying to act cool. "Yeah, a beer would be great. Anything."

Scott nodded and went to the kitchen.

A weird tension had filled the room. Kip didn't like it. What had he been thinking, bringing up an event they would both be attending in three weeks? It had been stupid. He shouldn't have assumed . . .

Scott returned and handed Kip a cold bottle of beer. "You want a glass, or . . ."

"Nah, bottle's fine." Kip forced a smile. He watched Scott fiddle a bit with his own bottle, his face twisting.

"I'm, uh, I'm looking forward to seeing you all dressed up at that gala." Scott gave Kip an adorably nervous smile.

Kip grinned back at him, relieved. "Yeah? I clean up real nice."

"I don't doubt it," Scott said, sinking to one knee on the couch and leaning forward to kiss him. Kip sighed and kissed back. He wanted Scott to cover him. He wanted to feel the weight of him everywhere.

He leaned back until he was lying down, then gazed up at Scott expectantly.

"Come here," he said.

Scott took Kip's beer out of his hand and placed it on the glass coffee table next to his own. He lowered himself carefully—too carefully—to cover him with his giant body.

"I'm heavy." Scott said it as if it would deter Kip from wanting to be absolutely smothered by him.

"I won't break." Kip wrapped an arm around his back to haul him closer.

When Scott settled his weight on him, Kip let out a whimper that would have been embarrassing, but he was too happy to care. Scott nipped at the sensitive skin of his neck, and Kip's cock stiffened for the fourth goddamn time this afternoon. He moved his hips to press it against Scott's thigh.

"God, Kip," Scott moaned against his throat.

Then his phone buzzed.

"Food's here," Scott said with an apologetic smile. "I'll be right back."

He headed down to the lobby, and Kip was left reeling on the couch.

Kip had thought he had this thing figured out: Scott needed someone to have sex with who wouldn't go to the press, or post online about it. He, for whatever reason, seemed to feel he could trust Kip with his secret. They would secretly hook up a few times, and then Scott would get back to being a giant superstar and Kip would go back to his sad joke of a life. Simple.

But, god*damn*, it was not going to be easy to walk away from this when the time inevitably came.

They ate their ravioli on the couch, and Scott turned on the television to catch a bit of the Pittsburgh vs. Boston game. It was interesting, watching hockey with Scott Hunter. Sometimes he would hunch forward, focused and chewing thoughtfully. Like he was working something out in his head. Kip wondered what he was seeing on the screen. What details he was noticing that almost no one else on earth would see.

"You're playing in Boston this week, right?" Kip asked.

"Yeah. Thursday," Scott said, his eyes still on the television. "We play in Philly on Tuesday."

"And back here for Saturday?"

"Yeah. Montreal plays here on Saturday."

"I'm, um, I'm not working on Saturday."

There was a pause, and then Scott seemed to register what Kip had said. He turned his attention away from the television.

"Oh."

"Yeah, I'm working Tuesday to Friday this week."

"Okay." His brow furrowed.

"I mean . . . I could maybe see if Maria wants to—"

"No! No, don't. It's silly, right?"

Kip shrugged. "If it's important to you, I could switch shifts."

Scott shook his head. "No, it's . . ." He put his takeout container down on the coffee table, switched off the hockey game, and turned to face Kip. "We should probably talk."

Kip's heart sank. He braced himself for the words he had been unhappily anticipating since they'd first hooked up.

"I'm, um . . ." Scott started, uncharacteristically fumbling for words. "You know I'm . . ."

"It's okay. You don't have to—"

"I'm closeted," Scott continued. "I guess. I mean, that's accurate. I need to hide that part of me. If it got out that I . . ."

"Right," Kip said, his eyes focused on the floor so Scott wouldn't see how dejected he felt.

"I've never . . . dated anyone."

Kip turned his eyes up, stunned.

"I've hooked up with men. Not here. I've never hooked up with anyone in New York. I've never brought anyone to my home before."

Kip's stomach flipped. "You haven't?"

Scott looked at him seriously. "No."

"Oh."

"Like I said, I've never dated anyone," Scott said. "I've never . . . I thought I didn't need to. That I could maybe live without that."

Kip heard the past tense in what Scott was saying. "And now?"

Scott exhaled. "I don't know. I feel like . . . maybe I hadn't met the right person yet, you know?"

Holy shit.

"I'm just saying," Scott said, "I don't think it's the smoothies."

Kip didn't say anything. He wanted to hear what Scott was going to say next.

"I want to. Date you. I know we barely know each other, but . . ."

Emotion bubbled inside him, pushing a lump into his throat. "Me too," he choked out.

Scott smiled at him, a little sadly.

"I mean, obviously, yes. I'm in," Kip said.

"I *want* to," Scott clarified, "but I don't know how we can."

"We'll figure it out," Kip said, still completely overwhelmed. "I can keep a secret, and it doesn't have to be . . . You know, it can be casual. Whenever you have time."

"You deserve better than that, Kip."

Kip laughed, because *seriously?* "I can settle for you."

Scott grinned and kissed him. Kip kissed back with everything he had, because he was pretty sure this incredible dream man had just asked him to be his *boyfriend.*

"You won't have to settle for anything," Scott murmured against his ear. "Not if I have anything to say about it."

They made it to the bedroom, but barely. Scott slammed Kip against the wall as soon as they were inside the door. They threw their shirts off, then Scott pushed up so hard against him that Kip's feet were almost being lifted off the floor. Kip was a tall, solid guy, but Scott made him feel small. He loved how Scott could manhandle him.

"What do you want?" he asked. "Tell me."

"Don't . . ." Kip stammered, breathless, "don't suppose you'd wanna switch it up?"

"You want me to fuck you?"

"Yeah. Would you?"

Scott made a low growl and kissed him again. "Absolutely."

Kip let out a relieved little laugh. He loved fucking Scott, but he *needed* to be fucked into that mattress, or against this wall, as hard as he knew Scott could give it to him.

They broke apart so they could get their pants off, then Scott pulled Kip to the bed, not roughly, but forcefully. Kip went happily, allowing himself to be shoved down onto the mattress, Scott immediately covering him. The weight of Scott's chest pressed down on Kip, just like on the couch earlier. It was exactly what he craved.

Scott moved his hips so the length of his huge, solid cock slid against Kip's.

"Please," Kip rasped. "I want it."

"Roll over," Scott ordered, sounding every bit like the respected team captain that he was. It sent a jolt of heat through Kip, and he couldn't obey fast enough. Once he was settled, Scott started kissing down his spine.

"You are," Scott murmured between kisses. "Absolutely. Stunning." He punctuated his statement by sinking his teeth into Kip's left ass cheek, biting it playfully but possessively. Kip moaned and grabbed fistfuls of one of Scott's pillows. He was so full of need he thought he might burst.

Scott kept nipping at Kip's ass, trailing down to his thighs and back up again. It felt so good, every part of Kip was tingling with anticipation. He wasn't sure if Scott was actually going to do what his mouth was hinting at. He knew he was relatively inexperienced, and maybe it would be too much to hope for him to—

But then Scott spread his cheeks with his strong hands, and ran his tongue down Kip's crack, slowly.

"Fuck," Kip moaned. "Yes."

Scott lapped at the sensitive flesh around Kip's hole, flicking the tip of his tongue over the tight opening as his hands gripped his ass. He coaxed him open with warm, wet strokes of his tongue, each one sending a delicious shiver through Kip's body.

God, let me stay in this moment forever.

When Kip had relaxed enough, Scott grabbed the lube and worked a slick, strong finger inside. His hands were *huge*, and his fingers were so long and thick. Kip wanted as many as Scott would give him.

Scott put a hand firmly on the middle of Kip's back—maybe it was more for his own balance, but Kip loved it. Scott must have noticed because he pressed down a little harder and gave him a second finger. Kip gasped at the increased pressure in both places.

"You like it, huh?" Scott rumbled.

"Yeah," Kip said hoarsely. "I love how big you are. Strong, fuck. Want you in me so fucking bad. Want you everywhere."

Scott responded by making a very manly, possessive growl and adding a third finger. Kip flinched and gasped.

"You okay?" Scott asked, stilling his fingers. "Too much?"

"No . . . no, it's fine. It's good. It's so good . . ." Kip was going to keep babbling. His mouth always ran away from him when he was this far gone. "I'm ready," he said. "I'm so ready for you, Scott. Please. I like it hard. Wanna feel it for days . . ."

Scott pulled his fingers out, and then Kip heard the frantic crinkle of a condom wrapper being torn. He turned to look over his shoulder as best he could, and saw Scott moving his hand over his sheathed cock, slicking it with lube.

Kip waited eagerly for the first press of Scott's cock entering him. It had been too long since he'd been fucked, and it had been a solid week of fantasizing about exactly this moment.

After a long minute of nothing happening, Kip glanced back over his shoulder. Scott was holding his hips, and was lined up, but he wasn't moving.

"You all right?" Kip asked.

"Yeah," Scott said. He was blushing. "Sorry. I just . . . I don't want to hurt you."

"You won't." Kip wriggled his ass playfully. "But if you don't start fucking me, I might die, so . . ."

Scott huffed out a laugh, but he still didn't move. "I've only done this once before," he confessed.

Oh my god.

Kip kept forgetting about Scott's lack of experience. It just seemed so . . . implausible.

"You won't hurt me," Kip promised. "I'll tell you if you do. But . . . I like it hard. I can take it."

Scott bit his lip and his brow furrowed, and Kip needed him to stop thinking.

"Trust me," Kip said. Scott locked eyes with him and nodded.

Finally, Kip felt the head of Scott's cock nudge his entrance, and it was all he could do to keep from slamming himself back onto it. He waited as patiently as possible as Scott slowly pushed in.

"God, yes," Kip breathed. "I've wanted this so bad."

Scott was *big*, and Kip stretched and burned around him in the best way. When he was all the way in, he returned his hand to the middle of Kip's back, putting weight on it. Kip moaned.

Scott was careful for the first few thrusts. Desperate for more, Kip offered some encouragement. "So good. So fucking good, Scott. Don't be gentle with me. You're perfect. Come on."

That worked. Scott began thrusting in earnest, one hand planted on the bed to anchor him, the other splayed firmly on Kip's shoulder blade. Kip was in heaven.

"So strong," he breathed. "Don't stop. I love it."

"You feel incredible. Fuck."

Kip felt Scott everywhere—his solid thighs pressing against Kip's legs, and his hand still firm on his back as Scott pounded him into the mattress. Kip loved how sweet and shy Scott could be, but right now he was fucking Kip like the star athlete he was. With each thrust, Kip's whole body got jolted, and his cock rubbed against the mattress in a way that normally wouldn't be enough, but this time . . .

It's going to work. God, I might even come first.

"Don't come," Scott said, as if reading his mind. "I want to see it. Don't come."

Kip moaned, loving Scott's authoritative tone, and did his best to obey. He lifted his hips up off the bed to reduce the friction, but damn if he didn't even need the friction, the way Scott was driving into him. It all felt too incredible.

"Don't know . . ." Kip choked out, "don't know if I can obey that order, Hunter."

Scott *snarled* and, without warning, pulled out and flipped Kip over. He hauled Kip's ankles up onto his shoulders and pushed back in, harder and faster than before.

"Holy fuck!" Kip cried out. "Holy *fuck*!"

"*Now* you can come."

Kip did. Not even a mattress was touching his dick now. He was just coming untouched because Scott told him to and because everything about this was so perfect and so hot. He watched, amazed, as his release splashed onto his stomach and chest.

"Oh my god. Fuck, Kip." Scott thrust into him a couple more times, then crumpled forward as he came inside him.

When the last tremors subsided, Scott gently pulled out and fell on the bed beside Kip. He was flushed and smiling. "That was . . ." he started, then just shook his head and smiled wider.

"Yeah," Kip panted. "Unreal."

It was the only word he could think of. He thought he'd known how good sex could be, but he was thrilled to learn how mistaken he'd been.

"I'll be right back," Scott said, planting a quick kiss on his cheek. "Don't move."

"Wouldn't dream of it."

Scott rolled off the bed and went into the bathroom, leaving Kip to grin at the ceiling and to try to commit every detail of what just happened to memory. He loved how quickly Scott had lost his inhibitions; he hadn't held anything back as he'd used his impressive strength and stamina to fuck Kip senseless.

This man is my boyfriend now.

Scott returned with a damp cloth and gently cleaned Kip's stomach. The warm fabric sliding across Kip's skin felt wonderful. He sighed happily, and reached for Scott. "Come here."

Scott smiled and kissed him. "That was incredible," he said. "*You're* incredible."

"I'm pretty sure you were doing most of the work that time."

"It's not work," Scott said, kissing Kip on the nose, and the cheek, and the corner of his mouth. "Not work at all."

Kip shoved him onto his back and climbed on top of him, kissing him with all the tenderness he felt at that moment.

They broke apart, and Scott looked up at him. He ran his fingers through Kip's hair and studied his face, clearly wanting to say something.

"What?" Kip asked.

"Can I buy you a tux?"

"Can you—"

"You don't have one already, right? Were you going to rent one? For the Equinox Gala?"

"Yeah. I mean, no, I don't own one. But you don't—"

"I'm going to call the Hugo Boss store tomorrow," Scott said. "I do ads for them."

"Yeah, I know."

"I'll call them. Tell them to expect you. Tell them you're a friend. They'll charge my account." Scott said the words like he was telling himself more than Kip.

"Seems a bit . . . generous. Isn't it?"

Scott stroked the backs of his fingers over Kip's face. "It's completely selfish, actually. I want to see you in a tux that was tailored to your gorgeous body. I might not be able to dance with you that night, but you'll know I'll be wishing I was."

Kip felt winded. Scott kissed him again and murmured, "I want you wearing the suit I bought you. And later, when we're alone, I want to take it off you."

Kip sucked in a breath.

"No," he said, with a tremendous amount of effort.

Scott pulled back. "No?"

"It's too much. And besides . . . won't it look weird? If you ask the store to charge your account or whatever for some random guy's tuxedo?"

"I—"

"I mean, it's not very discreet, right?"

Scott seemed to consider this. "They'd know, you think?"

Kip stretched luxuriously and grinned. "Oh yes. I'm much too pretty."

Scott snorted. "You are." He kissed him again. "What if you wore one of mine?"

"Why? How many do you have?"

"More than enough. You could take one and get it tailored."

Kip frowned. "But then you couldn't wear it again."

"I don't need it. I have too many."

Too many tuxedos was not a problem Kip had ever known someone to have. Not in his social circle, anyway.

"Fine," he said, with exaggerated exhaustion. "I will relieve you of one of your tuxedos. But only because I like to be helpful."

"Classic black?" Scott asked, stroking his thumb along Kip's jawline. "Or maybe midnight blue?"

"Your choice, Hunter."

Scott looked away and actually blushed a little. "It's kind of hot when you call me that," he said, "but it's really going to fuck me up when I'm hearing it on the ice."

Kip laughed. "Maybe I want you thinking of me during games."

Scott groaned. "You ever gotten hard while wearing a jock? Not pleasant."

"Sounds like *you* have."

Scott pressed his lips together.

"All right," Kip sighed, "Scott it is."

Scott leaned in. "I have a feeling I'm going to be thinking about you a lot anyway."

He looked so *happy*, gazing at Kip and stroking his hair. And Kip knew he looked the same way. It had only been a few days. This thing was so intense and way beyond Kip's wildest dreams.

"Will you be thinking of me?" Scott asked shyly.

Kip smiled. "Not sure I'll be able to think of anything else, *Hunter*."

CHAPTER EIGHT

"Three nines," Greg Huff announced, fanning his cards out on the table. "What you got, Hunter?"

"Fuck all," Scott said, tossing his useless cards down.

"Knew it," Huff said. "You're a terrible fucking liar, Scotty."

He gleefully swept up the small pile of twenties toward himself. Carter laughed and handed Scott a fresh bottle of beer. Scott took it gratefully.

"Your deal, Bennett," Carter said.

The four of them were gathered in Huff's hotel room in Philadelphia. Huff had kicked his young roommate out for a couple of hours so the four of them could enjoy an "old timers" poker game.

"So, Carter," Huff said, "how's it going with *Gloria Grey*?"

"It's nice. She's coming to New York this weekend. Gonna be at the game on Saturday . . . and at my apartment later that night and all day Sunday."

"Congratulations, man," Eric Bennett said, "that's great."

"Lucky bastard." Huff smirked. "How about you, Hunter? You been seein' anyone?"

"Why would I tell you assholes?" Scott deflected.

"Come on," Bennett said. "We're old and married. Give us something."

"Sorry to disappoint you guys."

"Scott here is saving himself for marriage," Carter said, placing a hand on Scott's shoulder. "And he's saving marriage for after he dies."

The others laughed.

"I'm just busy," Scott argued. "You guys know that."

"Yeah, and we've got nothing but time," Huff said. "Come on. Is there really no one? All those good looks going to waste?"

"Can we talk about something else?"

"He's seeing your sister, Huff," Bennett joked.

"You know I only have a brother," Huff said, "and I don't think Howie's his type."

They all laughed. Scott did too, though it was forced. It wasn't untrue, what Huff said. Scott had met his brother before and, no, he was not Scott's type. But that's not why his friends were laughing. It wasn't the idea of Scott dating Howie. It was of Scott dating *any* man.

"Fuck all of you," Scott said. Not in a serious tone. He loved these guys, really. They were just . . . guys.

They went back to playing poker and Scott's love life wasn't mentioned again.

Scott envied his teammates. He could only imagine what it would be like to not be burdened by his . . . otherness. He wished he could just magically be what people expected hockey players to be. But he considered the three men who were playing cards with him—NHL stars, all of them—and none of them quite fit the mold. Carter, most obviously, with his dark skin. Scott knew he had dealt with racist comments from players and fans his whole life. Huff was short. He was listed as five-eight, but Scott sometimes wondered if he had been measured while wearing skates. And Bennett seemed more like a kindergarten teacher than a superstar goaltender. He never drank or partied, and he had an English degree.

So maybe there was no "normal" way to be a hockey player. But that didn't change the fact that the favored insults thrown around the ice were homophobic slurs. In the world of hockey, being gay was considered, at best, a joke, and at worst, disgusting.

As long as Scott was careful—and he *was*—no one need ever know that he was different.

Scott went back to his own room before eleven. Evenings ended early when they had a game the next day. His roommate was in bed, reading.

Scott stretched out on his own bed and pulled out his phone. He sent Kip a message:

I miss you.

The reply was almost immediate.

KIP:
Already? 😉

Scott grinned and blushed. Had it really only been that morning that he and Kip had woken up together in Scott's apartment? The rest of the day had been a happy blur, as Scott had floated his way through a practice before boarding a plane to Philadelphia.

SCOTT:
Already.

The next reply came a little slower.

KIP:
Me too.

Scott rolled so his back was to his roommate. He knew the kid, a rookie named Gillis, wouldn't have the nerve to ask what his captain was smiling stupidly about, but still . . .

Scott wrote back. Was thinking about Friday.

KIP:
Friday?

SCOTT:
It's Valentine's Day.

KIP:
Oh!

SCOTT:
Will you come over that night? I want to cook you dinner.

KIP:
I'll check my schedule.

SCOTT:
Oh. Ok.

KIP:
I'm free. I was kidding.

Scott rolled his eyes. He felt like an idiot.

SCOTT:
Can I call you?

KIP:
Yes.

Scott sat up and said to his roommate, "I'm going to make a phone call. Be back in a bit."

He walked out of the room and took the elevator to the lobby. He ducked into the little business center room, which was empty, and called Kip. He sat in one of the desk chairs and swiveled from side to side while he waited for him to answer.

"Hi," Kip said, after two rings.

"Hey."

"Shouldn't you be in bed?" he teased. "Big game tomorrow."

"I will be soon. I just . . . wanted to hear your voice." Scott cringed at how hokey that was. He wasn't good at this.

"I miss you."

Scott smiled at his phone. "I miss you too. Did you find a tailor? I would offer to pay for it, but I have a feeling you'll turn me down."

"You're right. I would," Kip said. "I was going to ask Elena if she knew a good one, but then I thought . . ."

"Oh."

"Yeah. I don't want to . . . I mean, she kinda . . ."

"She knows?"

"No! No. She doesn't. I mean, I didn't tell her about us. I just . . . She's gonna figure it out, y'know? She's smart. And . . . she knows I like you. But, yeah. If she learns I somehow scored a free Hugo Boss tuxedo, she's gonna have questions."

Scott frowned. "Right."

"Maybe . . . maybe I should rent a tux. Just to be . . . safe."

"No, that's . . . No. You should . . ." Scott sighed, and hoped he wouldn't regret this. "You should tell her. If you want. You said she's your best friend?"

"Yeah."

"Tell her. I don't want us to come between you and your best friend."

"Thanks." Kip sounded relieved. "I really want to tell her.

And she can keep a secret better than anyone. She's the best. You'd like her."

"I'd love to meet her."

"Save her a dance at the gala."

"Deal. I'm a terrible dancer, though."

"She's an amazing dancer. She'll make you look good. Promise."

"Okay," Scott said absently. Kip sounded like a weight had been lifted, but Scott felt like it had been placed directly onto him. He chewed his thumb.

"So, Valentine's Day, huh?" Kip said cheerfully, changing the subject.

"Hm?"

"You wanna cook for me?"

"Right . . . yeah." Scott shook his head. *Get your head in the game, Hunter.* "Yes," he said, more convincingly, "I do."

"Didn't know you cooked."

"I can cook," Scott said. "I was a latchkey kid. I made a lot of the meals for Mom and me when she was working late at the grocery store. And later . . . when she got sick."

"Sorry," Kip said. He seemed genuinely embarrassed. "I should have figured."

"No! I wasn't saying that to make you feel bad. I just . . . like telling you things about me."

"I want to know everything about you," Kip said quietly.

Scott thought his heart might burst. He was so touched by Kip's words that he didn't notice that he hadn't replied, until Kip said, "Oh god. That was a bit intense. Sorry."

"Not at all," Scott said. "You can ask me anything."

"Anything, huh? How about . . . what are you gonna cook for me?" Kip's tone was relaxed and playful again.

"Not telling. It's a surprise." Scott grinned. "Oh, shit. Unless . . . Do you have any allergies?"

"Nope."

"Okay. Then it's a surprise."

Scott picked up a pen that was sitting on the desk in front of him and started absentmindedly doodling on a hotel notepad. "How was your day?"

"Fine. Not too exciting. Except, y'know, you."

"Tell me everything that happened. I just want to hear your voice."

Kip talked about the podcast he'd listened to on the way home from Scott's that morning, and about the woman he saw with an iguana in a baby carrier, while Scott listened and drew little swirls on the notepad.

"So, yeah," Kip said, when Scott's swirls had reached the edge of the page. "That's about it. Not a very exciting day."

Kip yawned, which made Scott aware of the time. "Oh god, I'm keeping you up. You have to work early tomorrow, right?"

"Yeah. Yeah, I should go to bed."

"Okay. Me too."

"But Scott? I'm glad you called."

Scott smiled into the phone. "I'm glad I did too."

"I'll watch the game tomorrow night."

"I'll score a goal for you."

"Fuck off."

"I will! First goal is yours. Remember that."

"All right. It'll be our secret."

"Yeah," Scott said quietly.

After they said goodbye, and after Scott pocketed the notepad he'd been doodling in, he exited the business room and walked back through the lobby. He was met by Frank Zullo. He had a young woman on his arm, and they both seemed pretty drunk.

"Evening, Hunter," Zullo said, with more than a little sneer in his tone.

"Zullo." Scott nodded. "Just getting in?"

"Sure. Just, ah, heading to bed, y'know?"

"Pretty sure you already have a roommate," Scott said, glancing at the young woman.

"Hey! Shit! You're that big superstar guy!" she slurred.

"Come on, darlin'," Zullo said, giving Scott a hard look as he guided the woman past him.

"Video meeting tomorrow morning at nine sharp," Scott called after him.

Zullo ignored him and got into an elevator.

Scott sighed. This was going to be a pain in the ass for Zullo's roommate. The team had a policy of placing older players with younger ones in hotel rooms on the road. Scott, as captain, usually roomed with rookies and new additions to the team. It was a system that typically worked well, and kept a lot of the younger players out of trouble. But sometimes the older players were the problems.

Scott took the next elevator up to the team's floor. He didn't know what room Zullo was in, so he walked the hall a bit until he heard a door open. Sure enough, Zullo's young roommate, a French-Canadian kid named Brisebois, wandered into the hall. He looked like he had been asleep.

If Scott knocked on the door and tried to talk to Zullo, it would just turn into a fight that would wake everyone on the floor up. He'd talk to him tomorrow.

"Hey, Breezy," he said to the sleepy young defenseman. "Come on down to my room. I'll get a cot sent up."

Kip sat across from Elena at a table in a little Mexican restaurant in midtown.

"So . . . does it look okay?" he asked.

"It's fine. I made some notes. I emailed them to you before I left to meet you."

Kip pulled out his phone.

"You can read them later, dummy," she said. "The cover letter was very good. Your résumé is fine. It's just a few notes."

"Okay."

"So what's this news you have for me?"

Kip grinned and then ducked his head to hide it.

"Oh my god. You're in love," she said.

"No!" Kip said quickly. "I'm not in *love*. I just . . . I've been seeing someone."

"Oh? *Seeing?* Not just *sleeping with*?"

"Well . . . mostly sleeping with. But it's becoming more than that. I think. I hope."

"All right."

"It's, uh, you know . . . Scott."

"Scott. As in—"

Kip's eyes darted around them and he leaned in. "Yeah. Exactly who you're thinking. And I know it's pretty unbelievable, but . . . yeah. We've been hooking up. And he wants me to . . ."

He trailed off. He suddenly felt embarrassed. Somehow, when Scott wasn't actually *there*, the whole thing seemed like a fever dream.

"He wants you to . . . go steady?" Elena guessed.

Kip rolled his eyes. "Sure. Or, like, *date*. Like . . . be boyfriends. Or whatever."

"Secret boyfriends?"

"For now," Kip said, with as much dignity as he could muster.

Elena smiled. "Well!"

Kip smiled too. "Yeah."

"Jesus, this is cute. I've never seen you like this, Kip."

"Like what? I'm not like anything!"

"Okay."

"I'm just . . . happy, is all. He's really—"

"You know what?" Elena said. "*This* just turned into a beer lunch. Tell me everything."

"That was interference!" Eric Bennett yelled. "He was on *top* of me! Come on, ref!"

"I saw it," the ref said. "It wasn't. Calm the fuck down."

Scott put a hand on Bennett's chest to stop him from crowding the ref.

"You can't be serious!" Bennett hollered over Scott's shoulder.

"I *am* serious, and I will give you a misconduct penalty if you don't back off, Bennett."

"Let's just move on, Bennett," Scott said. "Come on, we don't need a penalty right now."

Bennett glared at Scott through his mask.

"Please," Scott said. "We'll get them back by coming back and winning this game, all right?"

Bennett huffed, but skated back to his crease. Scott watched him tap the goal posts—right, left, and then right again—with his stick. A superstition that helped him gather himself and focus.

Scott turned to the ref. "For the record, that *was* interference."

"Don't you start on me, Hunter."

Scott skated back to the bench with the rest of his line to let Coach Murdock know what was going on. "Bennett's mad," he said.

"I can *see* that Bennett is mad. I'm *watching the game*."

Harv Murdock had once been a great NHL center himself. An outstanding goal scorer, and a pioneer for Black players at a time when there had been none in the NHL, Murdock's career had been cut short by a knee injury. He had returned to the game years later as an assistant coach, and had been the head coach of the Admirals for ten years.

"You know who else is mad?" Murdock continued. "Me. I'm mad because our defense decided to take the night off." His voice grew louder with each sentence. "I'm *mad* because we've given up three passes this period. I'm *mad* because we're down by two goals, and one of those goals was scored *shorthanded*. So fuck Bennett being upset about a guy running into him. Let's start playing hockey here, gentlemen."

"Good idea, Coach!" Carter said cheerfully. He and Scott skated over to the face-off circle together.

"He's not lying about our defense," Scott said. "Something is off with this team tonight. It's like we've never played together before."

"Yeah, well. I don't think it's a secret what's off," Carter said.

Scott grimaced. Things had gotten a little out of control at the team video meeting that morning. Scott had attempted to take Zullo aside and suggest that maybe he stop kicking his roommates out late at night, especially before game days. The discussion had escalated to the point that Zullo had informed Scott that his roommate, Brisebois, was "a fucking queer anyway," and that he "could have stayed and learned something." That had made Scott mad enough to shove Zullo, and well . . .

"Frank's not exactly a team player tonight," Carter said.

"When is he ever?"

"Only down by two, Scott," Carter said. "No problem at all. Let's turn this shit around."

"Yeah . . ."

Kip watched the game with his parents.

"Not looking too good tonight," Dad observed.

"No," Kip agreed. It was a definite understatement. By the third period, Philadelphia had buried the Admirals 6–2.

But Scott had scored one of those goals, and Kip had smiled at the idea that the goal was for him.

"Well," his mother said, "there's always the next game."

"Yeah," Kip said. The broadcast was showing a lot of close-ups of Scott's face. His jaw was clenched and his eyes were fierce. When a Philadelphia player skated by him and said something, Scott shot him a look that would turn most men to stone.

"Must be smoothie withdrawal, right?" his father joked.

"Must be."

The game ended, and Kip watched Scott and his team exit the arena and head back to their dressing room. Scott hit the blade of his stick hard against the wall, just before he disappeared from view of the camera. Kip winced. He'd never seen him look so angry.

"Can't win 'em all," his mother said, turning off the television.

"Guess not." Kip stood and stretched. It had been a long day. "I should go to bed. Work tomorrow."

"Goodnight, sweetie," his mom said, and kissed him on the cheek.

Kip knew he wouldn't hear from Scott tonight. He considered sending him a text, maybe try to cheer him up. All he could think of were unhelpful platitudes, though. And besides, it wasn't like he really understood how Scott felt right now. Hockey was Scott's whole life. It was his job to win games, and Kip may not know Scott very well yet, but he knew Scott probably took every team failure personally.

Exhausted but unable to sleep, he lay in bed and stared into the blackness of the room, listening to the bitter February wind blowing outside. He picked up his phone for a moment, staring at it in the dark before setting it back on his nightstand. Eventually his mind quieted down and he was able to drift off.

When the alarm on his phone woke him at five the next morning, he saw a message from Scott, sent at 1:30 a.m.:

I'd give anything to see you right now.

* * *

Kip had a lot of things on his mind at work on Wednesday.

There was the job at the museum that he'd finally applied for. There was the fact that he was going to be getting his tuxedo tailored after work—the tuxedo Scott had given him. The one Kip would be wearing to the Equinox Gala at the end of the month. Surreal.

And then there was Scott's message from last night. And the Valentine's Day plans for Friday.

Oh. And the fact that Kip was secretly dating Scott Hunter.

Kip had never smiled so hard in his life as he had when he had seen Scott's message that morning. It had completely unmoored him, and he'd been floating away, up into the atmosphere, ever since.

In response to Scott's message, even though it had been sent hours before, Kip had snapped a quick selfie. He hadn't even fixed himself up; he had still been in bed, hair disheveled and face sleepy. He'd wanted Scott to know he had woken up to the message, and how happy he had been to see it.

(He had to admit, the photo was kind of sexy too.)

Scott had replied just after eight, which Kip saw when he was in the back room at work.

SCOTT:

Wow.

And then, Thank you. I can't believe I didn't have a picture of you before.

Kip had written back, I can do better.

SCOTT:

No. It's perfect.

Then, But feel free to try. 😊

Kip had laughed and written, I don't have a picture of you, you know . . .

No response had come for a minute, and then he'd received a photo from Scott. It was an image of a Gatorade ad Scott had done.

KIP:

Fuck you.

Scott had ended the conversation with a winky face emoji and Kip had reluctantly gotten ready for work.

Kip was a complete space cadet during his shift, and of course, Maria noticed.

"What's fucking *you* up today?" she asked at the end of the morning rush. "I mean, besides Scott Hunter, who you are obviously in love with."

"No I'm not!" Not exactly a lie. Maybe.

"Sure," Maria said.

"It's just . . ." Kip decided to offer another secret to distract from the bigger secret. "I applied for another job. At the Museum of the City of New York."

"Whoa!"

"Yeah, well. There is no way I'm gonna get it. But . . . I don't know."

She punched his arm. "Kip! Look at you, improving yourself!"

"I mean it *would* be really great. *If* it happens."

"This is exciting!"

"Maybe, yeah. Don't tell anyone, okay?"

"Not a word," she promised. "Are you sure you want to leave this glamorous job behind?"

"As long as I can keep the apron."

At quitting time, Maria walked with Kip to the subway station. She was heading back to the East Village apartment she shared with three roommates. Kip mentioned that he was meeting Elena, and that she was going to help him with his tux for the Equinox Gala. He omitted a lot of details.

"I can't believe you're going to the Equinox Gala," she said. "That is fucking nuts. What if Beyoncé is there?"

"Then she will have the honor of dancing with me."

It was always a big deal when New York played Boston.

Boston had their own star center, a hotshot Russian named Ilya Rozanov. He was cocky, brash, flashy . . . everything Scott wasn't. And the fans *loved* him.

He was also an incredibly skilled player, with an uncanny ability to always be in the right place at the right time.

Scott knew better than to let him get under his skin. Rozanov antagonized everyone in the league. He had gotten good at ignoring the yappy Russian, but sometimes Scott just wanted to hit him into next week.

Coming off the embarrassing loss in Philadelphia on Tuesday, Scott was fired up. Coach Murdock had run them through a brutal practice yesterday after they'd arrived in Boston. Their defense had been especially punished, which Zullo had taken as well as expected.

Zullo was a problem. Scott had played with guys who were assholes but still got the job done on the ice. Zullo was getting the job done less and less. Scott didn't know how much longer he could put up with him. He was becoming a serious distraction, and not what they needed as the playoffs got closer.

Murdock knew how Scott felt about Zullo. The general manager knew how Scott felt. Scott tried not to let his teammates know because it was his job to keep the team together as a unit.

Scott was on a stationary bike at the arena two hours before game time, watching Rozanov playfully trash talk Scott and the Admirals on ESPN. Scott shook his head and fought a smile as he watched the television. He had to hand it to the kid—he put on a good show.

Scott was in a mood, though. If Rozanov rode him too much tonight, Scott might just punch him.

"Oof," Elena said. "That's gonna be five minutes."

They watched Scott being hauled off to the penalty box. He was still yelling what appeared to be *very* strong words at Rozanov over his shoulder.

"Rozanov deserved it," Kip said.

"You might be a bit biased."

"Rozanov is a fucking dick."

"Well, nice guy Scott Hunter just punched him in the face."

"Aw, whatever. Scott had gloves on. And Rozanov covers his whole fucking face with that visor anyway."

The ref made the hand gesture to indicate that Scott was getting a five-minute penalty for roughing.

"You should text him," Elena said, nudging Kip's thigh with her toe. "He's not doing anything for a few minutes."

"Shut up."

"Send him that photo I took of you in the tux at the tailor."

"No! It's not finished yet, and besides—"

"You want it to be a surprise."

Kip blushed a little. "Maybe."

"You're cute," Elena said, getting up. "You want more wine?"

"Nah, I gotta work tomorrow."

"You can stay here tonight, if you want. Cut your commute down in the morning."

Kip considered it. "Can't. I need to pack a bag before I go to work. I'm, uh . . ."

"Staying at Scott's tomorrow night?"

"Yeah," Kip said, grinning stupidly.

"Oh my *god*!" Elena exclaimed. "It's Valentine's Day tomorrow!"

"I know . . ."

"Are you going *out*?"

"No! No . . . we're not going anywhere. We, y'know . . . can't."

She rejoined him on the couch. "Are you sure you want this, Kip? I know he's *him*, but he comes with a lot of baggage."

Memories of the past week flooded Kip's brain: both of them naked in Scott's bed with their legs tangled together, Scott's fingers gently brushing his hair; Scott admitting that he'd never brought anyone to his home before; Scott wanting Kip to tell him about his day over the phone, just so he could listen to his voice.

And that late-night text message.

I'd give anything to see you right now.

"Yes," Kip said. "I do. He's worth it."

CHAPTER NINE

Friday finally arrived.

Scott had texted Kip that morning. Getting on the plane soon. See you tonight?

Kip had written back, I can't wait.

SCOTT:
Me neither. But I need time to cook!

KIP:
Ok. When?

SCOTT:
6?

KIP:
Ugh. Ok.

Kip finished work at two. He had an overnight bag packed, and four hours to kill. He had already planned on going to the gym after work, so he did that. After, he could shower there and get all fixed up before going to Scott's.

He had packed a nice outfit to change into for tonight. He didn't think Scott expected him to dress up; he'd decided to make a bit of an effort.

When Kip checked himself out in the locker-room mirror before leaving the gym, he thought he looked pretty good. He was wearing his best jeans, which were dark and slim-fitting. He paired them with a deep red shawl-neck sweater he had bought on sale at Old Navy. Nothing fancy, but appropriately cozy for a Valentine's night in.

And it would come off easily.

He still had an hour and a half, so he decided to go pick up some wine to bring over.

Should I bring a gift?

Jesus.

Kip had never actually *done* Valentine's Day before. What was an appropriate gesture for the man you had been secretly dating for about a week?

The *millionaire* he had been secretly dating for about a week.

A short while later, Kip stood in the wine boutique down the street from his gym, frowning at the bottles he typically purchased—inexpensive reds his parents liked, and eight-dollar whites that Elena had described as "drinkable." Could he really show up to Scott Hunter's home with one of these? What did that guy usually drink?

Kip considered a thirty-dollar bottle. Then a forty-dollar bottle. He considered the meager sum that sat in his bank account at the moment.

Maybe he could bring beer. It wasn't traditional, but . . .

Or flowers? Would flowers be weird?

Suddenly the seventy minutes he had left to kill didn't seem like nearly enough time.

* * *

Scott wiped his hands on a dish towel and admired the salad he had made. It was simple, just arugula and cherry tomatoes and pine nuts with a bit of Parmesan, but it was pretty.

He checked the time. Fifteen minutes until Kip would arrive.

He opened a bottle of chilled white wine and pulled out a couple of glasses. He wasn't even sure if Kip drank wine. There were still so many things he didn't know about him.

I want to learn everything.

These feelings were all so new to him. He hadn't had anyone to care for—or to care for him—since his mother had died when he was fifteen. His teammates were like family, and those bonds were important to him, but this all-encompassing desire to be with Kip was like nothing he had ever experienced.

He considered where he had been less than a year ago. Last August he had been in Spain. Torremolinos. Alone.

Scott had spent his days there anonymously exploring the small beach town, sometimes heading to the beach to swim or check out the . . . sights. He hadn't quite gathered the courage to go to the "gay" beach that he had known was there.

At night, the darkness making him brave, he had made his way to one of the many gay bars. He preferred the pubs. It was much easier to take a seat at a bar and nurse a beer than it was to embarrass himself on a dance floor.

He'd never had trouble attracting the kind of attention he had been secretly hoping for. He couldn't flirt to save his life, but he knew he had a good body. He would sit with his beer in the tightest T-shirt he'd dared to wear and wait for someone to approach. Someone had always approached.

Doing anything in public terrified Scott, so he had gone to their hotel room, or, on a couple of rare occasions, brought them to his. The encounters were provisional, educational. They were just . . . maintenance. They had filled a basic need, and they'd prevented Scott from losing his mind. There had been nothing romantic about them.

They had been nothing like the times he had been with Kip. Scott had carefully stored the memory of every kiss and touch and moan Kip had given him, and had filled the lonely hours on the road by replaying them over and over again.

He was smitten. That was the only word for it.

Water was heating up for the pasta, and the shrimp were all cleaned and ready to go into a pan of butter and garlic. His plan was to throw it all together after Kip arrived.

He checked the dinner table to make sure everything was perfect. He adjusted the lighting and lit a little candle in a glass holder in the middle of the table. He was nervous. He'd never celebrated Valentine's Day before.

He inspected himself in the hallway mirror. He'd dressed a bit beyond his usual T-shirt and jeans, going with nice charcoal-gray pants and a button-down blue shirt. He didn't expect to be wearing clothes for very long anyway.

But he wouldn't rush things. He had plans. Lots of plans.

He smiled to himself and went downstairs to greet Kip. He had been counting the minutes all day. All week, really. He'd lost count of the number of times he'd looked at the selfie Kip had sent him.

And then, there he was. Walking through the front doors of Scott's building with a shy smile that made Scott's heart race.

"Hi," Kip said.

"Hi." Scott wanted to hug him, but he worried if he made contact he wouldn't be able to control himself. Better to get behind closed doors.

In the elevator, a minute later, Scott said, "It's so good to see you again. You have no idea."

"I think I do."

He flushed and pressed his lips together. "Are you hungry? I have to boil the pasta, but it will only take a few minutes."

"Sure. Whatever you want to do."

"I mean, we could wait, but I was thinking we might want to get eating out of the way . . ."

Kip bit his lip, and just that small gesture turned Scott on so much.

He fumbled with the code to unlock his apartment. Kip was right behind him, leaving barely any space between them, but still not touching.

Finally the door unlocked and they slipped inside. When the door clicked shut, they stood facing each other for a moment, nervous and grinning. After a ridiculous few seconds, Scott huffed out a laugh and, with a gentle hand on Kip's face, guided them together.

They kissed deeply and openly for a long time. Scott heard Kip's backpack hit the floor before his hands wrapped around Scott's back. Scott dropped his own hands to Kip's back and pulled him tight against him. It felt so good to hold him. The frustration and stress Scott had carried all week drained away.

When they eventually broke apart, Kip laughed. "I missed you too."

Scott smiled and took his jacket from him to hang up. Kip had a red sweater on that made him look so handsome and cuddly . . .

"You look good," Scott said. "Really good."

"Was just thinking the same thing about you."

"Come on in," he said, extending a hand. Kip smiled and took it.

Scott led him to the dinner table that, he had to admit, looked pretty romantic. He had done a good job setting the mood, considering his lack of experience.

"Wow," Kip said. "All this for me?"

"I, uh, I'm sorry if it's a little much. I just . . . I've never celebrated Valentine's Day before."

"You know something?" Kip said. "Me neither."

"Really?"

"Really. Never."

"I find that very hard to believe."

Kip shrugged. "Never been in a serious relationship. I mean, there were a few guys that I saw for a little while, but never in February, I guess."

"Wow," Scott said. "Well, that takes a load off. I thought I'd have to live up to some stiff competition."

"No." Kip smiled. "And I have a feeling you would have won anyway."

Scott kissed him, because he couldn't help it. "I like winning."

He led him into the kitchen. He poured two glasses of wine and put on an apron, which Kip seemed to *love.*

"Look at you," Kip said, leaning back against the fridge with his glass in his hand. "A whole other side of Scott Hunter."

Scott rolled his eyes. "I have lots of sides." He dumped the linguini in the pot of boiling water and turned on a second burner. "This won't take long," he assured Kip as he placed a sauté pan on the burner.

"Take your time. I like watching you work."

They chatted while Scott prepared dinner. It was easy and comfortable, just how Scott had always imagined being in a relationship would be.

"Okay," he said when dinner was ready. "Go sit down. I want to bring it over to you looking all nice on the plate."

Kip did as he was told and Scott assembled the plates. He carried them to the table, and his breath caught when he saw how stunning Kip was in the dim light of the dining area.

He placed the pasta down next to the salad plates and slid into his chair. He held up his wineglass. "Happy Valentine's Day."

"Happy Valentine's Day. This looks amazing, by the way."

"Oh, thanks. I wanted to keep it kinda light, y'know?"

Kip's lips twitched. "I think I get it."

"I was thinking," Scott said after a couple of bites, "it's not just Valentine's Day that we're celebrating tonight."

"Oh?"

"It was also one month ago today that I met you for the first time."

"Wow," Kip said, "I didn't think about that."

"I'm really glad I decided to get a smoothie that day," Scott said, smiling.

Kip smiled back at him, that easy, sexy smile that always completely disarmed Scott. "Me too."

They ate and talked and laughed and drank more wine. Scott had positioned their chairs so they were facing each other across the table because he thought that would be the most traditional, but now he was regretting it. He wanted to be closer to Kip. As soon as they were done eating, he suggested they move to the couch.

Before he joined Scott in the living room, Kip paused and said, "Oh! Just a second."

He walked over to where he'd left his backpack by the door and came back with a small paper bag. "I got you something. It's . . . I mean, it's nothing. I just saw them and . . . Anyway, here."

He thrust the bag at Scott, who took it. "You got me a present?"

"Sort of. It's just dumb. I didn't know what to bring."

Scott opened the bag and pulled out . . .

"Socks," he said.

"Yeah, they're kinda like the color of blueberries. Or, like, the color of your smoothie that you get. I thought maybe you could wear them when you're on the road. It would be like bringing the good luck with you?"

Scott ran his thumb over the soft material of the socks, completely speechless.

"Like I said," Kip mumbled, "it's just dumb."

"No!" Scott stood to meet him. "No, I love them. They're . . . I love them, Kip. I'm going to wear them all the time when I'm away and I'll think of you. Thank you."

Kip looked relieved and delighted, and Scott kissed him, because how could he not? It might sound silly, but having these socks would help him a lot when he was away from Kip.

They kissed, and this time Kip's mouth moved from Scott's lips to his jaw, then up behind his ear. He sucked in a breath, completely overwhelmed with need for this beautiful, thoughtful man.

"So now that dinner is out of the way . . ." Kip breathed against his ear.

"There's also dessert," Scott said weakly. "I went to a bakery—"

Kip cut him off with a kiss that made Scott forget all about the macarons sitting in a box on his counter.

He was hard already. He'd been at least partway there since Kip had walked into his apartment, if he was being honest. It was ridiculous. He had previously gone *years*, and more recently *months*, without sex and now he couldn't go a few days without feeling desperate for it.

Kip wasn't going to make him wait anymore. He unbuttoned Scott's shirt, destroying the nice outfit Scott had so carefully put together. But Scott didn't care. He couldn't wait to be rid of these clothes. To feel Kip everywhere.

When the last of the buttons were freed, Kip hauled down the collar of Scott's undershirt and scraped his teeth along his clavicle. Scott shuddered and pressed his erection against Kip's stomach. If Kip didn't touch him there soon, he was going to start whimpering.

Kip laughed softly against his neck. "That for me?"

He slid a hand up Scott's thigh. When his hand finally made contact with Scott's cock through the fabric of his pants, Scott choked out a broken "Y-yes. God."

He was disappointed at his lack of discipline. He'd wanted to lead up to this. Draw it out. Savor it.

But Kip was already unfastening Scott's belt and unzipping his pants and slipping a hand inside and . . .

"I—have plans," Scott stammered.

Kip smirked at him and knocked a throw pillow onto the floor at Scott's feet. "Me too."

He dropped to his knees.

"Been thinking about this all fucking week," he said, nuzzling Scott's cock through his underwear—his *nice* underwear—and breathing hot on it. He slid Scott's pants down by running his hands firmly down Scott's thighs. Scott wished he had something to lean against, but he was standing between the couch and his coffee table with no walls in reach. It was going to take all of his strength to keep his knees from buckling.

Scott stroked Kip's hair and sighed happily as Kip slid a hand back up and cupped his balls, gently squeezing. Scott shuddered and sucked in a breath.

He had wanted to pamper Kip. To take it slow so they could explore each other. But maybe taking the edge off wasn't the worst idea . . .

Kip pulled Scott's cock out, and kissed the head. "Fucking beautiful," he murmured. "Look at you."

"Been that way since you got here, pretty much."

"Lemme help."

Kip's mouth was so warm and so slick, and Scott was so

turned on that he was going to come embarrassingly fast. A few minutes of Kip's mouth on him, and Kip's hands on his thighs and ass, and Scott was trembling.

"So close already, aren't you?" Kip brushed his fingers over Scott's balls, which were tight and heavy. He tongued at the precome that was leaking from the tip in fat drops.

Scott just gripped Kip's hair, unable to speak, and Kip took him deep into his mouth, sucking hard and relentlessly until Scott shattered and came. Kip continued to lap gently at the head until Scott took a wobbly step backward.

"That," Scott panted, "that was not how this was supposed to go."

"No?" Kip said, rising to his feet. "I'm pretty pleased with the results."

Scott laughed and shook his head. "I was gonna take it slow tonight."

"We can still take it slow. I'm in no rush at all."

Scott kissed him and then playfully hauled him down onto the couch with him. They landed all tangled up in each other. Scott shifted so his back was against one of the arms, one leg stretched out along the length of the sofa. Kip was mostly in his lap now, kissing him as he carefully tucked Scott back into his briefs.

They made out on the couch, hands pushing up under their shirts. Scott felt *wild*. Even in the afterglow of a (really excellent) blow job, he craved more. Kip's erection was hard against his hip now, and Scott reached for it, gripping him through his jeans. Kip moaned softly into his mouth and rocked into his hand. Scott moved to undo Kip's fly, but Kip stopped him with a hand wrapped around his wrist.

"You all right?" Scott asked.

"Yeah." Kip exhaled, his forehead pressed against Scott's shoulder. "I just . . . There's something I wanna do. And I don't want to lose my nerve."

Scott's curiosity was piqued, to say the least. "What do you want to do?"

"Can we go to the bedroom?"

"Yeah! Yeah, of course."

Kip untangled himself from Scott and led him to the bedroom. When they got there, he turned and started undressing. "Last time," he said, after pulling his sweater over his head, "you said . . . you wanted . . ."

"Last time . . ." Scott repeated, struggling to recall the specific request to which Kip was referring. He wanted a lot of things when it came to Kip. "Oh!"

"Yeah," Kip said with a crooked smile. "Said you wanted to watch me. Wanted to see how I get myself off."

"I did," Scott said, dazed. "I *do*. I want that. God."

"Well," Kip said, unbuttoning his fly, "have a seat." He gestured to the chair in the corner of Scott's bedroom.

"Yeah . . . yeah, okay. Jesus."

Scott sat in the chair. Other than his shirt being unbuttoned and his pants being open, he was still dressed. Kip, on the other hand, was already down to his black briefs. The imbalance made Scott feel very dirty. He was getting hard again already.

Kip piled up the pillows against the headboard and threw himself playfully onto the bed, his back propped up by the mountain of pillows.

Scott dragged the chair a little closer. He would abide by Kip's rules, but he'd be damned if he wasn't going to get the best view possible.

Kip closed his eyes, exhaled heavily, then slid a hand down his stomach and onto his thigh. He moved his hand in lazy circles on his inner thigh for a moment, then trailed it over to where his cock strained against his briefs.

He inhaled sharply and opened his eyes, first looking at his hand, and then up at Scott. Scott nodded slowly.

"Okay," Kip murmured, apparently to himself.

Scott could see the tension leave him as he moved his hand, gripping and fondling the bulge in his shorts. He sighed and chewed his lip, eyes fluttering closed, then open again to gaze at Scott under heavy lids.

"Been thinking about this a lot," Kip said, his voice sleepy and easy. "You watching me like this. Hot as fuck, I can tell you that."

"Yeah?"

"Mm. When I was jerking off . . . fuck, after we hung up the other night . . . I imagined you were watching."

"God."

"Almost . . . almost called you back. Wanted to Skype or something so you could watch me for real."

"Fuck, yes. We'll have to do that. Soon. When my roommate isn't there."

Kip laughed. "Right. Shit. Roommate. Forgot." He tugged at himself through the fabric, head rolling back against the pillows. He was so sexy and daring, and he was giving Scott everything he wanted.

"How're you doing there?" Scott asked, voice hoarse.

"So good, Scott. Feels so nice. I'm gonna take these off now." He hooked his thumbs into the waistband of his shorts, lifted his hips, and slid them off. And Scott was treated to the perfection of Kip's naked body, with his gorgeous, thick cock, which was so hard right now it was almost flat against Kip's belly.

Scott had had the foresight to place the bottle of lube on top of the nightstand. He hadn't wanted things to get interrupted once they got going. He was thankful for that bit of planning now, as he watched Kip reach for the lube and slick some onto his cock.

"Mm . . . that's really good lube. Have I mentioned that?" Kip asked, eyes closed again. "Feels incredible."

Kip's long fingers curled around his cock and slid down, then back up so his palm could twist over the head. His thumb pressed in a bit just under the head on the way back down. His other hand gently fondled his balls, sometimes pulling on them. It was all pretty slow and loose.

"You like to keep it gentle, huh?" Scott asked.

Kip opened his eyes and gave him a lazy smile. "I'm tryin' not to come right away. Wanna put on a good show here."

"You are." Scott shifted in his chair. It took all of his willpower to stay there. "You sayin' you're close already?"

"Sayin' I could be . . ."

Scott swallowed. "You look so fucking good, Kip. I wanna come over there. I want to touch you. But I want to watch you too."

"Maybe I'll let you . . . later . . . Ah . . . Jesus . . ."

Scott watched obediently from his chair as Kip's hand sped up and his eyes squeezed shut again. He was the most gorgeous thing Scott had ever seen, writhing on the bed, and completely focused on his own pleasure. His breathing was rough and he was making beautiful little moans.

Scott's own breathing was getting ragged. "Kip . . . fuck." He couldn't take it anymore. "Can I . . . can I sit on the bed with you?" he asked. "I won't touch you. I just want to be closer."

"Yeah, sweetheart," Kip drawled, head rolling back on the pillows behind him. "Come on over."

Scott blushed at the pet name, but it sent a giddy thrill through him at the same time. He moved over to the bed and sat on the corner, twisting so he could see Kip as he sat near his one extended foot.

And here he could see the beads of precome glistening at the slit. He could see the sweat that was dampening the edges of Kip's hair, the way the muscles in his neck strained, and the way his jaw clenched when something felt particularly good.

"Oof," Kip gritted out. "Tryna make this last, but fuck . . ."

"You don't have to," Scott said, mouth dry. He wanted to touch himself, but he also wanted to wait for Kip's hand later. Mostly, he needed to see Kip come.

Kip grunted and moved his hand faster.

"You're close, aren't you? You need to come? Trying to hold out for me, but you're right there, I can tell."

"I'm—Oh, *fuck*," Kip stammered.

"You gonna finish for me? Or do you want me to help?"

"Ah . . . god . . . I don't know . . ."

His chest was heaving and the muscles in his arm were straining as he pumped himself harder. He locked eyes with Scott, and Scott knew he was about to—

Kip's mouth dropped open and he let out a broken noise as he came. Long ribbons fell on his chest and stomach and ran over his fingers as he shuddered and slowed his hand.

"God, Kip. So beautiful. You should see."

Kip closed his eyes and sank, boneless, into the pillows.

Scott crawled over his body and hovered above his face. When Kip opened his eyes again, Scott kissed him, slowly and tenderly.

"Thank you," Scott said. "That was . . . I'm going to be holding on to that for a long time."

"Something else to take with you on the road." Kip smiled.

"Damn right." Scott kissed him again. "Now seems like a perfect time for the next thing I have planned."

"Shit, don't make me do anything now, Scott."

"You'll like this. Just a second."

CHAPTER TEN

Kip relaxed against the pillows, pleased with his successful exhibitionism experiment.

Scott came out of the bathroom with a damp cloth. He sat on the bed next to Kip and wiped him clean with gentle strokes. It felt heavenly.

So heavenly that it took Kip a while before he realized that Scott had left water running in the bathroom.

"What you got planned?" Kip asked.

"Thought we might take a bath . . ."

Kip liked that idea a whole lot. "You're pampering me."

"Do you mind?"

"Not really." Kip pulled him down by his unbuttoned shirt and kissed him. "You have a lot of clothes on for a bath."

Scott sprang off the bed onto his feet and quickly removed his shirt. He was down to his royal blue briefs in seconds. Kip didn't think he would ever get tired of Scott's incredible chest and abs.

Unlike the other parts of Scott's home, the bathroom had no windows. The room was far from claustrophobic, though. The lighting and the decor created a soothing atmosphere, a private sanctuary in a noisy city of millions.

The bathtub was in the middle of the room, and it was huge. Steam billowed from the water that was filling it. The room smelled amazing too—spicy and citrusy.

"I usually just use Epsom salt," Scott said, "but I thought maybe I'd use this fancy bath stuff I bought." He gestured to a slim, expensive-looking bottle that sat on the counter.

"You really are pampering me." Kip smiled. He wrapped an arm around Scott's neck and hauled him down for a kiss.

Scott got into the bath first, and Kip settled himself between his legs. Kip had tried, once, to take a bath with another guy, but the tub had been way too small for the two of them. The faucet had dug into his back, and he'd had nowhere to put his legs.

This was not a problem in Scott's tub, where the tap was on the side and there was enough room for both men to splay their legs out.

Kip tipped his head back so it rested on Scott's shoulder. Scott wrapped an arm diagonally across his chest, and kissed the top of his head.

"This is nice," Kip murmured. He could actually fall asleep in here.

"It's perfect."

They were quiet for a while, and then Scott said, "When I first looked at this place, and I saw this tub, I thought, 'It's big enough for two.' And I know it's dumb, but I always wanted . . . I imagined sharing it with someone."

Kip tangled their fingers together under the water.

"Not just the bathtub," Scott said. "All of it. This apartment. My life. I don't know . . ."

Kip was stunned. *His life?*

"Sorry," Scott said, "I know we've only been . . . I mean, I shouldn't be suggesting—"

"I don't know how I got to be so lucky," Kip interrupted, "but being able to share anything with you makes me really happy."

He pulled their joined hands up and rested them over his heart. Scott brushed his lips against his temple, and nipped the top of his ear. "I *would* share anything with you, Kip. Give you anything."

"Don't need anything. Except maybe to stay in this bath forever."

Scott chuckled against Kip's hair. "Do you want to come to the game tomorrow night?"

"I can't. I'm working an event. Serving."

"Oh."

"See? We both have full, busy lives." Kip laughed at his own joke. Scott was quiet.

"I hope you don't think . . ." he started. Kip could feel him tensing up. "I don't think you're beneath me."

"Technically *you're* beneath *me* at the moment."

"I'm serious. I just—I want to say this once, so you know. Because it's possible that you think that I'm just . . . taking a vacation, or whatever, with you. Like I'm trying to escape my high-profile life by hooking up with a, um . . ."

"Nobody?"

"No! I mean . . . you're not. That's what I'm trying to say—terribly. You're not some nobody. I'm not using you to escape anything. I love my life. I love my job. The fame part is a little much sometimes, but I don't mind it. I'm happy, is what I'm saying. But this? You? I feel like . . . like I found the missing piece."

Kip didn't know what to say to that.

"Geez," Scott said, "that's not—Sorry. I shouldn't have—"

"No! It's just . . . Really? You feel that way?"

"I do."

Kip turned around to face Scott, water sloshing loudly around them. "You don't owe me anything, okay? I don't expect anything. But I like you a whole fucking lot, so thank you."

"Thank *you*," Scott said, "for coming over. This is all new for me, and I'm trying really hard to take this slow and not get too intense, but I'm kinda used to charging ahead and going after what I want."

Kip grinned. "Works for me."

They kissed, and Scott ran his hands down Kip's sides. "You called me sweetheart," he said, his voice soft and dopey.

"Did I?"

"Yeah . . . when you were—"

"Aw, I say lots of dumb things when I'm that far gone. Sorry."

"No, I liked it."

Kip smiled at him. "Well, all right, sweetheart," he said, and then kissed him again.

He ended up moving to the opposite end of the tub so he could talk to Scott more easily.

"I saw the goal you scored for me," he said.

Scott grimaced. "I was hoping you hadn't watched those games."

"I watched both of them. They seemed . . . frustrating."

"That's one word for it," Scott grumbled.

"You want to talk about it?"

"No." Then, "It's just . . ." And he proceeded to rant about Frank Zullo for several minutes. Kip listened and absently stroked his fingertips along Scott's shin.

"Geez," he said when Scott was done.

"Sorry," Scott said. "I'm kinda ruining the mood here."

"Don't apologize. If something is bothering you, I want to hear about it."

Scott raised an eyebrow. "Even if we're in a bathtub together on Valentine's Day?"

"Definitely." It was true. Kip had hooked up with lots of guys, but he hadn't made a real connection like this before. It was frankly pretty sexy that Scott wanted to share his problems with him.

"So . . ." Kip said, "what did Rozanov say that made you punch him like that?"

Scott laughed, a little darkly. "Oh. Nothing really. I was taking out my frustrations on his face. He just yapped some dumb shit at me. Normal stuff."

"You're not gonna tell me?"

Scott sighed. "He told me he was disappointed because he'd heard I was, quote, 'good at hockey again.'"

"Ouch."

"Yeah, well. He didn't deserve a sucker punch like that."

They stayed in the tub until the water got cool, talking about different things and learning about each other.

"If it wasn't for hockey, what do you think you would have wanted to do with your life?"

Scott blew out a breath. "I can't even imagine my life without hockey. But I guess maybe something like social work?"

"You like helping people."

"I do. I've been lucky in a lot of ways. Maybe unlucky in others, but there are plenty of people who could have their whole lives changed with just a little help and support. I think I would have liked to have done something like that."

"You *do* do that," Kip pointed out. "You help people all the time. You give money to charity. You visit hospitals. You help your teammates." He smiled. "I've read all about your good deeds, Scott Hunter."

Scott shrugged. "My mom and I never had much when I was growing up, but she always did what she could to help people. She got the grocery store she worked in to start a holiday toy drive. And she was always giving her time, what little of it there was, to helping anyone who was having a hard time. She was really inspiring."

"She sounds amazing."

"She was. And she always made sure I could play hockey, even though it's a sport that demands a lot of money and time. I owe her everything. And I know she'd be proud of me, but I think I could do more."

"Like what?"

"I don't know. I'd like to maybe start a charity. I've been thinking about that. I wish . . ."

"What?"

Scott sighed. "Someday, maybe, I'd like to help gay kids. Or, um, you know, kids who aren't . . . heterosexual?"

"Queer kids," Kip said. "You can say that. It's fine."

"Oh. Yeah, well. I'm not really too knowledgeable about the whole . . . queer community thing."

"I've noticed. You want to be?"

"I would. Someday I would like to do something to help . . . queer kids . . . who play team sports? It's tough for them, you know?"

"I can imagine. I think that would be an awesome thing for you to do."

"Someday."

"Yeah. Someday."

"Let's get out of here," Scott said abruptly. He stood and the water ran off his huge, solid body.

Kip was definitely ready for whatever was next.

He dried himself with one of Scott's luxurious, fluffy towels and followed him back to the bedroom.

Scott opened the nightstand drawer and pulled something out. "Lie down," he instructed. "On your stomach. Get comfortable."

Kip did as he was told. He trusted Scott.

The bed sank as Scott joined him on it and straddled his lower back, his own strong thighs gripping Kip's hips.

Kip heard a cap being opened, and he smelled something

sweet and fruity. Then Scott's hands were on him, rubbing oil into his damp, clean skin.

"Blueberry massage oil," Scott said. "Couldn't resist."

"You bought that for me?"

"I did."

"Does it taste like blueberries or just smell like them?"

Scott's tongue ran up his spine, hot and slick. "Tastes like 'em," he confirmed.

Kip laughed and then moaned when Scott's big, strong hands dug deep into his muscles around his shoulder blades. "Oh my god. That feels incredible."

"Just getting started," Scott said. "I want you to relax and let me make you feel good."

Kip didn't protest. Scott worked in silence for a while, kneading Kip's muscles while Kip sighed happily and tried not to feel too bad about all the hard work Scott was doing.

"How are you feeling?" Scott asked after a bit.

"A little guilty, to be honest."

"Don't. I love doing this. I love touching you, looking at you. I've denied myself anything like this for so long . . . Don't feel guilty."

"Okay," Kip said. *God, that's so sad.*

"You're so beautiful, Kip. I've never . . ."

Kip waited.

"I've never *wanted* anyone like this before. I've had, I don't know, crushes. I've been attracted to men, of course. Hooked up with men. But you . . . I'm breaking all my rules with you."

Kip swallowed and tried to fight off the surge of emotion that coursed through him.

"What can I say?" he said, trying to remain playful, though his voice was cracking. "I'm irresistible."

"You are," Scott said in a low voice. He slid down to straddle

Kip's thighs. His hands began to knead Kip's lower back and then his ass.

"Mm . . . Might need to focus on that area," Kip slurred. "Lotta tension there."

"It has my undivided attention." Scott dug his fingers deep into Kip's cheeks, and Kip let himself drift away.

Scott rubbed him down for a long time, until Kip's whole body felt like jelly. He was mostly silent, aside from a few hushed, reverent words:

"Unreal, Kip."

"Gorgeous."

"Perfect."

Kip was nearly nodding off when Scott ran the side of his hand down his crack, slow and firm. He followed it up by making a fist and running his knuckles down the same path. He repeated it over and over, one fist, then the other, dragging knuckles over the sensitive flesh around his hole.

"That feel good?"

"Yes! Holy . . . Amazing."

"Good. I want to fuck you. Do you want that?"

"Yeah. Yes. God, yes."

"Roll over," Scott instructed gently. "I miss you."

Kip smiled to himself and flopped over, relaxed and completely ready to let Scott do whatever he wanted with him. Scott knelt on the bed, inching up Kip's body to straddle his waist again. Scott's cock was half hard, hanging heavy between his legs. He leaned down and kissed Kip, who wrapped a hand around Scott's cock, stroking it as they kissed and feeling it grow harder in his hand.

Then he placed both hands on Scott's ass and guided him forward until his thighs were stretched wide around Kip's chest. He tilted his head up and took Scott's cock into his mouth.

He kept his eyes up so he could see Scott looming over him,

one hand gripping the headboard. Scott was gazing down at him and murmuring praise in a low, gentle voice. "Yeah. Just like that. Fuck, you're gorgeous. Look at you. So good to me."

Kip closed his eyes and sighed around Scott's dick. It was so big and so hard now. He dug his hands into Scott's ass to push it deeper into his mouth.

"Holy . . . Wow. God, I want to let you keep going, but . . ." Scott slowly pulled out. He rested the tip on Kip's lips for a moment, considering, before he slid back down Kip's body. He nudged Kip's legs so he'd bend his knees, then he got up and grabbed the lube and a condom.

Kip was already relaxed from the massage, so it didn't take long at all for Scott to open him up with his strong, careful fingers.

Scott grabbed both of Kip's thighs and hauled him down to the end of the bed. He didn't even have time to react beyond wide-eyed gaping before Scott lifted his hips and ass and plunged into him.

"Ahh! Shit," Kip gasped. "God, that feels amazing."

"This is all I've been able to fucking think about since last time," Scott said, and *oof*, Kip loved the deep rumble of his sex voice.

"Me too. Want it hard. Just like last time."

Scott gave it to him, standing on the floor at the end of the bed with one of Kip's ankles on his shoulder. His thrusts were just on the edge of too hard, and Kip loved it.

"Yes. Fuck. Like that," Kip babbled.

He was on another plane, awestruck by the perfect physical specimen that was fucking him so eagerly. Sweat was forming on Scott's face and chest, slicking the muscles that tensed and rippled as Scott held Kip where he wanted him.

Scott was nailing his prostate with almost every thrust, and it was incredible. It was so fucking good. Kip started jerking himself hard and fast.

"Want to come . . ." he gritted out. "Gonna come on your dick. Want to . . ."

"Fuck, yes. Come on."

"You're perfect . . . Love you fucking me like this . . ."

"Could do this forever. You're beautiful, Kip. Thought you were gonna come for me . . ."

"I am. I am. I—Oh fuck!"

They both watched Kip's dick as it spurted all over his chest. Scott stopped thrusting.

"God, Kip. That feels amazing. Okay—Jesus . . ." He started moving again. "I'm close. I'm real fucking close . . ."

"Come on me," Kip said, still gently stroking himself through the last waves of his own orgasm. "I want to see it. Please."

Scott grunted, then quickly pulled out and tore the condom off, throwing it behind him. He lowered Kip's leg and stood over him as he furiously stroked his own cock. Within seconds Scott was coming, raining down on Kip's stomach and chest and neck.

Scott collapsed on the bed and Kip rolled on top of him, mess and all. They kissed, breathless and giddy, and when they broke apart after a minute, they were both smiling.

"Before I forget," Kip said, "I want to thank you for a lovely evening."

Scott laughed and kissed him again. "So I did okay at the whole Valentine's thing?"

"Absolutely. Hands down, best Valentine's Day ever."

They cleaned up and then got back into bed. Kip snuggled against Scott's body. The evening had been perfect, and he wished he could keep it going, but he was exhausted.

"Goodnight," Scott murmured, wrapping a giant arm around him. Kip couldn't remember ever being so comfortable.

He kissed Scott's hand. "Goodnight, sweetheart."

* * *

They slept in the next morning, neither of them needing to be anywhere until late afternoon. When they awoke, they stayed in bed, tangled up together and talking.

"What are you doing today?" Scott asked. He was on his side, head propped on his elbow, and his hair was an adorable mess.

"Nothing planned. You have any ideas?"

"Yeah." Scott smiled shyly. "I want to make you breakfast."

Kip was all for that idea, but then he started kissing Scott and quickly lost interest in anything that involved leaving the bed.

They were blissfully making out, Scott's hands and mouth exploring Kip's body and making him shiver, when Scott's phone started buzzing.

"It's nothing," Scott said, without looking at it. "They can call back later."

He continued mapping Kip's body, tasting the jut of Kip's hipbone, when the phone started buzzing again.

"Go away," Scott grumbled, still not picking it up, "I'm busy."

The third time it started buzzing, when Scott was sucking on Kip's neck with a hand sliding up his thigh, Scott sighed and said, "Sorry. I'm just going to see who it is."

He grabbed the phone. "It's Carter," he said, brow furrowed. He answered the call. "Carter?"

Scott was still close enough that Kip could hear the voice of Scott's teammate. "Scott, Zullo fucked up. He got arrested last night."

"What?"

"Yeah. Caused a scene at a bar in Jersey. Destruction of property. Assault. Resisting arrest . . . Probably some other things."

"Okay. Fuck. Where is he?" Scott got off the bed and walked to his closet, ending Kip's access to the conversation.

When Scott returned, he was fully dressed and off the phone. "I have to go. I'm sorry."

"Of course. Yeah. Jesus, are you all right?"

"I'm furious is what I am," Scott said, "but I really am sorry to have to leave you."

He sighed and kissed him. When he pulled back slowly, Kip leaned forward to chase his lips.

Scott shook his head. "If I kiss you again, I'll never leave. You can stay as long as you want. I don't know when I'll be back. I might not be back before the game, honestly. This is a real fucking mess."

"Okay. Don't worry about me. Go take care of your team."

"Thanks, yeah." He stood and moved toward the door, then looked back at Kip. "Why do you have to be so goddamn tempting?" he asked, smiling sadly.

Kip grinned and pulled the blanket up over his head, concealing himself completely. He heard Scott laugh. Then the door opened and closed, and Scott was gone.

CHAPTER ELEVEN

There was a small mob of reporters standing outside the players' entrance. Scott pushed past, ignoring them. When he got through the doors, he found Carter waiting.

"Coach is calling a team meeting," Carter said. "The message just went out to everyone. But he wants to meet with the captains first."

"Okay. Right. Where's Huff?"

"In the coaches' room already."

Scott followed Carter into the small room that was normally reserved for coaches' meetings. Greg Huff was sitting in one of the chairs.

"Hey, guys. How's your day going?" Huff asked.

Scott folded his arms and leaned against a wall. "It's kind of terrible now. Started out great, though."

"Is that so?" Huff asked, with a bit of a leer. Scott flushed and looked at the floor.

"What's going to happen, do you think?" Carter asked. "With Zullo?"

Huff turned his calculating gaze away from Scott. "Fuck knows, but it's gonna leave a hole in our defense if he's gone."

"Trade deadline's next week," Scott said. "Great fucking timing, Frank."

Coach Murdock entered then with the assistant coaches. He bent forward over the table, hands pressing down onto the wood, and glared at everyone.

"Zullo," he said, "is being put on waivers. He is no longer a part of the New York Admirals. We will be bringing someone up from Hartford to fill the vacancy until we can find a more permanent solution."

Scott's eyebrows rose. "That bad, huh?"

"That bad," Murdock confirmed. "We will be calling a press conference within the hour. I will be there; Zullo will not."

"What about the game tonight?" Scott asked.

"We will have to shuffle the defense lines around a bit, but we will make do."

Scott didn't like the sound of that, but what choice did they have?

"The rest of the team will be here for a meeting in half an hour," Murdock said. "You boys start talking like we're doomed, and we're doomed. Focus on the game tonight. This is no different from an injury. We'll adapt."

"No problem, Coach," Carter said.

"Of course," Scott said.

The three players left to wait in the dressing room for the rest of the team.

"Holy shit," Carter said when they were away from the coaches, "was not expecting that."

"Nope," Huff agreed.

Scott was still mad at Zullo, but he felt like a weight had been lifted too. This was definitely going to be a long-run positive for the team.

"It's for the best," he said, leaning back in his cubby until his head hit the wall. "We can't go into the playoffs with a distraction like Zullo."

"No question," Carter said.

The three of them sat in silence. Then Carter said, "So, Scott . . ."

"What?"

"You've got a glow about you this morning."

"What are you talking about?"

"Huff knows what I'm talking about."

Scott looked at Huff.

"It's true," Huff confirmed. "You've got a glow."

"Maybe I'm just glad Zullo is gone."

"Nah. You had it before that," Huff said.

"Mm," Carter agreed. "I think Scotty was getting some last night."

"Definitely," Huff said.

"I—" Scott started. Then he surrendered. "Maybe I was."

Carter clapped his hands together and beamed. "Atta boy, Hunter!"

Scott tried like hell to fight it, but he was grinning like an idiot within seconds.

"Look at this, Carter! He's blushing!" Huff said.

"Adorable."

"Mind your own business, guys."

"I don't need to know who she was," Carter said, "but I do need to know *how* she was."

"Well, you're not gonna find out," Scott said.

"Judging by the shade of red Hunter is right now, I'd say she was pretty excellent," Huff said.

"I'm not telling you guys anything. Shut it."

"It's no use," Carter lamented. "Scott's a gentleman."

"Damn right." Scott hunched forward and stared at his feet,

trying to control the heat that was turning his face beet red. Memories of the previous night and of that morning were rushing back, though, making his struggle futile.

He remembered waking up to find Kip propped on one elbow, gazing down at him all rumpled and sexy. The look on his face had been so . . . well, not *loving*, obviously, but . . . affectionate.

Then he remembered Kip touching himself for Scott. Getting himself off. His face when he came, all slack and euphoric. How beautiful he'd been in the afterglow.

"I'm, uh, I'm going to get a coffee." Scott strode quickly toward the lounge. There was no way he was going to let himself get aroused while he waited for his teammates to arrive. This meeting was going to be uncomfortable enough.

In the lounge, Scott loaded a pod into the coffeemaker and waited for the water to heat up. He texted Kip. You still at my place?

KIP:

No. Left about twenty minutes ago.

SCOTT:

Oh.

For some reason Scott had liked the idea of Kip being in his apartment, even when he wasn't there.

KIP:

Everything all right?

SCOTT:

I think it will be. I'll talk to you about it later.

KIP:
Ok.

SCOTT:
Sorry again for rushing off. I had a great night.

KIP:
Don't apologize. I had an amazing night. Thank you.

Scott smiled. When can I see you again?

KIP:
Insatiable!

SCOTT:
I am.

KIP:
Call me later? When you're done. We can figure it out.

SCOTT:
Deal.

Kip had been trying to relax at home all day, but he kept wondering how Scott was doing, and what was happening with Zullo. If Scott was upset, or worried about the game tonight. If he'd gotten to go for his game-day run, even if he couldn't buy a smoothie from Kip. Did the routine even matter to Scott anymore?

There had been a midday press conference, which Kip had watched in case Scott was there. Instead it had just been his coach, Harv Murdock, addressing the media.

Murdock announced that Zullo had been cut from the team. Kip didn't know much about Frank Zullo other than what Scott had told him last night, but Scott had to be at least a little relieved that he was gone.

While he'd been reading the updates on the Zullo situation online, Kip had also checked out the Admirals' upcoming schedule. It looked like Scott would be in town for a while. The Admirals played five games over the next week, including the one tonight. The next game was against the Brooklyn Scouts. Then there were two home games at Madison Square Garden, and an away game in Boston next Saturday.

Kip wondered how much of the next week he could spend with Scott. He didn't want to push.

He had expected it to be Scott when his phone rang around one o'clock, but instead he had been surprised by a call from the Museum of the City of New York. They wanted him to come in for an *interview*. Holy shit!

"Absolutely," he had stammered into his phone. "Definitely. Yes. Thank you."

He had cringed at himself and then scrambled for a pen so he could jot down *Monday, 3:00* on his hand. He'd have to go to the interview straight from work. Jesus, how was he possibly going to not look like a total wreck?

It was over three hours later when he heard from Scott. He was stretched out on his bed, reading a novel, when the phone rang.

"Hi. Sounds like you're having a day," Kip said when he picked up.

He heard Scott exhale into the receiver. "Yeah. It's been nuts."

"How are you?"

"Frustrated. Angry. Relieved. I don't know."

"Did you get to go for your run?"

"No. I hit a treadmill pretty hard here at the rink, but no. Everything is just a mess today. Can't quite get my head focused. I hate feeling like this."

"That sucks. Sorry."

"The day started out great . . ."

"You just gotta get your head back to where it was this morning," Kip suggested.

"That's exactly what I was trying *not* to do. But I kept getting . . . distracted."

"I know *I've* been thinking about it a lot."

Scott laughed a bit. "What are you doing? You heading to work yet?"

"Soon. The event is in Brooklyn, at the museum, so I've got time. I don't have to be there until six or so."

"Oh."

Kip wondered if he should tell Scott about his job interview. *Why? So when I don't get the job he can know exactly how big a failure his boyfriend is?*

Instead, he said, "Hey, I was thinking about seeing if Dad wanted to go to the game with me tomorrow afternoon. The one here against Brooklyn."

"Yeah?" Scott's voice brightened a bit with this news.

"Yeah. He's always been a Scouts fan, though obviously I'll be cheering for you."

"Obviously. I can probably get you tickets. Let me look into it."

"Oh. No. That's all right. I can—"

"It's no problem. Those tickets are expensive."

Kip frowned. "I can buy them."

"I know," Scott said gently. "I'm not trying to insult you. It's just, I mean, it's easy for me to ask for them and then you can save your money for something else. It's no trouble at all."

"Fine," Kip said, because he didn't want to get into an argument, and he really *could* use the money. But he wouldn't make a habit of accepting these sorts of things from his millionaire celebrity boyfriend.

"So what's your schedule like this week?" Scott asked, his voice a little lower.

"I work Tuesday to Friday. Nothing in the evenings, though."

"I'm in town all week."

"I know. I checked."

"I've got long morning practices on Monday and Tuesday. But you'll be at work anyway . . ."

"Maybe we could—" Kip said, at the same time that Scott said, "Will you come to my place tomorrow night?"

"Sure, yeah! Yeah, of course," Kip said. "Be kind of convenient for work the next morning too. If you let me get any sleep, that is."

"I will. I promise. Eventually."

They both laughed, then Scott said, "Shit. I have to go. Sorry. But . . . I'll see you tomorrow, right? And I'll let you know about those tickets."

"Yeah, tomorrow. For sure. And good luck tonight."

"Thanks. Talk to you later."

"Okay. Bye, Scott."

They ended the call, and Kip started to get ready for work while his boyfriend . . . got ready to lead his team to victory against Montreal.

Kip shook his head. When would this stop feeling so surreal?

Scott woke up alone on Sunday.

He'd been waking up alone pretty much his entire life (roommates aside), so it shouldn't have felt as jarring as it did.

He went to the kitchen to make coffee, then turned on the television to watch SportsCenter. They were showing highlights of the game last night, and there were a lot of them. The anchors were commending the outstanding performance by the entire Admirals team, especially given the circumstances.

It had been a hell of a game. Scott was extremely proud of his team, coming together for a massive win over Montreal.

The news on the television turned to the Zullo incident. There was footage of him leaving the police station, stony-faced and not speaking to the reporters.

For some reason it wasn't as satisfying as Scott had imagined it would be. Zullo was an asshole, no question, but it still made his stomach twist to see a teammate hit rock bottom like this. He sincerely hoped that Zullo would use the league's rehab program and get his career back on track.

But he didn't have time to think about Frank Zullo right now. Zullo was a grown man, and he had made his own bed. Scott had a game to get ready for.

Kip didn't spend nearly enough time with his dad. They lived in the same house, sure, but they never did stuff together anymore. Kip left for work most mornings before his parents were awake, and he tended to go to bed early. The dumb smoothie job really took a lot out of him.

Kip watched his dad as he cheered on his beloved Scouts. They were both drinking beer and eating Nathan's crinkle-cut fries from the concession stand. It was a good afternoon.

Scott had come through with the tickets. His dad had been thrilled that morning when Kip had suggested they go to the game. Kip had lied about where the tickets had come from, saying he'd bought them cheap off a friend who couldn't go. He wasn't sure if Dad believed him, but if he didn't, he wasn't saying anything about it.

The crowd was loud. They roared for every hit, every shot,

and every save. It was getting late in the season, and these games mattered.

By the third period it was 3–2 for the Admirals, and Scott had scored one of the goals. The building was tense as the game entered the final minutes. With just under six minutes left on the clock, the Admirals got a penalty. They would be short-handed for two minutes.

Kip leaned forward and chewed on his thumb. “You got this, Scott,” he said under his breath.

The Scouts weren’t going down without a fight. They kept the action in the Admirals’ zone and gave the goalie, Bennett, a workout. After one save, Scott shot the puck at the blue line to clear it out of their zone, but one of the Scouts defensemen caught it on his stick before it could cross the blue line. He fired it at the Admirals’ net, and Kip could see what was going to happen before it happened.

“No, Scott. Fuck. Don’t!”

As the puck rocketed toward the net, Kip could only watch, horrified, as Scott threw his body in front of it. He dove through the air and caught the puck somewhere in his midsection, where his padding was light.

He went down hard.

CHAPTER TWELVE

"That shot must have been a hundred miles an hour!" Kip's father said.

"Fuck, Scott, come on. Get up."

Scott lay crumpled on the ice in the fetal position, one leg slowly moving in and out. Kip felt sick. He wanted to run down and jump over the glass.

"Did it get him in the face?" someone behind him asked loudly.

No . . . Kip mouthed.

"Nah. Maybe the ribs," someone else said.

God.

Scott rolled, and Kip could see his face. His eyes were wide and his mouth was open and gasping.

"He can't breathe!" Kip said to no one and anyone. "He can't breathe! He needs . . ."

Scott put a gloved hand down on the ice, bracing himself before he slowly pushed himself up to his knees. He was wincing, with his eyes squeezed shut, but he seemed to be breathing. He wrapped an arm around himself, holding his side. One of his teammates hooked their arm under his and helped him up. Another picked up his stick for him.

Scott skated slowly off the ice, supported by his teammate, while the crowd applauded.

Kip slumped back into his seat with relief. *He's all right. He's all right.*

Dad put a hand on his shoulder and squeezed. "He's a tough one."

"Yeah." Kip exhaled. He watched as Scott was escorted by the team doctor down the hall behind the bench.

The game continued, but Kip was no longer paying attention. He kept his eyes on the bench, watching for any sign of Scott's return.

The final seconds ticked down, and the match ended 3–2 for the Admirals. Scott never came back from the dressing room. Kip wasn't sure what he could do. He was supposed to go to Scott's tonight, but . . .

As he and his father were leaving the arena, Kip sent Scott a text: Just tell me you're ok.

There was no reply, which Kip had expected. Scott probably wasn't anywhere near his phone right now.

On the subway, his father said, "Hunter's got heart, that's for sure. That act of self-sacrifice may have won them the game."

Kip chewed his lip. "Yeah . . ."

They trudged along the slushy sidewalks from the subway station to their house. He felt bad that he couldn't enjoy his dad's company right now. He'd been having a great afternoon, but now he was completely preoccupied with worry.

They had been home for almost an hour before Kip got a reply from Scott. I'm ok. Nasty bruise, but ok. Heading home now.

Kip sat on his bed, hard, and wrote back, Good. You scared me.

SCOTT:

Sorry. Looked worse than it was, probably.

Kip frowned. You still want me to come over?

His phone rang a second later.

"Yes," Scott said.

"You sure?"

"I'm sure. I mean . . . I don't know if I'll be able to . . . do much."

"I knew it! You *are* hurt!"

"It's not that bad. It's just a bruise. I put ice on it, and I'll put more ice on it when I get home. No fractures. No bruised ribs."

"You got an X-ray?"

"Yes, of course. They gave me an X-ray right in the arena. No fractures. Please come over."

"All right. You'd better have an ice pack on that when I get there."

"I will," Scott said. "And I like that you're so worried about me. It's really . . . sweet."

Kip blushed, because what was he doing? Telling an NHL superstar how to care for his injuries? "I just—I'm glad you're all right. I'll be right over. And I'm serious about the ice pack."

Scott chuckled. "I'll see you soon."

"All right, let's see it," Kip said. Scott had been unable to keep himself from grimacing as he walked Kip back up to his apartment. Kip, of course, had noticed.

Now Scott was laid out on the couch, and Kip was carefully lifting his shirt up.

"It looks worse than it is," Scott said. "Really."

"Oh my god!"

Scott glanced down and saw the massive black-and-purple welt that covered most of his right side. The puck had hit him just under his rib cage, just above the thick padding at the top of his hockey pants.

"It's not that bad." It had hurt like hell, and had completely knocked the wind out of him, but there were no internal injuries.

"Bullshit it's not! You're staying right there. I hope you have an ice pack ready to go on that," Kip said as he walked to the kitchen.

"I have several," Scott said, "always. I barely keep food in that freezer. It's all injury treatment stuff."

Kip returned with a fresh ice pack and pressed it gently to Scott's skin. Scott sucked in a breath at the initial contact, then relaxed and placed his hand over Kip's, helping him hold the pack in place.

"It's been a long time since anyone's fussed over me like this," he said. "It's nice."

Kip gave him a smile that was a little sad, and Scott squeezed his hand.

"Sorry I scared you," he said. "Hazard of dating me, I guess."

"Acceptable hazard." Kip slipped his hand out from under Scott's and stood. "I'm gonna make you some dinner. You have any food?"

"I have the stuff I bought to make you breakfast the other day. Bacon and eggs. It's still in there. Here, let me help—"

"No way. You're benched, Hunter. Stay there."

Scott rolled his eyes and stood up, slowly. "I'm at least going to move over to the kitchen so I can see you."

He made his way (with some discomfort) to the stools that lined the high counter separating the kitchen from the living/dining area. He sat and offered Kip helpful instructions about where to find things, and how to use his fancy gas range.

It was nice, having Kip here in his kitchen. Watching him prepare food for the two of them, and hearing him talk about his day.

"Over easy? Sunny-side up?" Kip asked. "I'm an egg expert."

"Over easy. It's okay if you fuck them up, though. I drown them in hot sauce anyway."

"I will *not* fuck them up!" Kip said as he carefully flipped the eggs. "You know, I used to do this professionally and . . . Aw, dammit! I broke a yolk!"

Scott laughed. "It's fine. I'll eat it, believe me. I'll eat just about anything."

Kip raised an eyebrow and pressed his lips together.

They sat next to each other at the kitchen counter and ate their bacon, eggs, and toast. Kip looked so happy and cute, and Scott lamented that he wouldn't be able to do much more than kiss him tonight.

Which reminded him of another annoyance.

"I should warn you," Scott said, "I'm going to be stressed out and distracted this week."

"Why's that?"

"The trade deadline is next Monday. Probably the most stressful day of the year for every player."

"But you're not . . . you're not gonna be *traded*, right?" Kip looked horrified at the thought.

"No, I don't think so. I mean, there's always a chance, but we're making a run for the cup this year, so I doubt they'll get rid of me. I'd be worried if the team needed to cut some costs."

"So why are you nervous?"

"Because someone will be leaving. With Zullo gone, we have a hole to fill in our defense, and to fill it we're going to have to lose a guy or two. We're like family, so it's hard."

"Right, yeah. I guess it would be like that."

They talked and ate, and Scott tried, but failed, to keep himself from visibly leaning on the counter for support.

"Come on," Kip said, after Scott wasn't able to conceal a wince. "You must be hurting. Let's go back to the couch."

Scott didn't argue. Kip helped Scott lower himself onto the couch, letting him stretch out on his back. Kip sat at one end so Scott could rest his head in his lap. They watched an action movie on television, and Kip brushed his fingers through Scott's hair.

And soon, Scott forgot all about trade deadlines and Zullo and nasty bruises.

Kip watched the credits roll on Scott's massive television screen. "Man, how much do you think it cost to make that dumb movie?"

Scott didn't answer. Upon closer inspection, Scott Hunter was, in fact, asleep in his lap.

Kip smiled to himself, and admired Scott's profile. He looked so peaceful and young. His long eyelashes brushed his cheekbones, and his full, pink lips were parted slightly. All of the tension Scott usually carried with him had left his face.

Kip reached and took Scott's hand in his. He didn't want to wake him, but his legs were asleep. "Hey," he whispered. "Come on, Scott. Time for bed."

"Mrmff," Scott said. Then his eyes fluttered open, and he gazed up at Kip and smiled shyly. "Sorry," he said. "Always pretty exhausted after games."

"S'okay. We should go to bed. I have to get up early." Kip helped him up, and kissed him. "I had a nice time tonight."

Scott lit up. "Me too."

They stripped down to their underwear and then crawled into bed. Scott needed to lie on his back because of his injury, and Kip lay beside him with a hand on his chest.

"G'night," Kip said.

Scott placed a hand over Kip's. "Will you come here tomorrow night?"

"You want me to?"

"Yeah. I do."

"I'll have to go home after work first. Get some clothes and stuff."

"You should keep stuff here," Scott murmured sleepily.

"Seriously?"

Scott seemed to wake up a bit, obviously realizing what he had just suggested. "Well . . . yeah. I mean . . . it would make sense, right? I live close to your work and—" he smiled shyly "—I like having you here."

Kip raised himself up so he could kiss Scott.

"I feel bad," Scott said. "Couldn't do much with you tonight. Want to make it up to you."

"You're not going to be healed by tomorrow night!"

"I know . . . but maybe—"

"Tomorrow night," Kip said, "we'll see. I'm not letting you do anything that might hurt you."

Scott sighed but smiled affectionately at him.

"Besides," Kip said, "I like talking to you."

Scott lifted Kip's palm to his mouth and kissed it. "Me too."

It was still dark when Kip's alarm went off. Scott was confused at first, then remembered that Kip had to go to work. Kip shifted next to him, slowly sitting up and grumbling quietly.

"Morning," Scott mumbled.

"Fuck, yeah. I guess so."

Kip got out of the bed and went into the bathroom, while Scott rubbed his eyes and tried to wake up. He was by no means a late sleeper, but it wasn't even five o'clock yet.

He finally forced himself to sit up, wincing when the pain reminded him of his injury. After a few minutes, Kip came out of the bathroom and started putting on his clothes.

"I'll make us some coffee," Scott said. "At least stay for that."

"Okay. How are you feeling?"

"Like I got hit by a puck. But other than that . . . I'm very happy."

Kip smiled and finished getting dressed. Scott went into the bathroom, stopping to kiss him on the cheek on his way past.

"Yikes," Kip said, making a face. "That bruise does not look great."

"Doesn't feel great either. But I'll live."

In the bathroom, Scott splashed water on his face, and stood back to examine his bruise in the mirror. Kip hadn't been lying: It had definitely darkened overnight into an angry midnight blue color.

When Scott had thrown on some sweats, he headed to the kitchen to make coffee. He paused when he saw Kip standing in front of the living room windows.

"You get this view every morning, huh?" Kip asked.

"More or less."

"It's not bad."

The first hint of light was showing itself over the Brooklyn skyline, softly illuminating Kip's lean frame. He stood with one arm stretched over his head, his hand on the glass.

"It's better now," Scott said. He wrapped his arms around Kip from behind, and kissed his neck. Kip sighed and turned to kiss him properly.

In that moment, Scott could imagine all of it. Being with Kip. *Living* with him. Going to bed and waking up together. Preparing meals and going to restaurants and traveling together. Not hiding anymore, just being happy and complete with a man he . . . cared about. Being brave enough to let the world know who he really was.

But even if he *was* brave enough, it was a lot to ask of Kip, who may not realize what he was getting himself into with Scott. It would be a *big deal* if Scott came out. It was unheard of in the NHL, and the media would want so much of them. Scott was used to being scrutinized by the public; he didn't want to drag Kip into all of that.

Besides, they had only been seeing each other for a couple of weeks. It was ridiculous to even think . . .

They broke apart, and Scott brushed a strand of Kip's hair aside and ran his palm over the light stubble on Kip's jaw. "I'd love to have a whole day with you."

"You will."

"Uninjured. Really take my time with you."

He could see the change in Kip's eyes. Dark lust creeping in.

Scott leaned in for another kiss, but Kip pulled back and shook his head. "I have to get going," he sighed.

"Coffee first."

As Scott fumbled with the fancy coffee machine that he rarely used, Kip lifted Scott's T-shirt and inspected the bruise.

"You aren't going to practice today, are you?" he asked.

Scott stepped away from him and tugged the hem of his shirt back down. "Of course I am."

"What? But you're hurt!"

Scott waved a hand dismissively. "I want to see how it feels to skate. I have a game on Wednesday, so I need to figure out how to play with this injury."

"You're going to *play* on *Wednesday*?" Kip looked horrified.

"Yes."

"Are all hockey players stubborn idiots?"

"Pretty much."

"God, if I had a bruise like that I would stay in bed for a month."

Scott laughed. "I've played with broken ribs before. I can play with this."

Kip looked like he had something to say about that, but Scott kissed him and pressed a travel mug full of coffee into his hand. "You need to go to work," he reminded him.

"Fine," Kip sighed. "I'll be here as soon as I can tonight, okay?"

"Okay."

"And please take it easy at practice today."

Scott smiled, touched once again by his concern. "I will."

They kissed one more time, and Kip was gone.

Scott ran his tongue over his bottom lip, trying to capture any lingering remains of their farewell kiss. Then he felt the heaviness that always landed on him whenever he and Kip parted.

He wanted more time.

In his head, Scott fast-forwarded to a time where Kip maybe didn't need to work. Maybe he could just . . .

Just what? Be Scott's stay-at-home boyfriend? Here whenever Scott needed him? As bored as some of his teammates' wives were? If Scott never gathered the courage to come out, Kip would basically be a prisoner. They'd never be able to go on proper dates.

"Dammit," Scott said to no one. He was already fucking this up.

Fucking Jeff had worked the day before, so absolutely nothing was prepped when Kip got to work.

"I hate him," Maria said. "I'm going to murder him."

"He sucks," Kip agreed with a yawn.

"How was your weekend?"

"Good. I went to the Scouts game with my dad."

"Oh, you mean the Scouts vs. *Admirals* game?"

"Yeah . . ."

"Such a fanboy. So cute."

Kip shrugged. "He's hot. Sue me."

"Can you imagine actually dating him?" Maria asked. "It would be amazing. Like Cinderella."

"Come on. My life isn't *that* shitty!"

"Well, it would be wild, anyway."

"Mm."

"You know, I was working on Saturday and he didn't come in. I wonder if he's found another silly superstition."

"Well, there goes my entire love life," Kip joked.

"I mean, all that shit went down with Zullo that day. He would have been distracted."

"Yeah. Maybe."

"When's the next home game?"

"Wednesday," Kip said, way too quickly.

Maria smirked. "So fucking cute. You ready for that interview today?"

"Nope. But I'm gonna do my best."

"You think Scott Hunter will start going to the museum all the time if you start working there?"

"No. Shut up."

"What if he *did*? Oh my god. That would be incredible."

"You're ridiculous."

Maria lowered her voice and did a truly terrible impression of Scott Hunter. "Oh, hey, um, I just like to keep things the same when my game is going well, so I'm gonna need Kip Grady to give me another private tour of the whole museum."

Kip couldn't help but laugh.

"Hunter, let's go. Lunch is on me," Carter said. They were the last two players in the locker room.

Scott had gritted his teeth through the practice. It hurt to bend. It hurt to shoot the puck. And it *really* hurt when anyone so much as brushed him. "I might have to freeze it on Wednesday," he said. "It's not a serious injury, but it's slowing me down."

"I mean, you *could* take a night off and actually let it heal, but hey . . ."

"Would *you*?"

Carter grinned at him. "No chance."

They went to a nearby sushi place that Carter liked.

"So," Carter said as they waited for the way-too-many maki rolls they'd ordered, "who's being traded, do you think?"

"I don't know. I really don't."

"They're gonna make a play for someone big. I figure we'll lose some young talent in exchange for an experienced defenseman."

"Well," Scott said, "that means *we're* off the hook."

"I was thinking Burke. He's not that young, but he's a good winger and we're rich with talent on the front lines right now."

"Yeah. Maybe."

"Who knows? Anyway, did you see? The paparazzi got us the other night. Me and Gloria. We were getting dinner at the new Nobu—have you been there yet?"

"No."

"Well, you have to. Anyway. We were leaving Nobu and the paps fucking got us. So our little secret is blown." Carter shrugged. "Matter of time, I guess. Turned out to not be a big deal because one of the Kardashians announced she was pregnant yesterday, so no one gives a shit about us anymore."

"Right . . ."

Carter launched into a detailed description of his Nobu meal, and Scott tried to listen, but mostly he thought about what Carter had just said. Carter had been trying to keep his new relationship a secret, but when that secret had come out, it had just been another gossip column item. Just two celebrities who had started seeing each other. People said "huh" and moved on.

That would not happen if the paparazzi caught Scott and Kip together. Sure, they could go to dinner maybe. Once. If it started to be a regular thing, it would attract attention. And what if they were caught . . . touching? Holding hands? *Kissing?* There'd be no way Scott could deny—

"They have this miso caramel sauce that—You listening, Hunter?"

"Huh? Yeah. Yeah, sorry. I'm just . . . hungry. Kinda hard to hear about food right now."

"Well, we've talked about hockey, we've talked about food, we've talked about *my* love life. How about *your* love life?"

"No."

"Seems like there might actually be something to talk about there."

"There isn't."

Carter studied him, and probably didn't miss the color in Scott's face, or the way Scott couldn't look him in the eye. "You're the worst liar in the world, Scott."

"I know."

"You don't want to tell me? Fine. I only want you to be happy. Guy like you should be with someone special."

Scott smiled to himself. "I'm happy."

"You bringing her to the Equinox Gala?"

"Are *you* going to the gala?"

"Yes, I'm going! Did you forget who I'm dating? Also, I am *very* famous and beloved."

Scott laughed, but inside he fretted. He hadn't been expecting any of his teammates to be there. That would only make things more complicated.

And, god, it wasn't fair. He wanted to tell Carter—his best friend—that he was bringing his boyfriend to the gala. His wonderful, gorgeous boyfriend who made him feel lighter and happier than he could ever remember feeling in his life. He wanted to dance with Kip, and kiss him, and introduce him to everyone so they would know how lucky Scott was.

Instead, Scott said, "Maybe. We'll see."

Carter smiled. "I hope so. I can't wait to meet her, man."

CHAPTER THIRTEEN

Scott and Kip woke up together the morning after the trade deadline.

They'd had the television on all day, turned to a sports channel that was devoted to the trade activity. At times Scott had given it his undivided attention, and Kip had known to give him space. Most of the day, though, he had been happy to let Kip take his mind off everything.

And Kip had been happy to do that.

He had also been happy to distract *himself* from the stress of waiting to hear back from the museum. The interview had gone surprisingly well. Both of the interviewers had seemed to really like him. By the end of it, everyone had been talking like he'd already got the job. He had left on a real high.

But he still hadn't told Scott about it. Maybe he didn't want to jinx it, or maybe he was just embarrassed about his pathetic attempt to improve himself. Scott's level of success made everything Kip did seem kind of ridiculous.

Scott had lost some teammates in a trade the anchors on television had called "huge." A guy named Burke and another forward had been traded to Tampa Bay in exchange for an enormous Finnish defenseman.

"Matti Jalo," Scott had said when he'd heard the news. "Wow."

"He's good?" Kip had asked.

"Yeah, he's . . . I didn't think we'd get somebody like that. He's probably the best defenseman in the league right now."

"Hey, that's great then!"

"It is," Scott had agreed. "Shows the management has confidence in us. They just bought us a really nice present."

"But, uh, the guys who are leaving . . . Burke, was it? And, um . . ."

"MacDow, yeah. Good guys. Sucks, but I figured Burke would go. It will be better for him, honestly. He's not getting time to shine here."

"So you're good?"

Scott had smiled at him. "I'm good."

"Feel like celebrating?"

"Absolutely."

Now it was just after five in the morning and Kip needed to go to work, but Scott's hands were on him, and his mouth was nipping along his jawline.

"Call in sick," Scott murmured against his skin.

"I can't! And you have a game tonight. You'll be busy."

"Go in late. I'll write you a note."

Kip laughed. "What would it say?"

"'Sorry Kip is late, but Scott Hunter was riding his dick.'"

Kip moaned. "God, we haven't done that. I . . . *Fuck*, I want that."

"Me too," Scott said, and moved Kip's hand to his solid cock to illustrate his point.

"Fuck," Kip breathed. Then, "No. No. I have to go. Not fair, Hunter."

He got up and got dressed before Scott could convince him to do something stupid like not show up for work.

"I'm not gonna see you until the gala tomorrow night," Scott sighed. "And even then it will be agony, not touching you."

"Sexy, though, right? Kinda?"

"Kinda."

Scott made coffee, as was their tradition, and they drank it together in the kitchen.

"You know it will be agony for me too, right?" Kip said.

Scott smiled sadly. "I'm going to want to leave early. I'll be making my excuses as soon as I get there."

"No you won't. We'll both have a wonderful time, and then we'll get back here and take each other apart."

Scott kissed him, and it was full of promise. When it was over, Kip shivered.

"I've gotta go," he said weakly.

"I'll see you tomorrow night."

Scott arrived at the restaurant early and ordered a coffee. He was meeting his agent for lunch, and coffee was important.

He liked Todd Wheeler—he wouldn't let him represent him if he didn't—but he truly hated talking about contracts and endorsements. He knew he was lucky to have so many opportunities to make so much money, but it wasn't why he played hockey.

Todd arrived just as Scott was draining the last of the French press the server had brought him. "So that was some shit with Zullo, huh?" he said, almost as soon as he'd sat down.

"Yeah." Scott nodded. "You could say that."

"It's over now, though. That's gotta feel good, right? I know you hated that guy."

"*Hate* is a strong word," Scott said. "A strong, accurate word."

Todd laughed. "And Matti Jalo's an Admiral now! Looks like a cup-winning team to me!"

"Absolutely," Scott agreed. "Jalo is going to be a huge asset."

"Huge is right. Jalo is a fucking monster. Good-looking too. New York is gonna love that guy."

"I hope so."

"Hopefully not too much, though! We've gotta make sure you're still number one in this town."

"Sure."

The server came and took their orders. Todd ordered a spinach salad without looking at the menu. Scott ordered a club sandwich, and then Todd abruptly said, "You know what? Fuck it. I'll get the club too."

After the server left, Todd said, "You bringing anyone to that Equinox Gala?"

"Why? You wanna be my date?"

"No, fuck you. I just thought you might be seeing someone. I'm *praying* every night that you'll start dating some actress. Maybe a model. Something that gets you in the papers, y'know?"

Scott grimaced. He definitely *would* be "in the papers" if anyone found out who he was dating. But probably not in the way his agent was hoping for. "Sorry to disappoint you."

"I could find you a date, if you want," Todd mused. "A New York–based ingénue who wants to boost her profile . . ."

"No, thanks, Todd."

Todd shook his head. "I don't understand you, Scott. You look like *that*—" he waved his hands to indicate Scott's entire body "—and you don't seem to be sharing it with anyone. Man, if I looked like you . . ."

Scott snorted. Todd had been an athlete, once, but the years away from competition had given him a bit of a gut. He was far from unattractive, though.

"I should have gotten the damn salad," Todd muttered to himself. "Not all of us are burning a million calories a day."

"You look fine," Scott assured him.

"We're not talking about me, Scott. We're talking about you and why you're not dating the gorgeous women of New York."

"I'm busy," Scott mumbled.

"We're *all* busy! I've got a wife and three kids and fourteen clients!"

"Why are we talking about this?"

"I want you to be happy, Scott. I've been representing you since you were seventeen and I've never known you to even go on a date with anyone. I've gone to a lot of my clients' weddings—you're all like family to me. You know that. Especially you, because . . . you know."

"Because I'm an orphan?" Scott asked flatly.

"I just want you to know I'm looking out for you, and I care about your happiness. That's all."

"Well, thank you. But I'm perfectly happy. Really."

"So . . . if my friend who represents a certain New York–based actress asked me if you might be looking for a date for the gala . . ."

"You should tell your friend that I'm not."

Todd sighed. "Fine. Don't you even want to know who she is?"

"Nope."

"Because if you're a leg man at all—"

"Oh, good! Our food is coming!"

Scott started asking about talk show bookings to keep the conversation away from his love life for the rest of the meal. Todd seemed to take the hint because he didn't bring it up again.

But less than half an hour after they parted ways, Scott received a text from him. It was just a red-carpet photo of a beautiful young woman followed by You sure?

SCOTT:

I'm sure.

Jesus. He *really* did not need the whole world to be interested in his love life right now.

Kip left work on Thursday and went straight to Elena's. He had brought his tuxedo there days ago after he'd picked it up at the tailor.

She answered the door with wet hair and a bathrobe on.

"Awesome," Kip said. "You've showered already. Can I take one?"

"Yeah, sure. We gotta be out the door in, like, two hours, okay? The limo will be here."

"Limo?"

"Equinox is sending one. They like me."

He showered and then left the bathroom wearing a towel. Elena was in her room with the door ajar. He knocked lightly. "Can I come in? Is my suit in there?"

"Yes. Come in."

He opened the door and found her sitting in front of a mirror putting hot rollers in her hair. Pop music was playing from a little speaker next to her.

"I'm putting on my underwear," Kip said. "Don't peek."

"Wouldn't dream of it."

"I can *see* you looking in the mirror, Elena!" He pulled on his *nicest* black briefs as quickly as he could. He could see Elena's reflection smirking.

"So what's the plan tonight? You and Scott pretend you don't know each other and then you go back to his place and—"

"Go to town on each other? Yeah. That's the plan."

"Kinky."

"A little."

"You sure you're okay with this weird relationship?" Elena asked as she put the last roller in her hair.

"Yeah, it's fine." Kip frowned. "I mean, obviously it would be nice to—"

"Go somewhere other than his apartment?"

"It's a *nice* apartment, but yeah. It would be great to actually go somewhere together."

"Do you think you ever will?"

"I don't know! I mean, it hasn't even been a month."

"That's a month longer than I've seen you date anyone else."

"Exactly! That's why it feels so serious. I've never—"

"Felt this way?"

Kip blushed because it sounded so sappy. "I like him a lot," he mumbled.

Elena stood and crossed the room. "I can't wait to meet him," she said, and kissed Kip's cheek.

"You're not going to give him one of your scary talks, are you?"

"Of course not. I just think it's fair to warn him that if he hurts you, it will be detrimental to his career. Because he'll be dead."

"Elena!"

"I'm kidding. Mostly. Listen, I have to paint my nails. Let's open some wine, crank some Rihanna, and get beautiful."

"God, yes."

Kip got out of the limo to a wall of bulbs flashing. They abruptly stopped when the photographers seemed to realize that he and Elena were nobody.

They quickly crossed the red carpet. "You look incredible," Kip said, offering Elena his arm so she could balance on him as she made her way up the short staircase to the entrance. "I know I keep saying that, but really. A lot of guys are going to be jealous of me."

She smiled at him. "I think a lot of guys are going to be jealous of *me*."

Elena *did* look stunning. She was wearing a black satin halter gown that had ombré ruffles down the side of the skirt, each layer fading into a lighter shade of gray. The ruffles parted when she walked, revealing a high slit that showed off her legs and strappy black heels. Her dark hair was swept into a curly side bun, showing off her sparkling earrings that at least *looked* like rubies and diamonds.

The party was hosted in an enormous historic building that had been recently restored and upgraded. It was now one of the most glamorous venues in New York. Kip had never been inside before, not even as a server.

"Impressive," he said, gazing around at the ceilings of the lobby.

"Just wait," Elena replied.

She led him into the most lavish room Kip had ever seen. It was full of high arches and marble columns, but Equinox had added their own modern touches to the event. There was a (probably famous) DJ on a platform up high, and 3-D holograms of floral centerpieces projecting from devices in the middle of every table.

The thing that struck Kip the most, though, were the little rolling robots that appeared to be serving the guests hors d'oeuvres.

"Equinox doesn't do anything on a small scale, huh?" Kip asked.

"No. They don't."

"Do I look all right?"

"You look absurdly handsome." She squeezed his arm. "We have time to mingle before we have to be seated for dinner. Let's see who we can find."

She led him toward the crowd of New York's rich and famous that had gathered near one of the bars. He wasn't great at clocking celebrities, but he vaguely recognized some of the people in the room.

Kip wondered if Scott was here yet.

Elena introduced him to some of her coworkers, and he made polite small talk, but no one seemed particularly interested in him. He was distracted when a robot server rolled up and offered him a canapé. Kip wasn't used to being on the receiving end of an hors d'oeuvres tray, and seeing the kind of work that made up the bulk of his résumé being so efficiently executed by a machine was . . . bleak.

"You tryna put me out of a job, buddy?" he asked it. The robot just rolled off to serve another group of guests, leaving Kip to reconcile the fact that he had more in common with the robots than with any of the actual guests at the party.

He went to the bar and got (complimentary!) drinks for himself and Elena. He brought Elena her martini and she nodded over his shoulder.

He turned and saw Scott across the room. He was talking to a small group, smiling, and standing head and shoulders over all of the others. He was dashing as hell in his classic black tuxedo.

Elena gently hit his arm, which caused him to turn back to her. "Stop staring!" she hissed.

"Okay! Can . . . can he see me? Has he spotted me yet?"

"Not yet. You guys need to be a lot stealthier if you're going to fool anyone."

"What are you talking about? I'm fine. Has he looked yet?"

"No. But if he *does* come over here—Okay, he sees you."

"How can you tell?"

"Because he just lit up like the goddamn sun. Jesus. You guys are doomed."

Scott couldn't move one inch without someone stopping him. Some of them he actually knew a bit, others were complete strangers, but everyone at the gala seemed to want their moment with him.

All night it had been the same impersonal small talk. "Yes, I feel really good about our chances in the playoffs.

"Very excited to have Jalo on the team. He should be a great addition.

"I don't golf, actually. Never have."

And to the few people brave enough to ask about Zullo: "I hope he gets the help he needs."

He could see Kip, barely. His back was turned to him, but Scott recognized him instantly. He was standing with a gorgeous woman who was turning heads even in *this* crowd. She was the woman Kip had taken to the Admirals game all those weeks ago. Elena.

It was getting close to dinnertime, when they would all need to be seated. Then there would be speeches, and who knew when he'd get a chance to talk to Kip. He just needed to *see* him.

Scott wrapped up a conversation with one of the New York Jets' star players by politely saying that he was going to the bar to get something. He moved through the crowd, pretending not to hear a couple of people who called out his name.

Kip finally turned and made eye contact with him, and Scott's heart stopped.

God, he looked handsome. Like a classic Hollywood movie star. Scott drifted toward him like a moth to a flame.

"Good evening," he said when he finally reached Kip. The suit fit him like a dream: dark blue and slim cut everywhere. You could barely tell it had once been tailored to Scott's body—had, in fact, been the tux Scott was wearing the first night he and Kip spent together. His hair was parted on the side, and he had a twinkle in his eye as he played along.

"Scott. Good to see you again. This is my friend Elena Rygg. She works for Equinox. Elena, Scott Hunter . . ."

"No introduction necessary," Elena said, extending her hand. "It's exciting to meet you at last, Scott."

"Elena," Scott said, shaking her hand. "Wow. You are very pretty."

Kip laughed.

"Sorry," Scott said. "I'm not great at talking to women."

"It probably doesn't come up often in your line of work." She smiled at him, a secret little smile that almost seemed like she was making fun of him, but it was warmer than that.

"No," he said, smiling back. "It doesn't, unfortunately."

Kip seemed to be taking him in. His eyes were roaming over his entire body, and he was chewing his lip. Scott tried to think of a reason to touch him. His thoughts were interrupted by the arrival of a woman he didn't recognize.

"Elena! You look gorgeous! How are you enjoying yourself?"

Elena embraced the woman, and they kissed each other's cheeks.

"The party's incredible, Jacqueline. You've done an amazing job," Elena said.

"You think so? I do like the contrast of old New York glamour and our cutting-edge technology." She turned to Scott and extended her hand. "Scott Hunter! Thank you so much for coming. Jacqueline Kane."

Ah. The CEO of Equinox.

"Of course. Thank you for inviting me," Scott said politely.

"I didn't know you two knew each other," Jacqueline said, pointing between Scott and Elena.

"We've just met," Scott said.

"Lucky you! Elena has been immeasurably valuable to the company this past year. We absolutely love her. And, I'm sorry, I'm being rude. We haven't been introduced." She extended her hand to Kip. "I'm Jacqueline."

"I'm, uh, Christopher. Grady." Kip shook her hand.

"Do you also work in IT, Christopher?"

"No—I, um—No. I don't."

Scott wanted to jump in and say something complimentary about Kip, but he wasn't supposed to know who he was.

"You're with Elena?" Jacqueline asked Kip.

"No! I mean . . . I'm her date, yes. We're friends. Good friends."

"Oh! All right. How about you, Scott? Did you bring anyone special tonight?"

Scott couldn't stop himself from glancing over at Kip before saying, "I came alone."

Jacqueline smiled and looked at Scott and then at Elena. "Well, I'll leave you to get acquainted. Enjoy yourselves!"

"We will. Have a good evening, Jacqueline," Scott said politely.

"You hadn't met Jacqueline before?" Elena asked.

"No," Scott said. "I get invited to all sorts of things by people I don't actually know." He chuckled. "It felt surreal, at first, being a poor kid from Rochester and suddenly being immersed in this whole other world. Rubbing shoulders with New York royalty."

"I can imagine," Kip said, with a small smile.

Scott frowned, because *did* Kip feel that way? It was easy for Scott to think of himself as just a guy from Rochester because that's what he *was*. But was this all surreal for Kip? It must be, at least a little.

One of the things Scott really liked about Kip was that he never seemed interested in Scott's money or fame. Being with Kip was the only time Scott felt like . . . Scott.

Elena must have noticed the awkwardness between them, because she quickly dumped the entire contents of her glass into her mouth. "Oh, look. My martini's gone. I'm going to the bar to get another one. Scott, what are you drinking?"

"Oh, um, a beer. Just a beer. Stella, I guess, if they have it."

"They have it," Elena assured him. She left them alone.

Kip was staring at the floor, and Scott desperately wanted to tuck a finger under his chin and tilt his head up. He wanted to kiss him. He wanted to tell him that he absolutely belonged here because he was important to Scott, and clearly important to Elena.

"Quite the party, huh?" was what he said instead.

"Yeah," Kip said, turning his eyes up to meet Scott's. "I feel like I should be carrying a tray around."

Scott frowned and kept himself from reaching for his boyfriend. He felt eyes and ears all around them. "You don't *look* like you should be carrying a tray around. You look . . ." He couldn't finish his sentence. Not with the words he wanted to use. Not here.

"Elena seems great," he said instead, changing the subject.

"She is. You'll dance with her later, right?"

"I'll do my best impression of dancing, yes."

Kip laughed a little. Then he sighed and gazed at Scott with so much affection and longing that Scott couldn't do anything but stare back. He knew he had a goofy, love-struck grin on his face, but he couldn't help it.

Throwing caution to the wind, he lowered his voice. "You look incredible."

Kip bit his lip. "Not so bad yourself."

Scott leaned a little closer, pushing his luck. "It's going to be a long night."

Kip was staring at his mouth. Scott watched his Adam's apple bob as he swallowed.

When Kip replied, his voice had shifted to that ragged Brooklyn drawl that Scott loved so much. "Should have a hell of an ending, though."

"I can't wait," Scott breathed.

"Me neither."

And thank god Elena returned at that moment or else Scott

might have done something very stupid. The pointed look Elena gave him as she handed him his beer told him that he and Kip had been standing much too close a moment ago.

"It's time to sit for dinner," Elena said. "Let's get you two separated."

Before they parted, Scott extended his hand to Kip, who stared at it for a moment before he grinned and took it, shaking it like two men might who have just met at a social function.

But Scott took the opportunity to gently brush his fingertips against the inside of Kip's wrist. He stroked the sensitive flesh as they shook hands, and he watched Kip's lips part. He watched his eyes ignite.

"I'll see you later," Scott said, "*Christopher*."

The dinner went on for far too long. Between courses, Jacqueline thanked everyone for coming, and explained the importance of providing early opportunities for kids to explore STEM careers. She talked about some of the good work the Equinox Foundation had already done in this area, and what plans she had for the future. She announced a massive endowment to local public schools to furnish them with state-of-the-art computers and other technology. Scott applauded along with the rest of the crowd.

He was seated with nine people he did not know. Even Carter had been placed at a different table. Scott was never particularly comfortable at these types of events, but tonight he was even more restless and distracted. It didn't help that he couldn't see Kip at all from where he was sitting.

As they waited for dessert and coffee, he decided he needed to get out of there for a few minutes. He excused himself and stood. He briefly scanned the room for Kip, but couldn't find him.

Scott went to the bathroom, but didn't feel like returning to the table afterward. He wandered around the area outside the main ballroom where the bathrooms were located and found an alcove that offered a third-story view of the city lights. No one else was in it, so he took a few quiet minutes to himself, standing against the glass and watching the traffic below.

He felt Kip behind him before he saw his reflection in the glass, just over Scott's shoulder. "Hey," he said in a quiet voice.

Scott closed his eyes and forced the fluttering in his stomach to calm down.

He turned. "We probably shouldn't be here together."

"Probably not." Kip stepped closer, invading Scott's personal space and taking over his senses. The spicy smell of his after-shave was intoxicating.

"They did a good job with your suit," Scott said shakily. "Really . . . fits you well."

"Mm."

Kip's mouth was so close, and Scott's lips parted completely on their own. It would be so easy to lean in and take what he wanted . . .

"Food was good," Kip said conversationally.

"Was it? I wasn't really paying attention."

"Distracted?"

"Maybe."

"You look like you're still hungry."

Scott shuddered out a breath. "Goddammit, Kip."

Kip gave him one of those sexy smiles that Scott normally loved so much, but here . . .

Kip's eyes darted down to Scott's crotch, and his smile widened.

We could leave. We could leave right now . . .

"I should get back," Kip said, infuriatingly casual.

Scott bit down on his tongue, hard enough to bring him back to earth. "You're in trouble later," he growled.

Kip's eyes widened, but he managed a smile before turning and leaving. Scott grinned as he watched him walk away, pleased that he was able to retaliate a little.

He took a moment to compose himself, then returned to the ballroom. It looked like he had missed dessert; the tables were already being cleared away to allow more room for dancing and mingling.

He didn't see Kip anywhere.

There was a commotion in the crowd when the lights came down and the stage Jacqueline had been speaking on before suddenly spun around to reveal a famous lounge-style singer and his orchestra.

Scott mingled for a while, chatting with A-list celebrities and some of New York's top CEOs. He had just wrapped up a conversation with an actual astronaut when there was a tap on his shoulder.

"I believe I was promised a dance," Elena said.

Scott smiled, genuinely glad to see her. He took her arm and they moved to the dance floor, which was quite full now. "I'm a terrible dancer," he warned her.

"I'll make up for it."

She *was* a fantastic dancer. Scott quickly found a rhythm as they danced an easy two-step while the band played "Fly Me to the Moon."

"You know, I was just talking to a real astronaut," Scott said. "I wonder if he likes this song."

Elena politely ignored his clumsy attempt at small talk. "Are you having a good evening?"

"Sure." He lowered his voice. "How's Kip doing?"

"I think he's focused on the after-party."

"Well, that makes two of us."

She studied his face. "You like him."

"I do. I . . . I *really* like him."

"Good," she said. "Because he's nuts about you. You need to understand how unprecedented this is for him."

"You think I'm going to hurt him?"

"I don't know. We've only just met. Convince me otherwise."

Scott sighed. He hadn't spoken to anyone about his feelings for Kip before now. It was nice to have someone to share them with, but it was also terrifying. "I can't explain it, because it doesn't make sense how quickly I've—"

"Fallen?"

Scott felt himself blushing. "Yeah."

She squeezed his hand. "You are asking a lot of him, you know."

"I know. I won't promise more than I can give, but . . . I'll give him everything I possibly can."

"In secret?"

"For now."

She raised an eyebrow.

"Like I said, I won't promise more than I can give. But this is new. I think, with time, I'll be able to give more."

She seemed to consider this. "Okay."

Scott cleared his throat. "Do you like working for Equinox?"

"I do. I get to do what I love, they treat me with respect, and the money is obscene."

Scott laughed. "Sounds like my job."

When the song ended, Elena leaned in. "You can kiss me, if you want. If you want to . . . divert attention."

He smiled, touched by the offer, and kissed her on the cheek. "Thank you. But I won't do that to you."

"Wouldn't have been such a hardship." Before they parted, she said, "Kip is the best person I know. And he's happier than I've ever seen him these days. I'm protective of him because I love him."

"I know." Scott wanted to tell her that he loved him too, but he'd never said that out loud before. He hadn't even let himself seriously consider the possibility, but as he walked Elena off the dance floor, and saw Kip sitting, relaxed in a plush chair, watching them . . .

. . . what else could this feeling *be*?

Scott and Elena looked stunning together, dancing, and Kip was envious. He wished he could be the one in Scott's arms. He consoled himself by remembering that he soon would be.

But it would be nice to dance with him. Kip didn't *need* people to know they were together. He wasn't interested in showing off, or being shown off. He just . . . wished he could share everything with Scott.

He watched them leave the dance floor. Elena was immediately asked to dance by someone else, and Scott disappeared into a crowd of people. Kip sighed. He was getting bored. He didn't want to drink anymore, and he felt too inadequate to engage in conversation.

He was observing the party, trying to enjoy the spectacle, when his phone buzzed.

SCOTT:

161912

Kip stared at his phone, confused. Maybe Scott had pocket-texted him by accident?

A second message came.

SCOTT:

Door code. Works for the elevator too.

Kip looked up. Scott was leaning against a wall on the other side of the massive room, typing on his phone.

SCOTT:

I'll meet you there. Text me when you're leaving.

Kip smiled. He was equal parts excited about moving things back to Scott's place, and touched that Scott had given him his access code.

He wrote back, I'm leaving now. Just gonna tell Elena.

Scott was trying to leave when Carter stopped him.

"Scotty! Was that her? Was that her? I *saw* you, man!" He threw an arm around Scott's neck and hauled him in. "I saw you! Fucking gorgeous lady, Scott! Nice work, my friend!"

Carter had clearly been drinking. "Don't worry," he said in a whisper that was louder than most people's speaking voices. "Your secret is safe with me."

"Uh, sure, thanks, Carter," Scott said, pulling his arm away. "I was just heading out, so . . ."

"I get it, man, I *get it*. She leaving in another car?"

"Um."

"I feel you. Have a good night, Hunter! A *good* night!"

Scott exhaled as he walked away. Things were getting complicated.

His car service was waiting for him downstairs. He let the blissful silence wash over him once he was alone in the back seat.

The driver took him home.

CHAPTER FOURTEEN

Kip considered removing all of his clothes and just waiting, naked, on Scott's bed for him.

Then he considered that he was wearing a very expensive suit and looked damn good. And hadn't Scott said something about wanting to strip him out of it?

Kip grinned into the empty apartment. He kept the lights low and sat on the couch, admiring the view of Brooklyn.

He got an idea.

He synched up his phone to Scott's Bluetooth stereo and put on a Spotify playlist of romantic jazz standards. He waited.

It was almost half an hour later when he heard the click of the door being opened.

He stood, but didn't move toward the door. He just stayed in the dimly lit living room with the lights of the city behind him. He would let Scott come to him.

"Kip?" Scott called out in a soft voice.

Kip didn't reply. He leaned a hip against the side of the tall entertainment unit that housed Scott's television and crossed his arms as Frank Sinatra sang "I've Got You Under My Skin."

Scott entered the room. "Kip. Oh my god." He strode over

to him like he was the first glass of water Scott had had in days.

Kip had expected to be thrown against a wall and kissed aggressively. He had expected to be punished for working Scott up at the gala. Instead, Scott placed a gentle hand on Kip's face and just seemed to take him in for a moment. There was an urgency in Scott's eyes, but when he finally leaned in and kissed Kip, it was slow and deliberate. It wasn't a conversation; it was Scott telling him something important, and making sure Kip was listening.

When their lips parted, Kip felt limp. "Wow," he breathed.

"I've been wanting to do that all night," Scott said. His voice was husky and he was gazing at Kip like he couldn't believe he was real, his brow furrowed and his face almost pained.

"Hey," Kip said, and kissed him. He rested a hand against Scott's chest, over the lapel of his jacket, and let his tongue explore his mouth, unhurried and reverent.

They kissed for a long time that way, with Kip pressed against the entertainment unit, never escalating. Etta James started singing "At Last."

"You wanna dance?" he asked.

"A little on the nose, don't you think?" Scott asked, nodding at the stereo.

Kip smiled. "Come on, show me what Elena taught you."

Scott shook his head, but took Kip's hand, and led him to the middle of the room. He placed his other hand on Kip's lower back, and Kip grinned and let Scott lead. He wrapped his free arm around him, sliding his hand up his spine and landing his fingers in the short hairs at the top of Scott's neck.

Scott was an awkward dancer, but Kip didn't care. He rested his head on Scott's shoulder and sighed happily.

"Wish I coulda danced with you there," Scott said.

"S'okay."

"It's not. I wanted to show you off. The most gorgeous man in the room was with *me* and I couldn't even tell anyone."

Kip smiled. "Didn't think you were one to brag."

"I'm not. I just . . ."

"I'd like to go out on dates with you."

Scott swallowed. "Where would you take me?"

Kip considered it. "A club," he said finally. "We would just lose ourselves in the music. I'd love to see it, you letting go like that. In public. Getting each other all worked up and then going home."

"God," Scott said. "I'd like that. I've never been to a gay club. Not in New York, anyway."

"I know a few good ones. Someday, maybe."

"Someday."

They danced, and Kip let himself drift. He drank in the romance of the moment, of being wrapped up in Scott, the luxurious fabric of his tuxedo under his hands. Of the light scent of whatever grooming products he'd used. Of the lights of the city all around them as they pressed as close as they could against each other, while their heads swam with imagined scenarios of being together outside the safe walls of this apartment.

They danced, and Kip turned his head so he could scrape kisses along Scott's sharp jawline. Keeping his mouth busy prevented him from blurting out declarations that were embarrassingly premature.

Scott's fingers tapped lightly on Kip's lower back, and Kip wondered if Scott felt like he did: too full of *feeling*. Full of words he couldn't quite imagine saying out loud. His own fingers were trembling a bit, so he curled them into Scott's hair.

Scott said, "I want to go everywhere with you."

And Kip could hear the sadness in the way Scott said it. He could hear the unspoken *But I can't*. But Kip would ignore it. Tonight, he would ignore it.

* * *

Scott was overwhelmed.

Somehow, dancing fully clothed in his living room was the most romantic experience of his life. He loved having Kip in his arms, in his home, wearing *his* suit. His senses were *full* of Kip.

When the song ended, Scott stepped back because he needed to look at him. He had to make sure that this wonderful man was really *here*. That he was actually his boyfriend.

Kip smiled shyly at him, and Scott was momentarily paralyzed.

"What is it?" Kip asked, barely above a whisper.

Scott shook his head. "Sometimes I—" He exhaled, trying to slow the pounding of his heart. "I can't believe you're real."

As soon as the words were out, he blushed. *What a stupid thing to say!*

But Kip just laughed and put a hand on Scott's chest, over his racing heart, and said, "I keep thinking I'm going to wake up."

Scott's throat tightened, and his heart beat impossibly faster. He tilted Kip's head up with a gentle finger and kissed him. It was just a soft brush of his lips against Kip's, but it sent a shudder through him.

What is wrong with me? He felt overloaded, like his body was hosting something huge and wild, and it was slamming against his ribs, desperate to get out.

He tangled a hand in Kip's hair, and curved the other around his hip. Kip grabbed onto his lapels, pulling him closer and opening his mouth to kiss him properly. The wet heat of Kip's mouth, and the urgent press of his body against Scott's, brought him back down to earth. This was real. Kip was real. And Scott needed to get him out of that suit.

After being thoroughly kissed within an inch of his life, Scott reached for the button on Kip's jacket. He undid it and slid his hands up under the shoulders to slip the jacket down and off, letting it pool on the floor behind him.

"Almost hate to do this," he said in a low voice. "You look so good. But my plans for the rest of the evening don't include clothes."

Kip gave him one of those devastating smiles, and Scott pulled apart his bow tie. The ends unfurled and hung down Kip's front. Scott tugged on them lightly before undoing the top button on his shirt. He undid two more, letting the collar hang open, exposing Kip's neck and the top of his undershirt. His fingertips ghosted over Kip's throat, brushing over his Adam's apple and making him suck in a breath.

Nina Simone sang "I Put a Spell on You."

Scott unbuttoned Kip's shirt the rest of the way and let it hang open. Kip's chest rose and fell, and he stared hungrily at Scott but said nothing. Scott took his left hand and pulled his arm straight out in front of him. He unfastened the cuff link and brought Kip's wrist to his mouth, kissing the sensitive skin and feeling Kip's pulse race in the veins just beneath. He did the same with the other wrist, then tucked the two cuff links into Kip's pocket. That made Kip smile.

Scott considered him for a moment.

"Take off your shoes," he said. "And your socks."

Scott stepped back as Kip followed his instructions. It was so easy to shift into this authoritative role, to cover his nerves with a firm, cool tone. And, god, the way Kip obeyed him so willingly. It made Scott's head swim.

When Kip was done, he stood up, barefoot with his pants still fastened, his dress shirt open to reveal his white undershirt. Scott's own tuxedo was completely intact, and Scott loved the imbalance of that.

The slim cut of Kip's pants was unable to conceal the bulge that had formed as Scott undressed him. Scott ignored it. For now. Instead, he slid the dress shirt onto the floor, letting it join the jacket.

He ran his hands down Kip's sides, slipping his fingers inside the waistband of his pants just enough to pull the hem of the undershirt out. He pushed it up, slowly, sliding his palms over the soft skin of Kip's stomach. Kip stretched his arms up so Scott could pull the shirt off over his head.

When the shirt was off, Scott trapped Kip's wrists together with one hand, keeping his arms extended over his head. Kip's eyes fluttered closed, and Scott crushed their mouths together. He kissed him messily, their mouths sliding against each other until he released Kip's wrists and stepped back.

Kip's breathing was heavy, and his eyes were dark. He looked like he wanted to say something but didn't want to break the deliciously tense silence that they had created. Instead, he bit his bottom lip and waited.

Scott smiled to himself as he walked around Kip until he stood at his back. He kicked the discarded clothing that had gathered there aside and kissed Kip's neck. Kip moaned and tilted his head to rest on Scott's shoulder. He reached back to hook his arm around Scott's neck, and Scott wrapped an arm possessively around his chest. With his free hand, Kip grabbed onto it, pressing it into himself.

"Kip . . ." Scott breathed against his skin, ending the silence. He couldn't help himself. He felt drunk.

He pressed his crotch into Kip's ass so he could feel how turned on Scott was right now.

"Fuck. Please," Kip gasped.

Kip grabbed Scott's hand and moved it to his crotch, and Scott moaned, loving how eager Kip was.

"Don't worry," he breathed into Kip's ear. "I'm going to give you everything you want."

Kip shuddered and Scott slowly pulled the zipper on his pants down over his straining erection. As soon as he had the pants open, Scott moved his hands to Kip's hips. Kip groaned in frustration, but Scott ignored him, instead dipping his fingers into the loose waistband and sliding the pants to the floor. Kip stepped out of them and turned, his cock fully hard and trapped by the fabric of his black briefs, the tip of it almost peeking out from the waistband.

Scott bit his lip, feeling overwhelmed once again. There were words he wanted to say, but not yet. Not when they were both wild with lust.

Instead, he removed his jacket and took off his shoes. He untied his bow tie and removed his cuff links. He removed everything, letting Kip watch. He didn't make a show of it, just slowly and carefully took off each item. When he was down to his own briefs, he stepped forward and kissed him.

As soon as their mouths came together, Scott lost the ability to play it cool. He wrapped himself around Kip, wanting him everywhere, and Kip responded by shoving his hands down the back of Scott's briefs, gripping his ass. Their kissing quickly turned wild and hungry, and Scott couldn't fucking wait anymore. It had been a whole night of teasing, and he needed it to end. He needed to be inside him.

In a move that surprised both of them, Scott hoisted Kip off the ground, holding him firmly as Kip wrapped strong legs around him. Scott carried him to the bedroom this way, as if Kip were half the size he actually was.

When they got to the bedroom, Scott dumped Kip on the bed and was on him immediately. He pulled Kip's arms over his head and pinned his wrists with one hand, then went right back to kissing him senseless.

"Oh, fuck, Scott," Kip gasped. "Yes."

Scott just wanted *so much*. He wished they had endless time. That they never needed sleep. God, tomorrow he was leaving for a fucking *week*. He needed to drink his fill now.

"Please fuck me," Kip said in small voice. "Please. I know we talked about you riding me, and I want that, but god, I *need* you to fuck me. The way you've been looking at me all night, undressing me . . . Fuck, *please*."

"I'm going to," Scott promised. "I want that. Believe me."

He quickly removed his own briefs. He was about to get the lube and condoms from the nightstand, when Kip grabbed his wrist.

"Let me suck you. Please. C'mere."

Scott groaned and moved up so he was practically straddling Kip's face, and his beautiful, greedy boyfriend wasted no time taking his cock in his mouth. Kip moaned happily around his dick, and his eyes fluttered closed.

"Jesus, Kip."

Kip teased Scott's cock with his tongue, letting it glide slow and lazy around the head, and dipping as far down the shaft as he could from that angle. It felt incredible. Scott heard the click of a bottle cap and realized that Kip was using slick fingers to open himself up beneath him.

Kip's face was so blissful. He was happily licking and sucking Scott while he fucked himself on his own fingers.

"God, you love it, don't you?" Scott rasped.

Kip answered him with a smoldering gaze, and pressed his tongue to Scott's slit.

Scott was feeling dangerously good, heat and tension already building below. He needed to move this along.

He pulled out of Kip's mouth and shifted so he could see his fingers working. Fuck, he could watch Kip touching himself forever. He looked so goddamn gorgeous doing it. Scott considered Kip's cock, which hadn't been touched yet. It bobbed excitedly, as if waiting for attention.

"God, look at you," Scott said.

"Want you . . . Want your cock . . ."

"How many fingers?" He had no idea where this boldness was coming from.

"T-two."

"One more," Scott instructed.

Kip whimpered a bit and added a third finger. He writhed as he worked himself open.

"Are you ready for me?"

"Yes. Fuck. Yes. Come on."

Scott rolled on a condom and considered his next move as he slicked his cock up. He had thought about getting Kip on all fours so he could just pound him from behind, but truthfully he wanted to see his face. He wanted to see him come.

Kip removed his fingers and Scott wasted no time. He hauled Kip's hips up and slammed into him, burying himself deep in one thrust. Kip screamed and Scott cried out, but when he was sure Kip wasn't hurt, he fucked him hard and fast.

Precome was forming already at the slit of Kip's cock. Scott still hadn't touched him there. Barely had all night.

"Oh, Scott. That's perfect. *Shit.*"

"Are you—Fuck, look at you. I haven't even touched you."

"I know. I know. Keep going."

Kip's eyes kept rolling back; he looked completely gone, and, in that moment, Scott was determined to make him come first. He wanted to see if he could do it, without touching his cock. Without letting Kip have any friction there.

"Can you do it?" Scott said. "Are you gonna come for me?"

"Fuck. I think so. Yeah."

"God, really? Shit, come on. Please."

"I'm close. Just . . . don't stop."

Scott pumped his hips harder, treating it like a challenge. "As soon as you come, I'm gonna come," he said, partly as encouragement, and partly just stating fact.

"Ah." Kip clenched the bed sheets in his fists. His eyes screwed tight, his teeth clenched.

"You gonna? Oh, fuck, Kip, look at you. You are, aren't you?"

"Yes!" he gritted out. "Fuck . . . *fuck* . . ."

Kip cried out, his eyes opening wide as he came all over himself. He spurted endlessly as they both watched, amazed. Then Scott, as promised, growled and came inside Kip, relief hitting him everywhere at once.

Scott kissed him and kissed him, then rolled them over so Kip could lie on top of him, and then kissed him some more.

Kip raised himself up to straddle Scott's stomach. "That was incredible."

"It really was," Scott said. "I—"

"It's one-thirty," Kip said, smiling and stroking Scott's hair. "We can probably get another round in tonight, don't you think?"

"Yeah." Scott smiled. He looked up at Kip, and he knew. He knew for sure.

Scott Hunter was in love.

CHAPTER FIFTEEN

Kip sat on Scott's bed and watched him pack for his road trip. He was wearing his own jeans and one of Scott's New York Admirals hoodies. It was too big for him, but he loved wearing it.

"Can I hold on to this?" he asked, tugging at the strings of the hoodie. "While you're gone?"

"Of course," Scott said, tossing some underwear into his suitcase. "As long as you think about me while you're wearing it."

"I'll be thinking about you no matter what I'm wearing."

Scott smiled and kissed him. He would need to leave by two this afternoon to catch the team bus to the airport. That only gave them another couple of hours together before they'd be apart for nine days.

"I was thinking," Scott said, "that maybe you could stay here while I'm gone."

Kip hadn't been expecting that. He didn't know what to say.

"Not the whole time, if you don't want," Scott said quickly. "I mean, you don't have to at all, obviously. I just thought—"

"Really? You want me to?"

"Yeah. I do. I like the idea of you being here while I'm

gone. At least sometimes. Plus, it would be easier for you to get to work, right?"

What Scott was polite enough not to say was that this apartment was a grown-up place to live, and not Kip's parents' house.

"If you're sure you don't mind, yeah. That would be great," Kip said.

"I don't mind. I can think about you sleeping in my bed while I'm in some lonely hotel rooms."

"You'll have your roommate," Kip pointed out.

"Not the same."

"And if you ever find yourself without a roommate, we could . . ."

Scott smirked. "Believe me, I'll be calling you. Every chance I get."

He held up the blue socks Kip had given him on Valentine's Day and placed them in the suitcase. Kip grinned.

"So," Scott said, "I'm back on a Monday. And I'll be in town for a week after that. How should we celebrate my return?"

"Well . . ." Kip said, "I kind of have plans that night."

"Oh."

"Yeah, I mean, it's no big deal, but . . . that Monday is my birthday. I'm just going out with some friends for a drink or whatever. But after that we could—"

Scott froze. "It's your *birthday*?"

"Yeah, but it's fine. Twenty-six isn't exactly a milestone. And, besides, why would you know when my birthday is?"

"Because I should have *asked*!"

"Well . . . you can remember it next year." Kip realized as he said it what his words implied. He glanced shyly at Scott, but Scott only reacted with a heartbreakingly happy smile.

"I will," he said.

Kip flushed a little. He fiddled with the strings on the hoodie, trying to distract himself from all these damn *feelings*.

He was in love. There was no question. He was head over heels in love with Scott Hunter. It was absurd, but it was real.

"So," he said unsteadily, "where will this trip take you?"

Scott sighed. "Too many places. Columbus first. Then Detroit, Toronto, Winnipeg, Ottawa, and Montreal. Short flights, at least."

"Yeah? That's good," Kip said. Then, for no particular reason, he added, "I've never been on a plane."

"Seriously?"

"I'm serious. Never had anywhere to go, really."

"Oh, Kip! And you studied history—there's so much you should see!"

Kip shrugged. "Figure I'll get around to it someday."

"I'd love to take you somewhere," Scott said.

"What, like, Winnipeg? Or Detroit?"

"All right, fuck off."

"Yes, sir."

Then Scott was on him. He'd knocked Kip backward onto the mattress and was covering him, all in one swift move. "Are you mocking me, Grady?"

"Of course not." Kip smirked. *"Hunter."*

Scott growled and kissed him, fierce and challenging. "I'm going to miss you. So. Fucking. Much." He moved his mouth down Kip's neck, teeth scraping.

"Give me something," Kip stammered out. "Gimme something to remember you by."

Scott sucked in a breath and pressed his hardening cock into Kip's hip. Then he sealed his mouth to the tender flesh just above Kip's clavicle and sucked hard. Kip squirmed happily under Scott's weight as he held him down and marked him.

Scott pulled away slowly, admiring his work. "That should last," he said. "Maybe even until I get back."

"I hope so," Kip said weakly.

Scott ran his thumb over the mark. His eyes were wild with lust.

"What do we have time for?" Kip asked.

"Anything. Fuck, let me—I don't know."

"Let me fuck you. I know you don't want any marks, but I can make you feel me, at least for a little while."

"Yeah. *Fuck*, yes. But just like this. Me on top of you."

"Fucking finally." Kip grinned.

Scott yanked off all of his clothing in a frantic whirlwind. Kip pulled off the hoodie and his T-shirt together, then hauled his pants and underwear off. They were naked in seconds, and Scott had already grabbed the lube.

They didn't have a lot of time for foreplay, so Scott got himself ready as quickly as possible. He tossed Kip the lube and a condom.

Kip slicked himself up, moaning a little as he slowly stroked himself. When Scott lowered himself onto his dick, it felt so fucking good. He was still so tight, and Kip could see in his face that it was hurting a bit, but Scott sank down carefully until Kip was deep inside him.

He sat there for a moment, which gave Kip a chance to admire him. He was all chiseled muscle and faded battle scars. Thick thighs, deep-cut abs and massive, solid pecs. His big hands stroked Kip's own chest, fingers tracing through his chest hair.

"You're so beautiful," Scott said, his voice quiet and reverent.

"You're perfect," Kip breathed. He brushed his fingers across Scott's cheek. "Unreal. All of you. Can't believe how lucky I am."

Scott smiled and started moving, pulling himself up and slamming back down. They both cried out, and Kip grinned up at him because this was fucking incredible.

He just enjoyed the show, watching all that muscle bounce on his dick. Watching Scott's face twist and relax, sweat forming on flushed skin. And Scott was riding him so hard, so relentlessly, that Kip could feel himself racing to the finish line without doing anything.

Scott's cock bounced in front of him, huge and hard. Kip reached for it, hands still slick from the lube he'd used on himself.

"Yesss . . ." Scott hissed.

Kip jerked him off, hard and fast to keep with Scott's rhythm. Scott threw his head back, and planted one hand firmly in the middle of Kip's chest. "Oh my god. Oh my *god*, Kip! I'm gonna . . . Fuck, I'm close . . ."

"Me too. I'm right there, Scott. I'm . . . Come on, sweetheart. Give it to me."

Scott cried out, and a second later Kip was being showered in his release. Scott clenched and fluttered around his cock, and that was it for Kip. He came inside him with a silent scream, so hard his ears felt like they'd burst.

"Kip . . ." Scott gasped. "Fuck. Holy . . ."

Kip lay panting on the bed, trying to return to himself. "Yeah. Yeah, Scott. Come here."

Scott pulled off him and fell beside him on the bed. Kip grabbed his face and kissed him giddily. He couldn't stop smiling. He felt unhinged. He felt . . . like a man who was very much in love.

Scott brushed his fingers over the mark he'd made on Kip's skin at the base of his neck. "Was that too much?" he asked. "It's bigger than I thought it would be—"

"No," Kip said, covering his hand. "It's perfect. Thank you."

"You haven't even seen it yet," Scott said affectionately.

"I don't care. I love it." *I love* you.

Scott kissed him again and then sighed. "I need to finish packing."

"Can't you call in sick?" Kip teased.

"Yeah, yeah. All right, Grady."

He rolled off the bed and went into the bathroom, leaving Kip alone to stare at the ceiling. Before Scott left for nine days, should Kip just . . . tell him how he felt?

He shook his head. What if it was too much? It *had* to be too much, right? If he told Scott he was in love with him now, Scott would have a week away from him to think about how weird that was. Kip could imagine Scott returning from his trip to tell him that it wasn't going to work out between them. It was devastatingly realistic in his mind.

Not fucking worth it.

He traded places with Scott in the bathroom and got himself cleaned up. He inspected the mark Scott had left on him. Scott hadn't been kidding about how big it was, but Kip was very happy with it.

He returned to the bedroom, where Scott was already wearing most of a striking gray suit.

"I do appreciate the NHL's dress code for team travel," Kip said, admiring the way the perfect tailoring showed off Scott's broad shoulders and trim waist.

"That makes one of us," Scott grumbled. He tied a Windsor knot with the ease of someone who had done it countless times since childhood.

As Kip retrieved his underwear from the floor, Scott said, "You said last night that you know some good clubs."

"Yeah," Kip said. Scott had once again said something he had not expected at all. "I do."

"I was just thinking. Do you . . . go to clubs often?"

"No, not really. Not for a while now."

Scott seemed to relax a little, which was weird. "Oh. Okay. It's nothing, anyway. Forget I said anything."

"Scott," Kip said. "Are you trying to ask me if I've been hooking up with other guys while we've been . . . ?"

"No!" Scott said, way too quickly. "I mean. I guess. Yes. But not because—I'm not going to tell you not to. I know I'm not always available."

"Scott," Kip said again. He walked up behind him and wrapped his arms around Scott's ridiculous chest.

"I'm sorry," Scott said. "I'm not . . . jealous. I just . . . I don't know how these things work."

"There aren't any rules," Kip said. "Unless we set some. But I don't need any."

"Okay."

"I haven't been with anyone since we met. Just for the record."

"Me neither."

Kip laughed. "Yeah, no shit."

Scott laughed too, then he turned and kissed Kip.

"You're enough for me," Kip said. "More than enough. I have no problem waiting for you."

"I know it's dumb, but I'm really happy to hear that," Scott said.

"It's not dumb. And to be honest, I think I'm developing an addiction to reunion sex."

Kip let Scott finish packing while he got dressed. At five minutes to two, Scott was kissing Kip goodbye at the door.

"Text me whenever you want," Scott said, "and I'll call as much as I can. Video. I'm bringing my iPad. We can Skype. Maybe even—"

"Yeah. I'd like that." Kip pulled him into another kiss. It was so hard to let him go. Harder than it had been before.

"Okay," Scott said finally, picking up his suitcase. "I'll see you. Nine days."

"Nine days."

"Bye."

"Bye."

Scott left quickly before either of them could reach for the other again. Kip blew out a breath and leaned back against the wall. Actual tears prickled his eyes, which was embarrassing. It wasn't like Scott was going to *war.*

He was surprised when, a few minutes later, the door clicked and opened. Scott slipped inside, looking a little lost.

"I, uh," he started. His face was pure anguish. He didn't have his suitcase. He must have gone to the car and come back. "I was thinking . . . Planes, y'know? And anything can happen . . ."

"Scott?"

"I love you," he said. "I just wanted to say that. Before I left."

Kip's jaw hit the floor.

"I don't expect you to, y'know, say it too or anything. I know it's probably a ridiculous thing to say or feel right now, but I am in love with you. And I wanted you to know that."

The tears that had been prickling were now *flooding* Kip's eyes. He was no longer embarrassed about them.

"Kip?"

Kip pressed his lips together and shook his head, trying to gather himself. "Sorry," he said, finally. "I just . . . I thought I was the only one who felt that way."

Scott's face lit up. All of the agony was gone instantly.

"You're not." He closed the distance between them and held Kip's face, brushing away tears with his thumbs. Scott's eyes were wet too.

"I wanted to tell you," Kip said.

"Tell me now."

"I love you. Scott, I'm . . . *completely* in love with you."

Scott beamed and kissed him, still holding his face. Kip reached up and did the same.

"Fuck," Scott breathed. "Now I really *do* have to go."

"I know."

"I'm glad I told you."

"I'm glad too."

"But it's really fucking hard to leave now."

Kip sniffed. "Yeah."

Scott kissed him one more time. "I'll call you," he said as he headed back to the door. "Tonight. I love you."

Kip laughed wetly. "I love you too. Go win six hockey games."

"You got it."

And with that, he was gone. But this time, when Kip leaned back against the wall, he was grinning from ear to ear.

Scott had decided to sit with his newest teammate, Matti Jalo, during the flight to Columbus. Even with the extra-wide leather seats on their private plane, it was a squeeze fitting his own large body next to Jalo's massive frame. It didn't help his comfort level that his ass was still sore from fucking himself on Kip earlier that afternoon.

Not that he minded.

Carter was sitting across the aisle from them. "You know what I call this trip? The bullshit trip. Six games in eight days and all of them in cold, miserable cities."

"The cold doesn't bother me," Jalo said cheerfully. "I'm Finnish. Ice runs in our veins!"

"Looks like big fucking ice in those biceps, son," Carter said.

Jalo laughed. "Where are you from, Carter? That you fear the cold?"

"I don't fear anything. I'm from all over. Bounced around, y'know? Military family. But I spent a lot of years in North Dakota, and there's no way Finland is colder than that place."

Jalo smiled. "Have you not been to Finland?"

"Haven't had the pleasure. Is it like Sweden? I've been to Sweden."

"No," Jalo said, suddenly serious.

Carter laughed.

"Bit of a rivalry, then, I take it?" Scott asked.

Jalo looked at him hard. "Finland is better than Sweden."

Scott put his hands up in surrender. "Got it."

The flight was a short one, which was good given how uncomfortable Scott was, wedged between Jalo and the window. The truth was he normally wouldn't have minded being pressed against all that muscle. Jalo was, in a word, blindingly hot. Taller even than Scott by at least a couple of inches, and probably outweighing him by twenty or so pounds of muscle, with piercing blue eyes, white-blond hair that he wore combed back off his face, and ever-present stubble. He was definitely a walking fantasy.

But Scott's mind wasn't on the hunk filling the seat next to him; it was on the secret boyfriend that he'd left behind. The secret boyfriend he *loved.*

He smiled to himself. He couldn't believe he had actually *said it.* And that Kip had said it back! Scott felt light-headed, and completely giddy.

The team was scheduled to meet in the hotel restaurant for dinner as soon as they had checked into their rooms. Scott was rooming with Jalo tonight, then Jalo would be rooming with his new defense linemate for the rest of the trip.

Spirits were high as the team enjoyed a meal together. Everyone was excited to have a superstar defenseman like Jalo on board. It helped that Jalo was a lot of fun. He was jovial and loud and loved to tell stories with his booming voice and lilting Finnish accent. He liked to drink beer and buy rounds (though Scott made sure there were only two rounds tonight, since they had a practice in the morning). Scott liked him. Everyone liked him. He was the opposite of Zullo in pretty much every way.

When the meal was over, Jalo was obviously in no hurry to return to the room. Instead, he held court with a group of younger players, who were hanging, starstruck, on his every word.

"I'm gonna head up," Scott said. "Don't let these guys stay up too late." He said it with a teasing tone, so he wouldn't sound like such a dad. But he knew his role on this team. He wasn't Jalo. He was the boring, responsible one.

The boring, responsible one who was going to call his fucking *boyfriend* right now!

Scott had hit *call* on his phone before the hotel room door had even clicked shut behind him. It was nearly ten o'clock.

"Hey," Kip said when he answered. His voice was quiet.

"Are you at my place?"

"No, I'm home. I'm gonna stay here tonight. Maybe your place tomorrow night."

"Are your parents going to . . . Will they be wondering where you are?"

"Are you asking if I've told them about us?"

"No!"

"I haven't. But I'm a grown man and they can probably guess why I don't come home some nights."

"Right. Yeah."

"Hey," Kip said shyly. "I love you."

Scott smiled and sat on the bed, any tension he had picked up that day leaving him. "I love you too. I've never said that to anyone before. Besides my mom."

"Me neither. Except Elena sometimes, but that's different."

"It feels good to say it to you."

"Yeah," Kip said. "It does."

Scott grinned stupidly at his phone and imagined Kip doing the same thing.

"So . . ." Kip said. "How's Jalo?"

"Jalo is great. Everyone loves him."

"I'll bet. I saw him being interviewed on ESPN. He's kind of bonkers hot."

"Off the record? Yes. He is."

Kip laughed. "I'm pretty jealous of your job. Just hanging out in locker rooms with ripped, sweaty men."

"Well, you're not gonna like this: Jalo's my roommate tonight."

"Okay, now I really am jealous."

"You have nothing to be jealous of."

"Maybe I should hop a flight to Columbus. See if you and Jalo wanna make a sandwich outta me."

"Oh my god. Kip, stop." Scott was turning beet red in his hotel room. Jalo was his *teammate*! And now he was picturing the three of them—

"Jesus," Kip said. "Now that's all I can think about. I might have to wrap this call up. Unless you—"

"No. He'll be back any minute. I can't. Not tonight."

"Your loss," Kip said in a low voice that went right to Scott's dick.

"Knock it off," Scott said. "Soon. I promise."

"I'll be watching the game tomorrow night. Call me after?"

"I'm getting on a plane to Detroit immediately after the game. But the Detroit game is in the afternoon. I can call you after that."

"Such a long wait," Kip sighed.

"I'll text you tomorrow."

"I miss you already. Send me a photo after we hang up, okay?"

"All right. You too."

They said goodbye and hung up. Scott snapped a quick selfie of himself lying back on the bed. He tried to make it a little sexy. He sent it to Kip and got an immediate reply.

KIP:

I meant of Jalo.

Scott laughed.

SCOTT:
Fuck you.

He got a cute photo of Kip back, relaxing on his own bed and wearing Scott's hoodie.

Scott smiled at it. He loved him so much.

SCOTT:
Thank you. I love you.

KIP:
I love you too.

"So," Carter said, coming to a stop that sprayed Scott's shins with snow, "tell me about your girl."

Scott rolled his eyes. "Nothing to tell, Vaughan."

They were lingering on the ice at the end of their morning practice. Scott was watching a couple of rookies gather up the pucks.

"Bullshit, Scott. You've been floating around with a dumb smile on your face, humming 'How Sweet It Is' all over the place. You got it bad."

Scott kicked at the ice. "No comment."

"Don't know why a girl who looks like that wants to be seen with your ugly ass, but—"

"All right."

Carter looked at him seriously. "I *am* happy for you, Scott. Even if you don't want to talk about her."

Scott turned his gaze to the ice, considering. He couldn't

talk to Carter about Kip, but he *could* talk to Carter about "Elena."

He chose his words carefully.

"I've never felt this way about anyone," Scott said. "It's just very new. That's all."

Carter slapped him on his heavily padded shoulder. "There you go!"

"We've been seeing each other for a few weeks and it's nice. I'm happy. But we want to keep it private, y'know?"

"My lips are sealed."

"Your lips are *never* sealed."

"Well, they're sealed about this."

"Thanks." Scott glanced at his teammate, his *friend*, and wondered if he could maybe tell him the truth. Not right that second, obviously, but soon? Carter was probably his best friend, and he'd always seemed accepting and open-minded. He was never overtly homophobic, anyway, which put him ahead of a lot of NHL players.

Scott would really like to tell him. He'd like to tell Huff and Bennett too. Hell, he'd like to tell the whole world, but . . .

"Come on," Carter said. "Let's go rest up before we fuck up Columbus tonight."

"I like him," Elena said. The words were out of her mouth as soon as he sat down with her at the Thai restaurant.

"Yeah?" Kip asked.

"Yeah. And he's head over heels for you."

"I know." Kip smiled. "He told me."

"Told you what?"

"He told me—" he leaned in "—that he loves me."

If Elena was surprised, her face didn't show it. "Did he?"

"He did!" Kip said, and proceeded to tell her the whole romantic story.

"Wow," she said when he had finished. "That's a big deal."

"I know!"

The server came and took their orders. After he left, Elena said, "Have you told Scott about your potential new job?"

"I will. If they offer it."

"And what if they don't offer it?"

"Then there's no reason to mention it?"

Elena rolled her eyes. "I mean what are *you* going to do if you don't get that job?"

"I don't know! Keep working at fucking Straw+Berry, I guess."

"You're wasting your talents there."

"No," Kip said irritably. "I'm earning *money* there."

"So you're not going to quit and live off your millionaire boyfriend who is in love with you?"

"Of course not! You know I would never do that. I feel bad enough that I have to depend on my *parents'* generosity. I know he's got money, but . . ."

Elena didn't say anything for a moment, but she looked at Kip approvingly. "I know you wouldn't throw your life, or your dignity, away for a guy," she said, "but I don't like seeing you selling yourself short either."

"I'll figure something out," he grumbled.

Later, when they were finishing their meals, Kip asked, "Did you dance with anyone interesting at the gala?"

"You mean besides your charming boyfriend?"

"Yes, and I was not jealous at all, by the way."

She smiled. "I did, actually." She leaned in and whispered the name of a somewhat famous young actor.

"Whoa! Good dancer?"

"Mm. He was good at sex too."

Kip nearly choked on his water. "I figured you'd be going home with someone that night."

"Oh yeah. Took me a while to round it down to my top five, but I think I made the right choice."

"You gonna see him again?"

Elena made a face and shook her head.

Kip laughed. He had always been deeply envious of Elena's game. She was just so *cool* about sex.

"Do you think it's weird?" he asked later, after they had stepped outside into the cold night.

"What?"

"That he told me that he loves me. That I told him that I love him. I know it's only been a few weeks."

"Are you in love with him?"

"Yes."

"Then it's not weird." She looped her arm through his and tugged him against her. "Come on. Let's go watch your man play hockey."

CHAPTER SIXTEEN

Detroit was cold as hell.

Not that it had been particularly warm anywhere Scott had been lately, but Detroit was unreasonably cold.

It ruined his plan of going for an evening stroll while he called Kip. His roommate seemed to be settled in for the night in their hotel room, and the lobby was oddly busy due to some kind of business conference. He didn't want to go anywhere too public, like a coffee shop, because Detroit was a hockey town and he would almost certainly get recognized.

He decided to play the fame card.

He went to the front desk and gave them his best Scott Hunter smile. "Excuse me. I was hoping you might be able to help me."

The young man behind the desk looked very excited. "Of course, sir!"

"I need to make a phone call and I was hoping for some privacy. But my roommate is asleep and . . ."

The young man smiled at him as if he were about to do a very big favor for him. "Come with me," he said. "I know where you can go."

He led Scott to a door that said *Meeting Room #3* on it. He unlocked the door and turned on the light. "Stay as long as you need," he said. "The door will lock behind you."

"Thank you," Scott said, glancing at his name tag, "Michael." He handed him a twenty-dollar bill, and Michael took it, beaming. He thanked Scott twice before leaving the room.

Scott sat in one of the meeting-room chairs and called Kip, who picked up right away.

"Two wins. Nice job," Kip said.

"Yeah, thanks. I'm proud of the guys."

"I love watching you play."

"Oh yeah?"

"Mm. It's sexy."

Scott grinned. "Where are you?"

"I'm in your bedroom. Where are you?"

"A hotel meeting room in Detroit."

"Oh."

"Yeah, sorry. Not tonight."

"That's okay. I'm snooping around your apartment."

"Snooping?"

"Yeah. Looking in your drawers." There was a pause. "Oh my god. Scott, do you keep your gold medal in your underwear drawer?"

"It sounds like you already know the answer."

"Why isn't it on display?"

"Like where?"

"I don't think I'd keep a gold medal in my underwear drawer if I had one."

"Where would you keep it?"

"I don't know. I'd probably wear it all the time!"

Scott laughed. "It goes with everything." Then, "So you're staying at my place tonight?"

"Yeah. If that's okay."

"Of course it's okay. It was my idea!"

"I know. It just . . . seems generous."

"Kip," Scott sighed, "you're my boyfriend. I'm in love with you. You can stay at my place whenever you want."

"Okay. I love you."

Scott smiled. "I like hearing you say that."

"I like saying it."

"I can't wait to be back home with you."

"Still got a lot of games to go there, Hunter."

"I know."

"You win 'em all and then come home to me. I'll give you whatever you need when you get back."

Kip's voice had gotten lower, and Scott shivered a bit. "Whatever I need, eh?"

"Mm. You think about it."

"I will." He exhaled. "Fuck, I wish I had my own room tonight."

"Me too. Coulda put on a show for you."

"I want to do that," Scott said. "For you."

"You ever done that before?" Kip asked. "Just let someone watch you get yourself off?"

"No. Never," Scott breathed. "But I want to. For you."

"I'd like that. Fuck, I'd *really* like that. Now I'm picturing you, all laid out . . ."

"Kip," Scott warned. "Don't. I can't get all turned on."

"But you are, aren't you? I'll bet you're getting hard right now."

Scott swore under his breath because Kip wasn't wrong.

"I am too," Kip purred. "Tell me what you'd like to do to me."

"No. Stop it."

"Fine. I'll just lie back on your bed here and we can talk about whatever you want."

"Thank you," Scott said. "Are you naked?"

Kip laughed. "Knew you wouldn't be able to drop it. Almost, yeah. Still have my briefs on."

Scott swore again. He was abso-fucking-lutely *not* going to jerk off in this hotel meeting room. He wasn't that creepy. "I *really* can't do this right now."

"That's okay," Kip said. "*I* can."

"Kip . . ."

"Shh . . . Just talk to me," he said, his tone drifting a little. "Love your voice, Scott. Tell me what to do."

Scott loved and hated this plan. He loved it because it was fucking *hot*. He hated it because he was going to be left with a very uncomfortable hard-on.

He glanced at the meeting-room door, then lowered his voice. "You touching yourself?"

"Yeah. I'm real fucking hard. Tell me what to do," Kip drawled, "*sweetheart*."

"Jesus." Scott adjusted himself through his sweatpants. "All right. Go slow. Don't take the shorts off. Not yet."

He could tell Kip was smiling when he replied. "Gonna be like *that*, huh? All right. I'm just rubbing myself real gentle. It feels nice."

Scott could picture Kip's thick cock straining against the fabric. He could picture Kip, nearly naked, sprawled out on his bed, eyes closed and thinking of Scott.

"You imagining it's me touching you?" Scott asked.

"Yeah. God, I wish it really was."

"Me too. Keep going."

Kip sighed and made breathy little moans that made Scott's dick twitch in agony. He cupped it with his hand to relieve some pressure.

"My shorts are getting wet," Kip said. "I'm leaking already. Can I take them off?"

"Not yet," Scott said, surprising himself with how much he was enjoying this control.

"Fuck, Scott."

"Are you cold?"

"Getting warmer."

"Your nipples must be hard." Kip had perfect, dark nipples that always stiffened into delicious little peaks.

"Mm. Yeah. Want me to touch them?"

"Yeah. Let go of your dick. Play with your nipples for a bit."

He heard Kip inhale sharply as his fingers made contact with his sensitive nipples.

"If I was there," Scott said, "I'd lick them and bite them until you were begging me to suck your dick."

"Fuck. *Fuck*."

"Are you still holding the phone?"

"Yeah."

"Put me on speaker and put the phone beside you so you have both hands."

"Okay." He heard rustling, and then Kip was back. "Both hands are free, Hunter. What should I do with them?"

Scott smiled and considered the question. "Take off your briefs. But don't touch your dick yet."

"Jesus, you're cruel."

"Tough but fair."

"I like this side of you," Kip said. "Okay, my shorts are off."

"Get the lube."

There was more rustling, then, "Got it."

"I want you to finger yourself. Open yourself up as if I was gonna fuck you."

"Okay. Okay. Shit. All right."

"Don't touch your dick," Scott reminded him.

"I won't. I won't. Okay, I'm, ahh, I'm—"

"Just relax."

Kip let out a long, slow breath. "Okay."

Scott imagined him with his knees bent, his slick fingers circling that tight ring of muscle. He swallowed hard and adjusted himself again.

"Please tell me you're gonna surprise me by walking through that door in a second," Kip said.

"I wish. Believe me."

Kip moaned and gasped as he worked himself open. Scott chewed his lip and resisted the urge to stroke himself under the harsh fluorescent lights of the hotel meeting room.

"Tell me when you're ready," he said.

"Ready for what?"

"You'll see. Pretend you're getting ready for me."

Kip blew out a breath. "Okay. Keep talking to me."

Scott glanced at the door again. He couldn't believe he was doing this. "If I was there, I'd be opening you up with my mouth. Real slow."

"Scott, god."

"Wish I could see you right now. You feel good?"

"Better . . ." Kip gritted out. "Better when you let me stroke myself."

"Soon, baby." *Baby?* "Tell me when you've got three fingers in you."

"Yeah . . . yeah. Almost. I'm . . . Oh fuck. I feel like I could come just from this. With your voice and imagining your fingers in me . . ."

Scott moaned. He almost wanted to let that happen. Just see if Kip could get himself off with his own fingers.

But he had other plans.

"Okay. I'm ready," Kip said. "What's next?"

"Open the nightstand drawer. There's a box at the back."

"All right. I see it. I've got it."

"Open it."

He waited a moment. Then Kip said, "Christ. Yes."

Scott knew the item well. A large black dildo that, for about a year now, had been his most reliable romantic partner.

"I want you to fuck yourself with that. Pretend it's me. God, I wish it was me."

"Me too. For the record, though, this is really fucking hot."

"Yeah." He blew out a breath, his heart racing like he'd just run a mile.

"You must be in agony," Kip said. "How are you doing there?"

"Hard as a fucking rock. But don't worry about me. Get that in you. When it's all the way in, you can touch your dick."

"Shit. Okay."

Scott leaned back in his desk chair, legs spread wide, and closed his eyes as he listened to Kip work the toy inside himself. Every gasp and moan was going straight to Scott's dick, but he still wouldn't touch himself.

"How are you doing?" he asked.

"Good. It's . . . it's big."

"I know. But you can take it."

"Yeah . . . yeah," Kip panted.

"You got it in?"

"Almost. Almost. Fuck."

Scott wished he had a glass of water or something. His mouth was bone-dry and he felt dizzy, probably from all the blood rushing directly to his cock. He gripped the edge of the table with his free hand, determined not to give in to the temptation to jerk off to Kip's moans.

"Okay. It's in. It's . . . Fuck, it's so good, Scott."

"Pull it out and push it back in. Fuck yourself."

"I am. I'm—Oh wow. It really hits that spot, huh? Fuck."

Scott knew exactly how well it hit *that spot*. He remembered using it on himself not that long ago, back when Kip had just been a fantasy—when he had just been the cute guy working at the smoothie shop and Scott had never in a million years thought he would actually have him in his arms and in his bed. He'd fucked himself with the toy, imagining it was Kip who was penetrating him. And, god, the thrill of having Kip use the same toy on himself now was intoxicating.

"You can touch yourself whenever you want now," Scott said, "but tell me what you're doing."

"Thank Christ. Okay, I'm—Ah! Mm. Finally. Fuck. I'm just gripping it. Running my thumb over the slit and—Fuck. I'm gushing over here."

Scott groaned. This was fucking torture. "Get a rhythm. Pretend I'm fucking you."

"I'm gonna go off fast, Scott."

"I know. That's okay. Just let me hear you."

"Oh fuck . . . Tryin' to do both things at once, but I kinda just wanna keep fucking myself here. Feels almost as good as you in me."

Scott let his imagination provide him with the visuals. He could picture the way Kip was stretched around his toy, arm muscles straining as he moved it in and out. He could see Kip's thumb working the slick head of his cock, and the way his mouth was probably hanging open, face slack and euphoric.

"So good, Kip. I'll bet you look so beautiful right now."

Kip wasn't talking anymore. He was just making gorgeous, needy sounds, and Scott drank them in.

"Come on, baby. Finish it. However you need to. Wanna hear you."

"Okay, fuck. I wish I could hear you too. Wish I could—Ah. I'm so close. I'm so—"

Scott was on fire, everywhere. If he so much as brushed his

cock, he was going to erupt. "Come for me. Come on. I love you so much."

He heard Kip start to reply, "I lo—" but he broke off with a strangled cry.

Scott's own mouth fell open. Relief washed over him as if he was somehow sharing Kip's orgasm.

"Oh wow. Fuck," Kip panted after he'd had time to come back to himself. "That was . . . Holy shit. I was not expecting *any* of that."

Scott laughed. "Me neither. I thought we'd just have a nice chat."

"I'm a real fucking mess over here."

"Mm. I'll bet you look incredible."

"You must be hurting, though. You sure you can't—"

"I'll take care of myself. Later. As soon as fucking possible."

"Wish I could help."

"You did. I'll be thinking of you, don't worry."

Kip exhaled loudly. "I love you."

"I love you. Can't believe the things you make me do."

He chuckled. "I'm all sleepy now."

"Go get cleaned up and go to bed," Scott said. "I should get out of this room anyway."

"You gonna be able to get back to your hotel room? Without poking someone's eye out?"

"I'll be fine," Scott said tersely. "Go to bed."

"All right," Kip yawned. "Well, thanks for the phone call."

They both laughed.

"Goodnight." Scott hung up and did his best to conceal the erection that was not flagging at all before making a beeline for his hotel room. He acknowledged his roommate with a quick nod and went straight into the bathroom.

It only took a few strokes with his hand braced against the

shower wall and the memory of Kip's moans filling his ears. He pulled his hand away from the wall and bit his fist as he came so hard he nearly lost his balance, panting hard as his release swirled down the drain.

Jesus Christ, Kip. What are you doing to me?

Kip checked his email when he got back to Scott's after work the next day. There was one from the Museum of the City of New York.

This is it!

But as he read the first lines of the email, his heart sank.

> Thank you for your interest in the position of Assistant Educator. We enjoyed meeting with you. Unfortunately, we have decided . . .

Kip swore and closed his laptop. "Of course," he muttered.

Fuck.

He called Elena at work. He normally wouldn't call, but this was an emergency. "I didn't get the job."

"What? Why not?"

"They went with someone who has their master's degree."

"Sorry. That sucks," she said. "You should get your master's degree."

Kip snorted. "How? I'm still paying off the last useless degree."

"It's not useless, and you can figure it out. People do it."

"Yeah, I know. I'll think about it," Kip said glumly.

He heard Elena sigh. "I *am* sorry, Kip. I was really hoping that would work out for you."

"I know. Thanks."

After they ended the call, Kip opened his laptop again. Just for fun, he went to the NYU website and looked at their graduate admissions page.

I could apply. No harm in trying.

He closed the laptop again. Maybe.

He slumped on the couch and flipped around television stations. Hanging around Scott's apartment by himself was nice, but it was also pretty boring. His boredom, paired with the aftermath of the disappointing email, brought on a sudden surge of panic. What if this was it? Obviously there were worse hardships than dating a superstar athlete, especially one he was so madly in love with, but what if he was always Scott's secret? What if that's *all* he ever was? What if he never went back to school and never got a better job and just stayed in Scott's apartment, hidden away until Scott had time for him?

Scott wouldn't do that. He just needs time.

Right?

Surely Kip wasn't looking at a life of attending events together, but arriving separately and pretending not to know each other. Was Scott going to keep letting the world believe that he was a confirmed bachelor? Or worse, would he marry a woman for appearances and keep Kip on the side?

No. Come on. What the hell would give you that idea?

What if Kip was just *convenient* for Scott right now? What if Scott *thought* he was in love because it was the first time he'd let himself be with a man for more than one night? What if he just needed to take this first step and then he'd feel free to date other men? Better men. Men who were in his league, or at least adjacent to his league. Kip was nobody.

Scott would realize it eventually, and if Kip put all of his eggs in this basket, he'd be left with nothing.

There was suddenly a lump in his throat. This was absurd. Where were these thoughts coming from?

He wanted to talk to Scott, but he wasn't even sure where he was right now. He wasn't playing tonight. A plane? Or maybe at a practice.

He didn't want to be needy. And he probably *was* just depressed about that fucking email. And Elena had a point—he should at least *try* to do his master's degree. Either that or find a better service industry job, and that prospect was beyond depressing.

Maybe he could do his Bachelor of Education. Be a teacher like his parents. That wouldn't be so bad, right? Respectable career.

Fuck, this apartment was lonely.

He sent Scott a text. Just a simple hi to let him know he was thinking of him.

Scott didn't reply. Kip turned off the television and flopped over onto his side on the couch. He kind of wanted to get drunk, but that was a terrible idea.

He loved Scott so much.

How could he ever be good enough for him?

He was feeling really fucking low. And Scott wasn't texting him back. And maybe Scott was realizing right now that he could be dating, like, a gay movie star or something.

He had been moping on the couch for almost an hour when Scott texted back. Hi! Can I call you?

Scott didn't even wait for a reply. Kip answered the call. "Hey."

"Kip! I just landed in Toronto! I have to tell you the funny thing that happened at the airport . . ."

Kip grinned and sat up. He listened to Scott's long, animated story, and by the end of it they were both laughing and he felt a lot better. Scott had been on a plane waiting to call Kip so he could tell him all about his day.

"How was *your* day?" Scott asked when he was done.

Kip's heart thumped happily in his chest.

"Better now."

CHAPTER SEVENTEEN

The siren signaled the end of the overtime period. The game had been grueling, ending in a 3–3 tie that would now go to a shootout.

Scott skated to the bench. He nudged Bennett when he got there. “You ready for this?”

“Nothing is getting past me, Hunter.”

“Damn straight,” Scott said, and he tapped his helmeted forehead against the front of Bennett’s mask.

“All right,” Coach Murdock said. “We’re starting with Vaughan, then Huff, then Hunter. Surely one of you millionaires can put this to bed.”

“No problem, Coach,” Huff said.

Bennett skated to his net. The Toronto goalie did the same. Toronto was the home team and they chose to shoot second, so Carter skated out to the center line.

The whistle blew, and Carter took off.

“Nice,” Scott muttered under his breath as Carter deked and swerved toward the net, fancy stickhandling being his specialty.

Unfortunately, it didn’t work and the goalie blocked the shot. Carter skated back, shaking his head. “Shit. Thought I had him.”

"Nice moves, Carter. Next time," Scott said.

Bennett stopped the Toronto shooter, and the Admirals bench breathed a collective sigh of relief.

The bench got rowdy as Huff skated to center ice. "Come on, Huff."

"You got this."

Huff did what he did best. He fired a quick shot at the top corner of the net that the goalie had no chance of stopping. The Admirals all pounded their sticks against the boards and bumped gloves with him as he skated down the line. If the Toronto shooter missed, the game would be over.

The Toronto shooter didn't miss, beating Bennett down low. Scott was up.

Kip had his hands over his mouth. He was on the edge of his seat on Elena's couch. "Come on, Scott . . ." he muttered.

It was surreal seeing Scott in this setting. On television, at this crucial moment, staring down the goalie and looking so determined. So intimidating.

"He's got it," Elena said calmly. "Watch."

They both watched as Scott moved like lightning toward the net. Kip held his breath. Everything was slow motion as Scott let off his shot.

It floated over the goalie's shoulder, pretty as anything.

"Yeah!" Kip said, jumping up from the couch. "Did you see that?"

"Amazing!"

He pointed gleefully at the television. "That man loves me! Me!"

"I don't understand it either."

He sank back onto the couch, resting his head on Elena's shoulder. "That's my boyfriend."

"Of course it is, sweetie."

Kip laughed. "It does sound nuts when I say it, right? It's so weird."

"It's very weird."

"He's so great."

"Yeah, well, you might wanna watch to see if this Toronto player scores, because the game ain't over yet."

"Oh."

"Yeah, superfan."

They watched the Toronto shooter skate down the ice and . . .

"He missed!" Kip exclaimed. "He-missed-he-missed-he-missed!"

"He did."

"They won! Scott won!"

"That's three for three on this road trip, isn't it?"

"Yes! I'm so proud of him!"

He watched Scott's teammates all hug each other. Scott's smile was wide and bright, and Kip wanted to leap into the television and kiss him all over his face.

"I wonder what Jalo's deal is," Elena mused.

"Oh yeah. You need to hit that if you can. Want me to ask Scott?"

"Nah, I'll figure it out on my own."

A half hour later, on his way back to Scott's place, Kip sent him a text. So fucking proud of you.

An hour later he got a reply. Three games down. I'll call you tomorrow.

Then, I love you.

Kip was never going to get tired of that.

"So," Scott said as soon as Kip answered his phone the next afternoon, "I have good news."

"Oh yeah?"

"I, uh, I'm at the hotel in Winnipeg and I managed to get a room to myself."

Kip sat up from where he'd been lying on the couch. "Really? How'd you swing that?"

"Well, Cameron just recovered from a fractured wrist and he's been cleared to play, so he flew up here to meet the team. But it means there's an odd number of us, so . . . I kind of lied about wanting some space to get focused or whatever."

"I'll give you something to focus on, if it helps you feel honest."

Scott laughed. "That's what I was hoping. You at my place?"

"Yeah."

"You wanna—"

"Absolutely. Yes. Let me just get my laptop. I'll call you back on Skype, all right? Give me a minute."

"Okay. Yeah."

They hung up and Kip ran to the bedroom. He set the laptop up on one corner of the giant bed, then opened Skype and fiddled with the screen, trying to find the perfect angle.

He grabbed the lube, buzzing with excitement—this was finally happening! And, man, did he need it.

He set the bottle on the nightstand, then stretched out on the bed so he was on his side, his face propped up on one elbow near the computer. He grinned from ear to ear when Scott's face filled the screen.

"Hi!" Scott said, smiling back just as widely.

"Nice to see you."

"Man, yeah. It's *really* good to see you. I miss you so much."

Damn, Scott had a way of turning everything inside Kip to mush with a few dopey words. "Me too."

Scott took an audible breath and blew it out, still smiling. "I almost forgot how cute you are."

Kip rested his chin on one fist and batted his eyelashes coquettishly. "Who, me?"

Scott laughed. "I, uh, I have to keep my voice down. I've got my own room, but there are teammates on either side of me."

"Yeah, no problem. We can just talk for a bit. You seem nervous."

"No!" Scott said quickly. "I mean . . . yes. A little."

"Nothing I haven't seen before," Kip teased.

Scott rolled his eyes. "I know. I just haven't ever—"

"I'll help. Don't worry. You're gonna love it, but let's talk first."

"Okay. Thanks. Um, how's New York?"

"Cold. How's . . . Winnipeg, did you say?"

"Yeah. *Really* fucking cold. Windy as hell."

"How's the team? How's *Jalo*?"

Scott laughed. "Jalo's good. Been a real asset. He's exactly what we needed on the blue line."

"And in the dressing room?"

"All right, enough."

"I'm gonna change positions. Hold on," Kip said. He piled up all the pillows against the headboard and fell back against them. He tossed one of the pillows on the bed near his outstretched knees and placed the laptop on top. "How's that? Can you see me okay?"

"Yeah. Hi."

"Hi."

Scott was clearly just holding his iPad in his hands and staring straight at it.

"You should find a place to put that thing," Kip suggested. "I wanna see more of you."

"Oh. Okay. Um . . . Oh! I've got an idea."

Scott put the iPad down and Kip was left looking at the ceiling of Scott's hotel room. He heard a rumbling, and then the iPad was picked up and set down on something.

"I pulled the rolling desk chair over," Scott explained, "next to the bed here. I can put the iPad on that with the little stand and it should be a good angle. I think."

He stretched out on the bed and now Kip could see him from head to thighs.

"That's better," Kip said. "God, you're enormous."

"Well, I'm no Matti Jalo—"

"You're perfect. It was so hot watching you win that shootout the other night. You have no idea."

"Oh yeah?"

"Mm. Been thinking a lot about the other night . . . on the phone."

"Me too. A whole lot, actually. Can't believe I said some of those things."

"You were incredible. So fucking sexy."

Scott smiled and probably blushed. It was hard to tell.

"Nice hotel?" Kip asked.

"It's all right."

"You're not even a little turned on right now, are you?"

"I'm nervous! I said!"

"All right," Kip sighed, then smiled. "You're adorable, you know that?"

Scott grinned and shook his head.

"Seriously," Kip said. "People think you're all tough, but look at you, all blushing and jittery about a bit of webcam action."

"Look, Grady . . ."

"I can't believe this was the same man who was giving me orders over the phone the other night. Where'd that guy go?"

"He's here! He's here. Just . . ." Scott closed his eyes and let out a long breath. "Just talk to me."

"Okay. You been wearing those blue socks?"

"Yeah, like every day. I've been washing them in the sink."

Kip laughed and his stomach fluttered. "Aw," he said.

"I really miss you," Scott said in a hushed voice.

"What time are you flying back on Monday?" Kip asked.

"Should be there before noon," Scott said, relaxing back into the pillows. "I hope so. Wanna show you a good time on your birthday."

"You got plans?"

"Maybe."

"Want me to be waiting here for you? At your place?"

"Yeah . . . Yeah, that would be . . . I'd like that."

"I will. I'll be waiting for you. I could be in your bed. I could even get myself all ready for you. Open myself up . . ."

Scott's face changed. It was subtle, but his darkening eyes and the way he swallowed told Kip he was getting Scott where he needed to be.

He smirked. "That working for you, big guy?"

"It's working. Keep talking."

"Sure. Why don't you take that shirt off?"

Scott obediently pulled his T-shirt over his head. "Only seems fair if you . . ." he said, pointing at the camera/Kip.

"Yeah, yeah." Kip removed his own T-shirt and winked at Scott.

"Oh," Scott said. "That mark is still there, huh?"

"Still there," Kip confirmed, brushing his fingers over it. "Might need a new one soon, though."

"I'll give you one."

Kip trailed his fingers over his chest to play with one of his nipples. "Maybe I could just be waiting by the door for you when you get home. Kiss you like I've been wanting to for days now."

"Mm. Would you still be naked in this scenario?" Scott

asked with a crooked grin. He threw one giant arm over his head, seemingly more relaxed.

"That would be kinda weird, but if you like . . ."

"Either way I'd probably end up fucking you against the wall in the hallway."

Fuck. "Fuck, Scott."

"Like I said," Scott said, his voice a little lower, "I miss you."

"What do you miss?" Kip slid a hand up the inside of his thigh, and Scott's eyes followed it.

"I . . . I miss your lips. Your mouth. The way you kiss me. The way you taste. I miss the way you smell."

"How do I smell?" Kip laughed.

"I dunno . . . Nice. Kinda spicy? Like whatever aftershave you use, I guess."

"It's nothing fancy, I can tell ya that."

"I miss your smile," Scott continued, which earned him one. "I miss the little freckles on your shoulders. I miss your perfect nipples and your belly button."

Kip actually giggled. "You're weird. Keep going."

"I miss your ass. Man, do I ever miss your ass. Have I told you how much I love it? It's just great."

"I can always hear it again," Kip said.

"I miss your thighs. Miss being between them."

"I love having you there." Kip moved his hand over to his cock and started casually fondling it outside his jeans. He watched Scott watch him. "How you doing there?" he asked.

"Good . . ." Scott said, his voice husky and quiet.

"Why don't you join me?"

Scott gave him an adorable smile and moved his hand to his own sweatpants. He massaged his cock through the fabric with one big hand.

"Yeah," Kip said. "There you go." He flicked the button on his fly open as he watched pleasure take hold of his boyfriend.

He was so beautiful, and Kip absolutely loved helping him shed the stress and responsibilities of his job and just lose himself. Every time.

Kip unzipped his own fly and peeled back the denim, leaving it hanging open. He gave his cock a squeeze through his briefs, then folded his arms behind his head as he settled in to watch the show.

Scott lifted his hips and shucked his pants. He was still wearing his gray briefs. Kip approved. For now.

"Jesus," Kip said, nodding at the solid bulge in Scott's shorts. "That didn't take long."

Scott grinned lazily and went back to rubbing himself. Kip watched his hand dip down to caress his balls through the fabric, gripping and pulling them lightly.

"You just gonna watch?" Scott asked, his speech slurring already.

"For now."

Scott slipped his hand inside the waistband of his briefs and grabbed onto his cock. Kip watched the shape of his hand under the cotton as Scott stroked himself.

"You do a lot of this," Kip asked, "on the road?"

"Mostly in the shower. I think about you every time now."

A wet spot was forming on the gray fabric of Scott's briefs. Already.

"How about you remove the curtain there?" Kip suggested. "I wanna see."

"You still have your jeans on," Scott pointed out, hand still moving inside his briefs.

"Fine," Kip said with an exaggerated sigh. He removed his jeans and underwear in one move, then bent the knee that was farthest from the laptop. He placed his hands behind his head again.

"Oh wow." Scott quickly removed his own shorts, and now

Kip had a spectacular view of Scott's naked body from his head to the middle of his thighs.

"Jesus, look at you," Kip said. "Fuck, I miss that beautiful cock of yours. Let's see it."

Scott stroked his hand over it, letting his thumb drag through the precome that had gathered at the tip, and smearing it all over the head.

"You got lube with you, Hunter?" Kip asked.

"Yeah, I brought some. It's right . . ." Scott leaned out of the frame for a second. "Here." He poured some out of the bottle directly onto his cock. Kip's own dick twitched.

Scott began stroking himself in earnest, the slick liquid allowing him to get a rhythm going. He watched himself as he jerked off, then gazed at Kip with hooded eyes. "You gotta . . . Kip, you gotta touch yourself too. Please. Do this with me, okay? I wanna see you."

"Mm, I want to. You look so fucking sexy, Scott."

"Do it. God, you're so hard. So gorgeous. Exactly what I think about when I'm alone."

That was enough for Kip to grab the lube from the nightstand and get to work. He curled his fingers around his aching cock and gave a few slow strokes.

"F-u-uck." Kip shuddered at the relief. He smiled and closed his eyes for a second as his head rolled back. When he opened his eyes again, Scott was grinning at him.

"Feel good?" Scott asked, breathless.

"Yeah. Feels real fucking good. Gonna go slow so I can watch you. Don't wanna miss anything." Kip sucked his bottom lip into his mouth and chewed it a little.

"C-can't wait 'til I'm back there with you. All I can think about is how much I want that dick in me."

"Oh yeah? Thought you were gonna fuck me against a wall."

"Can't decide. *Fuck*. Wanna do everything. I love you."

Kip gasped and involuntarily sped up his hand. "I love you too, Scott. Fuck, I love you so much. God, you're so sexy. I'm so fucking hot for you right now."

Scott was pumping his hand hard and fast. His arm muscles flexed and strained as he pushed himself closer to the edge.

"I'm gonna give you whatever you want when you walk in that door," Kip said. "Drop to my knees. Fuck, I'd like that. Right there in the hallway."

Scott whimpered and kept pumping. "I'm so close, Kip . . ."

He was making the lovely, desperate gasps he always made when he was riding the edge. Kip could see the flush on his chest, could see his thick thighs trembling.

It was all working for Kip. He felt his own climax start to take hold, curling and tightening deep inside. "Come on," he said. "You're so beautiful when you come. Let me see. Show me."

Scott panted and swore and gritted out, "Here . . . here."

He came in long, hot streams against his chest and stomach. Kip watched, making sure to glance up at Scott's euphoric face as he rode the waves of release.

"Oh, sweetheart. That's gorgeous," Kip purred.

Scott made a noise between panting and laughter, and slumped back against the pillows, eyes closed, still slowly stroking himself as his orgasm subsided. "Kip . . ." he moaned. "That was incredible. So fucking good."

"Yeah? It *looked* good."

Scott let go of his dick and opened his eyes. "Wanna see you. Are you close? You look like you're close."

"Getting there. I'm feeling really good over here."

"Good."

"Love you like that," Kip said. "All spent and happy. Look like you're drunk."

"I feel a little drunk. Want you to feel this way too."

"I'm gonna . . . Ah . . ." Kip moved his hand faster and used his other one to tug at his balls. "Fuck, god . . ."

He was close. He was really close. His balls tightened and blood rushed in his ears, nearly drowning out Scott's breathy encouragements. "Yeah, Kip. Come on. So pretty."

Kip looked at the screen, saw Scott's sex-drunk face and his thick, softening cock lying on his thigh. Saw the glistening white mess that streaked his muscular torso. And then he shattered and yelled out into Scott's bedroom as he came. His release covered his fist and trickled onto his thigh.

Kip sank back into the pillows, arms spread wide on the bed. "Goddamn," he panted.

"Feel good?"

"Fucking amazing."

They both laughed a little.

"How many days until you're home again?" Kip asked, knowing the answer.

"Four and a bit," Scott said.

"Too fucking many."

"I know." Then Scott snorted.

"What?" Kip asked.

"Nothing. Just, I've never come that hard from my own hand before. That was something else."

Kip grinned. "Happy to help."

"I want to spend a solid week with you in the apartment when I get home."

Kip laughed, but something unpleasant pinged inside him.

In the apartment. Like always.

His anxiety must have shown on his face, because Scott's tone was concerned when he said, "Kip?"

Kip blinked and forced a smile. "I should get cleaned up."

"Oh, yeah. Me too. I'll call you tomorrow, all right?"

"Okay. Love you."

"Love you too."

Kip ended the Skype session and frowned at the ceiling.

Don't freak out. You just had fantastic video sex with your boyfriend. Nothing is bad.

Except he would trade a hundred video sex sessions for one walk in the park with his boyfriend.

Or to be able to bring his boyfriend home to meet his parents.

Or to, you know, tell people that he had a boyfriend.

He pushed himself off the bed and went to the bathroom to clean up.

Maybe when Scott got home, things would be different.

CHAPTER EIGHTEEN

Kip waited just inside the front door of Scott's apartment, his phone in his hand. Scott had been texting him constant updates all morning.

SCOTT:
Heading to the airport.

SCOTT:
Taking off soon.

SCOTT:
Just landed.

SCOTT:
In the car.

SCOTT:
Crossing the bridge. Traffic heavy.

SCOTT:
Almost there!

Kip looked at his phone, waiting for another update. Would there be one, or would Scott just walk through the door . . . ?

He rolled his eyes at himself. This was so silly. They were grown men and they'd only been apart for nine days.

Another text came. Just pulled up. See you in a minute!

Kip ran a hand through his hair, set his phone on the coffee table, and went to the door. He was in his jeans and a new dark green Henley shirt that he'd bought yesterday—an early birthday present to himself.

The door clicked and opened, and Kip only had a split second to take in Scott's smiling face before Scott was on him. Kip was pressed back against the wall, Scott kissing him hard and hungry while he held Kip's arms with his giant hands.

"Happy birthday," Scott said when they finally broke for air.

"Thanks. I missed you."

Scott smiled, and kissed him again.

Kip felt weak with happiness. It was so good to have Scott's huge, solid body surrounding him.

"You did it," he said when they broke apart. "You won all six games!"

"I was motivated." Scott cradled Kip's face in his hands, brushing his thumb over Kip's cheekbone. "You said something about a reward?"

"I never said reward. I said I'd give you whatever you need," Kip corrected him.

Scott kissed him one more time. "You always do. But today's not about me. It's about you!"

"Does that mean I get to unwrap you?"

"Yes, please."

"I'm *starving*!" Scott said. He was toweling himself off after the shower they had enjoyed together (and after the sex they had enjoyed together).

"Thank god," Kip said. "Me too." He frowned. "Um, you might not have much for groceries here."

"Oh. Yeah, well, I was thinking . . ."

"Delivery?"

"Actually," Scott said, "I was thinking we could maybe . . . go somewhere?"

Kip lit up. "Really?"

"Yeah, I mean . . . one lunch wouldn't be too suspicious, right?"

"Right," Kip said, a little less enthusiastic. What had he been expecting?

"So where do you want to go? My treat!"

Kip rolled his eyes but smiled. "I dunno. Doesn't have to be fancy. You might know better than I do where you wouldn't be bothered."

Scott seemed to think about it.

"Get dressed," he said. "We're going out!"

The March weather was cold and damp and shitty, but Kip was so happy to be out of the apartment with Scott. They weren't holding hands or doing anything else that would suggest that they were a couple, but just being out in the world with him felt surreal and wonderful.

Scott led them to a diner a few blocks from his apartment. They sat in a booth, grinning at each other over their menus.

"What are you getting?" Scott asked.

"It's my birthday," Kip said. "I'm getting a damn patty melt!"

"Good man."

"And a milkshake."

"That sounds amazing. What flavor?"

"Vanilla. Why mess with perfection?"

"Yup," Scott said, closing his menu. "I'm getting the exact same thing."

They ordered, and then Scott said, "You know . . . I was thinking we could maybe go somewhere this summer."

Kip raised an eyebrow. "You were?"

"Yeah . . . Like, I told you I usually go away in summer, to places where I don't usually get recognized. We wouldn't have to worry so much," Scott said in a hushed voice, leaning in, "about people seeing us together."

"Right." Kip frowned at the table. "Yeah."

Scott started talking excitedly about some beach town in Spain or Italy he'd been to and didn't seem to notice that Kip was starting to spiral.

I don't want to hide our relationship anymore.

Is he even going to want me by the summer?

How long can I be in a relationship with someone in secret?

The server brought their food and Kip was grateful for the distraction.

"Man, it has been *way* too long since I've had a patty melt," Scott said. He was so cheerful.

"It's good," Kip said, forcing a smile. "Thank you."

There was no way Kip was going to let Scott take him on a luxurious vacation. Between the hockey tickets, the tuxedo, and the time spent in the penthouse, Kip had already accepted way too much from him. What could Kip possibly give him in return? An all-expenses-paid trip to some five-star incognito gay beach resort would only increase the debt Kip was keeping a running tally of.

I'd rather he just take me to a diner again. And we can split the bill.

"So where are you going tonight?" Scott asked, before taking a long pull from his vanilla shake.

"Oh, there's this pub, in the Village—the Kingfisher. I used to go there a lot, but I don't go out as much these days. When I do meet my friends, though, it's usually there."

"Is it, like . . . a *gay* bar?" Scott asked in a low voice.

Kip laughed a little. "Yeah. It's very much like a gay bar. But it's chill. It's just a pub with cute bartenders."

"You're meeting some friends there, you said?"

"Yeah, Elena. I asked Maria from work. And then some friends from college." He leaned in with a playful smile and whispered, "Some *gay* friends."

Scott rolled his eyes. "Fine. Make fun of me."

Kip laughed again and kicked Scott under the table. But he stopped laughing when he realized there was really nothing funny about Scott's closeted life. It was sad that he was nervous about going to a gay bar. That he had never gone out with a group of supportive friends, or enjoyed flirting with a cute server.

He decided to try something even though he knew it wouldn't work.

"I know all the reasons why you'll say no," he said, "but you should think about coming out with us tonight."

"Oh. No, I—"

"I know. But going to a gay bar doesn't mean you're gay. It's just a group of friends at a bar. It's no big deal. It's not like we're going to be grinding into each other on a dance floor or anything."

Scott seemed to consider it, but then shook his head. "Your friends would be wondering what I'm doing there. I mean, Elena knows, but . . ."

Kip deflated a little. Scott was right. Elena was one thing, but the others . . .

Scott would cause a commotion in the Kingfisher, even if everyone believed he was a straight guy hanging out with his gay friend. Even if no one knew who he was, he would attract a lot of attention. He kind of stood out.

"Well," Kip said, "if you change your mind, I'll text you the address of the bar."

Scott looked like he was about to say something, but they

were interrupted by two men who had approached their table, looking very excited.

"Hey! Scott Hunter!"

"Hello?" Scott asked.

"Holy shit! It's you, right?" One of the men held out his hand. Scott gave a small smile and shook it.

"I'm a huge fan," the man continued. "My opinion? You're taking us to the cup this year. All the way!"

"I share your opinion," Scott said, smiling politely at him.

The second man spoke. "Can we get a picture?"

"Sure," Scott said, standing up. "No problem." He gave Kip an apologetic glance, but Kip just waved his hand. He was actually enjoying this.

"Would you . . . ?" the second man said, handing Kip his phone.

"Oh, sure. Of course." Kip stood up so he could take their picture. Scott threw an arm around each of the men and they all smiled at Kip.

"Thanks, Scott!" the first man said. "You're first-class, man. Lookin' forward to seeing you hoist that cup for us. Enjoy your lunch, all right?"

"Thank you," Scott said.

The men left and Kip grinned at Scott. "That was nice."

"That was fine," Scott said. "Sometimes it's not so fine." His eyes darted around the restaurant. "We should probably get going soon. It always starts with one and ends with a mob."

They didn't talk on the way back to Scott's place. Scott's jaw was clenched the way it always was when he was worried about something, and Kip knew exactly what was bothering him.

He hates that people saw us together.

Kip shoved his hands in his jacket pockets, and walked quickly to keep up with Scott's long strides.

* * *

Scott was nervous. They were sitting on his couch, Kip stretched out at the opposite end with his feet in Scott's lap. He was replying to a birthday message from his sister. Scott waited until he was done.

"So, um," Scott started, "I, uh . . . I have a birthday present for you."

"Oh?" Kip said.

"Yeah." Scott pulled a slightly bent envelope from the back pocket of his jeans. He handed it to Kip, who sat up a bit and removed his feet from Scott's lap. He eyed the envelope suspiciously, glancing at Scott over his bent knees.

Scott watched him open the envelope, and readied the speech he had prepared. He could guess how Kip was going to react.

"Are you . . . *What?*" Kip said, visibly stunned. He had opened the little card and was holding the paper that had been tucked inside. "No. Scott. Come on."

"I'm not sure if I got the amount exactly right," Scott said calmly, "but I want to pay off your student loans."

"This is a check for fifty *thousand* dollars, Scott!"

"I know. I wrote it."

"No," Kip said again, shaking his head. "This is dumb. You can't just give me fifty thousand dollars for my birthday."

"I figured you would say that," Scott said, "but the thing is . . . I can. Easily. And you know it."

Kip was still staring at the check, dumbfounded. "It's too much," he said quietly. "*Way* too much."

"You mean your loan is less than that?"

"Well, yes. That too. But this is nuts!"

"You said you don't like your job. You said you want to move out of your parents' house. I want you to be able to do anything you want to do. So if that money can help you get started, I'm happy to give it to you. More than happy."

"Jesus," Kip mumbled.

"I don't want to make you uncomfortable," Scott said.

"Right. Um."

"You're uncomfortable."

"Yeah."

Scott sighed. He'd guessed it was going to go this way. "How about this? We'll go to the bank and I'll pay off your student loan. Forget the check if it's too much, but at least let me take care of your loan."

"That's kinda still too much, Scott."

"Please." Kip started to shake his head again, so Scott said, "Look, I know. I know how it feels to struggle for money, and then suddenly not have to do that anymore. But I make . . . I mean, my salary is public record. You probably know what it is. It's a whole lot of money. And then I have endorsement deals and all the rest. What I don't have—" Scott took Kip's hand "—or, what I *didn't* have, was anything worth spending it on. Or anyone to share it with."

Kip blinked at him.

"I give to charity," Scott continued. "I bought this apartment, and I travel a bit in the summers. Other than that, I just have a whole lot of money sitting in the bank. It would make me really happy to be able to help you with some of it."

Kip pulled his hand away and turned his eyes back at the check, his brow furrowed.

"No," he said finally. "Thank you, but no."

"Kip—"

"No. Look, I get what you're saying. I know it . . . I dunno, makes you happy to make me happy, or whatever. But . . . it . . ." He sighed. "I can't explain myself."

"It's not a big deal," Scott tried.

"It *is* a big deal, Scott! It's a *very* big deal! You can't just . . . change my whole life!"

"Why not?" Scott said softly. "You changed mine."

Kip looked dangerously close to crying, which was not at all what Scott wanted to happen.

"Hey," Scott said, placing a hand on Kip's shoulder. But Kip stood up and started pacing.

"I'm not—I'm not a *charity*. I've got a normal student loan to pay off—the same kind that millions of other people have. I've been managing just fine since I graduated. Maybe my job isn't impressive, and I live with my parents, but I have my fucking pride. And I was paying the loan off on my own every month before you just . . . just scribbled on a fucking piece of paper and shoved it in a birthday card and—"

"Hey!" Scott said, standing to meet him. He was getting angry now. He took a breath. "Look, I wasn't trying to insult you. It seems silly for me to have all this money and for you to have all these loans to pay off. It seems like a pretty obvious solution, right?"

"I can manage my own life, okay?"

"Okay," Scott said desperately. "Okay. Yeah. Fine. I'm sorry."

Kip rolled his eyes, but it seemed to be more at himself than at Scott. "Fuck, Scott. I know you're just trying to . . ."

"I only want you to be happy," Scott said quietly.

"I *am* happy," Kip said. "Maybe I'm not living my dream life, but who the fuck is?" Then he laughed roughly and gestured at Scott. "I mean, besides—"

"My life isn't perfect, Kip," Scott said tightly. "I thought you understood that."

Kip exhaled. "I'm sorry. I know. I'm being an asshole. I'm just touchy about this stuff."

Scott nodded, possibly a little frantically. He wanted to undo whatever was happening here. "It was too much. I get it now. I do. This relationship probably seems a little . . . unbalanced to you. But you give me *so much*, Kip. I love you. I love you and I know I rush into things, and I know I'm probably being way too intense about us, but please. Just know it's only because I care about you so much."

Kip seemed to consider this, then his face softened. "Okay."

"Yeah?"

"Yeah. But I'm tearing up this check."

"Deal," Scott said, relieved that the situation seemed to be defused.

"I'm sorry," Kip said. He slumped back onto the couch and buried his face in his hands. "That was a thoughtful and generous gift you were trying to give me. And believe me, a part of me *really* wants to say yes to it, but I can't."

Scott sat next to him and pulled him into his arms. "Let's just forget about it, all right? *I'm* sorry. I should have gotten you flowers or something."

Kip laughed against his shoulder. "It's always hard to decide: flowers, or fifty thousand dollars."

Scott laughed too, fully realizing now how ridiculous his gift had been. He really had no idea what he was doing.

"I want to try again," he said into Kip's hair. "Can I try again? I want to give you the perfect present."

"You don't need to."

"I want to. I love you, Kip. I'm sorry I'm so fucking bad at this."

Kip's gaze was soft and affectionate as he tilted his head and brought their lips together. The kiss was achingly slow and sweet, and Scott melted into it.

"I love you," he said, his lips brushing the light stubble on Kip's cheek.

"Love you too. So much. Fuck, I don't want to be mad at you. I missed you."

"I missed you too."

"I'll miss you tonight."

"I know. I'm sorry. And I'm so busy this week. I'm sorry about that too."

"What's on the schedule this week?" Kip asked, then started trailing kisses up Scott's neck.

"I've got a long practice tomorrow." Scott tilted his head back to give Kip better access. "And I've got a thing tomorrow afternoon."

"A thing?"

"Mm. *Sports Illustrated* interview."

"Oh."

"And on Wednesday I'm visiting kids at the hospital in the morning. And I'm playing that night. Thursday morning, we have a video meeting, and that afternoon I've got another thing . . ."

The kisses stopped.

"And what's *that* thing?"

"Oh. Um . . . just a photo shoot. New campaign for Gillette."

Kip leaned back to stare at him. "Seriously?"

"And then on Friday I play again and—"

"Then you're hosting *Saturday Night Live*?"

Scott laughed. "No! I turned that down. God, can you imagine?"

"No . . ."

Scott looked at him seriously. "You know that stuff is all just . . . None of it's important. It all seems glamorous, but all I really care about is hockey and the time I spend with you."

"The world loves you," Kip said, brushing a thumb over Scott's lips. "I've gotta share you."

"Just a little," Scott said. "They only get tiny pieces." He nipped Kip's thumb and flicked his tongue against it.

"Sucks to be them," Kip drawled.

CHAPTER NINETEEN

"I'm *so* sorry about the job," Shawn said as soon as he joined the table. "If you want, I'll never go to that museum again."

Kip laughed. "It's fine. I was way underqualified. Like I *said*."

"You aren't and it's *their* loss," Shawn said.

"Exactly," Elena said, raising her pint glass.

The bar was crowded for a Monday night. Kip looked around the table at his friends: Elena, Shawn, and Maria, plus Jimmy and Chuck, who had taken vacation time to come down to New York for this. It was the first time any of them had met Maria, besides Elena. Kip didn't hang out with her much outside of work, which was too bad. But she was here now, and Kip was surrounded by a wonderful group of people he was lucky to have in his life.

He just wished Scott could be there.

He tried not to dwell on that. It was not like any of his friends had partners with them. None of his friends had steady partners at all, that he knew of.

"Now that everyone is here," said Chuck in his booming, happy voice, "I propose a toast. To Kip! A guy you want to hate because he's so handsome, but you can't because he's so goddamn charming."

"To Kip!" everyone said.

"Yay! To me!" Kip cheered, raising his glass.

Their server was the same one who had flirted with Kip the last time he had been there with Shawn—Kyle. He was still very cute and still *very* flirty with Kip, who couldn't help but flirt back a little.

"Have you hit that yet?" Shawn asked after Kyle left to fetch them another round.

"Nah," Kip said.

"That's tragic," said Jimmy. "I will if you don't."

Chuck laughed. "As if, Jim. He doesn't even *see* you through the glow around Grady."

"Kip," Maria said, "you didn't tell me that *all* of your cute dude friends are gay. What is even the point of me being here?"

"I *did* tell you and, if you want, later we can go to Olive Garden or wherever straight people go."

She flicked an olive at him from the nachos they were all sharing.

They all drank and talked animatedly for a while. Kip began to feel pleasantly warm and sloppy, laughing easily and teasing his friends.

"All right," Chuck said, placing his hands on the table for emphasis, "the next round is gonna be bought by whoever has gone the longest without sex."

"That's not right," Elena said. "It should be the person who had it the most recently."

"Damn, Elena," Kip said, "you *really* want to buy the next round, huh?"

"I'm not sure it would be me," she said, looking at him pointedly. Kip shut up.

"Nope, my rules," Chuck said. "All right, spill it, everyone. Been two weeks for me."

"What counts as sex?" Jimmy asked.

"Getting off with the assistance of another person," Chuck said, with authority.

"Oh. Like three days, then," Jimmy said.

"Wait," Chuck said, "was it that accountant who—"

Jimmy nodded.

"Nice. All right, who can beat two weeks?"

Elena shook her head. "Last night."

"Sa-ame," Shawn singsonged.

Maria threw her head back and moaned. "Fuuuuuck!" she said. "A month. Over a month. Ugh."

"Uh-oh," Chuck said. "How about you, birthday boy?"

"Um . . ." Kip said. *A couple of hours . . .*

He looked at Elena for help. She just raised an interested eyebrow.

"Been, like, two months or something," he said finally. Elena was the only one who knew that it was a lie.

"Aw, shit, sorry, Grady," Chuck said. "Looks like you're buying the round on your own birthday."

"S'okay," Kip said. Because it *was* okay. He was pretending to be sex-starved when he was, in fact, in the best relationship of his life. There were worse problems to have.

He got up to place the order. He wobbled a little as he made his way to the bar. Kyle was there, cute as all hell in a tight white T-shirt.

"My favorite customer," Kyle drawled. "What can I do for you?"

Kip smirked and rested an arm on the bar. "Buying a round for the table."

"Is that everything?" Kyle asked, leaning in to meet him.

This was the point where Kip would normally say something like "For now," or be more direct and tell him to find him when his shift ended. But . . .

"Yeah," Kip said, backing away a bit. "That's all."

Kyle looked surprised, but quickly schooled his features. "Whatever you say," he said, still smiling and raking his eyes over Kip's body.

Kip went back to the table. It was nice to know that he still had it, even if "it" was reserved for a certain superstar athlete.

They were all quite drunk by the end of the evening. As they waited outside for cabs, Maria hugged Kip with her whole body. "Thanks for inviting me, Kip. I like you. Your friends are cool. You're cool."

"Thanks for coming," Kip said into her hair. "We should hang out more."

"Yes! Yes, for sure! Kip . . . Yes." She pointed at him as she walked backward toward her waiting taxi.

Jimmy, Chuck, and Shawn piled onto Kip in a group hug.

"Thanks, guys," Kip said. "Love you assholes, you know that?"

"We love you too, Kip," Shawn said. The three of them got into a cab together, and Kip was left with Elena.

"He's on his way." She was always eerily poised and coherent, even when she was drunk.

"Huh?"

"Scott. I texted him. He's coming to take you home."

"What? Why? How do you have his number?"

Elena stared at him like he was very stupid.

"You're scary, you know that?" Kip said.

"Good thing I'm on your side."

"It is. You are. I love you, Elena." He hugged her. She resisted at first, but finally accepted it.

"You didn't have to text him," Kip said.

"I did. You're drunk and I'm meeting someone soon." She was typing on her phone as she talked.

"Another famous actor?" Kip grinned.

"Just a guy from my gym," Elena said, "who is also a backup dancer for Rihanna."

"Get it, girl!" Kip said, and raised his hand for a high five. Elena ignored him.

"Looks like your ride is here." She nodded at a very nice SUV that had pulled up.

"Thanks, Elena. You're the best!" he said, meaning it completely.

He opened the back door of the SUV and was surprised to see that Scott wasn't there.

"Um, up here," Scott's voice said. Kip turned and saw Scott sitting behind the wheel.

He closed the back door and instead got into the passenger seat. He grinned sloppily at Scott. "Didn't think you knew howta drive," he slurred.

"I can drive," Scott said. "Man, you're a mess."

"'M fine. You have your own car?"

Scott laughed. "Yes. I don't use it very often, but I own this one. It's, um, easier, to use a service. Not having to worry about parking and stuff."

"Mm," Kip said sleepily. Parking or car ownership was not a thing he had ever had to worry about.

They drove in silence for a minute, and then Scott said, "Did you have fun?"

"Yeah. Yeah. My friends are awesome."

"Good. Sorry I couldn't be there."

"S'okay."

"No, I . . ." He sighed. "Never mind. We can talk about it when you're not . . ."

"Talk about what?"

"Nothing."

Kip could see the way Scott's jaw tightened, even through his hazy vision. "I love you," he said.

Scott relaxed a little. "I love you too. Even when you're shit-faced."

"Not shitfaced. Just a little tipsy."

"Mm."

"Thank you," Kip said, concentrating hard at making his words as clear as possible, "for picking me up. Didn't have to—"

"Of course," Scott said. "I was glad Elena texted me. Not sure how she got my number—"

Kip waved a hand. "Fuck knows. She finds out everything."

"Well, I'm glad she texted me. Made me feel . . . like what we have . . ."

Kip was losing the thread.

Scott stopped at a red light and looked at him. "I know it sucks keeping things secret. It sucks for me too. Tonight was really hard for me."

"Scott . . ."

The light turned green.

"Anyway," Scott said, turning his attention back to the road, "it was nice to get that text from Elena. Made it all seem more real."

Kip placed a hand on Scott's thigh. "It's real."

Scott's lips quirked up. "Yeah," he said. "Now let's get you to bed."

"Good morning," a blurry Scott-shaped blob chirped. "Glad to see you're alive."

Kip blinked and rubbed his eyes. He was parched.

"Here," blurry Scott said, and handed him a glass of water. Kip gulped it down.

"Thanks," he said, handing the glass back.

"How are you feeling?"

"Wonderful," Kip rasped. He flopped back onto the pillow.

"You were cute last night," Scott said. "Real cuddly. Until you fell asleep on me."

"Sorry," Kip said.

"Don't be. I'm glad you had fun." Scott ran his fingers through Kip's hair, and Kip closed his eyes and sighed happily.

"Do I smell bacon?" he murmured.

"Yes! I made French toast and bacon."

"Oh my god. You are the best."

"It's ready whenever you are. Coffee too. I have to leave pretty soon."

Kip sat up. "Right! Sorry, I forgot about your practice. Okay. I'm just gonna take a real quick shower."

He stood under the shower just long enough to shampoo his hair once and run soap over his body. He felt a lot better when he got out.

He walked into the kitchen in sweatpants and a T-shirt and wet hair. Scott handed him a mug of coffee, and Kip kissed him.

"Seriously," Kip said. "Best boyfriend ever."

They sat at the kitchen counter and ate (incredible) French toast, and he told Scott a bit about his evening. "I remember," he said, "in the car last night. You said you had a rough time?"

"Oh." Scott looked at his plate and blushed. "It's nothing. I was in a weird mood last night. Don't worry about it."

"No, come on. Tell me."

Scott put his fork down. "I think maybe it was the first time I really felt . . . I mean, the gala was tough, but you going out with your friends for your birthday . . ."

Kip reached over and put a hand on his forearm.

"I should have been there," Scott said. "That's what was bothering me all night. I wish I could just . . ." He sighed. "It doesn't matter. No point in crying over things I can't have. Should just be thankful for what I do have."

Kip was very close to asking Scott if he was *sure* he couldn't have those things. If it would be so bad if he publicly came out. But he'd promised himself he wouldn't push that issue. Scott understood the stakes far better than Kip.

Instead, he said, "You need to be ready."

Scott's face was miserable. "I *want* to be ready."

"You will be. Soon," Kip said, squeezing his arm.

Scott nodded and gave him a tight smile. "Sorry. Like I said, it was just a weird, lonely night. Imagination started running a little wild."

"I've been there. I understand."

Kip kissed him, and Scott deepened it immediately, placing a hand on his face and sliding off his stool so he could stand over him. Kip's neck strained up to meet him as Scott explored his mouth with his tongue.

"You're good at that," Kip breathed when they broke apart.

"Must be all those years of practice," Scott said dryly.

"Stop it." Kip hit him lightly in the chest. "When do you need to leave?"

Scott looked at his watch. "Now, pretty much. Car is gonna be here in a couple of minutes."

"Nuts," Kip said. "I'm working until two today. You're busy this afternoon, right?"

"Yeah. *Sports Illustrated*."

"Right."

"And I'm busy the next few afternoons too."

"Well . . . we'll figure it out. Do you want me to stay here tonight?"

"I do," Scott said. "Can you?"

"I'll make you dinner."

"Oh yeah? I might be a little late."

"That's all right," Kip said, grinning up at him. "Good luck with your interview."

"Thanks. I kinda hate doing them."

"There gonna be a photo shoot?"

"Yeah. Not today, but yeah. Soon. It's the cover story."

"Well, now!"

Scott grimaced. "Yeah."

He threw a leather jacket on and kissed Kip by the door. "Oh! I thought of something! For your birthday present," he said excitedly. "I was thinking that maybe on Saturday we could go to the Met together?"

"The Met? Like . . . the museum?"

"Yeah," Scott said. "I thought you might like that?"

Holy shit. "I would *love* that."

Had Scott figured out the thing that Kip hadn't been able to bring himself to say: that all Kip had wanted for his birthday was to go somewhere he loved with his boyfriend?

"Okay then," Scott said, smiling. "It's a date."

"Really?"

"I mean, obviously we will need to be . . . discreet."

"Oh. Yeah. No, I know." Kip deflated a bit.

"I'll take you back here after and make it up to you, all right?"

Kip nodded, and tried to keep his face cheerful when he said, "Sounds great." He kissed him. "Go be a superstar. I'll be here when you get home."

CHAPTER TWENTY

"So who's this guy?" Scott asked. "What's his story?"

"I don't know!" Kip laughed. "I don't know everything!" He leaned in to read the museum's description of the ornate set of silver armor. "Italian. Sixteenth century. Just a guy. A knight."

"Just a random knight, huh? Pretty small knight."

"Everyone was small back then. I wonder if he was wearing this when he died."

"Geez, can you imagine how long it must have taken to make this thing? And they had whole armies of these guys?"

"They probably reused the armor. High job turnover."

Scott laughed at Kip's dark joke. Scott was in incognito mode: a Yankees hat pulled as low as possible without covering his eyes, a basic charcoal zip-up hoodie, and jeans. Kip wasn't so sure his disguise was going to work; he was still the hottest man in any room. He was going to attract attention no matter what.

Scott's shoulders were hunched, and he kept shoving his hands into the pockets of his sweater, as if to stop himself from reaching for Kip.

"My dad used to bring me here, when I was a kid," Kip said. "He taught high school history and English."

"So you got it from him?"

"Definitely," Kip said. "My sister, Megan, was more into novels, but I was always interested in history."

"What do you like about it?"

Kip wasn't sure how to answer a question that enormous. "It's . . . I mean, it's one long story. One *really* long story. And there have been millions of people over thousands of years who have helped to tell it. To record their own little piece of it, or to try to fill the gaps or make corrections to the parts that came before them. Like, some people try to record their story in a way that makes them look better—or that makes someone else look worse. But then historians work to fix that. And that's what I want to do—work to make sure the right stories are being told."

"Wow," Scott said. "That's cool. I like that."

Kip shrugged, a little embarrassed by his weird ramblings. "I just find it interesting."

"So sixteenth-century Italian knights aren't your area of expertise?" Scott asked.

Kip shook his head and smiled. "Not really, no. I'm more interested in peasants. But soldiers definitely interest me."

"Tell me," Scott said. "I want to hear about what interests you."

"Oh. Mostly I'm just interested in people. Not so much the big names in the history books, but how people lived during different periods. In different places. Who the soldiers were in the wars. Who the workers were. That sort of thing. Marginalized groups, especially. People who haven't had their history told properly."

Scott nodded thoughtfully. "Like gay people?" he guessed.

"Sure, yeah. For one. I wrote my undergrad thesis on marginalized groups being drafted into wars." Kip examined the detailing on a sixteenth-century glaive, and waited for Scott to change the subject.

After a minute, Scott surprised Kip by asking, "Do you have a copy of it somewhere? I'd like to read it."

Kip blinked at him. "You want to read my thesis?"

"Of course. If you wrote it, I want to read it."

God, that was sweet. Kip really wanted to hug him. Would Scott be angry if he hugged him? "It's, like, ninety pages long," he said, instead of lunging for his big, adorable boyfriend. "And probably boring as hell."

"I can read ninety pages," Scott said, smirking. "I'm an athlete, not a moron."

Kip rolled his eyes. "I know you're not dumb, Scott."

Scott smiled, and then his eyes darted around the room for the millionth time. He seemed to be forcing himself to have a good time, but was obviously uncomfortable. It was bumming Kip out.

He put a hand on Scott's arm, then snatched it away when Scott flinched.

Kip did his best not to be annoyed. He wanted to tell Scott to relax, but instead he turned and led him to another suit of armor.

"Hey, have you seen this before? This was always one of my favorite things here. This was worn by Henry VIII."

"I've heard of that guy!"

"See? Not dumb at all!"

Scott frowned at the golden armor. "I thought he was fat. Wasn't he, like, a big fat guy with a beard? This suit looks really small."

"This was his armor when he was a young man," Kip said. "Over here . . ." He gestured for Scott to follow him. "We see another one of his suits, which he wore twenty or so years later. Big difference."

"I guess he spent those twenty years eating."

"And fucking. And killing his wives."

"Well, I was on board until that last part."

Kip laughed. Scott beamed at him. "You should work here," he said. "You'd be great at it!"

"Yeah. That'd be awesome," Kip mumbled. He had never bothered to tell Scott about the fruitless job interview at the other museum. No reason to make himself seem even less impressive.

"What do you need to work somewhere like this? You have a history degree already."

"Oh, I don't know. A master's degree at least, probably. Depends on the job."

"And you don't want to do your master's?"

"I don't know," Kip said, pretending to be interested in a fifteenth-century gauntlet. "I mean, yes. I would like to. I just can't—" He stopped himself.

"Afford it?" Scott finished for him.

"Don't start," Kip warned.

"I'm not! But if money is the only thing holding you back—"

"It's not. For one thing, I would have to actually be accepted somewhere."

"Have you applied?"

Kip couldn't think of a reason to lie. "I sent in a few applications a couple of weeks ago."

Scott's eyes went wide with surprise, but he smiled. "That's great!" Then his face fell a bit. "Um . . . whereabouts?"

"Oh, just around here," Kip said quickly. He dropped his voice and smiled. "You thought I was gonna leave you?"

Scott looked at him seriously. "I would miss you like hell if you went away for school, but I would understand."

Kip *really* wanted to kiss him, or at least squeeze his hand. This sucked.

"Thanks," he said. "But I'm happier staying here. And besides, I might not get into any of them anyway."

"You will."

Things took a turn later when they were in the European sculpture gallery. In the bright lighting, and the wide-open spaces, people started to notice the celebrity in their midst. Suddenly the museum patrons seemed a lot less interested in the statues of Greek gods and began snapping covert photos of the modern-day Adonis who walked among them.

Kip leaned in close to Scott and said, "Those guys are—"

"I know," Scott said tightly. "I see them."

It wasn't long before two young women approached them and asked if they could take a selfie with Scott. Kip could tell that he wanted to politely decline, but instead he forced a grin and said, "Sure!"

Kip could hear the mutterings bouncing around the quiet, marble atrium. "Did you see Scott Hunter over there?" "Is that really Scott Hunter?" "Who is that with him, do you think?"

More people approached Scott and had their picture taken with him. Scott signed a few museum guides, which seemed like an absurd request to Kip.

After a family of four took photos with him, Scott turned to Kip and said, firmly, "We should go. Sorry, but this is only going to get worse."

They left quickly. They had planned on getting lunch nearby, but Scott was already calling his car service as they walked through the lobby of the museum.

"No lunch then, I guess," Kip said, keeping his voice as cool as possible.

"Nope." Scott's tone was less cool, and his posture was tense and angry. Kip wanted to put a hand on him to soothe him, but he didn't dare.

Back to the apartment. To hide.

Well, it had been a nice couple of hours of pretending he was in a normal relationship.

By that evening, the Scott Hunter fan accounts were full of cell phone photos—most of them taken without permission—of Scott and Kip at the museum. There were even a couple of celebrity gossip sites that were posting them. Kip only knew about them because, at just after eight o'clock that night, he received a text from Shawn.

SHAWN:
Kip! WTF is this you???!!!!!!!!

It was a picture of Scott gazing (a little too lovingly) at Kip as Kip stared up at a statue of Perseus. The scene definitely looked romantic, and the statue's marble penis hovering between their faces didn't help tone things down.

Most people wouldn't notice any of that, right?

KIP:
Yes.

SHAWN:
You want to tell me why you're on a date with Scott Hunter?

KIP:
It wasn't a date!

A total lie.

SHAWN:
Explain yourself.

KIP:

We met at work. We're friends. It's nothing.

Shawn sent back a gif of a *RuPaul's Drag Race* contestant making a "bitch, please" face.

KIP:

It's nothing! I'm serious! As if Scott Hunter would want to date me. Come on!

SHAWN:

Hmmm . . .

KIP:

Does he seem gay to you? Even a little?

He hated every word he was typing. He didn't want to lie to his friends.

SHAWN:

Hmmm . . .

KIP:

It's nothing.

SHAWN:

Well, next time you and your straight friend Scott are doing "nothing," you should invite me. And maybe go to the beach or something. Or a pool. Or a bathhouse.

Kip rolled his eyes and then sent the eye-roll emoji.

SHAWN:

He looks like he wants to eat you. That's all I'm saying.

KIP:

He does not.

(Even though he completely did.)

He decided not to tell Scott about the photos being online. Scott didn't even have any official social media accounts. There was a good chance he would never find out about these.

Overall, they weren't a big deal. All of the focus was on Scott Hunter being spotted in the wild. No one even mentioned Kip except to label him an "unknown friend."

No reason to tell Scott. It would only stress him out.

At nine-thirty that night, Scott said, "Are there pictures of us online? From the museum?"

"Um . . . I don't know," Kip lied. "Why?"

"Carter just texted me one."

Fuck. Kip pulled out his phone and made a show of opening Twitter, as if he hadn't checked it all day.

"Oh. Yeah, there are a few. Nothing . . . I mean, they're mostly pretty blurry. I don't know why people are even bothering to post them."

He waited for Scott's reply, and hoped Scott didn't notice how flushed he was. He had already lied to Shawn about these dumb photos; now he was lying to Scott about them. In truth, Kip just wanted to look at them, and be a little proud of them. He had never seen a picture of the two of them together before.

"Why was Carter sending you one of them?"

"Just . . . making fun of me, or whatever. He knows I hate this kind of attention."

"So he doesn't think—"

"I don't know! Fuck!" Scott threw his phone down on the couch and started pacing. "We shouldn't have gone! It was stupid. I just wanted . . . Fuck. What was I thinking?"

"Hey," Kip said, trying to sound soothing. "It's not a big deal. It's nothing. It's not like we're making out in the pictures."

"What if we *were*? I mean, not making out. But what if I touched you in some obvious way by accident? Or what if I . . . looked at you the way I know I always do?"

Kip hoped to god that Scott never saw the photo that Shawn had sent him.

"It's too fucking hard to be careful," Scott said. "I should never have . . ."

"Right," Kip said tersely.

It was fucking ridiculous. Their "date" couldn't have been more chaste, and here Scott was having a meltdown over the fact that they had been spotted standing near each other in a public place.

For the first time, Kip seriously considered leaving to go home for the night. He was filled with so much more than irritation with Scott. His usual fear that there was no way this was going to work between them in the long term was overtaking him.

He loved Scott so much, and he would do almost anything to stay with him. But he couldn't lie about who he was. And he didn't want to lie about who Scott was to him.

"I think . . . I'm gonna head home, all right?"

"What?" Scott seemed completely caught off guard by this. "Why?"

"I just . . ." Kip chewed his lip. He didn't want to get in a fight about any of this, but if he stayed, they *would* fight because Kip couldn't pretend he wasn't upset. "I've got stuff to do at home."

It sounded like the lie it was.

"Please don't go," Scott said.

Kip was going to insist that he needed to leave, but then Scott said, "I'm sorry."

Kip sighed. "You don't have to apologize, Scott."

"Well . . . I feel like I do, all right? And I wish I could promise things will be better, but the truth is . . ." He scrubbed a hand over his face and swore under his breath. "I'm trying. I swear, I'm trying. It probably doesn't seem like it, but every tiny step we take is a huge leap for me."

"I know," Kip said. He did know. Scott even attempting a public outing with him had been a big deal. They had only been dating a few *weeks*; how much could Kip really ask of him?

"Things are going to get more hectic for me when the playoffs start," Scott said. "I just want to know that we're okay."

Kip nodded. "We're okay."

"Please stay," Scott said. "I love you so much, Kip. I need you. Please be patient with me."

And how could Kip resist that?

"I'll stay."

CHAPTER TWENTY-ONE

The crowd was deafening, but Kip still managed to hear Elena when she leaned over and said into his ear, "I think *someone* is going to have great sex tonight."

Kip blushed and smiled even wider than he had been already. The Admirals had just won their fourth game in a row in the first round of the playoffs, sweeping the higher-ranked Pittsburgh and moving on to the next round. Kip watched Scott celebrate with his teammates on the ice. He was so proud of him.

Scott had had less and less time for him as the playoffs had grown closer. Though Kip was spending most nights at Scott's place, Scott was only home for about half of them. Kip had told his parents that he'd been crashing with friends in Manhattan. He'd needed to tell them *something*.

Their relationship was still new—just two months old, really. Kip reminded himself of that whenever he felt frustrated about it. He did wonder sometimes if Scott would ever be ready to come out. To let them be a real couple.

In private, though, when Scott *did* have time for him, things were wonderful.

The two teams lined up to shake each other's hands. Each

player on the Pittsburgh team seemed to take a moment to say something to Scott when they had their turn with him. He even received a few quick, manly hugs from some of them. It showed how well respected Scott was, even by his opponents.

Kip loved him. And he *was* expecting great sex tonight.

Kip was brushing his teeth in Scott's apartment when he received a text from him.

Going out with the guys. Will probably be pretty late.

Kip tried to not feel disappointed. The Admirals had just swept Pittsburgh out of the playoffs! Of course Scott would want to celebrate with his team.

He sat on the edge of Scott's bed and wrote back. Ok. Have fun.

He sighed. The truth was he'd been spending a lot of time alone lately. It wasn't like he didn't have friends; he just didn't have friends who knew about Scott, besides Elena. His *family* didn't know about Scott. His family that he technically *lived* with.

It was getting harder.

As nice as Scott's penthouse was, it was also empty and lonely. Plus, it didn't belong to Kip. He'd moved some clothing and basic toiletries in, and his laptop spent most of its time here, but he was still a guest.

Any sexy thrill of having a secret relationship that had once existed had definitely faded. The disastrous museum outing had probably killed the last of it. Kip had grown tired of being careful when he spoke to his friends and family. He was tired of the lies and half-truths. Mostly he was tired of avoiding everyone because he didn't *want* to lie. He had always been a very social guy. He didn't like this.

Scott seemed to be a lot more comfortable than Kip was with their weird relationship. He very obviously loved coming home to Kip, always greeting him with a warm smile and a kiss. Even the most basic domestic activities like preparing food or watching television appeared to make him very happy. They made Kip happy too, but he'd been feeling very . . . compartmentalized. He fit into Scott's life at home, and it was definitely important to Scott that Kip attend the games, but beyond that there was nothing. Kip wasn't telling his friends about Scott, and Scott sure as hell wasn't telling *his* friends about Kip.

Not that their relationship was *bad*. Kip was in love. Totally and completely in love. And he had no doubt that Scott loved him too. Plus, their sex life was still amazing. For a guy with limited prior experience, Scott sure found new ways to surprise Kip in bed.

It would be ridiculous for Kip to say that he felt like a *prisoner* in Scott's apartment. It wasn't that. It was just that their relationship really only existed within the walls of Scott's home. It was the most important thing in Kip's life, and he couldn't carry it beyond the front door. Now that the playoffs had started, Kip had given up hope that Scott might make their relationship public anytime soon. And when the playoffs ended, Scott's plan was to sneak off to Europe with him.

And then what? The next hockey season would start and Scott would get busy and maybe Kip would start school . . . or worse, maybe he'd just continue working his shitty job and continue pretending to not be dating anyone. Pretending he wasn't sharing his life with a man he loved. Letting his parents think that he was couch surfing in Manhattan, or sleeping with an endless parade of random men.

Kip threw his phone down on the mattress. He was being selfish. The city was celebrating the Admirals' victory tonight.

He should be nothing but proud, and *grateful* that Scott gave him whatever he could.

Scott loved him. He knew that. He just wished it didn't have to be so complicated.

Kip heard the unmistakable thud of Scott bumping into the dresser, followed by the sound of him swearing under his breath. Kip turned on the bedside lamp.

"Hey," he said, his voice scratchy.

"Hi," Scott whispered. "Sorry to wake you. Go back to sleep. Jus' gettin' undressed."

"You're a little drunk, huh?" Kip asked with a slight grin.

"A bit. Not really. Maybe."

Kip sat up, grinning wider now. "I've never seen you drunk before."

"Not that drunk," Scott muttered. "Just . . . had a good time."

"Mm."

Scott pulled off his shirt and pants, and went into the bathroom to brush his teeth. Kip watched the door, waiting for him.

"Go back to sleep," Scott said again when he returned. "You have work tomorrow."

It was true. Kip had to get up for work way too soon.

Scott got into bed and quickly kissed Kip on the cheek before turning off the light. Kip frowned into the darkness, wanting to say something but not knowing what. And the middle of night when your boyfriend is at least a little drunk and you have to go to work in a couple of hours probably wasn't the best time.

"Congratulations on the win," he said finally. "I'm really proud of you."

But Scott was already asleep.

* * *

It hadn't helped that a couple of weeks ago there had been an Admirals team dinner where wives and girlfriends were invited to attend. Part of Kip had wanted to argue that a private event like that, where Scott would be among the people he considered to be his family, could be a perfect opportunity to introduce him. Maybe coming out didn't need to be a big deal. Maybe Scott could just . . . show up with Kip. Let his teammates draw their own conclusions.

He didn't bring this up with Scott, and Scott never even hinted that he might bring Kip along. Instead, he'd only apologized when he told him about the dinner. He had told him he wished he could bring him, but that was it.

Kip had been a little low ever since.

A customer had left one of the free newspapers they give out in subway stations on a table at work. A photo of Scott, jubilant after one of the two goals he'd scored last night, filled the front page. When Kip glanced at it, he felt both guilty and emotional. He was an asshole. His boyfriend was a fucking *hero* and he was an ungrateful jerk who expected Scott to jeopardize everything he had worked for his whole life? For him?

He looked at Scott's exuberant face on the cover of the newspaper and was filled with the gut-wrenching truth that there was no way this thing with Scott would possibly last. How could it?

This was the exact headspace that Kip was in when Maria said, "So . . . I have to tell you something."

"Oh?"

"I put in my notice."

It took Kip a moment to register what she had said. "Shit. Really?"

"Yeah. Um, my friend got promoted to manager at one of the Starbucks in Midtown, and they were hiring . . ."

"Oh."

"I'll still have to get up at ass o'clock, but the pay is better and there are benefits, you know? Health insurance."

"Yeah. No, yeah. That's great. Good for you." His enthusiasm was beyond forced.

"Aw, Kip. I'm sorry. I should have given you a heads-up. I just didn't want to say anything until I knew for sure."

"No, it's fine. Don't be. It's fine! I'm happy for you. Really."

"Hey," she said brightly, "if they're ever hiring again, I'll put in a good word for you. If you want."

"Oh, sure. Yeah. Maybe. Thanks."

"I probably won't work there for too long," Maria said. "I've been thinking about . . . police academy."

"Seriously?"

"It's probably dumb . . ."

"No! Maria, you'd be great! And we could use more good cops, y'know?"

Kip worked the rest of his shift in a daze. He couldn't tell what was truly bothering him: that he would miss working with Maria, or that he resented her leaving while he was stuck here.

You could quit too, dummy.

When he went back to Scott's apartment after work, Scott wasn't there. He hadn't received any texts from him all day.

Resigned to endure another lonely evening, Kip dragged himself into the shower and came out feeling a little better. He wondered if Scott would be home for dinner.

It wasn't unusual for Scott to not keep in touch. Not lately, anyway. The playoffs and everything leading up to them had understandably consumed him. He had apologized to Kip in advance for how little time he'd be able to give him, which was ridiculous. It was the Stanley Cup *playoffs* and Scott was the biggest star in the league, for chrissakes. Adding to that was the fact that Scott, despite his many achievements, had never actually *won* the Stanley Cup.

Yeah, it was important that Kip be cool about this.

When Scott got home later that evening, he looked exhausted.

"Hey," Kip said, kissing him quickly. "What were you up to today?"

"Oh, just . . . ESPN asked me and a couple of the guys to record some promos for round two of the playoffs. Took longer than I thought it would."

"Ah."

"I'm gonna—" Scott gestured toward the bedroom. "Long day. And I've got an early morning tomorrow."

"Sure. Yeah." *My day sucked, thanks for asking.*

Scott disappeared into the bedroom, and Kip sank onto the sofa. He knew he was probably overreacting because he had been in a bad mood to begin with, but in that moment he felt like Scott's fucking *pet.*

And then he became angry with himself, because why the fuck *had* he been waiting for Scott to come home? Why was this his life now? He used to go to the Kingfisher all the time—at least once a week. And he went out to clubs. And dinner with friends. And lunch with friends. And brunch with friends. Now he just left work and went to Scott's apartment and waited for him to come home. And if Scott was away, he went to Scott's apartment and watched television alone until he fell asleep.

He loved Scott. Absolutely. But this could *not* be his life long-term. He was *twenty-six*!

For the past few weeks, Kip had been bracing himself for Scott's inevitable realization that he was too good for Kip. Or, at least, that Kip was not worth risking his whole career for. But maybe he shouldn't be waiting for that moment. Maybe *he* should initiate the conversation. Because the painful truth was that if Scott had no plans to change things, then Kip couldn't stay in this relationship.

Kip almost wanted to march into the bedroom right then

and just ask Scott, point-blank, "Are you ever going to come out? Am I worth it?" but the timing would be terrible. Scott was obviously drained.

And what was the answer Kip was expecting to hear? *Yes. Absolutely. I will come out publicly tomorrow. Let me get on the phone so I can call a press conference*?

So Kip didn't say anything. He just watched television for a while, then slipped into the bed next to Scott's sleeping body. He stared into the darkness for hours, worrying.

Scott wrapped black hockey tape around the blade of his stick using the exact same method he'd perfected when he was a teenager. It was two hours before game time in Boston.

"Hey," Carter said, testing the blade sharpness on his own skates with his thumb, "did you hear what your boyfriend was saying?"

Scott nearly dropped his stick. *"What?"*

"Rozanov. Mouthing off again."

"Oh." He relaxed, feeling stupid.

"Said he'll feel bad about taking away your first Stanley Cup victory."

He rolled his eyes. "All right."

"Said he'd be nice and give you one of *his* rings."

"Charitable."

"I don't know about you," Carter said, "but I'm looking forward to shutting him up."

Scott ripped the tape off the roll with his teeth. "Hell yes."

Besides wanting to beat Rozanov, round two was the point when the Admirals had been eliminated from the playoffs last year, so it was important to Scott that they make it to the third round.

Huff walked into the dressing room, eating an apple. He sat and pulled out his phone. "Who wants to see a cute picture of my kids?"

"Do we have a choice?" Carter asked.

"Nope! Check it out!" Huff passed his phone to Carter, who glanced at it and handed it over to Scott.

"Nice," Scott said, looking at the smiling faces of Huff's son and daughter, chocolate smeared all over their mouths. "They're getting so big!"

"I know. I miss so much," Huff sighed. "I feel like I have at least another season in me after this, but then I gotta think seriously about getting Laura that ranch she's always wanted." He smiled. "You can take the girl out of Alberta . . ."

"Well, let's get you another Stanley Cup ring first," Scott said. "Then you can think about retirement."

"How many will this be?" Carter asked. "Four?"

Huff waved a hand. "Who the hell can keep track?"

Carter chuckled. "Fuck you, old man."

Scott knew for a fact that Huff had already won four Stanley Cups with three different teams. None with New York. It was four more than either Carter or Scott.

Scott sat and pulled out his own phone. He brought up a couple of recent photos of Kip that he'd taken. It was probably a risk even having these on his phone, but he had to give himself *something*, for fuck's sake.

He let himself look at Kip's sexy grin for a minute, enjoying the warmth that flooded him every time he saw it. Then he pocketed the phone and went back to pretending that part of his life didn't exist.

CHAPTER TWENTY-TWO

Kip had expected Elena to attend the upcoming home games with him, but when he mentioned it to her, she texted back, Can't. I'm not in town.

KIP:
Where are you?

ELENA:
L.A.

Kip frowned and sent back a question mark.

ELENA:
Work. I'll explain when I get back.

This was not great news. Elena was literally the only person he could bring without having to answer a lot of questions about how he had two prime tickets to a sold-out game.

The Admirals had won the first game against Boston. Boston

had won the second. They would be playing the third game tomorrow night in New York.

Scott should be home soon.

Kip picked up the copy of *Sports Illustrated* from Scott's coffee table. The glamour shot of Scott stared back at him. Scott had been embarrassed about the cover, but he had seemed to warm to it a bit when he'd seen how much Kip liked it.

The cover had Scott, shirtless and wearing hockey pants, holding a hockey stick across the back of his shoulders and neck. He stared straight at the camera, cold and challenging and absurdly sexy. The dramatic lighting showed every groove of his muscular torso and arms.

The copy on the cover said *THE RETURN* in big, white letters. Kip had read the article several times. It mentioned that Scott was unmarried, and didn't have any surviving family. It was just a brief sentence or two, almost offhand, but it gave the reader the impression that Scott might be very lonely.

Kip wondered if the interviewer had asked Scott if he was seeing anyone. What would Scott have said? Just a simple "no"? Or would he have blushed a bit and fidgeted and mumbled "no comment"? Or would he have said that he *was* in a fulfilling relationship, but he had chosen to keep it private?

From this line of thought, Kip's imagination jumped to a possible future scenario where Scott came out publicly and their relationship became known. What would the articles about Scott look like then? Certainly his love life would take up a lot more of the page than a couple of sentences.

Kip closed the magazine. The kernel of dread that seemed to be living in his stomach lately began to grow.

Scott's whole life could be ruined because of him. Or he could finally be whole and happy. Or he could be whole and happy with someone else . . .

Kip scrubbed his hands over his face. He hated thinking these things.

Scott walked through the door about forty minutes later. He smiled tiredly at Kip, who went to him and kissed him. Scott's beard had filled in quite a bit.

"I watched the game last night," Kip said.

"I'd like to get that one back."

"You'll win the rest," Kip assured him.

"You're coming tomorrow night, right?"

"Yeah. Alone, though. Elena's in L.A."

"Oh. That's too bad," Scott said absently. He seemed distracted. Probably because he was an important person with actual problems that mattered. He didn't need Kip's insignificant worries piled on top of him.

"Rozanov bothering you?" Kip asked.

"Yeah," Scott sighed. "He's a real pain in the ass."

"You wanna take a bath and unload all your problems on me?"

Scott gave him a small, grateful smile. "Yeah. Okay."

Kip listened to Scott vent all evening. He kept his own problems to himself.

"It's getting quiet in here," Rozanov said, feigning confusion. "Why is it so quiet? There are so many people here! It should be loud, yes?"

"Shut up, Rozanov." Scott bent to take the face-off against him.

"It *was* loud earlier. But since we scored that fourth goal it has been quiet. Is weird, I think."

Scott gritted his teeth and made sure he won the fucking face-off.

Rozanov wasn't wrong. The energy had been sucked out

of Madison Square Garden. The hometown crowd was understandably unhappy with the 4–1 lead that Boston now had over the Admirals. It would be the second game in a row that Boston won in the series, unless by some miracle New York scored three goals in the next seven minutes.

Scott and Carter charged toward the net, Huff hanging back slightly. They executed the play they had perfected in practice: Scott passed to Carter, Carter immediately knocked it back to Huff, who took the shot and—

Stopped by the Boston goaltender.

"Sorry, Scott," Huff said. "Fuck."

"That was a cute move!" Rozanov chirped as he skated by Scott. "I fucking love old-timers hockey!"

He nudged Scott, which prompted Scott to shove him. *Hard.*

Rozanov stumbled backward, then moved like he was going to shove Scott right back. The referee, Hal Coleman, stepped in. "Come on, guys. Rozanov, stop being a dick. Hunter, stop listening to Rozanov."

"How many minutes would I get if I just killed him?" Scott grumbled as he watched Rozanov skate away.

"I'd have to give you at least ten," Hal said dryly. "Not worth it in the playoffs."

Scott skated to the bench.

"Good effort, Hunter," someone said, and others said similar things in agreement.

Scott sat down hard on the bench and resisted the urge to slam his stick against the boards. This game was a complete fucking embarrassment and it was infuriating.

He glanced across the ice to where Kip was sitting. He was easy to spot because he was next to one of the only empty seats in the building. He was sitting hunched forward, with his hands clasped in front of his mouth. Just one of thousands of anxious, disappointed people in the building tonight.

Tomorrow the team would review, they would practice, and they would regroup. In two nights they would make this crowd *roar*.

Kip walked out of the subway station near Elena's apartment and trudged through the chilly April drizzle. Elena was back from California and had invited Kip over to watch the fifth game of the New York vs. Boston series. He was looking forward to seeing her. He was looking forward to seeing *anyone*.

The Admirals had rallied and won the second home game against Boston, tying the series at two wins each. NHL playoff series were all best of seven, so the series would go to at least six games.

Scott had been very distant the past few days. He barely spoke, and didn't seem to be listening when Kip said anything to him. Besides the games, he'd had meetings and practices and gym sessions. He was focused on beating Boston, which Kip completely understood.

And that was why things were a little chilly between them. That was the only reason. He told himself that almost constantly.

Scott had left for Boston yesterday while Kip had been at work. He hadn't even really said goodbye.

Kip was glad Elena was back.

"Aw, you're all cold and wet," she said when she opened the door. "Come on in. I ordered pizza. I have beer."

"I love you."

She waited until the first intermission to drop a bomb on him. "I have some news," she said. "Equinox is opening up a West Coast headquarters."

"Oh yeah?"

"Yeah. And . . . they want me to manage the cybersecurity team there."

It took Kip a moment. "You're *moving*?" he asked.

"I'm afraid so."

"When? I mean . . . *What?* You're leaving?"

"Next month."

"Next *month*?"

She placed her hand over his. "Yes," she said. "I'm sorry to spring this on you like this."

"Fuck. That sucks. I mean, congratulations, but . . ."

"Thank you."

"No, really. I'm proud of you. Just . . . Damn."

"I know. I'll miss you too."

"That doesn't even begin to describe it," Kip said miserably.

"Aw, sweetie. You'll come visit. You and Scott both, okay?"

"Yeah . . ." Would that day ever happen, where he and Scott could travel together as a couple in North America? "Shit, I can't believe you're really leaving. It'll be like . . . losing my leg or something."

She squeezed his hand. "It's much worse than that," she said with a wry smile.

"Hey, what's up?" Scott asked. It sounded to Kip like he had caught Scott at a bad time. But he had waited until the morning after game five in Boston (which the Admirals had won) to call.

"Sorry. Are you . . . I can call later?"

"It's fine. What is it?"

Kip was a little taken aback. Scott never asked him why he was calling. They just . . . called each other.

"Just . . . had kind of a shitty day yesterday."

"Oh. Okay. What happened?"

"Elena is moving to California. She got a promotion and Equinox is opening a new division there."

"Good for her!"

"Yeah. It is. But . . . sucks for me."

"Right. Yeah."

"Yeah."

"Sorry," Scott said. "I guess I'm used to my friends moving. Being traded and stuff."

"Oh."

Their conversation was so stiff. Kip hated it.

"Is that it?" Scott asked.

"Is what it?"

"Elena moving. Is that the only reason your day sucked?"

Now Kip was getting angry. "It's a pretty good reason."

"I know . . . Just . . . I have to go. We're heading to the airport . . ."

"Sure. Yeah. Sorry."

"Don't be—" Scott sighed. "I'll talk to you later, all right?"

"Okay."

They ended the call and Kip walked miserably out of the break room at work. He immediately checked the fridges to see what needed to be restocked. He didn't feel like dealing with customers right now.

What the fuck was he even mad about? That his shitty life was changing? That the people around him were bettering themselves? It wasn't like he wanted everything to stay the same forever. He'd had his heart secretly set on that museum job until recently. Even now he was waiting to hear back from grad schools. He couldn't possibly be mad at his friends for moving on.

He wasn't mad. He was just frustrated and feeling sorry for himself. And mentally preparing himself to be rejected from the schools he'd applied to at the same time as his friends announced new, better jobs.

Maybe having to keep quiet about his relationship with Scott was making him long for some news that he *could* talk about.

Maybe if he didn't have to keep quiet about his relationship with Scott . . .

Fuck. At this rate there probably wouldn't *be* a relationship with Scott to keep quiet about.

When Scott got back to his apartment in Manhattan, Kip wasn't there.

Scott knew he wouldn't still be at work. He wondered if he was out somewhere, or if he just wasn't staying there anymore. He hadn't spoken to him since their tense phone call that morning.

He decided to text him. Hey. Just got home. You staying here tonight?

It took a few minutes to get a reply.

KIP:

No. I'm home tonight. Family stuff.

Kip hadn't mentioned any family stuff. Scott had the distinct impression that he was being blown off.

SCOTT:

Oh. Sorry to hear that.

He waited.

KIP:

Congrats on the win last night.

Scott relaxed a little. That was *something* at least.

Unless Kip was being sarcastic . . .

But that would be ridiculous. Right?

SCOTT:

Thanks.

He tried to think of something to add that wouldn't sound pushy or angry or desperate or paranoid or . . .

SCOTT:
Hope to see you soon.

Ugh.

KIP:
Ok.

Whoa. That wasn't good.

SCOTT:
Are you home now?

KIP:
Yes.

Scott chewed his thumb, trying to decide what to say next.

SCOTT:
Are you coming to the game tomorrow night?

KIP:
If you want me to.

SCOTT:
Of course I do! Are you mad at me?

There was a long pause, and then:

KIP:

No. I'll see you at the game.

Scott's brow furrowed. He had no idea how to deal with this. He was used to having the freedom to focus on his team and his game, on his own health and fitness, and his contract and business agreements. He had never focused on his own *happiness*. And having someone else's happiness be affected by him was just . . . terrifying. Probably a recipe for disaster.

He had no idea what was going on, or how to fix it. What he *did* know was that he really didn't need any distractions right now.

Kip hadn't been lying about the family stuff. His sister and her boyfriend were joining them for dinner, so he'd made sure he was there too.

The meal had been fine, with a lot of talk about the puppy Megan and Andrew were hoping to adopt. Kip had been worried that the conversation would be focused on him, and that he would have to lie to his family even more than he already had been. As a result, he asked way more questions about the puppy than he normally would.

It was after dinner when Megan cornered him. Andrew went into the kitchen to help with cleanup, and she grabbed Kip's arm and pulled him upstairs.

"So what's going on with you anyway, Kip?" she asked. "Mom says you're almost never here anymore. Are you seeing someone or something?"

Fuck.

"Nah," he said as smoothly as possible. "Just, you know, couch surfing mostly. Saves time commuting to work in the mornings."

"Hm," she said.

"What?"

"Are you happy, Kip?"

He shrugged. "Sure. I don't know."

"I worry about you."

Kip made a face. "Why? We barely even talk anymore. I'm fine."

"You're still my little brother. You can't be happy living here with Mom and Dad, sleeping on friends' couches, hooking up with random dudes and working that job you hate."

"Jesus, Meg. Anything else?"

"I'm sorry. I just want to see you happy, is all."

"I'm *fine*," he said again. He sighed, and added, "I applied to some grad schools, all right? Just waiting to hear back. Don't tell Mom and Dad."

"Awesome! That's great!"

"Good. Get off my back."

He liked Megan a lot. They had always gotten along well, even if they had drifted apart a bit these past few years. He wanted to tell her that he had actually been staying at his *boyfriend's* apartment. He wanted to tell her that he was in love for the first time. He imagined her face if he told her he was dating Scott Hunter.

At that moment, he didn't *feel* like he was dating Scott Hunter. Things had grown tense and distant between them lately, and Kip was sure he knew why.

At ten o'clock he got into bed. He had to get up extra early for work the next day, since he'd be commuting from Brooklyn again. His stomach clenched around the dread that sat like a lump inside him. He was so certain that his relationship with Scott was doomed that he felt compelled to just rip the bandage off quickly. Just end it now so he didn't need to suffer later.

And maybe, one day, he could wake up in his bedroom in his parents' house, drag himself to his shitty job, and fondly remember the brief time in his life that he'd lived the fantasy of being Scott Hunter's boyfriend.

CHAPTER TWENTY-THREE

"Good evening, Ilya," Scott said. He was standing opposite Rozanov at the face-off circle, ready for the first puck drop of the game.

"Don't worry, old man," Rozanov said with a grin, "I know you must be getting tired. I'll make sure you lose so you can get started on your summer vacation."

"My only summer plans involve a Stanley Cup parade."

They bent for the face-off, and Scott winked at him.

Scott won the face-off.

He had two good reasons to win this game. Obviously, he wanted to win the series and move on to the next round of the playoffs, but winning tonight would also give him a couple of days off here in New York. And he wanted to use some of that time to fix whatever the hell was going on between him and Kip.

He could see Kip sitting in his usual seat. That was comforting. Scott wasn't sure what seeing that seat empty would have done to him, psychologically. He was already struggling to stay focused.

He would win this game. He would talk to Kip. He would go on to the next round clearheaded. He would win that round, and the next round, and he would finally, *finally* lift that cup over his head.

When Scott got home after the game, Kip wasn't there. It was the second night in a row. Something was definitely wrong.

He sent Kip a text. Will I see you tonight?

The answer took a few minutes. No. Sorry. I'm just really tired.

Fuck.

I think you are mad at me, Scott wrote.

He watched the three little dots flicker on his screen for what seemed like an eternity. Then, Can we talk? Tomorrow?

Yes. Come over here as soon as you can tomorrow. Ok?

Ok.

Scott sat down hard on his bed. He felt sick. And a little angry. What the hell had he done to deserve this cold shoulder?

He guessed he would find out tomorrow.

Kip took a deep breath and opened Scott's apartment door. "Hello?" he called out.

Scott appeared immediately. He was dressed in cozy sweats. His beard was really full now, making him look rugged and gorgeous. Kip set the backpack that he had optimistically brought with him on the floor.

"Hi," Scott said shyly.

"Hi. Congratulations. That was a great game." Kip sounded as awkward as he felt.

"Thanks. I'm glad you were there."

Kip nodded, not sure what to do or say.

Scott stepped closer. "Can I kiss you?" he asked. "I feel like

I need to ask you now, and I don't know why that is, but . . . can I?"

Kip exhaled, trying to relax his nerves. "Yes. Of course."

Scott smiled and closed the distance between them. He held Kip's face for a moment, gazing at him with sad eyes, before he brushed his lips against Kip's. The beard tickled Kip's face, and he sighed and deepened the kiss. It felt so good.

When they broke apart, Scott said, "We should talk, I guess."

"Yeah. I think we should."

They went to the couch, and Kip sat and stared at his folded hands.

"I feel like I've done something wrong," Scott started. "Being with someone is new for me and I'm pretty sure I'm screwing it up. But I can't figure out exactly what I've done, so I was hoping you could tell me."

Kip turned quickly to face him. "You haven't done anything," he said honestly. "I can't even put my finger on why I've been so . . . upset. I just . . ."

"Please," Scott said. "Give me *something*."

"All right . . ." Kip said slowly. "I don't like lying to my friends and family, or hiding my relationship with you. This . . ." He gestured between them. "*Us.* It's the biggest thing in my life. It's . . . the *best* thing that's ever happened to me. And I have to keep it a secret."

"I know. And I've told you—"

Kip held up a hand. Scott stopped talking.

"This isn't how relationships are supposed to work. This is how . . . *affairs* work. Dirty secrets. I'm not ashamed of you. At all. And I'm not ashamed of *me*. I've never been ashamed of myself, and I've been out since I was eighteen."

Scott bit his lip. "I've been honest with you this whole time. I wanted to make sure you knew what you were getting into."

"I did. I do. But I also know this isn't how I want this relationship to be. I don't want to be your secret. But . . . I'm worried, that if I push you—if I pressure you to come out and be honest about us, or at least about *you*—that you'll realize I'm not worth the hassle."

Scott looked like Kip had gut-punched him. "God," he said in a tiny voice. "No, Kip. No, I would never think that!"

"Being with you has been amazing, but it's also . . . lonely. And . . ." Kip swallowed. He needed to get this next part out. "I don't know how much longer I can do this."

Scott looked at him pleadingly. "I know I'm being selfish, asking you to keep this secret. I'm so sorry for that. But I'm also protecting you. I don't think you realize how much your life would change if this got out."

"My life has *already* changed. And not only in a good way, Scott. I feel like I've been shoved back into the closet. It's not you being famous or whatever that's making this hard for me. I've never been with someone who is ashamed of who they are."

"I'm not *ashamed*!" Scott argued.

Kip folded his arms and gave him a pointed look.

"I'm not!" Scott said. "I don't think there's anything wrong with me. With being . . . gay. I definitely don't think there's anything wrong with being in love with you. But my life has very little to do with what *I* think. There's a lot of responsibility on my shoulders. I represent something important to a lot of people."

"And you can't do that and also be gay?"

"Not according to most of them, no."

"So show them that they're wrong!" Kip said it way too loudly. His voice bounced off the walls of Scott's condo.

He thought Scott would yell at him, but instead he seemed to deflate. "I just don't . . . Our time together has mostly been away from all of that. It's been . . . nice."

"An escape, you mean?"

"No! I've already told you that's not what—You're a *part* of my life. Not a distraction from it. Never, Kip. I promise."

"But I am *separate* from the rest of your life," Kip argued, "and worse than that, you're hiding who *you* are."

"I have to."

"Do you?" Kip demanded. "Are you *sure*? What's the worst that could happen?"

"I can't! Not now. The playoffs . . ."

Kip took a breath. "I'm not asking you to do anything right now, but you need to start to think seriously about coming out. Or at least not hiding. You don't have to make a grand statement."

Scott's posture stiffened. "Do you have any idea how huge the media circus would be if I came out? If people knew I was dating you?"

Kip shrugged. "So your plan is to keep this a secret forever?"

"No."

"Or until you realize you're way out of my league and move on?"

"Kip—"

"You just expect me to hide out in your apartment until you need me?"

"No!" Scott said. He was angry now. He stood up. "I can't believe you're even suggesting any of this! Have I treated you badly? Have I not shown you how much you mean to me?"

"I can't mean *that* much to you. You're obviously embarrassed to be with me."

Kip knew he should *not* have said this the moment the words left his lips. But instead of backing down or apologizing, he glared at Scott and crossed his arms, waiting.

"Is that really what you think?" Scott asked. His voice was

quiet, but there was rage and hurt in it. "That I'm *embarrassed* to be seen with you? You *know* that's not it."

"I don't know anything, Scott! I just *wait here*. In your *penthouse*." He swept a hand across the spacious living room for emphasis. "I hole up here alone and imagine what it would be like to be able to go on normal dates with you, or to, I don't know, tell my *parents* that I have a boyfriend!"

"Tell them!" Scott yelled. He threw up his hands. "Fuck, tell the whole world, Kip! I guess you know what's best!"

"I know this isn't who I am!"

"Do you know who *I* am? I don't get to just be Scott from Rochester, all right? I've been a fucking commodity since I was a teenager. I've been a *brand* for almost as long. I don't have the luxury of just being me. I can't make decisions about my life independently. People *depend* on me!"

"Right. Don't want your brand to suffer. Don't want to tarnish it with your gayness."

Scott snorted. "You have no fucking idea, Kip. None."

"I guess not," Kip said tightly.

"It's the *playoffs*. I don't know if you get how big a deal that is. I've got a team—a *city*—depending on me. It's *everything* to me, all right?"

The sting of tears finally hit Kip's eyes. He nodded and clenched his jaw. *Everything.*

"I'm gonna go," he managed to say.

Scott reached out a hand like he was going to stop him, but instead he dropped his arm, nodded, and said, "Fine."

Kip picked up his backpack and left.

CHAPTER TWENTY-FOUR

Kip was drunk.

Scott was in Detroit, and Kip was drunk.

He had watched one period of the Admirals away game before leaving his parents' house and taking the train to the Village. He'd thought about texting Shawn to see what he was up to, but he didn't actually want to talk to anyone anyway.

Now he was on one of the bar stools at the Kingfisher. Cute, wonderful, flirty Kyle had been setting pints in front of him all night.

It was late. Kip noticed, with some surprise, that there weren't many people left in the bar.

"Last call, sexy," Kyle drawled. His lips curved up into a suggestive little smile that had Kip mesmerized.

Kyle's hair was blond, like Scott's. His eyes were blue, but not like Scott's. Kyle's were a washed-out gray-blue. They were really nice. His bangs kept falling into them. Kip wanted to reach out and brush the hair away.

He was way too drunk.

"S'okay," he said, with a flirty smile of his own, "was gonna head out anyway."

"You got plans?" Kyle asked.

"I dunno. Home, I guess."

Kyle grinned and leaned forward with his elbows on the bar. His face was suddenly very close. "Which way you headed?"

"Brooklyn."

"Looks like we're going the same way, then. I could walk with you to the subway?"

And Kip should have stopped the whole thing right there. It had bad idea written all over it.

But, fuck, it felt good to flirt like this. To just have someone be so open and honest about who they were and what they wanted. Kip felt like his old self.

"I'll be done here in about twenty minutes. Then I'll make sure you get home safe, okay?"

Kip was ready to politely decline, but instead he heard himself say, "Okay."

Kyle smiled and slid a glass of water in front of him. "Drink this. I'll be with you shortly."

The water was cold and Kip hadn't even realized how much his body had been craving it. It was nice of Kyle to think to give it to him. Kyle seemed nice.

God, Kip wanted to feel *anything* other than the all-consuming despair that had gripped him since he'd walked out of Scott's apartment. He shouldn't have left. He should have stayed and talked it out with Scott. He knew that now.

But it was too late. Obviously, it was too late. By now Scott had for sure figured out that Kip was not worth the hassle.

At least there was Kyle. Kyle in his faded jeans and his tight V-neck T-shirt. Kyle with the floppy bangs and the winter eyes and the flirty smile. Kyle wouldn't judge Kip for completely fucking up the best thing that had ever happened to him—that *would* ever happen to him. Kyle was going to walk him to the subway station because he was nice, and helpful. And cute, but that part wasn't important.

Suddenly, Kyle had his jacket on. He wasn't behind the bar anymore. He was standing beside Kip's bar stool. "Come on, tipsy."

Kip slid off the stool and followed Kyle outside. They walked together down the block a bit, and Kip enjoyed the cool night air. Kyle didn't talk much, which was nice because Kip was sleepy and he didn't think he could carry on a conversation right now.

Kyle's hand curled around Kip's bicep as they walked. "Hello, muscles," he teased. "You have beautiful arms, you know. I've been admiring them."

"Oh?" Kip smiled sloppily. He *did* have nice arms, dammit, and he appreciated that someone had noticed.

"Mm. And a gorgeous smile. Look at those dimples!"

Kip grinned wider, showing off the dimples a little. Compliments were awesome.

Kyle stopped walking. "I'd really like to kiss you," he said. "Can I?"

Oh.

No.

"Um . . ."

Kyle's brow furrowed. "Is that not what you want? I thought we were—"

Shit.

Kyle's face was so close, and Kip's eyes landed involuntarily on his lips. This was bad, wasn't it? Kip was with *Scott*. *Was* he with Scott?

Kyle must have taken whatever was happening on Kip's face as an invitation, because he leaned in and pressed their lips together. And for a second, Kip was too stunned, too confused, too *drunk* to do anything but kiss him back.

Kyle was a good kisser.

But *holy shit, no!*

Kip shoved him away, and stumbled forward.

"Hey, what the fuck?" Kyle said, catching himself before almost landing on his ass.

"Fuck," Kip mumbled. "This was . . . I can't do this. I wasn't looking for—I'm sorry."

"Are you all right?"

"Yes! Just . . . I need to go. Where's the—Fuck. Where's the subway?"

"That way. Do you want me to—?"

But Kip had already taken off at a run.

"You all right, man?"

Scott turned his head to be met with a concerned-looking Carter. "Yeah. Fine. Why?"

"You look a long way from fine, Scotty."

Scott faced the front of the bus. His team was en route from the hotel to the arena in Detroit to begin the next round of the playoffs, and now was *not* the time to think about his personal problems.

"I'm fine."

"You sure you're not getting sick or something? You look tired."

"Drop it," Scott snapped. In truth, he was exhausted. He hadn't slept well in days.

And now he was thinking about his personal problems. *Dammit, Carter.*

He still wasn't sure what the hell had gone wrong—if he was mad at Kip, or at himself, or at no one. He was thoroughly miserable. He felt like he was in actual physical pain, but not like a bruise or an injury; he could endure *those*. This was searing every part of him at once. He wanted to scream, or cry, or punch something. Or just hide where no one could see him.

Unfortunately, he had a team to lead to victory.

Goddammit, Kip.

Had Kip been unfair? Had he been wrong?

Definitely, about some things. Like, how Scott was *ever* going to think that Kip wasn't worth it? If someone asked Scott what he'd be willing to give up for Kip, Scott's knee-jerk reaction would be *everything*.

But when he thought about it, that wasn't really true. And when he thought about it some more, he realized that no one *was* asking him to give up everything.

Besides, Kip had given up a lot. He had distanced himself from his friends, from his family. He had adjusted his life to accommodate Scott. What had Scott adjusted?

Nothing. He had just been trying to tuck Kip wherever he would fit into his ridiculous, high-profile life.

He didn't think he had been unreasonable, asking Kip to be patient with him while he figured out a plan. There was no way Kip should expect him to just announce his sexuality to the world. They had only been dating a few *months*.

But a few months or not, Scott was in love. Before that first glorious kiss, he had resigned himself to a life without romance. He had never expected any of this to happen. It had flipped his whole world upside down. And now he loved Kip so much that he could barely remember the lonely years before. He knew, in only a few short weeks, that he wanted to share the rest of his life with Kip. It was staggering.

He'd wanted to, but now Kip was gone. And Scott had no idea how to get him back because he had no experience with this sort of thing. And maybe it wasn't fair to Kip to go after him. What could Scott promise him that would be different? He was in the middle of the damn playoffs; there was no way he was going to come out before they were over. And after that . . .

He really didn't know. When he tried to imagine coming out, it filled him with dread. For one thing, if he did that he would always be "the gay hockey player." Even if his teammates, and the fans, and the press, and the sponsors accepted him, his achievements on the ice would always take a back seat to his sexuality.

Scott was as private a person as he could possibly be, under the circumstances. He didn't have any social media accounts. He didn't go out to clubs or even restaurants all that often. He didn't try to be *seen* (much to his agent's chagrin). He didn't do probing personal interviews, and he generally didn't talk about himself much.

He had been able to hold on to some of his privacy because he had convinced the world that there was nothing interesting about him. He was good at hockey, he tried to be a good person, and that was it.

Being gay would, without a doubt, be something the world would find interesting.

He couldn't think about any of this now. He needed to focus. His team, his *city*, was depending on him.

"Enough, Hunter! Enough!"

The referee roughly pulled Scott away from the man on the ice. Scott struggled against him, but a linesman took hold of his other arm and helped haul him away from the bloodied Detroit player.

Scott looked at the man's pummeled face, and at his own busted knuckles. The adrenaline started to fade and the realization of what he'd just done set in.

"Shit," he said.

Fighting in the playoffs was *bad*. It was stupid and reckless and potentially costly. Scott wasn't usually the kind of player to get into actual fights on the ice. He was much too valuable for that.

His opponent got up, slowly. Scott was relieved when he was standing. He would be fine.

Scott's face hurt. He spat blood onto the ice and was hit with another wave of regret.

He let the officials take him to the penalty box. Huff skated over with Scott's gloves, helmet, and stick, retrieved from the ice. He didn't say anything. Scott nodded at him, and looked away.

Fuck.

They were down 4–1 in the third period. Scott hadn't slept more than a few hours in days. He was a powder keg, and number fourteen on the Detroit team had been playing with matches all night.

The one that had finally ignited Scott's rage was the word he'd been so good at blocking out since he was a teenager. And Scott had just lost it. The word that got thrown around—on the ice and in the locker room—so often that it barely meant anything had suddenly meant a whole lot. And when Scott's fists had been colliding with that asshole's face, he'd wanted to tell him. He'd wanted him to know *exactly* who it was that was beating his face in. A cocksucker. A homo. *Yeah, a fucking faggot is about to break your fucking jaw.*

But now that it was over, now that Scott had traded blows with the guy in front of the crowd and television cameras until he'd landed a punch that had dropped him to the ice, and then kept hitting him and hitting him . . .

Fuck. Goddammit.

Some fucking role model.

Scott picked up a water bottle and sprayed his face, cleaning away the blood and sweat. He squirted some into his mouth and spat it out. He looked at his hands. There were cuts, but nothing serious, though his knuckles would be swollen a bit for sure. He flexed his fingers. Nothing broken.

He felt sick. He felt *humiliated*, sitting in the penalty box for the next five minutes, the whole crowd having just witnessed him completely losing his mind.

He *was* losing his mind. He was untethered. He needed to find an anchor.

For now, he could only sit in the damn penalty box and watch his team lose. Again.

In an attempt to make himself feel slightly less miserable, Kip dragged himself to the Union Square Barnes & Noble after work. He normally found bookstores soothing.

It wasn't working this time.

It had been a week since he'd walked out of Scott's apartment. A week since he'd had any contact with Scott. He'd seen that the Admirals had lost the first two games of the series against Detroit and couldn't help but feel partly responsible, even if that was ridiculous.

Scott would be back in town today, if he wasn't already.

Kip wanted to see him so badly it hurt. The train he had taken that morning had been full of Scott's most recent Gillette ads. Kip had kept his eyes on the floor so he wouldn't have to look at Scott's rugged, chiseled jawline. Or his soft lips. Or his blue eyes.

Was it really over between them? Was that possible? Should he reach out to Scott?

A toddler shrieked somewhere in the store, and Kip realized he had been staring, eyes unfocused, at a shelf in the European history section for probably five minutes. He blinked, took a step backward, and collided with someone.

"Oh god. Sorry." Kip turned to face his victim. It was a young man with blond hair and glasses and a light scarf wrapped around his neck.

It was Kyle. Kip had stepped on Kyle.

"Oh. Um, hi," Kip stammered.

Jesus. What are the odds?

"Kip!" Kyle said, clearly shocked that he couldn't even go to a fucking bookstore without having to deal with Kip's messiness.

Kip took a breath. *Might as well get this over with.* "Listen, about the other night . . ."

"Forget it," Kyle said, waving a hand dismissively. "You're obviously going through something and I'm not interested in making it worse. And I'm sorry if I *did* make it worse. I shouldn't have come onto you like that. It was irresponsible of me."

"It's fine," Kip said. "I mean, I'm flattered and everything, but, yeah. Like you said. I'm kinda going through something."

Kip's eyes were suddenly stinging, which was great because he hadn't embarrassed himself enough in front of this guy.

"You like history?" Kyle asked. It was an obvious attempt to change the subject. Kip appreciated it. Kyle was nice.

"Yeah. I majored in it. I'm, um, I'm hoping to do my master's degree in the fall."

"No kidding? I'm doing mine now. Part-time, anyway."

"In history?"

"No. That was my undergrad degree; I'm doing my master's in ancient art and archaeology. At Columbia."

Kip was impressed. "That's awesome! I had no idea."

Kyle smiled. "Well, we've never really talked much beyond drink orders and flirting."

Kip looked down, embarrassed. "I'm sorry if I led you on the other night," he mumbled at Kyle's (really nice) boots.

"Forget about it. I'm just glad you got home safe. Or got somewhere safe, anyway. I was worried."

"You were?"

"You seem surprised."

Kip flushed a bit. He felt like he was being an asshole, maybe. He probably shouldn't be talking to anyone. "Sorry. I'm a total mess right now."

Kyle seemed to consider him a moment. "Do you want to get a coffee?"

"Oh, um, I'm not . . . I mean, normally I would, but . . ."

"Relax. You just seem like you could use a friend. Maybe we could talk about whatever is troubling you. Or about grad school."

Kip wasn't sure he *could* talk about his problems with this near stranger, but he sure didn't have anything better to do. "All right. Sure. Thanks."

They went to the in-store Starbucks and brought their lattes to a table against the wall.

"I didn't know you wear glasses," Kip said.

"Just one of many fascinating things about me."

"And you were a history major!"

Kyle gently pulled the lid off his cup and blew at the foam. "History and Latin, actually. Double major. But enough about me. What's making you so sad, Kip?"

"I . . ." It wouldn't hurt to try this. Maybe an impartial stranger was exactly what he needed. "I've been seeing someone. For a few months now. And . . . I love him. We're in love. Or, we were. I don't know anymore."

"Tell me about him."

"He's . . ." Kip smiled a little. "He's gorgeous. I mean, really. He's ridiculously hot. And he's smart, and caring, and generous, and just . . . wonderful."

"And he's, let me guess . . . married?"

Kip shook his head. "No. But he *is* closeted."

Kyle gave him a knowing look. "Word of advice, based on personal experience: Don't mess with the closeted ones."

"You know, I definitely would have agreed with you before. But he's worth it. I think."

"Why is he closeted?"

"His line of work is . . ." Kip sighed. "He thinks it would hurt his career. I don't know. It probably would, I guess."

"So he's putting the career first?"

"Well, it's . . . You know."

"Complicated?"

"Extremely." Kip raked a hand through his hair, agitated. "It's just . . . There's a big difference between us. Like, I'm not good enough for him. At all."

"He said this?"

"No! No. Never. But it's the truth. He's successful. Rich. Impressive."

"And closeted."

"Yeah."

"Older?"

"Not much. A couple of years."

"Jesus. And he's rich and successful?"

Kip squirmed. Was he giving too much away? Kyle wasn't trying to guess who his mystery man was, was he?

"His money and stuff . . . It doesn't matter to me. And he says he doesn't care that I don't have any. But it just makes the relationship so off balance, you know? I always feel uncomfortable with him paying for anything. And besides that, since we've been together I've felt like I've been shoved back in the closet instead of bringing him out of it."

"And I assume you've talked this all out with him?"

Kip chewed his lip. "Sort of. We had a fight. Last week. And I . . . walked out."

"Oof."

"It was our first real fight."

"It was your *first* fight, and you walked out?"

"Yeah." Kip was feeling stupider by the second.

"Have you tried to talk to him since?"

"No."

Kyle shook his head and smiled sadly. "Oh, Kip."

"You think I should?"

"Are you really in love with him?"

"Yes."

"Then you have to try."

Kip fiddled with his cup. "But what if he's never ready to come out? You just said you know from personal experience that I should stay away from closeted guys."

"Yeah, well. My situation was a huge mess, but I wasn't *in love* with the guy."

Kip nodded. "I'll talk to him. You're right. I have to try."

"Good boy. Now, where are you going to grad school?"

"Oh, I don't know yet. I applied to a couple of schools, but I'm hoping for NYU. That's where I did my undergrad."

"Shame. I thought we were getting along," Kyle teased.

Kip smiled. "I'm not sure how I'm gonna pay for school, exactly, but I'll figure it out. I definitely need a better job."

Kyle looked at him curiously. "Do you have any food-service experience?"

Kip laughed. "Yeah. That's about *all* I have."

"The Kingfisher needs a new server."

"Really?" Kip considered this. It would still be food service, but it might be cool working at his favorite pub.

"Mm-hmm. And there will be even more hours soon because I'm doing a summer program in Italy."

"Oh!"

"The tips, I can tell you, are *fantastic*. Especially when you're cute and charming." He swept a hand playfully across his own face. "Why don't you drop by tomorrow, late afternoon, with your résumé? The boss will be there then. I'll introduce you and put in a good word."

"You don't even know if I'm a good worker," Kip pointed out.

"Are you a bad worker?"

"No."

"Well, I don't think you're a liar, so I'll go with that."

"All right. Thanks. I'll be there tomorrow. And I really do appreciate this."

"Good. Now go call your gorgeous, successful boyfriend."

Kip didn't call Scott. He had pulled his phone out several times with the intention of doing that, or of sending a text, but he was scared. What if he sent a text and Scott ignored it? What if Scott had blocked his number? What if Kip called and Scott answered and told him not to call him again?

At least now, as miserable as he was, he had hope.

He was sitting on his bed at home, Kyle's words from earlier that day running through his head.

You have to try.

He should text Scott. Just text him.

He typed out, Can we talk?

He stared at it.

What if Scott wrote back *No*?

Maybe Kip should let him make the first move. Scott was the one with all the stress and responsibility heaped on his shoulders right now. Kip didn't want to add to that. But the Admirals were playing the following night. It would be their first home game since Kip and Scott's fight, and it felt so wrong not to be going.

He couldn't dwell on that. He needed to give Scott some space. Instead, Kip would go to work in the morning, and then he would stop by the Kingfisher with his résumé. He would use this time productively.

There was a knock on his bedroom door. "Kip?"

"Yeah, Dad. Come in."

The door opened and his father stepped in, holding an envelope. "This came from NYU," he said with a little smile. "You wouldn't happen to know anything about that, would you?"

"Probably just asking for money," Kip lied. *Probably just rejecting my application.*

"It's from the admissions department."

Oh god. Oh god. I can't take bad news right now.

"Give it." Kip's hand trembled slightly as he reached for the envelope. Dad crossed his arms and leaned back against the doorframe.

Kip gave him a pointed look, but when it was clear that his father had no intention of leaving the room, he sighed and opened the envelope.

"Holy shit," he said quietly to himself.

"Kip?"

Kip leaped to his feet. "I got in! I'm going to grad school!"

And suddenly the world felt a little less awful. He beamed and hugged his father.

"I'm proud of you. And very jealous," Dad said.

Kip shook his head, bewildered. "I didn't think I'd get in."

"Why not? Your grades were excellent. You're a fantastic writer, a hard worker. Any school would be happy to have you."

"I just . . ." And Kip now had tears in his eyes. "Things haven't been great, Dad."

"I know." Dad hugged him again. "I didn't want to intrude, but . . . are you boys fighting?"

"Boys? Who are you—?"

Dad smiled at him knowingly, then his face sobered. "I know he must be busy right now, with the playoffs, but it seems like maybe something worse than that is going on."

What the hell?

"What are you—?"

"Scott Hunter," his dad said calmly. "You've been seeing him."

"Dad, come on. There's no way that Scott would ever—I mean, Scott Hunter isn't—"

"I don't know anything about Scott Hunter, but I know you. And I like to think I'd be able to tell when my son is in love."

"I'm not—" *God. Fuck it. Does it even matter anymore?* "How did you know?"

"Remember when I broke my wrist slipping on the ice in our walkway?"

"Sure. Yeah . . ." Kip had no idea where he was going with this.

"The look on your mother's face was the same as the look on yours when Hunter got hurt at that game we were at."

Kip blushed. "Maybe I'm just a big fan?"

"Maybe. But I don't think so. You also bolted out of the house that night after making a phone call that included the words *X-ray* and *ice pack*. I'm good at picking up on subtle clues like that."

So maybe Kip hadn't been as careful as he'd thought he'd been.

"He's not . . . No one knows. And it might not be anything, so please—"

"Of course."

Kip's own words filled him with a fresh wave of despair. *It might not be anything. Oh god. It can't really be over, can it?*

He pressed the heel of his palm to his forehead and squeezed his eyes shut, trying to fight off a complete breakdown. "Does Mom know?"

"No, I've been keeping this one to myself."

"Thank you. I've wanted to tell you. Both of you. But now things are . . . I don't know." He sniffed, and turned his eyes up to the ceiling. *Keep it together, Kip.*

"You're on the outs?"

"Yeah. It's a mess right now. I want to clean it up so badly."

Dad smiled and patted his arm. "You will."

To his credit, Kip was able to keep himself from falling apart until after his father had left his room. As soon as the door clicked shut, he sobbed into his pillow like a teenager. God, he'd gotten into *grad school* and even that wasn't enough to cheer him up.

He needed to fix things with Scott. He had to at least try.

CHAPTER TWENTY-FIVE

"Holy shit," Maria muttered. "He's back."

Kip turned from where he'd been restocking the bananas to see—"Scott!"

He was standing there, in his running clothes, face sweat-slicked, just like the first time he'd walked into the shop. Except with more beard.

Kip hadn't meant to say his name like that. Surprised. *Familiar.* He'd just been thrown. Hopefully Maria would chalk it up to his supposed fanboy crush on Scott Hunter.

"Hey," Scott said, his voice soft and uncertain.

"Um, can I . . . help you?"

"Yeah," Scott said, with a shy smile. "I was thinking it might be good to . . . return to basics."

"Oh." *What does* that *mean?* "So . . . blue smoothie, then?"

"Please."

Kip made the smoothie and Maria smirked at him. He ignored her.

He handed the drink to Scott, whose eyes darted over to Maria, and then back to Kip. He could almost *see* the "fuck it" pass through Scott's brain.

"I, um . . . I wanted to see you."

"Oh." Kip braved a glance at Maria. She looked like the cat that caught the fucking canary.

"The game's tonight, and I was hoping . . ."

"Oh." Kip deflated. "You need your good luck charm there or something?"

"No! No, that's not—" Scott's eyes darted to Maria again. He lowered his voice, not that it mattered. Maria was very obviously hanging on every word. "I want to talk to you. Alone. Soon. Please, Kip."

Kip saw the anguish in Scott's eyes and a flicker of hope sparked inside him. Was it possible that Scott wanted to fix this as badly as Kip did?

"All right," Kip said.

"Can we meet somewhere? After you're done here?"

"I actually have somewhere to be this afternoon."

Scott looked devastated.

"No, I mean it," Kip said quickly. "I'm not brushing you off. I really want to talk to you. Really. A lot. Like . . . so much."

"Okay. I've got the game tonight and all, so . . . maybe—Would you come to the game? Do you think?"

"Yeah," Kip said. "Sure. I'll be at the game tonight."

Scott nodded. "Good. Okay. And maybe after we could . . . get together. Somewhere?"

"Sure. I'd like that."

Scott's face brightened. "Yeah? Well—" He leaned in, just the tiniest bit, and Kip's breath caught. But then Scott took a quick step backward and said, "—I'll see you then."

"All right."

Scott left and Kip waited as long as possible to turn and face Maria.

"What. The. Fuck," she said.

"Okay, that probably looked—"

"So you two are—?"

"Sort of. I don't know. Just please don't tell anyone."

"Holy shit!"

"I'm serious! Don't say a word. Promise me, okay?"

"I promise! Of course I promise! But you have to tell me *something*. I need some details!"

"One detail."

"One?"

"One."

She made a face that implied that she was thinking very hard, then grabbed a cucumber out of the fridge and laid it on the counter. She picked up a knife and held it near the center of the cucumber. "Okay, you tell me when I hit the approximate length."

"No."

She moved the knife a bit.

"Come on. I'm not doing this."

She moved it again and raised an eyebrow.

Kip glared at her and then rolled his eyes and said, "A bit farther."

Maria screamed. "Oh my god! I knew it! You lucky bitch!"

"All right. Enough. Seriously. Keep this to yourself, okay?"

"I will. I will. I promise," she giggled.

Kip laughed a little, relieved that there was someone else who knew about his relationship.

His relationship that he was going to make damn sure he fixed tonight.

Scott felt good.

His hands were bandaged inside his gloves from the fight the other night, but he felt good. Centered. Focused. They were going to win tonight. He had no doubt of it.

He had been ignoring the headlines, and the commentary

on the sports talk shows. He knew it was there, though. *What exactly is wrong with Scott Hunter?*

He shut it all off. None of that mattered. Each game was a fresh start. They were down two games, they would win the next four. No problem.

His teammates seemed to sense the change in him too. They weren't looking at him with concern in their eyes; they were looking to him for strength. They were nodding back at him, silently communicating, *You've got this. We're with you. All the way.* Kip was here, at the game. Seeing him here in his usual seat filled Scott with strength and confidence. It wasn't superstition; it was love.

He would work things out with Kip tonight. He would make sure of it.

"Whoa, shit," Elena said. "Looks like Scott got his groove back!"

They were standing and applauding wildly with the rest of the crowd. Scott had scored his second goal of the game, making it 5–2 for the Admirals late in the second period.

Maybe it was the hometown advantage, or maybe Scott had managed to find his focus. Or maybe the smoothies were magic, after all. Either way, Kip was relieved and happy.

And really fucking proud of him.

Kip received a text from Scott shortly after the game.

Would it be all right if we met at my place?

Kip had been hoping he might suggest it. Sure. You want me to go there now?

SCOTT:

Yeah. I'll be there as soon as I can.

Elena hugged him and wished him luck. They'd had a long conversation before the game. Her opinion was that Kip and Scott were both idiots.

It was weird how much Scott's luxurious apartment building felt like home to Kip now. He had to remind himself, as he walked into the enormous living room, that it *wasn't* his home. But it was comforting to be in the familiar space again.

The wait, however, was agony. He knew Scott would be a while, but it seemed like an eternity. Kip sat on the couch, and then at the kitchen counter, and then paced around the living room. When the door finally clicked open, he was standing at the windows.

For a moment, Scott stared at him as if he couldn't believe he was really there. Then he said, in the softest voice, "Kip."

"Hey."

He was wearing one of the bespoke suits he was required to leave the rink in. His beard was thick and his hair was longer than usual. He looked so fucking good.

Scott crossed the room until he stood an arm's length away.

"Congrats on the win," Kip said awkwardly.

"Thanks." Scott's hands, his bandaged fingers, were flexing at his sides. He was staring at Kip like he'd come back from the dead. "I've missed you."

Scott's voice broke on the last word. Kip did the only thing he could think to do—the only thing he *wanted* to do: He opened his arms. And Scott fell into them.

"I'm so sorry," Scott whispered into Kip's shoulder. "I never wanted you to leave. Please give me a chance to make it better."

"Shh." Kip kissed the top of Scott's head.

They stayed that way for a while, wrapped up together and breathing each other in.

"Let's sit," Kip said, taking Scott's hand. He held it gently, brushing his thumb over the bandages as he led him to the couch.

"I've been doing a lot of thinking," Scott said.

"Me too."

"I've been miserable."

"Me too."

"I'd be lying if I said that the idea of coming out doesn't still terrify me."

"I know," Kip said. "I'm putting too much pressure on you, especially now. So maybe I can back off a bit and be more patient."

"But you were *right*, Kip. You were right about everything. You shouldn't have to hide. You shouldn't be my secret. You deserve so much better than that."

"*You* deserve so much better too, Scott."

"I know I do. I'm just . . . scared."

"Can I ask," Kip said carefully, "what exactly it is you're afraid of? You keep saying, your career, or your privacy, but I know the NHL has, like, Pride nights and stuff."

Scott scrubbed a hand over his face. He looked exhausted.

"Sorry," Kip said quickly. "I just . . . I guess I feel like maybe there's something I'm not understanding here."

"You're right," Scott said, "about the league. They *are* trying. And teams are supposed to have a zero-tolerance policy about homophobia, but . . ." He sighed. "When I was a kid, I mean, hockey was my whole life. And, in that world, being gay—that was the worst insult. The lowest thing you could be. I can't even tell you how many times I had to hear . . . well, every homophobic comment imaginable. It was pretty relentless."

"Aimed at you?"

"At me, at everyone. It was just what you said if you wanted to get under a guy's skin. Or if you were mad. And everyone accepted that. But when I started to realize that I might *be* that thing that my teammates all considered so repulsive . . ."

Kip took Scott's hand. Scott swallowed and continued, "You have to remember, I went to boarding school—a hockey-focused boarding school—so there was no escape. And I hid. I hid my secret as deep as I could because I couldn't hide the rest of me. I was the biggest star at that school, with NHL scouts coming to watch my games even then. And I knew—I mean, I thought, but I probably would have been right about it—that if I was caught with another boy, if anyone even *thought* I wanted another boy, it would all be over."

"Was there a boy?" Kip asked quietly.

Scott smiled sadly. "There was a boy. Later. In Junior. My teammate Jacob."

"Did you guys . . . ?"

"No. I don't know if he was . . . But I think, maybe. He might have been looking at me too. But neither of us would have acted on it. The risk was way too high."

"But you wanted him."

"Desperately." Scott laughed, humorlessly. "I thought I was in love with him."

"God. That must have been agony."

Scott shrugged. "I forced myself to ignore it. Focus on what was important. Get to the NHL."

"And the NHL wasn't any better?"

"I can't really explain it. It's one thing for the NHL to wave the Pride flag and talk about inclusion—and that's great, really, I'm not saying it isn't—but the locker rooms, and on the ice, and on the road with the guys . . . I don't know. I never felt comfortable being honest about that part of my life. I don't think I'd be looked at the same way again."

Scott shook his head and continued, "And the thing is . . .

Not to sound dramatic, but for my entire adult life, my teammates have been the only family I've had. So the thought of losing their respect and support is terrifying."

And now Kip really felt like shit for pushing him. But he still wanted Scott to take the leap.

"That all probably sounds like a weak reason to not come out," Scott said. "I'm not expecting to get beat up in the locker room or anything. It's just—It's a big fucking line for me to cross. And there's no going back."

"No," Kip agreed. "There's no going back. But, let me tell you, there are some pretty amazing things on the other side of that line."

Scott smiled. "I know. I want to see them. I want to have them all. With you."

"Me too. And whatever happens, Scott. You know I'll be right there beside you, right? I can take it. Whatever you are afraid of, we'll fight it together. I am so *proud* to be your boyfriend. If you think the world finding out how much I love you is scary to me, you're dead wrong."

Scott's face crumpled a bit. His eyes were wet. "I love you. Kip, I don't know what I'm doing, but I just love you so much and I can't lose you. I just . . . can't."

Kip's heart felt like a big, warm puddle. "I love you too, Scott."

"Can you wait until the playoffs are over? Is that too much to ask?" His tone was sincere, not angry.

"I can wait," Kip said. "But when the playoffs are over, we need to figure out what happens next."

Scott nodded. "That's fair. Yeah. All right."

"Okay."

"And can you promise to stop thinking that I'm going to think you're not worth it? Or whatever? Because that is so far from the truth, I can't even tell you."

Kip gave a relieved, wet smile. "Deal."

Scott closed his eyes and pressed his face against Kip's palm. He took Kip's other hand in his, and Kip curled their fingers together, squeezing reassuringly.

"What happened to your hands, anyway?" Kip asked. He lifted one of them to his lips and gently kissed Scott's bruised knuckles.

"You didn't watch that game?" Scott sounded a little hurt by that.

"No. I tried to watch the first one, but it . . . I just couldn't. I'm sorry."

"Don't be. It was only a fight. It was stupid."

"A fight? You don't fight. I've never seen you fight."

"I don't, usually. Not for a long time. And I shouldn't have the other night, but . . ."

"What happened?" Kip asked, tracing his fingertips over the bandages.

"He called me a . . . Well, you can probably guess. Which," Scott said quickly, "is really not that big a deal. Like I said, words like that are so common on the ice that they don't even mean anything."

"Until they do," Kip said quietly.

"Until they do."

Kip cradled Scott's big hands in his own.

"I wanted to tell him," Scott said. "I wanted him to know *exactly* who it was that was beating his face in."

Kip looked at him, surprised. "Well, that's one way to come out. Not sure it's what I'd recommend."

Scott laughed. "I shouldn't have done it. Fought him, I mean. I wish I hadn't. But I was . . . You know."

"Miserable?"

"Yeah. And I hadn't been sleeping."

"I'm sorry. I shouldn't have walked out after that argument."

"Don't apologize. I'm going to figure this out," Scott promised.

"I know. You're going to win the Stanley Cup, and I'm going to get my master's degree, and we're going to be amazing together."

"Unstoppable," Scott agreed, and kissed him again. "Wait . . . did you get into school?"

Kip smiled. "I did! NYU!"

Scott wrapped him in his arms and squeezed almost too hard. "I'm so proud of you."

"See?" Kip said into his shoulder. "Unstoppable. But . . . maybe, for now, it would be best if we give each other some breathing room, y'know?"

Scott released him, which made Kip laugh. "No, I meant, like, for the next few weeks. Until the playoffs are over, so you can focus. You're traveling so much anyway, maybe it's better if you just . . . forget about me for a while."

He could see Scott tense up.

"Not gonna forget about you," Scott said.

Kip smiled. "A little. Besides, I've got stuff to deal with in my own life. I, um, I got a new job."

"What? Really? Like . . . a history job?"

"No," Kip said. "Nothing that great. But a better job than the smoothie shop for sure. It's at the Kingfisher. You know, the pub I go to."

"Oh. The, um—"

"Gay bar. Yes."

"Right. That's . . . I mean, that's great. You're happy about it, right?"

"Yes. I think it will be fun. Late nights, for sure, but I'll take that over ridiculously early mornings. And the money will be better. Good tips."

"Well, congratulations then. Have you put in your notice at work?"

"Yeah. I sent an email yesterday. As soon as I was offered the job."

"Oh."

"Are you all right?"

"Yeah," Scott said. "It's just . . . I have fond feelings about that smoothie shop."

"Aw. You'll have to visit me at my new job."

He waited for Scott to get weird about that.

Instead, Scott said, "I will. I promise. As soon as I . . . can."

"Something to work toward."

"Yeah."

Kip leaned forward and kissed him.

"Will you stay here?" Scott asked. "Tonight?"

Kip ran his fingers down Scott's necktie. "Yes. Of course."

Scott shuddered out a breath and Kip moved his lips over to brush the shell of his ear. "What do you want to do?" he murmured.

"I don't know."

"How about this?" Kip said. "How about you take off this sexy-as-hell suit, go lie down on your bed, and I spend a couple of hours kissing every inch of you?"

He could feel Scott smiling against his shoulder.

Scott shivered on the bed. He felt both cold and hot, skin exposed to the air and Kip's mouth and hands searing him and making his blood run like lava.

What Kip was doing to him, so slowly and carefully kissing and licking every part of him—cataloging him—it was almost an out-of-body experience. Kip would press kisses up the inside of one thigh, tantalizingly close to his cock, then switch and nip the inside of Scott's wrist. He would flick his tongue over one nipple until Scott thought he would die, then he would lovingly comb his fingers through Scott's new beard.

It was heaven and agony and possibly the most sensual experience of Scott's life. He would need to return the favor someday.

Finally, Kip curled his tongue over Scott's balls. He hummed as he took one into his mouth. Scott gasped and arched.

"I love you," he said. "I love you so much and I'm going to fix everything. I promise. I'll—"

"Shhh," Kip said, replacing his mouth with his hand. He caressed him and lightly kissed the head of Scott's swollen cock. "Don't worry about anything. Just relax. Let me take care of you."

Scott sighed and closed his eyes. Kip wrapped his plush, bruised lips around his cock and put his tongue to work taking Scott apart.

The buildup had been exquisite and eternal. Scott let himself feel everything that Kip was doing with his mouth and fingers. He felt the way it made his body tighten, the way it made his heart race. He wanted to come, and he wanted this to last forever.

He wanted so many things.

But now he could feel himself racing to the edge.

"Kip," he said hoarsely.

Kip pulled off, replacing his mouth with his hand. "Want to see it," he said. "Show me. Come on, baby."

Scott came, silent and awestruck, as his gorgeous, perfect boyfriend watched. The thick white ribbons of his release splattered across his stomach and up onto his chest.

"So beautiful, sweetheart," Kip said. He crawled up and kissed Scott, who kissed him back gratefully.

"You're so good to me," Scott said. "I love you. Don't forget that, all right? I love you."

"I won't."

Later that night, they lay in the dark. Kip was asleep with his head on Scott's chest. He'd given Scott so much that night. He'd wrung himself *out* for Scott. And now he was curled against him, his body heavy and exhausted.

Scott held him, and made a silent promise that he would be the man Kip needed him to be. Then he slipped blissfully into sleep.

CHAPTER TWENTY-SIX

Scott slept well for the first time in a week.

As he blinked awake, he heard a content little sigh next to him. He rolled to find the man he loved sleeping peacefully. The single white sheet that was covering them had slipped down to the dip of Kip's bare lower back. His soft brown hair fell messily into his eyes, a couple of loose wavy tendrils brushing against the slight stubble on his cheek. His face was relaxed and beautiful, his lips slightly parted. Scott propped himself up on one elbow and just looked at him for a while.

He watched him sleep until he was no longer able to stop himself from gently brushing the backs of his fingers over the line of Kip's jaw. In his sleep, Kip flinched and made a drowsy, irritated noise. Scott smiled and kissed the shoulder that was closest to him. When Kip didn't stir or protest, Scott continued to press soft kisses down the length of his back.

He would happily stay in this quiet moment forever.

But he was also lonely, so he moved his mouth so he could lightly nip Kip's side, just above his hip, where Scott knew he was ticklish.

Two scrapes of Scott's teeth and Kip was squirming away from him. Scott grinned. "Good morning."

"Fuck off," Kip murmured into his pillow.

"Sorry," Scott said. "Couldn't resist." He moved back to his original position of lying on his side next to him.

Eventually, Kip turned his head and looked at him. "Hey," he said, his voice soft and happy.

"I like waking up to you."

"Mm." Kip rolled onto his back and stretched. Scott enjoyed the way the muscles in his arms and chest tightened, and the way the thin bedsheet slipped farther down his hips.

"What time is it?" Kip asked.

"Hm?" Scott asked, his eyes following the trail of dark hair that ran from Kip's belly button down under the bed sheet. "I don't know. Eight, maybe?"

Kip closed his eyes and groaned. "Shit. I've gotta get up. I said I'd go in to work at nine to help train a new hire."

"You sure?" Scott asked, moving so he could kiss the side of Kip's neck.

"Sooner I start, the sooner it's done," Kip said, his voice a little strained. Scott moved his mouth to suck lightly on the pulse point, and felt his boyfriend's heartbeat quicken.

"Okay," Scott said, letting his mouth travel down to Kip's collarbone. He kissed the dip just above it, and Kip shivered.

"You're a bad influence," he complained.

In response, Scott put a hand on Kip's knee and slid it up, letting his fingers drag along the sensitive skin on the inside of his thigh.

"You have fifteen minutes," Kip said with a breathless laugh.

Scott covered Kip's body with his own and looked straight down into his eyes. "Is that a challenge?"

"I know you love them."

"I do."

Scott kissed him on the mouth, and it was immediately obvious that Kip had no real objections to Scott's advances. The kiss was open and hot and frantic, and just the feel of Kip's tongue curling against his own made Scott so wild with desire. Every time.

Kip was angling his hips so their erections rubbed together. Scott groaned into Kip's mouth. They moved like that for a while, until Kip broke away and said, with a playful smirk, "Ten minutes."

Scott accepted the challenge and slid down Kip's body, taking the sheet with him. He took his cock into his mouth, and Kip's hips jolted up as he gasped into the room.

Scott brought his A-game. He put to good use all of the knowledge he had gathered about what made Kip absolutely lose his mind in bed. He attacked the sensitive spot under the head of Kip's cock with rapid flicks of his tongue while he tugged at Kip's balls with his hand. Then he relaxed his throat and sank down, taking Kip as deep as he could.

Scott sincerely loved sucking Kip off. He loved how quickly he could reduce him to moans and gorgeous, sexy babbling.

"Mm, oh fuck, baby. So fucking good. God, your mouth. Love your mouth, Scott . . ."

After a few minutes, when Kip was pulled tight and trembling beneath him, Scott pulled off and asked, "How much time I got left?"

"Jesus. Fuck you, Scott. Come on!"

"Just checking!"

"You're an asshole. Get back to work."

Scott laughed and did as he was told. He finished Kip off quickly and flopped back down beside him.

Kip was breathing heavily and grinning at the ceiling. "Good job, champ," he said.

"Thanks, Coach."

"Come on," Kip said, sitting up and swinging his legs over the side of the bed. "I'll pay you back in the shower."

"The shower?"

"I've gotta multitask! I'm already late!"

"I'm a distraction."

"The best kind, though. Come on."

As soon as their plane took off from New York, Scott's confidence splintered.

They had just won the two games in New York, tying the series at 2–2, but he couldn't forget how terribly he had played in the first two games in Detroit.

But now he and Kip were back together, and he was going to make sure they stayed that way. And that meant being brave and making good on his promises to the man he loved.

That night, Scott lay on top of his hotel bed, worrying about what would happen when he came out. It had been his most closely guarded secret for so long, he almost couldn't imagine life without having that burden to carry.

He needed to clear his head, so he left his room and wandered around the hotel a bit until he ended up at the pool. There was no one in there, so he sat sideways on one of the lounge chairs and enjoyed the quiet.

Gazing at the still water of the pool, he let himself focus on something other than fear. He thought about Kip. Kip, who was being so patient with him. And Scott knew he had asked Kip to wait until the playoffs were over, but suddenly that seemed too far away. Scott didn't want to push their relationship out of his mind during the playoffs; he wanted their relationship to make him *stronger*. To make him a better player.

He thought about making a home with Kip—making a *life* with him. He thought about Kip's adorable dimples and the way he put his hand over his mouth when he was reading. He thought about waking up with Kip every morning after he retired, and traveling the world together. Going to restaurants and museums and for walks in the park without caring if people knew they were together. Maybe even *wanting* people to know they were together.

The desire for all of that burned so bright inside him that he was overcome with the need to get started on making it happen. He knew what he had to do.

It was time.

"Jesus, Scott," his agent griped into the phone. "It's almost midnight here!"

"I know. It is here too. I'm only in Detroit, you know."

"Is something wrong?"

"No. Not exactly. I was going to wait until I was back in town, but I don't want to wait."

"Wait for what? Hold on . . . What the fuck? After all these years you're just going to—?"

"No," Scott said quickly. "You're not fired, Todd. Nothing like that. Of course not."

"Well, then?"

Scott sat down on the bench in the empty locker room in the hotel fitness center. He had no idea how he was going to word this. As usual, his brain had made a sudden decision and he was going to go with it.

"I'm thinking about making an announcement," he said.

"An announcement? What, you're retiring? Scott, you've still got *years* left—"

"No. Not that. A . . . personal announcement."

Todd sighed. "Look, Scott. It's late. You wanna just cut to the chase here?"

Scott glanced around the locker room one more time, just in case. He was alone.

"I'm gay," he said, for the first time ever.

There was silence.

"Todd?"

"I heard you. Just give me a minute here."

"Sure."

More silence. Then Todd exhaled loudly. "All right. You're gay. Got it. Now tell me that isn't what you want to announce."

"It is."

"Scott," Todd said wearily. "No. You can't do that."

"Why not?"

Todd actually laughed. "You *know* why not! Jesus, do I really need to explain it to you? Do you know how many players are lined up to take your sponsorship deals? You think I'm not fighting Matti fucking Jalo's agent for this shit now? You're only the second-biggest heartthrob on the team these days, and that's not going to get better as you get older. Right now, you need to grab as much as you can. You're in your prime and it's not going to last. An injury, another slump—"

"I know. I understand," Scott said tersely.

"I'm just saying, there's no reason to *push* sponsors and fans away. Not when there are so many other ways for it to happen that you can't control."

"I get that," Scott said, "but I think some things are more important than all that."

"More important than everything you have been working your whole life for?"

"I don't know. Maybe." Scott was a little less sure.

"All right, let me try another angle: Have you thought about what an announcement like this would do to your teammates?"

"Do to them?"

"You think it wouldn't be weird for them? Knowing that you're, you know—"

"What? Checking them out in the locker room? I'm not."

"It's just, with some of these guys, it's like their biggest fear, right? I know it's not rational. I'm an open-minded guy, Scott. You know that. I'm only being real here. *Some* of your teammates, at least, are going to be weirded out. And that's going to affect the team dynamic, and performance. You're the goddamned *captain*. It's your job to consider these things!"

"Right," Scott mumbled. "Yeah. I know."

"Can I ask why the hell you are even considering this?"

"I don't want to lie anymore."

"Why not? Everyone lies. You think you're the only gay guy in the NHL? No chance. You're just the only one who's considering telling the fucking world. Don't do it, Scott. You'll lose everything."

"Come on," Scott said. "I wouldn't lose *everything*. And isn't it *your* job to make sure I don't?"

"I'm not a fucking wizard! I can only do so much. Now, granted, an announcement like this—being the first openly gay NHL player—might open up some new marketing opportunities, but I can't see you being on the cover of video games, or even representing the big athletics companies . . ."

"I think you're wrong about that. I think the world might be ready."

"Well, you're a lot more optimistic than I am."

"We knew that already."

Both men laughed.

"Listen," Todd said, his voice a little softer. "You've gotta be careful, all right? If you're spotted . . . You know. With a man . . ."

"I *am* careful. Of course I'm careful! If I wasn't careful, do you think I would have been able to keep this a secret for so long? From my teammates? From the media? From *you*?"

"I suppose not."

"I'm tired of being careful," Scott sighed.

Neither man said anything for a moment, then Todd said,

"How would you even do it? Make the announcement, I mean? Did you have a plan?"

"I don't know. I was thinking about seeing if *Sports Illustrated* wanted the story. Maybe doing it that way?"

"They will definitely want the story. I'll bet we could get a high bid for this thing, but we'd have to be smart about how we shop it."

"No," Scott said. "I'm not looking for money for this. That's not why I'm doing it."

"Yeah, but you may as well—"

"Todd. Stop." He smiled. "But I like that you're considering a strategy now."

"I still don't think you should do it."

"Noted."

"Fuck. You're gonna do it anyway, aren't you?"

"Probably."

"Jesus Christ. I'd better re-up on my antacid pills. Just . . . don't do anything without telling me, all right? Preferably, don't do anything at all. Ever."

"Stay in the closet forever. Got it."

"What's wrong with the closet? It's a wonderful place crammed full of professional athletes."

"Goodnight, Todd."

When Scott woke the next morning, he stayed in bed longer than usual, replaying his conversation with his agent. The part of what Todd had said that he couldn't get out of his head was:

You think you're the only gay guy in the NHL?

No. Scott was *sure* that he wasn't. But he felt like he was. All the time. It was a lonely, horrible feeling. And those other secretly gay players must be feeling it too.

Maybe he could change all that. Maybe he could make it easier for them, as well as for himself.

He frowned. Could he really change anything? Just by coming clean with the world about who he was? Would it have an impact? Or would Todd be right? Would the sponsors walk away? Would his teammates distance themselves? Would the fans turn their backs? Would his game suffer?

And then what would happen to those other gay players? It certainly wouldn't make them feel *better.*

Fuck.

"What's eating you, Scotty?" Carter asked over a hotel buffet plate of scrambled eggs and toast.

"Oh," Scott said, snapping back to attention. "Nothing."

"You're a shitty liar, Hunter. I keep telling you."

Scott smiled and poked at his eggs. "Has it been easier for you since your relationship was . . . outed?"

"Ah," Carter said, putting his fork down. "Tired of keeping your girl a secret?"

"Sort of," Scott said with a grimace.

"Sure, it was maybe getting a little old, the sneaking around. Sexy, for a while, but you can't keep love down."

"Love, huh?"

Carter shrugged. "I'm not ashamed."

"Glad to hear it. I guess that . . . Yeah. Love. It's a whole big thing, huh?"

"You can't cage it, Scott. You gotta let it loose for the world to see."

"Right."

"Listen," Carter said. "Why don't we do a double date or something next time Gloria's in town? You could ease into it, you know? We'll go somewhere low-key, if you want."

"Maybe," Scott said, knowing there was no way. Was there?

"What are you worried about? It's really not a big deal. You think she can't handle a few cameras?"

"I'm just a private person. Or, as private as I can be, anyway."

"Well, it wouldn't hurt for you to be seen with *someone*. Otherwise they're gonna start saying you're gay!" Carter laughed. Scott didn't.

"Jesus, Scott. Lighten up. No one is saying that. Relax."

Scott stood. "I'm gonna—" he said, making a vague gesture toward the elevators. He retreated to the privacy of his hotel room.

Back in his room, Scott made a list on the hotel stationery of what he stood to lose if he made his announcement.

Money, respect, endorsements, fan support, friendships, privacy, and, in a worst-case scenario, his career.

He made a list of what he stood to lose if he *didn't* make the announcement.

His sanity, his self-respect, Kip.

Kip.

When he put the two lists next to each other, it was no choice at all. Especially when he reasoned that the items in the first list were things that he wouldn't necessarily lose. The three items in the second list he would *definitely* lose.

Okay then.

Where to start? He'd said he wouldn't do anything until the playoffs were over, but now that he'd made his decision, that seemed like an eternity away.

He needed to do something now. Even if it was only going partway. He couldn't stand pretending Kip didn't exist, and he couldn't keep letting his friends believe he was dating a fictional woman. Enough.

He gathered his courage, and sent out some texts.

Twenty minutes later, Scott was joined in his hotel room by his three best friends. Bennett was the last to arrive.

"All right," Carter said with a raised eyebrow, "we're all here. What's up, Scott?"

"Um," Scott said, "why don't you have a seat?" He gestured toward the beds, where Huff was already sitting. Bennett and Carter joined him. They all watched Scott, waiting.

"Okay," Scott said to himself.

"Jesus, what's going on, Hunter?" Huff asked.

"Nothing," Scott said quickly. "Nothing . . . bad. It's not . . ." He must have looked terrible. He could feel sweat forming on his brow, and knew his cheeks were already pink. His throat was dry, and his stomach was churning. He glanced down at his blue socks, and found some courage.

He took a breath. "I have something that I want to tell you guys. I want to tell everyone, really. But I want to tell you guys first."

And, yeah, he *definitely* looked nervous, because Carter didn't even interrupt with a joke.

"I know this is weird timing, but I just have to . . . It's affecting my game. I need to—"

"Scott," Bennett said calmly, "just say it."

Scott steeled his nerves and said, for the second time ever, "I'm gay."

His teammates looked at him, then at each other. The few seconds of silence that followed were one of the most agonizing things Scott had ever endured.

"You serious?" Carter asked, finally.

No! Haha. Just kidding!

"Yes."

"Whoa," Huff said.

Bennett didn't say anything, but his face looked . . . normal. Not disgusted, anyway.

Now that he had cleared the biggest hurdle, Scott continued,

"I know you'd probably prefer to . . . not know. But I needed to tell someone. So I'm telling you. You guys are my best friends. So, yeah. There it is."

"You're serious?" Carter asked again.

"Yes," Scott said.

"Are you—?" Huff started, then seemed at a loss for words. "Sorry. I'm not trying to be a dick about this. It's just, you know. Wow, right?"

"I know," Scott said.

"To be honest," Bennett said slowly, "I kind of thought that you might be. Maybe."

"You did?"

"Yeah. Don't get me wrong, I'm still shocked over here."

"Are you planning on telling anyone outside this room?" Huff asked.

"Eventually, yes. I don't want to lie anymore."

"Shit," said Huff. "That's gonna—You sure you want that heat?"

"I *don't* want that heat," Scott said, "but I'll take it. I can't live like this anymore. And maybe—maybe I can make it easier for others. By going first."

"Maybe." Bennett nodded thoughtfully. "That's a lot to take on, though. Your life is hectic enough, isn't it?"

"Gay?" Carter said, still clearly not over it. "But I thought you were with that sexy dark-haired girl . . . Elena?"

"No," Scott said. "I'm actually . . . with her friend."

"What now?"

"I've been seeing someone. For a few months now."

"Wait. *What?*"

"I'm dating someone. I'm . . . in love with someone."

"Someone, like . . . a *man* someone?" Carter asked.

"Yes. A man someone."

Carter blew out a breath.

"Look, I don't expect you guys to be okay with this right

away or anything. I know it's a shock and maybe it wasn't fair of me to—"

"Scott," Carter said, holding a hand up. "Shut the fuck up for a second. I'm gonna process this shit, and then I am gonna give you a manly hug. But just shut it for five seconds."

Scott suppressed a grin. "All right."

Huff slapped his hands on his knees and stood. "Okay, I'm over it. And I'm happy for you, Scott. Good to hear you've found someone. And if anyone gives you shit about who you are, they're gonna have to deal with me."

Scott's eyes stung a bit. "Thanks, Huff."

"Me too," Bennett said, also standing.

"Yup," Carter said, finally standing to join them. "Me too. Let's hug it out, Hunter."

They hugged, and the other two piled on.

"Hey," Bennett said, after they separated, "what's his name?"

Scott grinned. "Kip."

Carter looked suddenly delighted. "Kip!" he said. "That is the cutest fucking thing I've ever heard! Are you *kidding me* with that shit?"

"Thank god," Huff said. "I thought you were gonna say you were secretly dating Rozanov."

"Rozanov wishes," Scott said.

"You got a picture of Kip?" Huff asked.

"Kip!" Carter exclaimed again.

"Yeah," Scott said shyly. "Yeah, I do. Just a sec . . ." He pulled out his phone and brought up his favorite picture of him. It was the first one Kip had ever sent him, when he was sleep-rumpled in bed.

"Good-looking guy," Huff said. "He an athlete?"

"No. He's smart."

"Oh. Not a dumb motherfucker like us?" Carter asked, mocking offense.

"He's just . . . He's getting his master's degree. In history. He's—"

"Wait a minute," Carter said, and grabbed Scott's phone. "This is the dude from the museum! Those pictures on the internet! Man, I never even thought—"

"Well, good. I was trying to be discreet."

"So this dude is so great that he's making Scott *Hunter* consider coming out publicly."

"Yup," Scott confirmed.

"Shit. I think I've gotta meet this guy."

"This really will be a huge deal," Bennett said, "if you come out."

"I know. And I promise I won't do it until the playoffs are over. Not publicly. We don't need that right now. And we don't have to tell the team either."

"You know," Huff said, "my brother-in-law's gay. Good guy. Great with the kids."

"Oh," Scott said. "I didn't know that."

Huff shrugged. "Not all hockey players are homophobic assholes."

"For the record," Carter said, "if you had to choose between the three of us—"

"No," Scott said.

"Come *on*," Carter said. "I mean, I assume it's me, but—"

"Bennett," Scott said, just to bother Carter.

"Makes sense." Huff nodded. "Bennett seems like a cuddler."

They all laughed and it was good. Scott loved them all.

"We've got your back, Scott," Huff said as they were leaving. "Whatever you decide, we're with you."

Scott nodded, and swallowed the lump in his throat. He closed the door behind them before they could see him cry.

"Hat trick!" Kip exclaimed, pointing at the television. "That's a hat trick! Yeah!"

Scott had scored his third goal of the game, making it 6–2

for the Admirals in the third period. He had been in top form all night. Kip was thrilled.

The Admirals were going to win this game. And then they would only have to win one more to move on to the finals.

"He's so handsome," his mother said, to no one in particular.

"Yeah," Kip breathed. His father chuckled.

"I'm happy for him," Mom said. "He seems like such a nice man."

Kip smiled to himself.

"I suppose they'll be back in town tomorrow," Dad said conversationally, "to get ready for game six."

"Yeah, I think so," Kip said, as if he didn't know for certain.

Scott had texted him that morning. Nothing much, just a quick Thinking of you.

Kip had written back. Not too much I hope. 😊

To which Scott had replied, Gonna win tonight.

Kip had smiled at that. He liked seeing Scott so confident. It was sexy. I'll be watching. I love you.

I love you.

Scott made good on his promise.

The following evening, there was a knock on their door during dinner.

"Who could that be?" Kip's mother asked, already up and making her way to the door.

"Probably just Annette," Dad said to Kip, meaning their next-door neighbor. "They just got back from vacation today, I think."

Kip shoveled some mashed potatoes into his mouth. Then he heard Mom exclaim, "Oh my goodness!"

He stood. "Mom?"

"It's—it's Scott Hunter!"

CHAPTER TWENTY-SEVEN

Kip moved like lightning. Sure enough, there was Scott, filling the doorway of their modest little Bay Ridge home.

"Scott?" Kip said.

"Hi," Scott said shyly.

Mom looked between them. "Well. I suppose you'd better come in."

"Thank you," Scott said. He stepped in and Kip's mother closed the door behind him.

"Scott?" Kip said again.

"Yeah, sorry for just dropping in like this," Scott said. "I got your address from Elena. I thought—I thought we could maybe go for a walk."

"A walk?"

"Yeah."

They stared at each other stupidly until Mom said, "Well, get your shoes on! Honestly, Kip!"

Scott grinned, which made Kip smile.

Dad appeared. "Ah." He stuck out his hand. "George Grady," he said. "Nice to meet you."

"Scott," Scott said, shaking his hand.

"Yes," Dad said.

"Scott, this is my mom, Margaret."

"Hello," Mom said, bewildered.

"Scott is my . . . friend," Kip said, "if you're wondering why he's here."

"Actually," Scott said, "I'm his boyfriend."

Kip was stunned, but he smiled at Scott. "Yeah," he confirmed, "we're, um . . . together."

"Oh my lord!" his mother said, her hands clasped together over her mouth. "Oh, Scott, you have chosen so well!"

They all laughed, and Scott smiled affectionately at Kip. "I know it, ma'am."

"Ma'am!" Mom exclaimed. "Oh, I *like* him!"

"I'm sorry," Scott said, "were you having dinner? I should have called first. It smells delicious in here, though."

"It's fine," Kip said, still dumbfounded.

"Have you eaten, Scott?" Mom asked. "It's just meat loaf, but you're welcome to join us."

Scott looked at Kip. "If it's no trouble."

"No trouble at all! Come on in," Mom said. She squeezed Kip's arm excitedly as she passed him.

"Um," Kip said, "maybe we should . . . talk. First. For a moment. Upstairs?"

"Yeah," Scott said, "all right."

"We'll be right there, Mom," Kip called out. "Scott and I just need to talk for a minute."

He felt giddy and oddly nervous. He gestured for Scott to follow him, and they climbed the narrow stairway to the second floor.

When they got inside Kip's bedroom, he closed the door behind them and turned, ready to hear whatever the reason was that had brought Scott here. "What—"

That was all that Kip got out before Scott was on him,

crowding him against the door and kissing him hungrily. Kip grabbed whatever he could—Scott's T-shirt, his neck, his arms, his hair—and kissed back. He loved the feel of Scott's soft beard against his face.

Scott picked him up so Kip's legs were straddling his waist. He carried him over to the wooden desk that had sat in Kip's bedroom since he was six years old, and sat him on it. He spread his legs and kissed him harder, pressing Kip back against his bookshelf.

Kip felt hot everywhere. He couldn't get enough of Scott's mouth or hands. And, yeah, maybe he was getting a little too turned on, considering they were in his childhood bedroom, but this was fucking *hot*.

"Fuck, Scott," he managed when they finally broke apart. "What's going on?"

"I can't lose you," Scott said, kissing him again. "I can't."

"Okay."

They kissed some more, and Scott's thumbs slid up the insides of Kip's thighs. Kip decided to do the responsible thing.

"We can't," he panted. "We have to stop. Holy shit. My parents are waiting for us. Fuck."

"I know." Scott let out a breath and stepped back. They both had very obvious erections, which would be awkward to take to the dinner table.

"Let's sit for a minute," Kip said. "Just . . . talk to me."

They sat together on Kip's bed, and Scott said, "I like your room."

Kip glanced around at the familiar—and embarrassingly juvenile—décor of his bedroom. He still had his grade school spelling bee and academic awards on a shelf above his desk. And that wasn't a humiliating thing for your NHL superstar boyfriend to see.

"It's pretty glamorous, yeah," he joked.

"It's very . . . you. I like it." Scott took Kip's hand. He let their clasped hands rest on the bed between them. "I told some of my teammates."

"You did?"

"Yes. I told my three closest friends on the team."

"What did you tell them, exactly?"

"That I'm gay. That I'm seeing someone. That his name is Kip. That he's wonderful."

Kip blushed and smiled. "Really?"

"Yes."

"What did they say?"

"They were great. Maybe a little surprised. But great. Encouraging."

"Good! That's awesome, Scott!"

"It is, yeah. And I'm going to go public after the playoffs. As soon as possible."

"Wow. That's . . . wow."

"I don't want to wait anymore," Scott said, turning slightly toward Kip and brushing his fingers over his cheek. "I'd make the announcement right now if it wouldn't distract the team. I want to be with you in the way that you deserve. In the way that we *both* deserve."

And now Kip was tearing up. "Me too."

They kissed, softer and more tenderly than before.

"Will you come to my place tonight?" Scott asked.

"Yes," Kip breathed. There was nothing in the world he wanted more.

They joined Kip's parents a few minutes later, and if they had heard the two men crashing into each other upstairs, they didn't let on. There was already a place set for Scott, with a plate that was heaping with food. Kip's plate looked like it had been topped up a bit too.

"Thank you for having me," Scott said. "It's nice to finally meet you."

"We're very honored to have you." Mom was very obviously bursting with pride. "We're big fans, you know."

"Oh. Thank you."

"I'm a Scouts fan," Dad said, "but I can make an exception."

Scott smiled. "I grew up a Buffalo fan. I consider myself an Admirals fan these days, though."

Everyone laughed and Kip beamed. It was thrilling and surreal, having Scott sitting here at his family's table. Watching his parents laugh at his dry humor. The same dry humor that Kip loved so much.

"This is delicious," Scott said. "I can see where Kip gets his cooking skills."

"He's cooked for you?" Mom asked, delighted. "That's nice to hear. So how long have you two been seeing each other, then?"

Kip wasn't sure how to answer her. "Since, um . . ."

"We met in January," Scott said. "I met him at his work, actually. I wanted a smoothie, and, well—"

"January! Christopher *Grady*! This has been going on since *January* and you haven't told us?"

"We needed to keep it a secret," Kip protested. "Scott's not . . . You know."

"I'm, um—" Scott started, "I've decided to come out. Publicly. Soon."

"Oh," Kip's mother said. "Goodness."

"That will be a pretty big deal," Dad said.

Scott nodded. "Believe me, I know. And I didn't want to . . . I don't want Kip to be dragged into anything he's not ready for, but—"

"I'm ready," Kip said. "Anything that happens, I'm ready."

Scott gave him a small, grateful smile. "I'm in love with your son, ma'am. I don't care who knows it anymore."

Kip blushed because *sheesh*.

Now his mother was crying.

"Oh, honey," she said, "I'm so happy for you. Both of you."

Kip smiled at Scott. "Me too."

Scott didn't even wait for them to get to his apartment. As soon as they stepped into the elevator, he had his mouth on Kip's. Every cell in his body screamed with raw, violent need. He wanted this man *all the time*, and he wasn't interested in hiding that anymore.

The second they were inside the apartment, jackets and shirts were shed and strewn about the floor. Scott tried to walk toward the bedroom, but Kip pulled them back together and then they were kissing each other wildly against a wall. When Scott took a step back to suggest they leave the front hall, Kip started unfastening Scott's belt.

"God, Kip." Scott loved that Kip was as fevered as he was. He helped Kip strip him down to his briefs.

"Bedroom," he finally managed to say. "Please. Wanna do this right. Been thinking about this for days."

Kip nodded, mouth wet and bruised and slack, and *fuck*, Scott wanted those lips wrapped around his cock. He wanted everything.

Kip toed off his own sneakers and followed Scott to his bedroom. It would be *their* bedroom soon, if Scott had anything to say about it.

When they were in the bedroom, Kip slid a hand down inside Scott's briefs, gripping his ass. His other hand played with one of Scott's nipples while he kissed his neck.

Scott closed his eyes and tilted his head back. He reached behind and grabbed onto Kip's ass, pulling them tighter together so he could feel Kip's hard cock dig into him.

Kip hummed and moved his hand around to cup Scott through his briefs. Kip's hand made contact with his aching cock, and Scott cried out in a way that was embarrassingly needy.

Kip fondled him through the fabric for a while, then hooked his thumbs into the waistband and pulled the underwear down. He sat Scott on the end of bed, and dropped to his knees on the floor.

"Fuck," Scott whispered. "Yes."

Kip wet his lips and kept his eyes locked with Scott's as he swirled his tongue over the head of Scott's swollen cock. He flicked his tongue against the slit, lapping up the precome that was already beading there. It was all so slow and deliberate, it was absolutely destroying Scott in the best way.

"Fucking love you so much, Kip," he babbled. "Couldn't do it. Couldn't stop thinking about you. So scared I was gonna lose you. I need you. I need you. *Fuck!*"

Kip had swallowed most of his cock and was bobbing his head, still slowly, but it was enough. It was more than enough. Scott was on fire, everywhere. He gripped the mattress and watched Kip's gorgeous mouth take his cock, in awe of how hard he worked to make Scott feel incredible.

There was so much Scott wanted. He wanted to come and he wanted to get Kip all worked up until Scott was ready to go again. He wanted to fuck Kip and make him come and then cuddle the hell out of him.

But first . . .

"So good, Kip. So fucking good. Shit . . . I'm gonna . . ."

The orgasm ripped through him and he came down Kip's throat. Kip took it all, humming his approval after he swallowed. Scott gazed at him, dumbstruck, as Kip slid his beautiful lips off. *I can't lose him. Not ever.*

"Not gonna lose me," Kip said. Shit, Scott must have said that out loud.

Kip rose off his knees and climbed onto his lap, causing Scott to topple backward. Kip fell on top of him and kissed him. "Can't believe you told your teammates," he said. "And you told them about *me*?"

"Yup. Showed them a picture, even."

"Shit. Really?"

"Mm. Wanted to make 'em jealous."

Kip laughed and his nose wrinkled—it was so cute. Scott kissed him.

He rolled over, flipping them both so Kip was on his back. He kissed his way down Kip's body, lingering at all his favorite spots.

Kip watched him, grinning, with his hands behind his head. "So what's next?" he asked playfully.

"I'm going to fuck you," Scott said, matter-of-factly.

"So soon?"

"Mm . . . Just give me a minute." He kissed Kip's belly, and Kip giggled.

"Your beard tickles," he said. "I like it, though. It's sexy."

"Does it make me look like a hot lumberjack?"

"You remember that?" Kip laughed. "Man, I was trying to be smooth. Didn't actually think there was a chance with you, but I had to at least let you know that I might be interested."

"It worked," Scott said, crawling back up to meet Kip's lips. "Couldn't stop thinking about you after you said that."

"Glad I said it, then."

They kissed and it was sweet and tender.

"I think it might be your turn," Scott murmured.

"Mm. Yes, please."

Scott reached for the lube that he kept in his nightstand and shuffled down the bed. He wrapped a slicked-up hand around Kip's cock and stroked him as he watched his face change. The flirty little grin melted into a slack-jawed, blissful expression.

"I wanted you from the moment I laid eyes on you, you know that?" Scott said wistfully.

"Really? Wasn't I asleep or something?"

"I thought you said you weren't sleeping? Just resting your eyes?"

"I wasn't. I, *ah*, just closed my eyes for a second. But I opened them, and I didn't know who you were. Just thought you were really fucking hot."

"And when you found out who I was, what did you think?"

"That there was no way I had a chance with you."

Scott slicked up his fingers and started to gently work Kip open. Kip gasped at the first press of Scott's fingers against his hole.

"When I came back the second time," Scott said, "I thought maybe . . . I thought I caught you looking at me."

"You definitely did."

"And the third time," Scott said, slowly pushing a finger inside, "when you were alone . . . I came up with a dumb excuse to stay. I don't even know why. I just wanted to look at you."

"God," Kip said, his body squirming on the mattress. "Should have sat in your lap right then and kissed you."

Scott's stomach flipped, imagining it.

"What would you have done," Kip asked, "if I had done that?"

"I don't know. I would have been so . . . shocked. I don't think I would have been very smooth. But . . ."

"But?"

"I'll bet I would have kissed you back. At least for a second. I wouldn't have been able to help it."

"And then?"

"Then I probably would have run out of there."

Kip closed his eyes and sighed as Scott added a second finger. "You would have come back."

"Yeah," Scott said softly. "I would have."

"You invited me to that game. I still wouldn't let myself believe that I had a shot with you."

"I loved seeing you in the crowd."

"I was fucking obsessed with you for a couple of weeks there," Kip confessed. "I, uh . . . I jerked off a few times. Thinking of you."

Fuck. Scott's dick started to fill again. "What did you think about?"

"Imagined what it would be like to—" His words were cut off when Scott curled his fingers to stroke his prostate. "Ah, fuck. So good, Scott."

"This what you imagined?" Scott asked, bolder as he became more aroused. "Or was it what I'm about to do? Burying myself inside you, fucking you as hard as I want because you can take it?"

"Yes." Kip's voice was high and wild. "Imagined you fucking me against a wall. Fuck, maybe at work. I don't know. Just wanted to feel how strong you are."

Scott sucked in a breath. "I thought of you too. On the road, when I didn't even really know you. I wanted your dick in my mouth. I imagined what you'd sound like when you came. I imagined kissing your beautiful mouth. I wanted so much . . . Fuck. Okay."

He opened a condom and got himself ready, then grabbed one of Kip's legs and put his ankle on his shoulder and entered him as quickly as he dared.

Kip cried out, arched his back, and reached out for him. Scott leaned forward enough that Kip could touch his face and shoulders. Then he pulled back and rammed back into him.

"Yes! God, please," Kip cried. "Just like that, sweetheart. So good."

Scott fucked him hard and fast, and Kip gazed at him with so much love in his eyes.

"So good, Scott," Kip said again. "So fucking good. Love you so much."

Tears prickled Scott's eyes, which was ridiculous. He felt so good and Kip was so wonderful and he was so happy . . .

"Touch yourself," he said, slowing down a little. "Show me what you used to do when you thought about me."

Kip grinned and started stroking himself. "Still do, sweetheart," he said. "Can't tell you how many times this week I did this."

"Yeah," Scott breathed.

"I wanna come," Kip said, head rolling back on the pillow. "I'm so close."

"Wanna see it. Gonna fuck you right through it."

"Yes, oh fuck. Yeah, Scott. Fuck, I'm—"

"Come for me, baby. Come on. Show me."

"Ah! Ah, fuck," Kip cried, trembling and clenching around Scott's dick. He slowed his hand as he came. The white strands fell on his stomach. Then Scott sped up his thrusts, suddenly desperate to come.

Kip was still clenching hard around him, and Scott was right on the edge, so fucking close. Just needed that push . . .

"Come on me, Hunter. Come on. Mess me up."

Scott growled and pulled out and tore off the condom, barely in time to let his own release fall over Kip.

"Oh my god," he panted, staring at the mess they'd both made on Kip's stomach. "So fucking hot, Kip. I love you."

"I love you. You're amazing. Come here." Kip pulled him down and kissed him.

They got cleaned up, and Scott made good on his promise to himself to cuddle Kip to death.

Kip settled into Scott's arms and rested his head on his chest.

"You're so comfy," Kip murmured.

"Move in with me," Scott blurted out. *Oh god.* He hadn't meant to say that at all. Not so soon.

"What?"

"Move in with me," he said again. "I want you to live here, not just stay over. I want this to be *our* home."

Kip lifted his head. "You serious?"

"Yes."

He didn't say anything for a minute.

"Please," Scott said, bracing himself for Kip's rejection.

"Okay," Kip said softly.

Scott *beamed*. "Yeah?"

"Yeah. I . . . Are you sure, though?"

"I'm very sure. I want to share everything with you, Kip. I want to do this for real."

"All right then."

Scott was giddy. "I can't wait! I'll set up one of the spare rooms as an office for you so you can study and do your work. I'll get some bookshelves installed. How soon can you move in?"

Kip laughed. "I don't know. Anytime, I guess. It's not like I have much stuff to move."

"We can decorate the place. Together. It's always been kind of sparse."

"I'd love that."

The more Scott thought about it, the more excited he got. "We could have people over," he said quietly. "Friends. I've never . . . I don't really do that ever."

"We could," Kip agreed. "That would be nice." He shifted so he was propped up on an elbow, looking up at Scott. "You sure you're ready for what's next?"

"Yes," Scott said. "Are you?"

"Absolutely," Kip said.

CHAPTER TWENTY-EIGHT

The Admirals had defeated Detroit in game six, knocking them out of the playoffs. New York was moving on to the Stanley Cup finals against the Western Conference champions, Los Angeles. The series would open in New York in three days.

Today, Scott was going to talk to Coach Murdock. He had asked his coach before the team's video meeting if he could meet with him privately afterward.

"If this is bad news, I would really rather not hear it," Murdock said, as soon as Scott had entered the man's office. His tone was deadly serious, but he was a lot softer than he seemed. He'd want to know either way.

"It's not," Scott assured him, and he sat in one of the two chairs across Murdock's desk from him. "It shouldn't be, anyway."

"You've got twenty minutes. Shoot."

Scott exhaled, and started the speech he'd prepared. "There's something I want to tell you about myself that will probably become public knowledge soon enough. I know the timing isn't great for this, but I really do think it's for the good of the team and for myself that I—"

"Jesus Christ, Hunter," Murdock said. "Can I get the bullet-point format of this thing?"

"I'm gay."

Murdock froze, and stared at Scott like he'd just told him he was a wizard.

Please don't yell at me. Not about this.

"You're gay."

"Yes."

Murdock tented his hands in front of his face and leaned back in his chair. When he lowered his hands, he was smiling. "How many times have you said those words out loud?"

Scott smiled shakily back, relieved. It was going to be okay.

"Before now? Twice. The first time was to my agent. The second time to Carter, Huff, and Bennett."

Murdock nodded. "Smart, telling them first."

"I thought so."

"And you're telling *me* because . . ."

"I didn't want you to hear it from someone else. I want to go public. Soon."

Murdock's face turned serious again. "When, exactly?"

"After the playoffs," Scott said quickly. "I promise. I don't have to tell the rest of the team just yet. I'm not trying to distract anyone."

Murdock seemed to consider this. "Why now?"

"Because I don't want to live a lie anymore. And . . . I'm with someone. It isn't fair to him."

"Ah. You're in love. That makes sense. Love makes men do all sorts of dumbass things."

Scott gave a small smile. "I think this actually might be the smartest thing I've done."

"You know what's going to happen, right? When this gets out? You got a plan for that?"

"Kind of."

Murdock swore under his breath. Scott wondered if maybe they were done. Then Murdock said, "When I played, I was one of about two non-white players in the league."

Scott didn't say anything.

"My road to the NHL was . . . challenging, let's say. I don't think there was a single game where I didn't hear a player, or a fan, or a parent, or, hell, even a ref, have something to say about a Black man playing hockey."

"You were a trailblazer," Scott said.

"Sure. In retrospect, maybe. Didn't feel like that at the time. I just wanted to play hockey. Didn't think much about my legacy beyond being the greatest center the game had ever seen."

Scott laughed.

"Funny thing is that the press, all they wanted to talk about was my skin color. How revolutionary I was. How I was changing the game. How I had overcome so many obstacles. It was all just noise to me back then."

"And now?"

"Now I look back and I can see why all that noise was important. And I *know* it was important because players like Vaughan tell me that they were inspired by me. I made them feel a little more certain that they belonged in this sport that we all love."

Scott nodded. "I know there's going to be a lot of . . . noise. I'm prepared for that. I'm focused on my game. On my team. On winning. But if I can make even one kid more comfortable with who they are, make them a little braver about living their life without shame . . . I'm not going to run from that. I want that."

"So what's the plan?"

"I don't know. I was thinking about offering *Sports Illustrated* the story rather than a press conference. Do it quietly, y'know?"

Murdock blew out a breath. "I don't envy you—which is not something I ever thought I'd say—but I certainly respect the hell out of you, Hunter. I've got your back if anyone comes for you."

"Thank you, Coach."

They shook hands, and Murdock said, "It's not Rozanov, is it?"

"Jesus. No! Why does everyone—?"

"Good. I don't need that kind of circus."

Scott laughed and left the office. He ran into Carter in the hallway.

"How'd that shit go?" Carter asked.

"Good, actually. I wish I thought everyone would take the news as well as you guys have."

"Yeah, well . . ." Carter shoved his hands into the pocket of his hoodie, and looked at the ground. Scott knew he had been struggling a bit to accept Scott's sexuality. He had been . . . quieter than usual.

"Listen," Carter said. "I want you to know—if I've been acting weird, or whatever, it's not because you're . . . You know. Gay and shit."

"It's okay."

"No, I'm serious. I don't have a problem with that. But I guess I do have a problem with you not thinking you could tell me sooner."

Scott hung his head. "I know. I should have told you. I *wanted* to. I was just scared."

"I just hate thinking you were, like, all alone. All that time."

Scott glanced up at his friend. *God, I've been such an idiot.*

He put a hand on Carter's shoulder, and Carter stepped forward and hugged him.

"Thanks, Carter."

Carter thumped him on the back, and they broke apart.

"Hey," Carter said. "I, uh, I had this reservation for tonight. It's a very *private* restaurant. Dark, little nooks, expensive as all hell. Anyway, Gloria has to work late, so I was thinking . . . maybe you could take your man."

Scott was stunned. "I . . . I don't know. I mean, we haven't—"

"Take your man out on a damn date, Scott. You're gonna come clean about this shit anyway, right? Ease into it a bit. Like I said, this place is discreet and also romantic as fuck. And delicious. Shit, actually, can I be your date?"

Scott laughed. "I'll ask him if he wants to go."

He had no doubt Kip would want to go out somewhere with him. He was less sure that Kip would want to go to a restaurant that was "expensive as all hell." But he recognized this gesture from Carter for what it was.

"Thanks, man," he said. "It means a lot. Really."

Carter punched him in the arm. "Go be happy, asshole."

"How fancy is this place?" Kip asked Scott over the phone. "I don't think I have anything to wear that's nice enough . . ."

"Don't worry about it," Scott assured him. "Not to sound arrogant, but you're with me. You can wear whatever you want."

"I wanna look nice for you." Kip added a dark blue button-up shirt to the "maybe" pile on his bed.

"You always look nice. Did you get the address I sent you?"

"Yeah. I went to the restaurant's website. It looks fancy . . ."

"It's just a restaurant. Carter chose it, so it's probably good. He knows food."

"Yeah, okay." He made a face at a small hole in the sleeve of a black sweater he'd been considering.

They had agreed to meet at the restaurant, because if they met at Scott's place, there was a really good chance they would never make it to dinner.

"The car is going to pick you up at seven," Scott said. "That okay?"

"Sure. You don't have to send a car. I can take the train." He tossed a gray sweater onto the pile.

"I'm sending a car. It's a special night!"

Kip smiled. "Fine."

"I'll see you in a few hours, then."

"Yeah. Can't wait."

"Me neither."

They ended the call and Kip sighed, frowning again at his sad wardrobe. He hadn't been able to believe it when Scott had asked him if he wanted to go out to dinner that night. Scott had said he was going to loosen up about their relationship and eventually come out to the world, but Kip hadn't expected to be going on actual dates like this so soon. He was thrilled, but he was also woefully unprepared to be taken anywhere this posh. The only truly fancy clothing he'd ever owned had been the tux Scott had given him, but that was, he assumed, back at Scott's apartment. Kip had kind of lost track of the suit after Scott had stripped him out of it.

Besides, nice restaurant or not, the tuxedo would probably be a bit much.

He finally settled on an outfit comprised of his darkest jeans, a dress shirt, a dark tie, and a V-neck sweater in deep plum. He snapped a quick photo of himself and sent it to Elena.

KIP:
This look ok?

ELENA:
For what?

KIP:
Dinner with Scott!

ELENA:

Where are you going?

He told her the name of the restaurant.

ELENA:

Oh yeah. You're good.

Kip nodded at his phone, relieved. Elena sent another message. You look hot, by the way.

He smiled.

This was going to be the best first date ever.

Scott sat alone at the cozy table for two in the dark corner of the restaurant and tried not to care if anyone was looking at him.

Being alone in public often opened him up to being approached by strangers. He was fine with it most of the time, but tonight was for him and Kip, not for them. This restaurant was very exclusive, though, and Carter hadn't been kidding about how dark and private the tables were. It was an ideal place for Scott to test the waters a bit. Had Carter invented the story of not being able to use the reservation himself? Maybe he had just booked this with Scott and Kip in mind in the first place. Scott appreciated the gesture, either way.

He sipped some water and glanced again toward the front of the restaurant. Kip should be here any minute.

Scott had spent an absurdly long time getting ready, as if this were a blind date and not dinner with the man he was madly in love with. The man he'd been sharing his life with for months. The man he *hoped* to share his life with forever.

Finally, at just after seven-thirty, Kip was guided to the table by the maître d'.

Scott's heart did flips in his chest. Kip looked so handsome, and so happy to see him.

"Hi," Scott said, standing to give him a quick hug.

"Hi. You're wearing a suit! I *knew* I'd be underdressed . . ."

"You look good," Scott said, letting his eyes travel over him. "Perfect."

"If you say so," Kip grumbled, sliding into the semicircular booth. Their thighs brushed together, but Scott refused to flinch.

"This place is nice," Kip observed.

"Yeah, uh, Carter said it's . . . romantic."

Kip smiled at him, and Scott blushed.

"I'm just happy to be somewhere with you," Kip said. "Wouldn't matter where. But this is nice. Thank you."

"I'm a little worried that Carter might show up here," Scott said. "I think he's sort of keen to meet you."

"That's sweet, right?"

"Yeah. It is. I want to introduce you to everyone, but not tonight."

Kip tapped his foot against Scott's. "Not tonight."

"Hey, um, do you want some wine? Or a drink? After tonight I'm abstaining from alcohol until after the finals, so . . ."

"Is that your rule, or your coach's?"

"Coach's. But I would have made the same rule for myself anyway."

"Tough but fair."

"Hey, some coaches make their players abstain from sex."

"Shit. You ever had a coach who did that?"

"Yeah. Once." Scott leaned in. "The hardest part for me was pretending it was difficult."

Kip laughed, but it sounded a little sad. Scott touched their knees together under the table and saw a heat in Kip's eyes that drew him in automatically. He wanted to kiss him.

"Any questions about the wine menu?" the sommelier said, interrupting the moment. Scott snapped backward, and immediately felt bad about it.

He clumsily ordered some wine, with the assistance of the eager-to-please sommelier. People expected Scott to know about things like wine, or to at least be interested, because he had money. He didn't care about it.

He ordered a bottle of "The first thing you said. That one. Sounds good," and the man left.

"Sorry," Scott said as soon as he was gone. "I know I kinda . . . jumped back, just then."

"It's okay."

"No—It's—I didn't mean to. I guess I'm not used to the idea of . . ."

"Not expecting you to suddenly be comfortable with everything," Kip said. "We'll take it slow."

Scott smiled gratefully at him. Impulsively, he covered Kip's hand with his own, on top of the table for anyone to see. Kip grinned and flipped his hand over, tangling their fingers together. It felt good. It was exhilarating, but it wasn't scary.

Kip squeezed his hand, then pulled his own away to pick up his menu. "So what's good here?"

"I have no idea," Scott said. "I was checking out the menu a bit before you arrived. I understand about half of it."

"I'm only going to say this once, because I know it makes me sound like trash, but this place is fucking *expensive*."

"You know," Scott said, "I still balk at prices like these. Even though I can easily afford them, I still instinctively look for the cheapest thing on the menu."

"There is no cheapest thing on this menu."

"Order whatever you want," Scott said, "obviously. I think I'll get the halibut because at least I know what that is."

"Jesus. Is it stuffed with hundred-dollar bills?"

The wine arrived, and Kip was obviously trying not to laugh as Scott went through the charade of tasting it and pretending to know if it was any good. He nodded at the pleased sommelier and the man filled their glasses. He left, and their server came and they ordered, and then they were finally alone again.

"Hey," Kip said in a soft voice, raising his glass. "To whatever's next."

"To whatever's next."

They had a nice dinner. They drank wine and ate ornate plates of weird food that tasted fantastic. They talked and planned for the future. The wine made everything pleasantly fuzzy, and made Kip seem to glow in the romantic lighting of the restaurant.

Between their main courses and dessert, Scott leaned in and said, "I love being here with you."

That slow, sexy smile that Scott loved unfurled across Kip's face. "Me too, sweetheart."

"I want to take you everywhere. What you said about going dancing. At a club . . ."

"We will. Anytime you want."

"Bet you look real good when you're dancing."

Kip leaned closer. Scott could smell his aftershave. He wanted to bury his face in Kip's neck.

"I'd put on a real good show," Kip drawled. "Everyone would be watching us. But it would all be for you. No one else."

Scott shifted in his seat. He felt warm. "Damn right," he growled.

Kip's eyes widened. Scott had the dim thought that anyone who might be watching them would have no doubt that they were two men who were sexually interested in each other.

Sexually *obsessed* with each other, really.

Did he care anymore? God, he wanted to kiss Kip.

"What are you thinking about right now?" Kip asked.

Scott took the dare. "Kinda want to blow you under the table."

Kip smiled and bit his lip. It was the sexiest thing Scott had ever seen.

"Well, that should get everyone's attention," he said, his eyes glittering with mischief.

Where the fuck was that stupid dessert they'd ordered?

"You're a bad influence, Grady."

"Mm. Corrupting New York's perfect boy."

"I was so sweet and innocent before I met you," Scott smirked.

"If they only knew what kind of filth falls from those pretty lips when you're—"

The server arrived with their desserts. Scott blushed and sat straight up, thanking him a little too forcefully when he set the plate down.

After the server left, Kip smiled and Scott shook his head and let out a shaky laugh.

"This is the problem with taking you anywhere," Scott said.

"I don't know what you're talking about."

"I'm talking about how you have exactly three minutes to eat that dessert because I am getting you back to my place as soon as fucking possible."

"What, no coffee?"

"I'll make you coffee in the goddamn morning."

CHAPTER TWENTY-NINE

Kip bounced his way back to Scott's (*their?*) apartment after his final shift at Straw+Berry. He tossed his strawberry baseball cap into a garbage can on the way.

It would be a quick stop at home to change because he was heading out to meet Maria and Elena for a celebratory drink. But he wanted to see Scott first because tonight was game six of the finals, and there was every chance that the playoffs would end tonight with the Admirals winning the Cup. Kip would be at the game later, of course, but he was hoping to steal a quiet moment with Scott before what was sure to be a hectic and exciting evening.

Scott had had a team meeting that morning, but he said he'd be home in the afternoon for a nap and to generally try to relax before the big game. The long flights and time zone differences between New York and Los Angeles had been adding to the stress of the series.

In the apartment, Kip found Scott in bed.

"Hey," Scott said, hoisting himself up on an elbow. Messy hair, thick beard, muscles everywhere—Kip still couldn't believe this was his boyfriend. "How was the last shift?"

"Uneventful," Kip said. "But I brought you something. For luck."

He held out a blue smoothie. The last one he would ever have to make.

"Aww," Scott said, reaching for it. "I hope the new staff can make them this good."

Kip feigned horror. "You would let *another guy* make you a smoothie?"

Scott smiled around the straw. "I'd be thinking of you the whole time. I promise."

Kip kissed his hair. "I gotta head out in a minute. Maria and Elena are meeting me in, like, half an hour." He pulled his grubby T-shirt off.

"I guess I have to head to the rink soon anyway," Scott sighed. "Are you guys gonna be talking about me?"

"Definitely," Kip said, as he pulled a fresh pair of jeans out of the dresser. "Maria has been calling this the Secret Meeting of the Society of People Who Know about Scott and Kip. I expect at least a hundred questions from her."

Scott chuckled and shook his head. "Not gonna be a secret much longer, I guess."

Kip pulled a clean T-shirt on, and walked over to the bed. He tilted Scott's face up, and gave him a slow, adoring kiss that tasted like blueberries. "When you're ready," he said gently. "Even just having my parents and some of my friends knowing about us makes me feel a lot better. No rush for the rest of the world."

He turned to walk to the bathroom, but Scott grabbed his wrist. Kip turned back.

"Thank you," Scott said. His face and his tone were very serious. His eyes looked like they were trying to say more, and Kip wished they would because he had no idea why Scott was thanking him.

"For what?"

"Everything. I don't know what will happen tonight—if we'll win, or if I'll be getting on a plane to L.A. right after the game—but I want you to know that I wouldn't even be playing tonight if it wasn't for you."

Kip's brow furrowed. "Of course you would be. What do I have to do with—?"

Scott shook his head. "I was miserable, Kip. I know my life seems pretty great—and it is, in a lot of ways—but I was so *lonely*. And it got harder every year. This season, before I met you, it was like . . ." He seemed to struggle for words. Kip took his hand and squeezed it.

"It was like," Scott continued, "I had lost my love of hockey. Like . . . the fire went out, y'know?"

Kip sat on the bed beside him. "And you think you found it again . . . because of *me*?"

"Yeah. I do. I hated myself for feeling so miserable because I had achieved my dreams and I have all this success and money and I live in this great city, but . . . I mean, nine seasons of coming home from road trips to no one. Of summers with no boyfriend to travel with, and no family to visit. Nine seasons of not having a date to team functions, or to the NHL Awards. Of not having someone I love in the crowd at games. It was weighing on me."

Kip's heart broke a little. He hated thinking about Scott during those years.

"I wish we had met nine years ago," he said with a sad smile.

Scott laughed softly. "Yeah, well . . . I probably wouldn't have been ready, back then."

"If you want to play twenty more seasons," Kip said, "I'll greet you at home after every road trip. I'll be in the crowd at as many games as I can get to. And I'll be your date for anything you want to bring me to."

Scott smiled. "And the traveling in the summers?"

"As long as I can help pay for it."

Scott rolled his eyes. "You know, *you* could work on your stubbornness about letting me pay for things."

Kip kissed him. "I know. I'll try to relax about it. I promise. I've agreed to live with you, haven't I? That's progress!"

Scott kissed his nose. "It is. Now go meet your friends."

"Okay. Go win the Stanley Cup."

"Deal."

"So," Maria said, as soon as their server had delivered their micheladas, "what should we talk about? Oh! I know! How about we talk about how your *boyfriend* is playing in the *Stanley Cup finals* tonight!"

Kip shook his head, but he couldn't keep himself from grinning. "I guess that's interesting," he said mildly.

"It's going good with him, right? You're still totally in love with each other? You can't screw this up, Kip!"

"It's going good! We are totally in love. I won't screw it up. Again."

Her eyes narrowed, and she pointed a tortilla chip at him menacingly. "You'd better not. I'm living vicariously through you."

"Oh god. Don't say that."

Kip glanced at his phone. Elena had texted twenty minutes ago to say she'd be a little late. He had no choice but to sit there and face the onslaught of Maria's questions.

"What's his house like? Is it enormous? Does it have, like, twelve bathrooms?"

"It's a penthouse, and it has *three* bathrooms."

She groaned. "You're so lucky. When are you moving in?"

"Well, now, I guess. I mean, I still have a couple of boxes of random things at my parents' house to move over, but I live with Scott full-time now."

She shook her head, looking bewildered. "You say *Scott* and I can't believe you mean . . ." She glanced around, and whispered, "Scott *Hunter*. Like, you just call him Scott, as if he's a normal person!"

"He *is* a normal person. He just happens to be very good at playing hockey."

"And he just happens to be a gorgeous babe."

"Yes. That too."

"Is he a good kisser? Just tell me that he's a good kisser."

Kip rolled his eyes. "Oh my god. Where is Elena?"

"Does anyone else know?" Maria asked. "Have you told Shawn?"

"No." He stirred the salsa absently with a tortilla chip. He felt bad about lying to Shawn, but, "Shawn is a gossip and having to keep this secret might actually kill him. It's kinder not to tell him."

At least, that was what Kip told himself. He hoped Shawn wouldn't hate him once he found out.

"Okay, so, scale of one to ten . . ."

"No."

"One being the worst kisser in the world, aka my prom date—"

"No."

"And ten being, like, that *Brokeback Mountain* kiss where Heath Ledger broke Jack Gyllenhaal's nose by kissing him so hard . . ."

"*What?* Is *that* a good kiss?"

"Yes. So where does your boy land on that scale?"

"Um, better than a kiss where my nose gets broken?"

"So an eleven? Fuck, I knew it."

Kip laughed. "He's a good kisser, all right? Stop being weird."

"Who's a good kisser?" Elena had finally decided to show up.

"Kip's perfect boyfriend," Maria grumbled.

"Oh, he's not perfect," Elena said cheerfully, taking the empty seat. "His jaw is too chiseled."

"Mm," Kip said. "And he's way too tall."

"And broad," Elena added.

"And his thighs are way too thick," Kip pointed out.

"Just terrible," she agreed.

"You guys are assholes," Maria said. "Let me know if any of his teammates are looking for an adorable Latina to take care of."

Kip snorted. *"Adorable?"*

"Tell them adorable. By the time they realize I'm a total grouch they will already be in love with me and it will be too late."

They all laughed.

The three of them spent a few hours eating Mexican food and drinking (but not too much because Kip didn't want to be drunk for the game). They talked about Elena moving to California, and Maria's new job, and about Kip's new job, and about Kip going back to school. He felt good. For the first time in years, he felt confident about his future. His life was more or less on track, even without the perfect dream boyfriend.

But he *did* have the perfect dream boyfriend. And more than that, he was in love, and no matter how he imagined his future now, it always included Scott.

"We should go," Elena said, tapping him on the arm. "We need to go see the man you're obviously daydreaming about play hockey."

"I wasn't—Okay. Yes, I was." He turned to Maria. "I'm sorry I couldn't get a third ticket, but this game is super sold out."

"Yeah, no shit. The tickets are going for, like, five thousand dollars online," Maria said.

"I'll text you a selfie from the game, all right?"

"Oh, fuck you."

When they were out on the street, Maria hugged him. "I'm happy for you, Kip. I mean it. I act like a bitch, but you're one of the best people I know and you deserve that fantasy man."

He kissed her cheek. "Thank you. Maybe next time we go out Scott will come too."

"Tell him to leave his shirt at home. And to bring a teammate!"

Kip laughed. "Will do."

Maria headed toward the subway, and Kip and Elena headed in the opposite direction.

"After tonight, you might be dating a Stanley Cup champion," Elena said.

"Finally, a reason to be impressed by him!"

She took his arm and tilted her head onto his shoulder. "I'm glad you'll be in good hands when I'm gone."

"Me too. But I am going to miss you so fucking much."

"I know."

"And . . ."

He couldn't see her eyes, but he was sure she rolled them. "I'll miss you too," she said. "Not to get all emotional, but I like you."

Kip laughed and nudged her. "Thanks, pal."

The third period was agony.

Scott could feel the tension radiating from the crowd. He certainly felt it on the bench, and in his own stomach.

The period had started with L.A. scoring a quick goal to make it 2–1. With ten minutes left in the period, Huff had scored off an assist from Scott to tie it 2–2. The crowd had roared while the Admirals had breathed a collective sigh of relief.

Then came the real nail-biting stuff.

First, New York got a penalty, so they'd been shorthanded for two minutes. It seemed to last for twenty minutes, but they'd managed to kill it off without giving up a goal. There had been five minutes left on the clock.

Another minute had gone by and L.A. *almost* scored, but Bennett made an amazing save that kept New York in the game.

Then, with two minutes left, Scott had gotten the puck and he would never remember how exactly it happened, but suddenly he was on a breakaway. He raced toward the net, completely focused on his target, and sent the puck just over the L.A. goaltender's right leg.

Now Scott stood behind the bench with the rest of his teammates and watched the clock tick down the final seconds of the game.

Eight . . . Seven . . . Six . . .

Holy shit.

We did it. We're going to win the Stanley Cup.

Five . . . Four . . .

The roar of the crowd was deafening; eighteen thousand people on their feet, cheering for their home team. It was everything Scott had ever dreamed this moment would be.

Two . . . One . . .

And it was over. Scott vaulted over the boards, nearly crashing into two of his teammates as the whole team spilled onto the ice together. Sticks and gloves and helmets flew in all directions as they made a beeline to where Bennett stood in front of his net with his arms raised in victory. Within seconds, all of the Admirals had piled onto their goalie in a joyous, thrashing mess of ecstatic hockey players.

Players took turns hugging each other and thumping each other on the back. Scott could hear Carter screaming "Yeaaaaahhhh!" behind him, and when he turned to embrace his friend, he was nearly knocked over by the force of Carter jumping up into his arms. He wrapped his legs around Scott's waist, forcing him to hold him for a second.

"We fucking did it, Scotty!"

"Hell yeah, we did."

Carter released him and dropped back onto the ice. "Shit, we should probably go line up, huh?"

Scott glanced over at center ice, where the devastated Los Angeles team was waiting in an awkward huddle for the traditional handshakes.

"Right. Yeah. Let's go."

He called to his teammates to line up, and they quickly but respectfully shook hands with the L.A. players. A lot of the Los Angeles guys had tears in their eyes. Scott understood. He had been in their position before.

But not tonight. Tonight he had achieved the dream he'd held since childhood.

He waited impatiently as the Stanley Cup was carried out and the league commissioner gave a boring speech. Scott was announced as the playoff MVP, which was an honor, but wasn't the trophy he wanted to be holding. Besides, it felt ridiculous to be singled out when his entire team had worked so hard to get here. Scott wasn't a big fan of individual awards.

Finally, *finally*, Scott, as team captain, was handed the Stanley Cup. He took the giant silver trophy in his hands and it was . . . awkward to hold, actually. Heavy, but also hard to grip. But Scott certainly wasn't going to let it slip out of his hands now. He kissed the Cup and then hoisted it triumphantly over his head, turning so the whole crowd could see it. It belonged to New York now: the team *and* the fans.

And that's when the tears came. Scott let them happen. Everything about the moment was surreal and overwhelming and he had so many thoughts at once.

But mostly, *I wish my mom was here to see this.*

She would have been so proud of him. And it was her, as much as anyone, who had gotten Scott to this moment. All the hockey schools and trainers and agents in the world wouldn't have gotten him to the NHL if she hadn't laid the foundation with her support, and her long hours working at the grocery store so he could afford secondhand hockey gear.

Scott wasn't religious, but he turned his eyes up to the rafters and quietly said, "This is for you, Mom."

He handed the Cup to Carter, who kissed it, like, five times before raising it high above him. Scott found Kip in the crowd, across the ice, standing and cheering with everyone else. Scott gave him a little wave. He wasn't sure if Kip saw it.

It was later, when the ice started to fill up with the wives and girlfriends and children of his teammates, that Scott started to feel it. Mixed with all of his happiness was a troubling feeling of *wrongness*. He watched his teammates kiss their partners, and hoist their children up, and Scott wanted to be able to share this moment with *his* partner. With the man he loved.

And what would be the harm in having Kip come down onto the ice? The place was a zoo anyway: hockey players and staff and reporters and photographers and family members. Who would even notice if Scott's boyfriend was among them?

Decision made, he skated over to the glass near Kip. He waved his hands, which a lot of people seemed to notice, but not Kip. Then Scott saw Elena nudge him and say something to him, and point at Scott. Kip looked, and smiled. Scott's heart fluttered. God, he loved him.

Scott gestured toward the penalty box. Kip made an exaggerated *what?* face, and Scott gestured again. He saw Elena, again, say something to Kip, and then Kip nodded and pointed toward the penalty box. Scott nodded back, and took off to meet him.

From the box, Scott watched Kip make his way through the crowd. People seemed to be watching this little sideshow they were putting on with great interest.

So much for being subtle.

When Kip reached the glass that separated the seating from the penalty box, he was flushed and grinning and adorable.

And Scott knew he wasn't going to be able to stop himself from doing something very stupid in a moment.

But . . .

"Climb over the glass!" Scott yelled. "I'll catch you."

"Okay!" Kip stepped onto the ledge and hoisted one leg over the glass. Scott helped him over, and Kip fell into his arms.

"You did it!" Kip said.

"I did it," Scott agreed.

They stood there for a moment, still holding each other and smiling, and maybe it was the adrenaline pumping through him, or maybe the whole night had just felt like such a wonderful dream and there was only one thing that could make it perfect and that was . . .

He could see the surprise in Kip's eyes as Scott leaned in and kissed him. Scott thought it might just be a quick peck, but as soon as their lips touched, he just went for it. He kissed Kip like they were alone and maybe hadn't seen each other in months. He kissed him like a man who had everything he had ever dreamed of.

When they broke apart, Kip gaped at him. "Holy shit!"

"I don't care," Scott said. "I love you."

And it was true. He didn't care. Well, he cared that now he *may* have pulled focus from his teammates and their achievement a bit. He knew he'd feel bad about that, especially when he glanced up at the giant scoreboard screens and saw a live shot of himself and Kip, wrapped up in each other.

"Well," Kip said giddily, "I guess the cat's out of the bag now."

"Mm. May as well go for broke, then."

Scott kissed him again, and everything around them disappeared. It was just Scott and the man he loved, making out in a penalty box.

But then, reality. Which was also pretty excellent at the moment.

"The press is gonna want a word with me, I think," Scott

said, glancing at the ice. There were a lot of stunned faces staring at them.

"Go," Kip said, "I'm so proud of you."

"Okay, but listen: I'm going to the dressing room with my team in a few minutes, and we can bring in family and friends soon. Come talk to Huff's wife, Laura. She'll tell you where to go. She's done this a few times."

"Scott. *Go.* For fuck's sake, stop worrying about me. You just won the Stanley Cup!"

Scott beamed. "I just won the Stanley Cup!"

"Yes. Get out there and be a hero, Hunter!"

But Scott refused to leave him behind. Not yet. This place was too chaotic, and he had to make sure Kip would be taken care of. He grabbed onto his hand and pulled him onto the ice with him. Kip slipped a bit when his sneakers hit the ice, and Scott steadied him with an arm around his waist.

There was a microphone in Scott's face almost immediately. He let go of Kip and gestured toward Huff, who skated over.

"You must be Kip," Huff said.

"I am, yes."

"Figured. The kissing gave it away."

Kip blushed and Scott smiled—he probably wouldn't *stop* smiling for days. Maybe months.

"Welcome to the extended Admirals family, kid," Huff said. "Come meet the Huffs."

Scott watched Huff as he led Kip away from the media throng that had formed. Huff was truly the best.

Scott turned toward the reporters and cameras.

"So," he said, "any questions?"

If Kip had thought the game had been wild, it was nothing compared to the party in the locker room after.

The room was *packed* with excited, sweaty men, proud

wives and girlfriends, sleepy kids, the press. Beer and champagne were flowing—Scott and his teammates were drinking champagne out of the Stanley Cup. Men were singing, men were yelling, men were crying.

Scott and Kip had gotten separated quite a few times, and it had given Kip an opportunity to notice the stares he was receiving from . . . basically everyone.

But he refused to shrink away. Scott wanted him there, so there he was.

Carter Vaughan caught him when Kip had been standing alone. "Here's the guy I've been wanting to meet! Come here, man!"

Before Kip knew what was happening, Carter enveloped him in a sweaty hug. "Kip, Kip, Kip. I love that fucking name, you know. So, what the fuck, right? Did you and Scott Hunter really just make out in front of the whole damn world?"

"We really did." Kip was still buzzing about it.

"That'll get a few tweets."

Kip smiled. "I expect so."

"Scott Hunter's got a boyfriend." Carter shook his head, grinning. "Man, I can't even imagine what it's like dating a dude that perfect."

"It's pretty great."

Someone handed Carter a beer, and Carter said, "Hey, get one for my man Kip, all right?"

When whoever it was returned with a beer for Kip, Carter asked, "So what's your story, Kip? Scott said you're a student?"

"About to be again, yeah. Starting my master's degree in September."

"You play sports at all?" the beer guy—who was drinking a Coke himself—asked.

"Nah."

"Sorry," Carter said, "this rude asshole is Eric Bennett. You don't recognize him because he usually has a mask over his face."

"Hi," Bennett said.

Kip nodded. "Nice to meet you. Congratulations."

"You a hockey fan?" Carter asked.

"I am now, for sure. I've always liked watching hockey. Hadn't been following too closely, until . . ."

"Until you started dating the biggest star in the game?"

"Right. Yeah."

Carter looked at him with some curiosity. "So you're not a Scott Hunter fanboy. You just happened to meet him?"

"Yeah. He didn't tell you?"

"Nope. Is it cute?"

Kip shrugged. "It's probably boring. One day he just came into the place I worked. It's, uh . . . it's a smoothie shop. Anyway. He got a smoothie, and then he came back the next day . . . and again . . ."

"That," Carter said with a wide grin, "is fucking cute. He picked you up at *work*? I didn't think Hunter had any game!"

"He didn't, really. Pick me up, I mean. He just kind of kept coming in. And I sort of . . . hinted . . ."

Carter shared a knowing look with Bennett. "Yeah, that makes a lot more sense. He was probably hoping you might just trip and fall on him or something if he kept showing up."

"Maybe. It all worked out in the end, anyway."

"You ready to be in the middle of a media storm when this gets out?" Bennett asked.

"No," Kip said, straightening his spine. "But I'll be there. Right by Scott's side."

Carter laughed. "All right, stand down, soldier. We've got

your back. I like you, Kip. Almost as much as I like saying your name."

"Thanks."

Scott joined their little circle, draping a heavy arm across Kip's shoulders. "Are these guys bothering you?" he asked with a sloppy grin. It was possible he'd had a lot of champagne already.

"We're just trying to figure out how a guy this great ended up with a mess like you, Hunter," Carter joked.

"I don't know either, but I'm sure glad he did," Scott said, and he kissed Kip on the cheek. Kip turned bright red. He glanced at Carter and Bennett, expecting them to be looking away, but they were both just smiling at them.

Scott dipped his head to speak directly into Kip's ear. "They're kicking out everyone who isn't on the team, but I'll see you at home, right?"

"Definitely. But I don't expect you anytime soon. It's your night. Have fun, okay?"

"I will. I love you."

"I love you."

And then Scott had kissed him quickly on the mouth. It was just a peck, but it was no small gesture, given where they were standing.

Kip practically floated all the way home, replaying the last couple of hours in his head and dreaming of the future.

Kip spent a few hours back at home staring at his phone.

He had received a *lot* of texts that night.

MARIA:

Aaaahhh!!! What the FUCK???!! That was the cutest thing I've ever seen?????

SHAWN:

You. Fucking. Bitch. You lying fucking bitch. We're getting lunch together. SOON.

KYLE:

First of all, congratulations and I am happy for you. Secondly, holy fucking shit!

MEGAN:

Um . . . WHAT?!

He'd also gotten texts from people he hadn't talked to in months. There had been a couple of missed calls from his parents. He would return them tomorrow.

Elena had left the game at some point, but she had texted him. Congratulations. You boys just made history.

A second text said, Seriously, though, I almost cried.

Kip kept watching the same video over and over again. It was the interview Scott had done on the ice, immediately after they'd kissed. It, along with many photos and screengrabs of them kissing, had gone viral.

"Sure, yeah," Scott had told the interviewer, who had asked him if he wanted to comment on what everyone had just witnessed. "I was just celebrating a little with my boyfriend."

"I don't think that the world was aware that you're . . ."

"Gay? Yes, I'm gay. I was planning on making some sort of official announcement, but what the hell, right? Everyone is here now."

The interviewer had been silent a moment, seemingly stunned, before she blinked and said, "And . . . are you . . . Is there anything you want to tell us about him?"

"Absolutely. He means the world to me and I love him."

Kip grinned like an idiot every time he watched it. Scott's voice was so steady. So confident, like he had no regret at all. No looking back.

Kip tried not to pay too much attention to what social media was saying about it, but a glance told him that there seemed to be more people who were thrilled than who were disgusted. Definitely a lot of shock on both sides, though.

"This is going to be fucking nuts," Kip muttered to his phone. Starting tomorrow morning, his life was going to be *very* different.

But tonight he was at home, madly in love, and so fucking happy. He was proud of Scott for so many reasons.

He watched the interview again.

Scott was surprised, but not really, to find Kip sitting on one of the stools at the kitchen counter, and not in bed, when he got home. It was almost three-thirty in the morning.

He was wearing sleep pants and a tank top, and he was everything Scott wanted to see at that moment.

"You're awake," Scott said stupidly.

"Of course. You seem less drunk than I was expecting." Kip slid off the stool and crossed the floor to meet Scott.

"I stopped drinking a while ago." Scott put his hands on Kip's waist.

"I'm really fucking proud of you," Kip said. "For everything tonight."

Scott kissed him and it was exactly what he had been craving all night. Even while celebrating winning the goddamn *Stanley Cup* with his teammates, he'd been consumed with the need to kiss his boyfriend.

"Kinda jumped off the cliff there," he said, after they broke apart. "Sorry. I should have talked to you first, maybe."

"It's fine," Kip said. "Scott, it's *fine*. I wasn't expecting it, but . . . I mean, that was romantic as hell!"

Scott laughed and buried his face in Kip's neck, kissing just under his chin.

"I love you so much," he said. His voice had gotten very raspy over the course of the night. He'd done a lot of yelling.

"Love you too, sweetheart. Now come on. Always wanted to take a Stanley Cup champion to bed."

EPILOGUE

Scott felt Kip's hand squeeze his own. He returned the gesture, reassuring him.

I'm fine. I've got this.

They sat together in the audience of the NHL Awards in Las Vegas. The nominees for the final award of the night, the league MVP, were being read from the stage, Scott's name among them. Winning would be nice, but he wasn't concerned about that as much as he was hoping for an opportunity to speak.

"And the Hart Trophy goes to," said the presenter, "Scott Hunter!"

Scott exhaled and stood. *Here we go.* Kip released his hand and smiled at him, and Scott found strength in that smile. He ignored the fluttering in his stomach as he turned and made his way to the stage. He took the trophy from the presenter and held it up for a moment before setting it carefully on the floor next to the podium.

"Hi," he said when the applause had died down. There was scattered laughter.

"First of all, thank you for this. All of my fellow nominees are just as deserving. Even Rozanov." There was more laughter.

He looked down for a moment, gathering his thoughts. He

probably should have written something out, but that sort of planning was never really his style.

"A few weeks ago," he started, "I achieved my lifelong dream of winning the Stanley Cup. Those of you who have done that know how it feels. I really can't describe it. But . . . something else happened that night. Something that, you've probably noticed, got a lot more attention than the Admirals winning the Cup."

The audience was very quiet now. He could feel the tension in the room. *Is he really going to talk about this? Here?*

"It's been an interesting month," he continued. "In case you somehow missed it, I came out as gay in a ridiculously public way. I don't regret that, and I never will. I know it was a shock to most people. And, sadly, it's been a disappointment to some. I know people have been burning their Scott Hunter jerseys, which, by the way, is not a good idea. Those are polyester, and are full of chemicals."

The crowd laughed. They sounded relieved.

"I, uh, I got a Twitter account a couple of weeks ago," Scott said. "I've always been a very private person. Or, as private as I can be, considering. I love meeting fans, but I never shared my life in any public way. What I've seen, these past few weeks, is that maybe it's important that I do, a bit. Fans have been sending me messages, a lot of young fans, telling me how much it meant to them for me to come out."

Scott didn't mention that he had also received emails and phone calls from a few fellow NHL players, saying similar things. He wasn't here to start rumors or speculation.

"I love hockey. I love being able to do this for a living. But," he said, "I know what it feels like to not fit in.

"When I was a teenager, when it started to look like a career in hockey was a real possibility, two things happened. One was that my mother died. The other was that I began to realize that

I might be that *thing* that every hockey player liked to throw around as an insult. The kind of language I heard on the ice, and in the locker room, every day was a constant reminder that I was different. Maybe it made me a better player. Maybe it gave me another reason to prove myself. But it also made me terrified that someone would find out my secret."

The room was silent.

"When you have a secret that you work as hard to protect as I did," Scott said, "it's exhausting. It's a nonstop effort, trying to keep it hidden, and the fear of people finding out consumes you. It also makes you lonely."

He paused a moment. He was probably overstaying his welcome, but he wasn't done.

"I've been extremely fortunate. I have a lot, and I'm grateful. But I was always missing something very important in my life. And this year, I found it."

Scott's eyes landed on Kip, and he could see that his lips were pressed together and his eyes were wet.

"I've attended a lot of my teammates' weddings over the years, and I listened to a lot of speeches about love, or finding that person who changes everything for them. I never really got it, though. I'd assumed that I never would get it. It wasn't for me. But this year . . . I met someone. I met *that* person. The person who changes everything. And he gave me the confidence, and the strength, and the *need*, to be honest about who I am. Fear is a powerful thing, but this year I found the thing that is more powerful."

People were turning to look at Kip now. There was probably a camera on him too, for the live broadcast.

"So I share this honor with my teammates, and my coaches," Scott said, needing to wrap it up, "but I also share it with you, Kip. You have made me better, in every way. I love you."

Kip mouthed *I love you too* back at him.

"And, uh, one of the gay clubs here in Vegas is having a Scott Hunter Night tonight, so that's where I'll be later, if any of you wanna come dance."

There was scattered laughter, and a distinct "whoop" that Scott was sure was Carter. He smiled.

"Thank you," he said. Then he picked up his trophy and left the stage to wild applause.

Scott drummed his fingers against his knee, possibly to the thumping beat of the club music. More likely to the internal rhythm of his racing heart.

He was in a club. A *gay* nightclub. Which was packed with people who were ostensibly celebrating *him*.

He could be cool about this. Absolutely.

It helped that he was surrounded by friends. *More* than helped. He didn't have words to describe how much it meant to him to have the people who meant the most to him here with him tonight.

Carter and Gloria sat on the couch across from him in the cozy VIP section. Beside them sat Huff, with Bennett relaxing in a chair by himself. Matti Jalo stood at the railing, watching the dance floor below them.

Scott's invitation had been sincere; he would have loved to have seen anyone from the audience of the NHL Awards here at the club tonight. He hadn't honestly been expecting anyone to actually show up, beyond Carter, Huff, and Bennett. Even Jalo was a surprise.

"Elena said she loved the speech and wishes she could be here," Kip said as he set his phone down on the table in front of them. He shifted a little closer to Scott, pressing their bodies together on the couch and giving him a reassuring pat on the knee. "How are you doing?"

"Good," Scott said. "Really. I'm happy."

And he was. It was weird, being famous for a whole new reason. For just being who he was. He had fans now who didn't even watch hockey.

It was going to be an interesting summer.

Scott was going to be doing a lot of press that summer, including a *Sports Illustrated* feature. This time the focus would be almost entirely on his sexuality and private life. It was nerve-racking, but he understood why it was important.

Kip had argued against a European vacation; he was determined to work as many shifts at the Kingfisher as he could before school started. Scott knew better than to fight him on that, but Kip *had* been getting better about letting Scott pay for things. Things like this trip to Las Vegas, which had been Kip's first time on an airplane. Scott was happy he was there for that, and he looked forward to experiencing many more firsts with Kip.

He also really enjoyed visiting Kip at work. The Kingfisher now had named a drink after Scott. Only Kip and Scott knew why it had blueberry juice in it.

"You look incredible tonight," Scott said in a low voice, his lips brushing Kip's ear. "Have I told you that yet?"

He *did* look incredible. He always looked perfect to Scott, but this was the first time he had seen him *done up* to go out. He looked effortlessly sexy—sensual—in a way that Scott was sure he could never achieve himself. He was wearing a deep V-neck black T-shirt and charcoal jeans that were so tight Scott wondered how he had managed to put them on and, with some concern, how they might be removed later. His hair was messily arranged to create a look that appeared both careless and meticulous.

But the thing that was *really* distracting Scott tonight was the touch of eyeliner that Kip was wearing. There was something about it that excited Scott, like he was leveling up. He was officially, *boldly*, staring down the homophobic stereotypes that got thrown around locker rooms and saying, yes, Scott

Hunter—captain of the New York Admirals and model of rugged masculinity—was going to a gay nightclub with his pretty, painted boyfriend.

Scott tangled their fingers together and held tight. Let the world make no mistake: Kip Grady was his.

"This is fun, yes?" Jalo's voice boomed, even over the pounding music. "Scott Hunter Night!"

"I was expecting more," Carter complained. "Where's the theming?"

Kip laughed. "What were you expecting?"

Carter shrugged. "Go-go dancers in jocks, maybe? With hockey sticks? Maybe an ice sculpture in the shape of Hunter?"

It was true that Scott Hunter Night seemed to mostly consist of Scott being in the building, but still. It was nice.

"I'm going to hit the bathroom," Scott said to Kip. "Be right back."

A few minutes later, as he was making his way back to his friends through the throngs of people, he glanced to his left and noticed a tall, fit man leaning elegantly against a pillar, just outside the VIP area. It took Scott a moment to recognize him, and when he did, he couldn't believe his eyes.

"Rozanov?" he asked. Ilya Rozanov grinned lazily as Scott headed toward him.

"What are you doing here?" Scott shouted over the music.

Rozanov shrugged. "Wanted to see what Scott Hunter Night was. Is not as bad as it sounds."

Scott snorted and shook his head. "Did you really come to a gay bar in Vegas just to make fun of me?"

Rozanov ignored his question, and instead swept a hand through the air and said, "So. This is you now?"

Scott wasn't exactly sure what he meant, but he nodded. "This is me. I mean, this has always been me. But now I'm . . . better at being me."

Rozanov seemed to consider this. "Is good. What you did. It will be good for . . . others."

There was something in Rozanov's eyes that caught Scott's attention. He hadn't ever seen that look on his face before. Was it gratitude, maybe?

"I hope so," Scott said.

Rozanov held his gaze for another second and then looked away.

"I'm here with some of the guys," Scott said. "From my team, I mean. You, uh, you wanna join us?"

Scott knew Rozanov was trying very hard to look like he didn't care one way or the other, but, as Scott expected he would, he accepted the invitation.

"Hey! The star of Scott Hunter Night is back!" Carter whooped. "And what the fuck is *that guy* doing here?"

Rozanov smirked and gave a little wave.

"I invited him to join us," Scott said. He shot Carter a pointed look that he hoped said *drop it*.

Carter did drop it, beyond a few suspicious glances at Rozanov. They all sat and talked as well as they could over the music. Carter ordered some fancy bottles of various things, and it wasn't long before Scott was feeling very loose and relaxed. Within an hour, Kip was snuggled against Scott on the couch and talking to Bennett, Gloria was perched on Carter's lap and talking to Huff, and Matti was chatting animatedly with Rozanov.

"Let's go downstairs," Kip murmured in Scott's ear. "I wanna dance with you."

Scott nodded and stood. "We're gonna . . ." he said to the group, but no one seemed to care at all that they were leaving.

Downstairs, they stood on the edge of the dance floor, the beat of the music thrumming through Scott's body. Kip leaned against a pillar, hands behind his arched back and his head tilted up, offering himself. He looked so fucking sexy, peering up at

Scott with those dark-ringed eyes as the colorful lights of the club played over his face.

Scott braced a hand against the pillar and leaned in, pressing Kip against it and devouring him. Knowing that they were in public. Knowing his dick was swelling in his pants, creating a bulge that anyone would be able to see. Knowing that Kip was getting hard too.

"Can't control myself when you look like that," Scott breathed into Kip's ear.

"Come dance with me," Kip murmured back. Scott kissed him under his smooth jaw, and Kip shuddered. Kip had shaved tonight, and the smooth skin added to the soft innocence of his look. Feminine, almost, except for his gravelly, Brooklyn drawl, and for the hardness that pressed into Scott's hip.

The music was loud, pulsing, and relentless. The massive dance floor was packed with men, many of whom were probably attractive. But Scott wasn't looking anywhere but at the man who was leading him by their joined hands.

He was terrified and excited, mentally preparing like he was about to play a game, shutting everything around him out. Focusing on the goal.

Kip found their spot in the sea of bodies, and turned to face him. It was so crowded that they were pressed together, and Kip wrapped his arms around Scott's neck and smiled at him. Scott smiled back and placed his hands on his waist, then awkwardly tried to match Kip's slow movements.

It didn't take long. After a minute, Scott was lost in the way Kip rolled his body, the way his fingers found their way into Scott's hair, and the intense heat in his eyes. Scott moved with him, and it was easy. He let go of his nerves and just allowed himself to feel his way.

Scott had never been high in his life, but he imagined it had to feel something like this. The onslaught on his senses of swirling lights and pounding bass, the sweltering heat of the club, and the strong scent of sweat and dry ice filling his head. The dulling effect of the alcohol, smudging his thoughts and giving him a feeling of relaxed euphoria. The rush of arousal coursing through every part of him. The thrill of possibility.

Kip must have seen it all in Scott's face, because he stopped moving and leaned in to brush his lips over Scott's ear. "Where are you?"

Scott swallowed and turned his head to reply. "I'm right here."

Kip tilted his head back and Scott pressed hot, open kisses under his jaw. He put a possessive hand on Kip's ass and pulled them flush together. He could feel Kip's heart race against his chest, and in the pulse point under his tongue.

He felt Kip's hands slide up under his T-shirt. He knew his skin was damp with sweat underneath. Kip leaned in and kissed him. Were they even dancing anymore, or just making out in the middle of a bunch of people? Scott didn't care.

It was madness. They were in *public*, safe space or not, and Scott felt completely out of control. He needed to get out of here, or make peace with the fact that he was going to fuck Kip against a wall in front of god and Ilya Rozanov.

Kip stepped back and laughed. "Easy, sweetheart. There'll be time for that later."

At least that's what Scott thought he said. It was hard to hear between the music and the molten need that was throbbing through him.

He glanced up at their VIP booth, and saw Carter, Bennett, and Huff leaning over the railing, grinning at him. That cooled him off. Kip turned and gestured for them to come join them. Minutes later, their booth was empty and they were all on the dance floor together.

Carter danced with Gloria *very* closely, and Scott smiled to himself at how obvious it was that he wanted everyone to be clear he was there with a woman. It didn't matter. Carter was *there*, and Scott appreciated it. Eric just danced by himself, oblivious to the guys who were trying to engage him, and seemed to be enjoying himself immensely. Huff was moving a little awkwardly, and it looked like he was edging slowly off the dance floor. Matti, on the other hand, was gamely dancing with anyone who approached him. Scott was pretty sure he was straight, but he was definitely a good sport.

And Scott didn't have much experience at clubs, but the way Rozanov moved against the men he danced with seemed a lot more deliberate and practiced than someone who was just trying to get into the spirit of the place.

Huh.

It was maybe unimpressive in size, this little resistance group of hockey players who had chosen to join Scott tonight, but it felt like a revolution. A year ago—hell, a *month* ago—Scott would never have imagined this scenario. Out at a gay club with his best friends—his *teammates*—and his *boyfriend* and, uh, Ilya Rozanov. Dancing. Laughing. Celebrating his sexuality instead of hiding it. It was surreal and wonderful.

Kip tilted his chin up, and Scott kissed him because he loved him, and he loved being here with him, and there was nothing to be afraid of anymore.

"You're happy," Kip observed.

Scott leaned their foreheads together. "I feel invincible right now."

"Me too. Let's change the fucking world."

Scott kissed him, hard, because Kip had described exactly how he felt.

"Yeah," he said. "Let's do that."

Keep reading for an excerpt from Heated Rivalry.

BLUE MOON OVER BROOKLYN SMOOTHIE RECIPE

As served at Straw+Berry

KIP APPROVED

Ingredients

1 cup frozen blueberries

$^{1}/_{2}$ cup frozen pineapple

1 ripe banana, or 2 if you like it extra creamy

1 handful fresh kale, stems removed, or 2 if you hate yourself

$1^{1}/_{2}$ cups milk of choice

$^{1}/_{2}$ cup pomegranate juice

1 teaspoon honey, option to lick it off a chest

Directions

1. Leave them in bed.
2. Make smoothie.
3. Take off shirt.
4. Bring them smoothie.
5. Receive reward.

Note: To make it sweeter, make them wait longer (or add more honey).

ACKNOWLEDGMENTS

I first want to thank my amazing editor at Carina, Mackenzie Walton, for her extremely helpful and enthusiastic feedback and guidance through the editing process of my first book. I would like to acknowledge the hard work of this book's original editor, Carole Ann Galloway. Her edits and advice improved *Game Changer* enormously.

I would also like to thank my friend Melissa Buote for coming up with the name Straw+Berry for the smoothie shop. It still makes me laugh every time I see it.

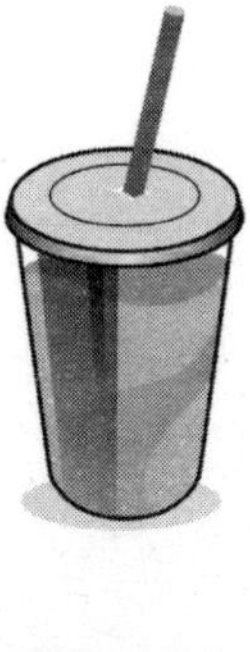

PROLOGUE

October 2017—Montreal

Shane Hollander was as close to losing it as he ever allowed himself to get.

He'd endured two periods and twelve minutes of one of the most frustrating hockey games he'd ever played. It should have been a glorious win at home for his Montreal Voyageurs against their archrivals, the Boston Bears. Instead it had been a grueling humiliation, with the score standing at 4–1 for Boston with less than eight minutes left on the clock. Shane had had no less than five beautiful scoring chances. He'd taken shots that should never have missed. But they had. And the Bears had capitalized on the Voyageurs' mistakes.

One man had capitalized more than anyone. The most hated man in Montreal: Ilya Rozanov. The near-century-old rivalry between the Montreal and Boston NHL teams had, over the past six seasons, become personified by Hollander and Rozanov. Their intense animosity was clear even to the fans in the farthest, cheapest seats.

Hollander bent at the face-off circle now, facing Rozanov as the referee prepared to drop the puck after the Russian's second goal of the game.

"Having a good night?" Rozanov asked cheerfully. His hazel eyes sparkled the way they always did when he was talking shit.

"Fuck you," Hollander growled.

"Still time for a hat trick, I think," Rozanov mused, his English barely comprehensible between his thick accent and his mouth guard. "Should I do it now, or wait until the last minute? More exciting that way, yes?"

Hollander grit his teeth around his own mouth guard and didn't answer.

"Shut up, Rozanov," the referee said. "Last warning."

Rozanov stopped talking, but he managed to find an even more effective way of getting under Hollander's skin: he *winked*.

And then he won the face-off.

"Fuck!" Jean-Jacques Boiziau, the Voyageurs' giant Haitian-Canadian defenseman, hurled his stick at the wall of their dressing room.

"That's enough, J.J.," Shane said, but there was no real threat behind it. To make it clear that he was in no mood to fight, or even argue, with anyone, he slumped into his dressing room stall.

Shane's left-wing line mate, Hayden Pike, sat on the bench next to him, as always. "You all right?" Hayden asked quietly.

"Sure," Shane said flatly. He tipped his head back until it met the cool wall behind him and closed his eyes.

Using the word *passionate* to describe Montreal hockey fans would be an understatement. Montreal loved the Voyageurs to the point of absurdity. Their arena was one of the toughest places for visiting teams to play, because they faced not only one of the best teams in the league, but the loudest fans in the league as well. The fans also had no problem letting their own beloved team know exactly how disappointed they were with them.

But when Montreal fans were really devastated, like they had been tonight, they were almost silent. And that was Shane Hollander's least favorite sound.

"You know what would be sweet?" Hayden asked. "You know that movie *The Purge*? Where you get to, like, break whatever laws for one night with no consequences?"

"Sort of," Shane said.

"Man, if that was real, I would murder the fuck out of Rozanov."

Shane laughed a little. He couldn't disagree that bludgeoning that smug, Russian face would be at least a little satisfying.

Their coach entered the room and voiced his disappointment with remarkable calm. It was early in the season—this had been their first regular season matchup against Boston—and they had been playing well most games. This was a glitch. They would move on.

Then it was time to face the press. At that moment, Shane would have preferred to see a pack of starving wolves enter the room, but he knew there was no avoiding the reporters. They always wanted to talk to him, specifically, after every game, and especially after games where he faced Rozanov.

He pulled his sweat-soaked jersey off over his head so the CCM-branded athletic undershirt would be seen on camera. Part of his endorsement contract.

A semicircle of cameras, lights and microphones formed around him.

"Hey, guys," Shane said tiredly.

They asked their boring questions, and Shane gave them boring answers. What could he even say? They'd lost. It was a hockey game, and one team lost, and that team was his team.

"Do you want to know what Rozanov just said about you?" one of the reporters asked gleefully.

"Something nice, I assume."

"He said he wished you'd been playing tonight."

The crowd of reporters was silent. Waiting.

Shane snorted and shook his head. "Well, we play in Boston in three weeks. You can let him know that I will *definitely* be at that game."

The reporters laughed, delighted that they had gotten their Hollander versus Rozanov sound bite for the night.

An hour later—showered, changed and finally alone—Shane drove himself home. Not to his Westmount penthouse, but to the one that nobody knew about.

Shane only spent a few nights a year at the small condominium in the Plateau. It was where he went when he wanted to be sure of total privacy.

He parked in the tiny lot behind the three-story building, let himself into the back door and quickly climbed the stairs to the top floor. He knew the other two floors were unoccupied because he owned those, too. The bottom floor was rented to a high-end kitchenware boutique, which had closed for the night hours ago.

The condo on the third floor looked like what it was: a demo condo that had been decorated by a professional house stager. Technically, this was the condo that would be used to sell this one and one below it. If Shane was ever interested in selling. Which, he told himself, he definitely would be doing. Soon.

He had been telling himself this for over three years.

He went to the stainless-steel fridge and took out one of the five bottles of beer—the only things in the pristine refrigerator. He twisted the cap off and sat himself on the black leather sofa in the living area.

He sat in silence and tried to ignore the way his stomach churned on nights like this one. He drank his beer quickly, hoping the alcohol would help at least numb the disappointment he felt in himself. The disgust at his own weakness. He needed to dull it because he knew he sure wouldn't be doing anything to fix things. He'd been trying for seven years.

The knock came at the door almost forty minutes later. It had been enough time that Shane had almost convinced himself to leave. To put an end to this foolishness. But, of course, he hadn't. And if the knock had come hours later, even, Shane would still have been on that sofa, waiting for it.

He opened the door.

"What the fuck took you so long?" he asked, annoyed.

"We were celebrating. Big win tonight, you know?"

Shane stepped back to let the tall, smirking Russian into the apartment.

"I got away as soon as I could," Rozanov said, his tone less teasing. "Didn't want to draw attention, right?"

"Sure."

And that was the last word Shane got out before Rozanov's mouth crashed into his. Shane gripped his leather jacket with both hands and pulled him closer as he kissed Rozanov breathless.

"How long do you have?" Shane asked quickly, when they had broken apart for air.

"Two hours, maybe?"

"Fuck." He kissed Rozanov again, rough and needy. God, he needed this. This horrible, fucked-up thing.

"You taste like beer," Rozanov said.

"You taste like that horrible gum you chew."

"Is so I don't smoke!"

"Shut up."

They grappled and maneuvered each other until they reached the bedroom, where Shane shoved Rozanov roughly against a wall and continued kissing him. He felt the familiar slide of his rival's tongue in his mouth, and slid his own tongue over teeth that had been fixed and replaced god knew how many times.

He wanted a lot tonight, but they didn't have time for a lot. Rozanov grabbed him and pushed him down onto the bed; Shane watched the other man drop his jacket on the floor and pull his T-shirt off over his head. A gold chain hung crookedly around Rozanov's neck, the shiny crucifix resting on his left clavicle just above the famous (ridiculous) tattoo of a snarling grizzly bear ("For Russia! I had it before playing for Bears!") on his chest. Shane would make fun of it later. Right now all he could do was watch Rozanov strip his clothes off, and belatedly realize that he should be doing the same.

They both took off everything, and Rozanov fell on top of Shane, kissing him and moving a hand down to grasp his already embarrassingly rigid cock. Shane arched up into his touch, making stupid, desperate noises.

"Don't worry, Hollander," Rozanov said, his lips brushing Shane's ear, "I am going to fuck you like you want, yes?"

"Yes." Shane exhaled, a mixture of relief and humiliation sweeping through him.

Rozanov slid down his body, kissing, sucking, licking, until he reached Shane's cock. He didn't tease any further. He took him into his mouth, and Shane was grateful that they were alone in the building because his moan echoed throughout the sparsely decorated room.

He propped himself up on his elbows so he could watch. Part of him wanted to lie back and close his eyes and let himself believe that it was *anyone* other than Ilya Rozanov making him feel so good. But most of him wanted to see *exactly* who it was.

Rozanov was a stunning man. Light brown curls that were always a mess fell into his playful, hazel eyes and over his dark, thick eyebrows. His strong jaw and cleft chin were covered in stubble. His smile was lopsided and lazy, and his teeth were unnaturally white due to most of them not being real.

His nose was crooked, having been broken more than a few

times, but the fucking thing only made him look more rugged. And for a Russian living in Boston, his skin was a lot more golden than it had any right to be.

Shane fucking hated him. But Rozanov was really good at sucking cock, and he was, for whatever reason, willing.

Shane hated *this*, but he had taken great pains to protect it, and he would continue doing so as long as Rozanov was willing. Their lives being what they were, this was not an easy thing to get. Maybe, when they had started seven years ago, they hadn't expected their lives, their famous rivalry, to get to the point it was at now. Maybe they should have stopped by now. But, despite the wrongness of it, this was comfortable. This was familiar. And it was as close to safe as either of them were going to get.

That's all it was.

Rozanov worked his talented mouth on Shane's cock, and Shane tossed the lube down the bed from the well-stocked nightstand. Rozanov took it, without pausing what he was doing, and poured some onto his fingers so he could get to work opening Shane up.

This was never Shane's favorite part because he felt so fucking vulnerable. He felt weak and ridiculous every time they were together like this, but he always felt it most acutely when Rozanov had his fingers inside him. As a result, the preparation usually took a while.

Rozanov, on the other hand, always seemed completely at ease. He was good at this, and he knew it. He slid his mouth off Shane's cock with a parting lick to the head that sent a jolt straight through Shane's body and said, "Relax, yeah? Is not much time, but enough."

Shane took a deep breath and let it out slowly. He hated that voice so much on the ice, and in the interviews he saw on television where Rozanov mocked him in an obnoxious, teasing tone. But here, in this bed, Rozanov's tone was patient and gentle, his voice soft and his accent wrapping elegantly around boxy English words.

Shane relaxed as Rozanov opened him with strong fingers and pressed openmouthed kisses on the insides of his thighs. When he was ready, Shane wordlessly handed Rozanov a condom before rolling over and getting on his hands and knees. He couldn't look at Rozanov. Not tonight. Not after that humiliating loss.

Rozanov seemed to understand. He entered him carefully, not taking him roughly like he had many times in the past. This was slow and considerate. Shane felt big hands on his hips and waist, holding him steady as Rozanov pushed inside. He even felt Rozanov's thumbs brush gently over his lower back.

"There. This is what you wanted, yes?"

"Yes." Because it was. It was what he always wanted.

Rozanov started to move and Shane cried out. It never took long for him to just give in and start moaning and gasping and asking for more.

"Fuck, Hollander. You love it."

Shane responded by turning, he was sure, beet red. But he couldn't deny it.

Rozanov fucked him hard with one strong hand pressing between his shoulder blades—pressing him down onto the mattress. They were both *loud*, and if he didn't know the building was empty besides the two of them, Shane would have been worried about it. But he felt safe here, so he let himself go. He cried out with every thrust and maybe said Rozanov's name a bunch of times.

Shane *really* hoped no one could hear them.

When Rozanov reached around to take Shane's cock in his slick hand. Shane became desperate for release and started bucking back against him. This was the point where he was always reminded why he couldn't give this up. It was too good.

"You gonna come for me, Hollander?"

Hollander *was* going to. And he did. He punched the mattress and swore loudly and coated Rozanov's fist with his release.

Rozanov picked up speed behind him, sending aftershocks rocketing through Shane's body with each thrust. Just as it was becoming too much for Shane, Rozanov stilled and cried out and pulsed inside him.

Afterward, they lay on their backs next to each other, and Shane felt the familiar aftermath of guilt and shame creep in.

"Well, you won at *something* tonight," Rozanov mused.

"God. Fuck off." Shane lifted his arm to hit him, but Rozanov grabbed his wrist and pulled him over so Shane was on top of his chest, looking down at him. Rozanov's playful smirk faded as he held Shane's gaze, and Shane felt suddenly breathless.

"Still have that stupid tattoo, I see," Shane said quickly, to distract himself from whatever the fuck was happening.

"Aw," Rozanov said, the obnoxious little grin returning to his face. "He missed you."

Shane snorted.

"He *did*," Rozanov insisted. "Give him a kiss."

Shane rolled his eyes, but he did dip his head to Rozanov's chest. Instead of pressing his lips to the tattoo, though, he trapped Rozanov's nipple lightly between his teeth and tugged.

"Fuck," Rozanov said, sucking air between his teeth.

As an apology, and also because Shane knew it would work him up even more, he brushed his tongue over the sensitive nipple. Rozanov put a hand in Shane's hair and guided their mouths back together. After a long, oddly tender kiss, Shane lifted his head and saw that Rozanov was, again, looking at him very seriously. He swallowed, but didn't say anything as

Rozanov brushed fingers through his hair. He hoped the fear he felt wasn't showing on his face.

"You are very beautiful," Rozanov said suddenly. It was said very matter-of-factly.

Shane wasn't sure how to react. They didn't really *say things* to each other. Not like that.

"Hottest Man in the NHL, according to *Cosmopolitan*," Shane joked. It was the only way he knew how to talk to Rozanov, besides yelling obscenities at him.

"They are idiots," Rozanov said, the spell broken. "They put me at number five. Five!"

"It does seem generous."

Rozanov rolled over, pinning Shane onto the mattress. Shane looked up at him, laughing.

"I have to go," Rozanov said, and he sounded like he truly regretted it. "Shower first, but then I have to get back to the hotel."

"I know."

They showered together and Shane dropped to his knees because he couldn't let Rozanov go without tasting him. Rozanov murmured his approval as he loomed over Shane in the spacious rainfall shower. His strong hands cradled Shane's head and long fingers curled into his wet hair. Shane turned his eyes up and found Rozanov gazing down at him with that damn crooked smile. Shane immediately closed his eyes and felt his cheeks flush and, to his embarrassment, his own cock get harder.

It was bad enough that he loved being fucked so much, that he loved having a dick in his mouth. But for it to have to be *this* son of a bitch, to the point that on the extremely rare occasion when it wasn't, Shane was left wanting . . .

So maybe it wasn't *just* that this was convenient. But that was something Shane didn't want to think about.

He brought Rozanov right to the brink and then pulled off,

catching the man's release on his chin and lips and probably on his neck. The evidence was quickly washed away, down the drain, and Shane fell back to a sitting position against the shower wall. He scrubbed his hands over his face and pulled his knees in. He heard Ilya panting in Russian.

"Shit," Rozanov said, still standing with his head leaning back against the tile opposite where Shane was sitting. "You been practicing that, Hollander?"

"No," Shane grumbled.

"No? You been saving it for me?"

Shane didn't reply, which was as good as confirmation.

Rozanov laughed. "You need to get laid, Hollander. Waiting for a quick fuck every couple of months is not healthy."

"I'm *not* waiting," Shane said. It wasn't quite a lie. He obviously wasn't one hundred percent straight, but having sex with women didn't *repulse* him. It just didn't do it for him like men did.

One man, in particular.

But women were safe and easy and *everywhere*. And maybe if he kept trying he might find one he'd like to spend more than a single night with. Someone who could finally put an end to . . . whatever *this* was.

Rozanov turned off the water and reached a hand out. Shane rolled his eyes and took it, letting Rozanov pull him to his feet. They stood, chest to chest, and Shane watched the water that dripped from Rozanov's hair onto his shoulder and down toward his navel.

Rozanov rested a hand on Shane's face and tipped his head up. He looked at him fondly, with a little smile on his lips, and then he kissed him.

"I have ruined you," Rozanov said when they broke apart. "No one else will do."

"God, fuck off."

"Such a mouth on you."

"Don't say it."

"I preferred it when it was on me."

"Dammit, Rozanov." Shane pushed the other man back against the shower wall and kissed him aggressively. It was always like this. Shoving and cursing each other and battling for control until one or both of them gave in and allowed themselves the release they both craved.

"I do have to go," Rozanov said, but even as he said it he was scraping his teeth along Shane's jaw.

"I know."

"I'm sorry."

"Why? I don't care. I think we're done here anyway, aren't we?"

Rozanov stopped kissing him and looked at him, considering. "I suppose we are."

They left the shower and got dressed quickly. Shane stripped the comforter from the bed and loaded it into the washing machine. He would make sure the place was left as spotless as he had found it.

"Three weeks, then," Rozanov said as he stood at the door, ready to leave.

"Yup."

Rozanov nodded, and Shane thought that was going to be it, but then the other man grinned and said, "Was it me tonight?"

"Was what you?"

"Distracting you. On the ice tonight."

It took Shane a moment to realize what he was suggesting.

"Fuck. You."

Rozanov's smile spread. "Couldn't play at all, thinking about my dick, right?"

"Good night, Rozanov."

Rozanov blew him a kiss on his way out the door, leaving

Shane furious and strangely relieved. It was good to be reminded of the fact that they didn't actually like each other.

Shane pulled another beer out of the fridge and sat on the sofa to wait for the comforter to be clean. It was late and he was exhausted, but he wouldn't sleep here. He should really talk to a Realtor about selling this building.

He would sell the building, and he would stay in his goddamn hotel room when they played in Boston and not slip out into the night to Rozanov's penthouse. He would end this, and he would move on.

He realized, as he was making this plan, that he was brushing his fingertips over his lips. They still tingled from the memory of the other man's mouth pressed against them.

He knew making plans to end this was pointless. As long as this was being offered, Shane would never be able to say no.

Don't miss Heated Rivalry, *the next book in Rachel Reid's Game Changers series, available wherever books are sold.*